LEVEL 1 DEMON LORD & ONE ROOM HERO

VOLUME 3

STORY & ART BY toufu

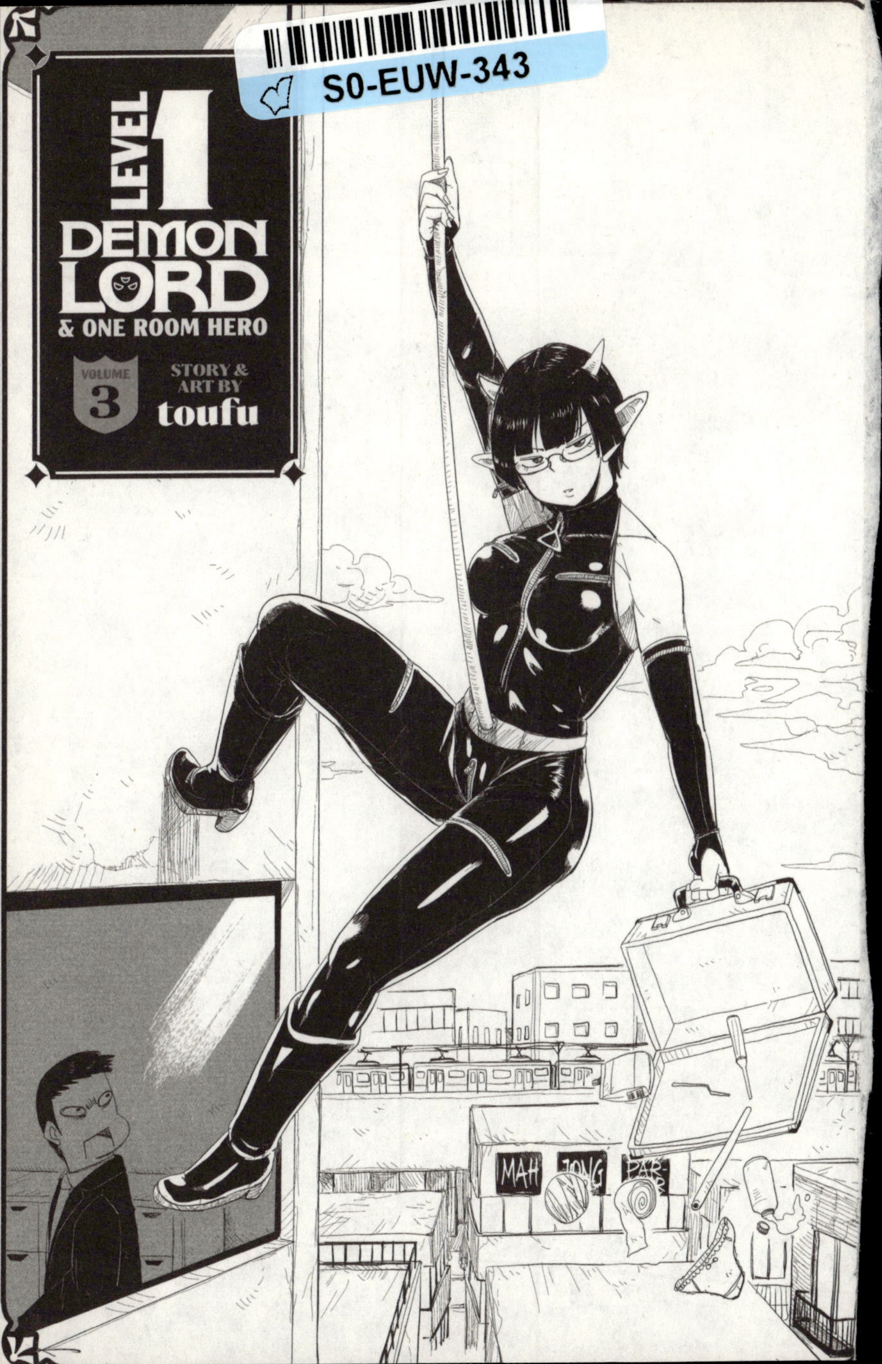
MAH
JONG

LEVEL 1 DEMON LORD & ONE ROOM HERO

◆ CONTENTS ◆

Episode 15	The Secretary at Work	003
Episode 16	The Secretary Captured	021
Episode 17	Sinister Developments	043
Episode 18	Call of the Eagle	077
Episode 19	Fallout	105
Episode 20	The Hero's Dilemma	131
Episode 21	Fred's Solo Campaign	153

3

STORY & ART BY
toufu

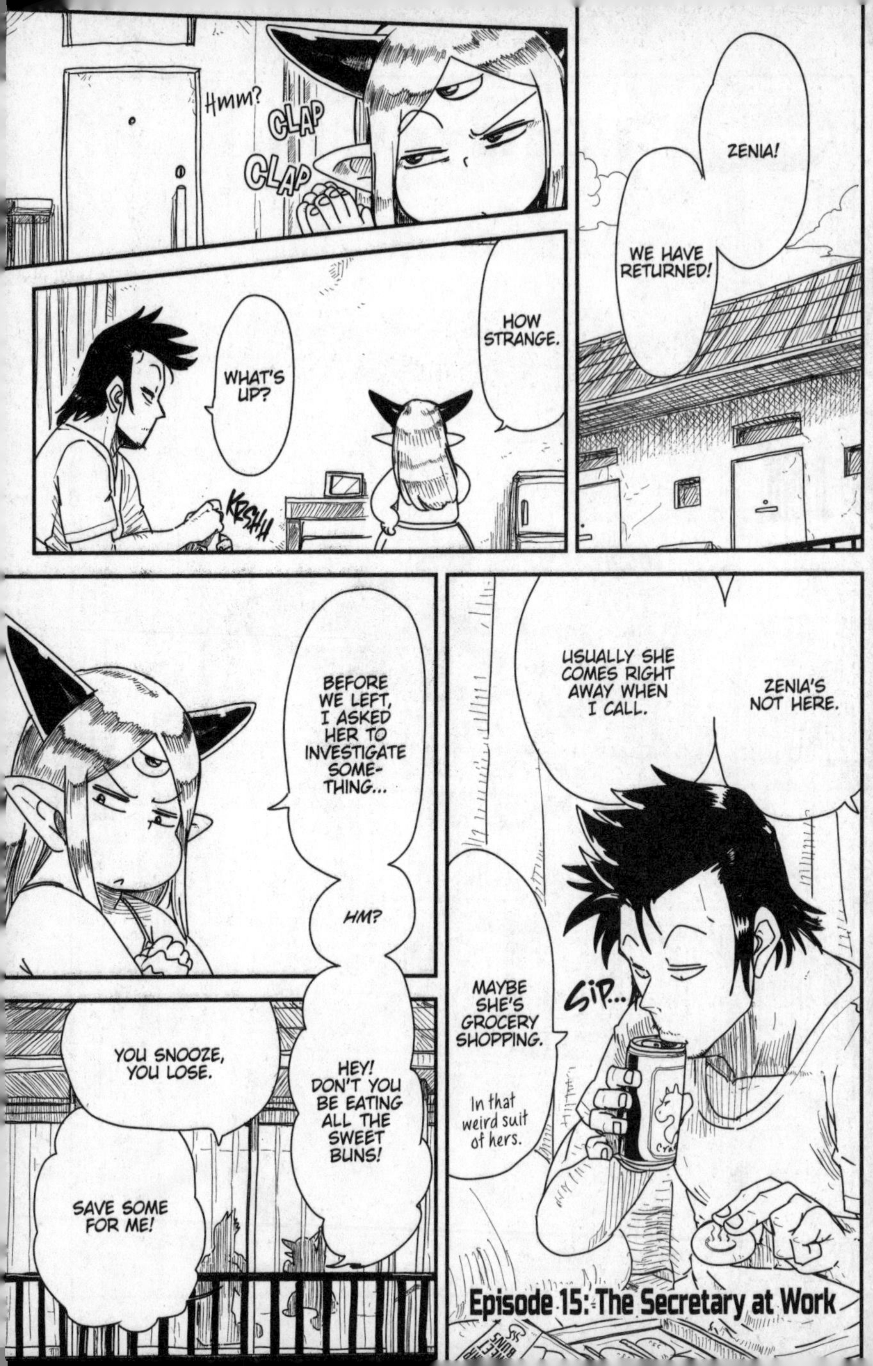
ZENIA!
WE HAVE RETURNED!
Hmm?
CLAP
CLAP
HOW STRANGE.
WHAT'S UP?
KRSHH
ZENIA'S NOT HERE.
USUALLY SHE COMES RIGHT AWAY WHEN I CALL.
MAYBE SHE'S GROCERY SHOPPING.
In that weird suit of hers.
SIP...
BEFORE WE LEFT, I ASKED HER TO INVESTIGATE SOME-THING...
HM?
HEY! DON'T YOU BE EATING ALL THE SWEET BUNS!
YOU SNOOZE, YOU LOSE.
SAVE SOME FOR ME!
SWEET BUNS

Episode 15: The Secretary at Work

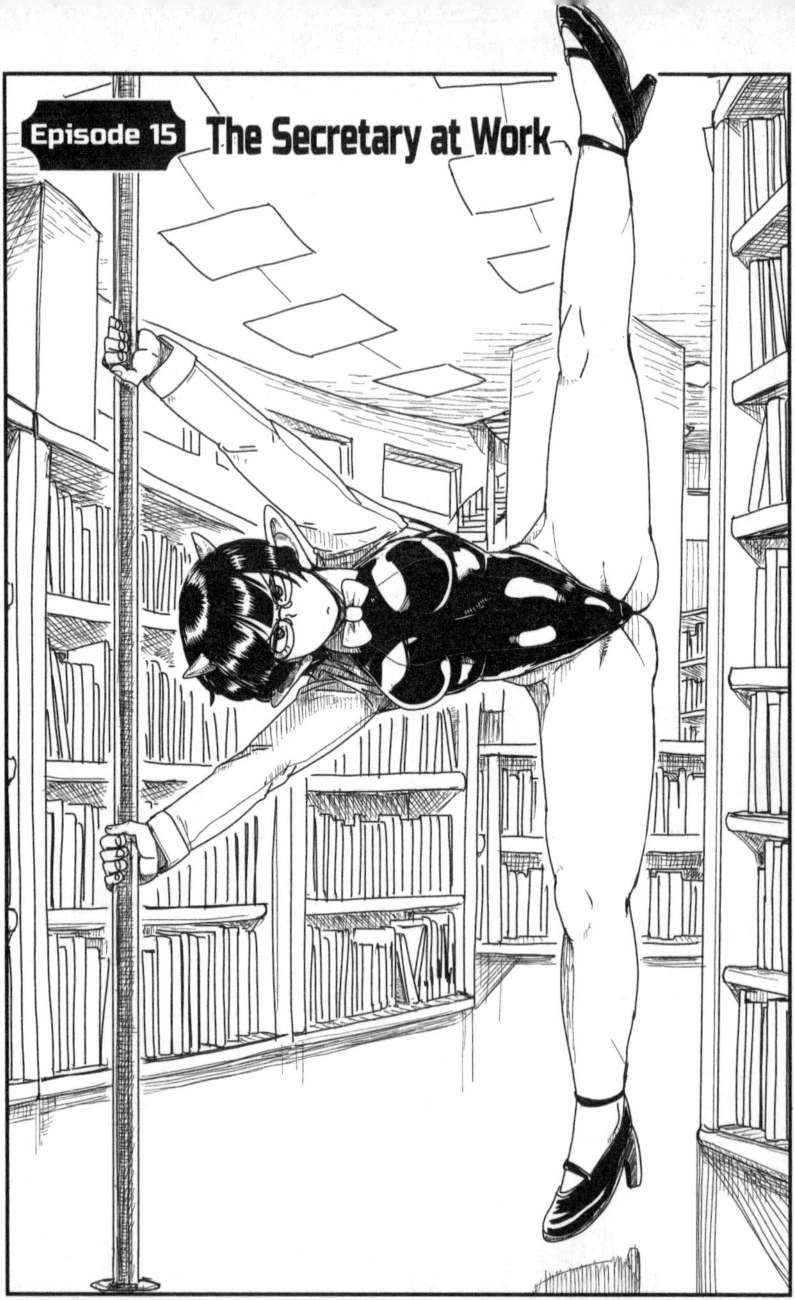
Episode 15 The Secretary at Work

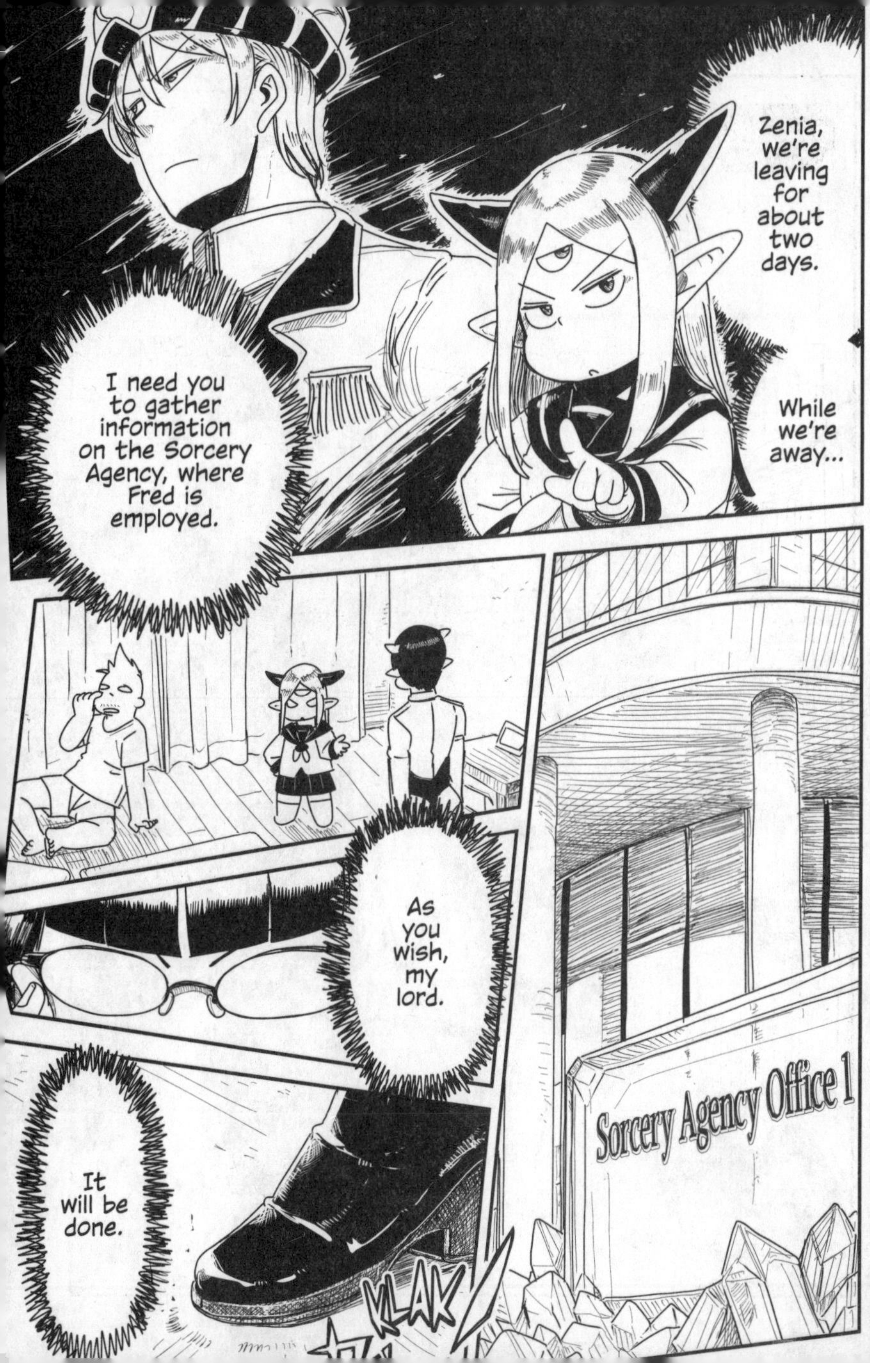
Zenia, we're leaving for about two days.
While we're away...
I need you to gather information on the Sorcery Agency, where Fred is employed.
As you wish, my lord.
It will be done.
VLAK
Sorcery Agency Office 1

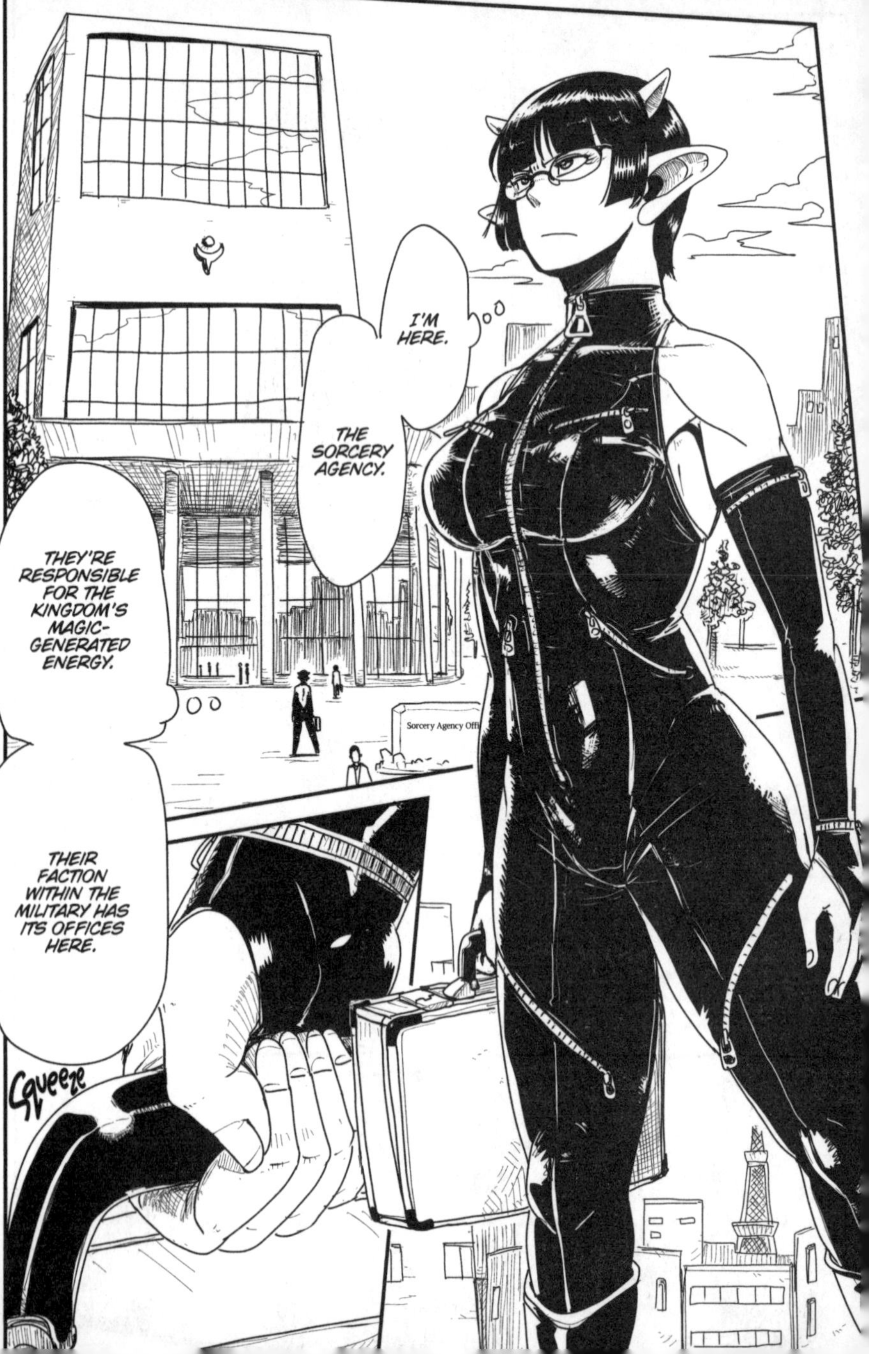
I'M HERE.
THE SORCERY AGENCY.
THEY'RE RESPONSIBLE FOR THE KINGDOM'S MAGIC-GENERATED ENERGY.
THEIR FACTION WITHIN THE MILITARY HAS ITS OFFICES HERE.
Sorcery Agency Offi
Squeeze

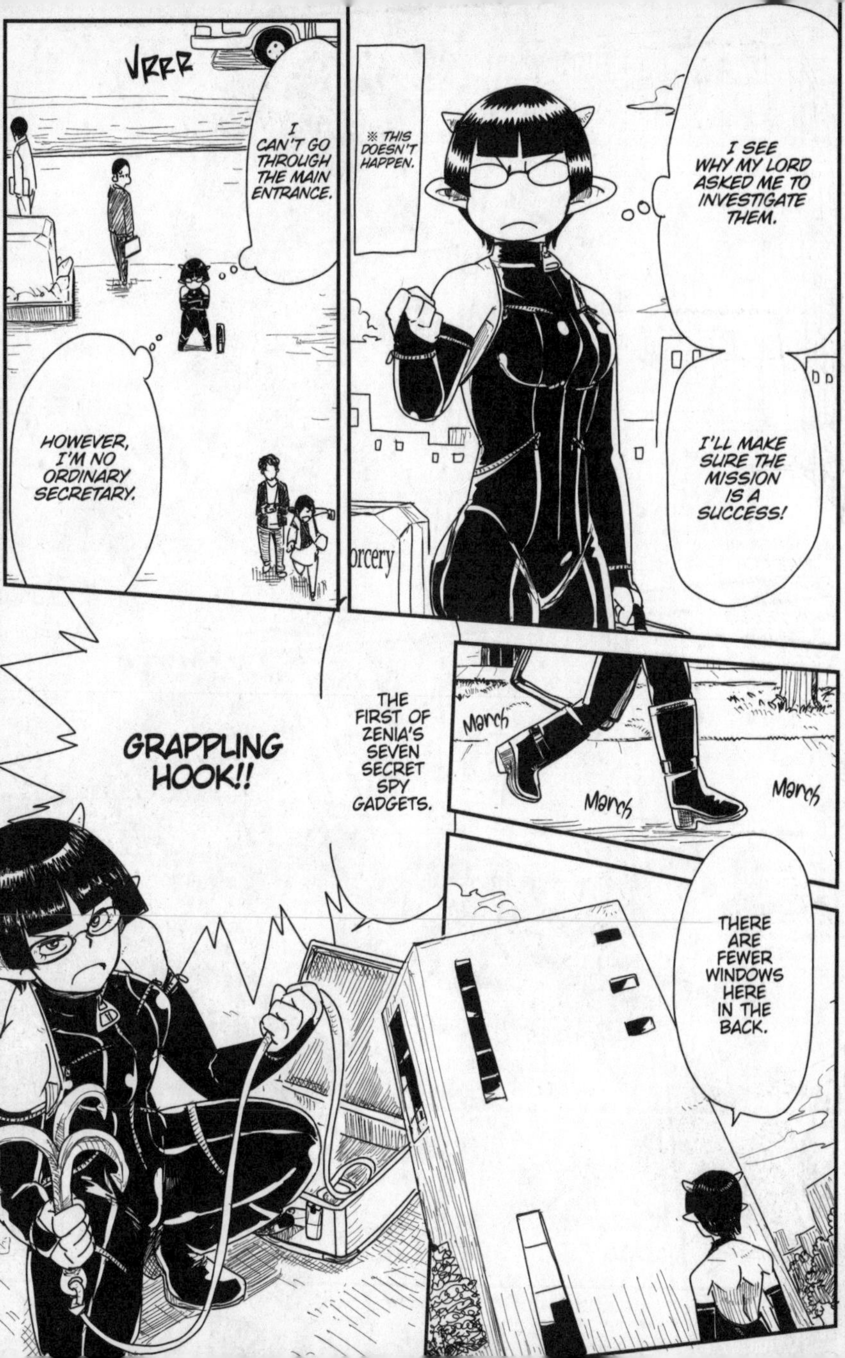
I SEE WHY MY LORD ASKED ME TO INVESTIGATE THEM.
I'LL MAKE SURE THE MISSION IS A SUCCESS!
※ THIS DOESN'T HAPPEN.
orcery
VRRR
I CAN'T GO THROUGH THE MAIN ENTRANCE.
HOWEVER, I'M NO ORDINARY SECRETARY.
March
March
March
THERE ARE FEWER WINDOWS HERE IN THE BACK.
THE FIRST OF ZENIA'S SEVEN SECRET SPY GADGETS.
GRAPPLING HOOK!!

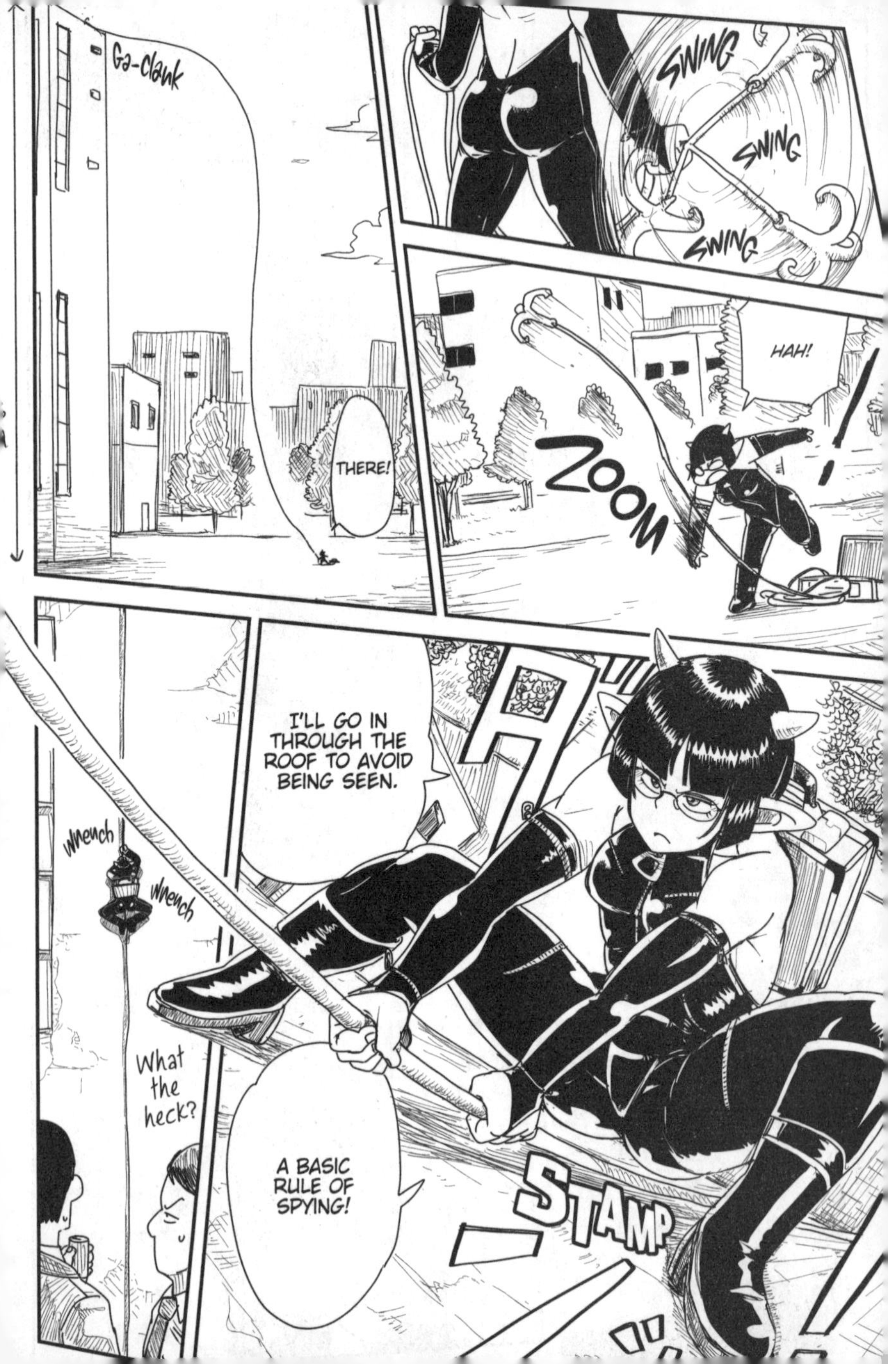
SWING
SWING
SWING
HAH!
ZOOM
Ga-clank
THERE!
I'LL GO IN THROUGH THE ROOF TO AVOID BEING SEEN.
A BASIC RULE OF SPYING!
STAMP
wrench
wrench
What the heck?

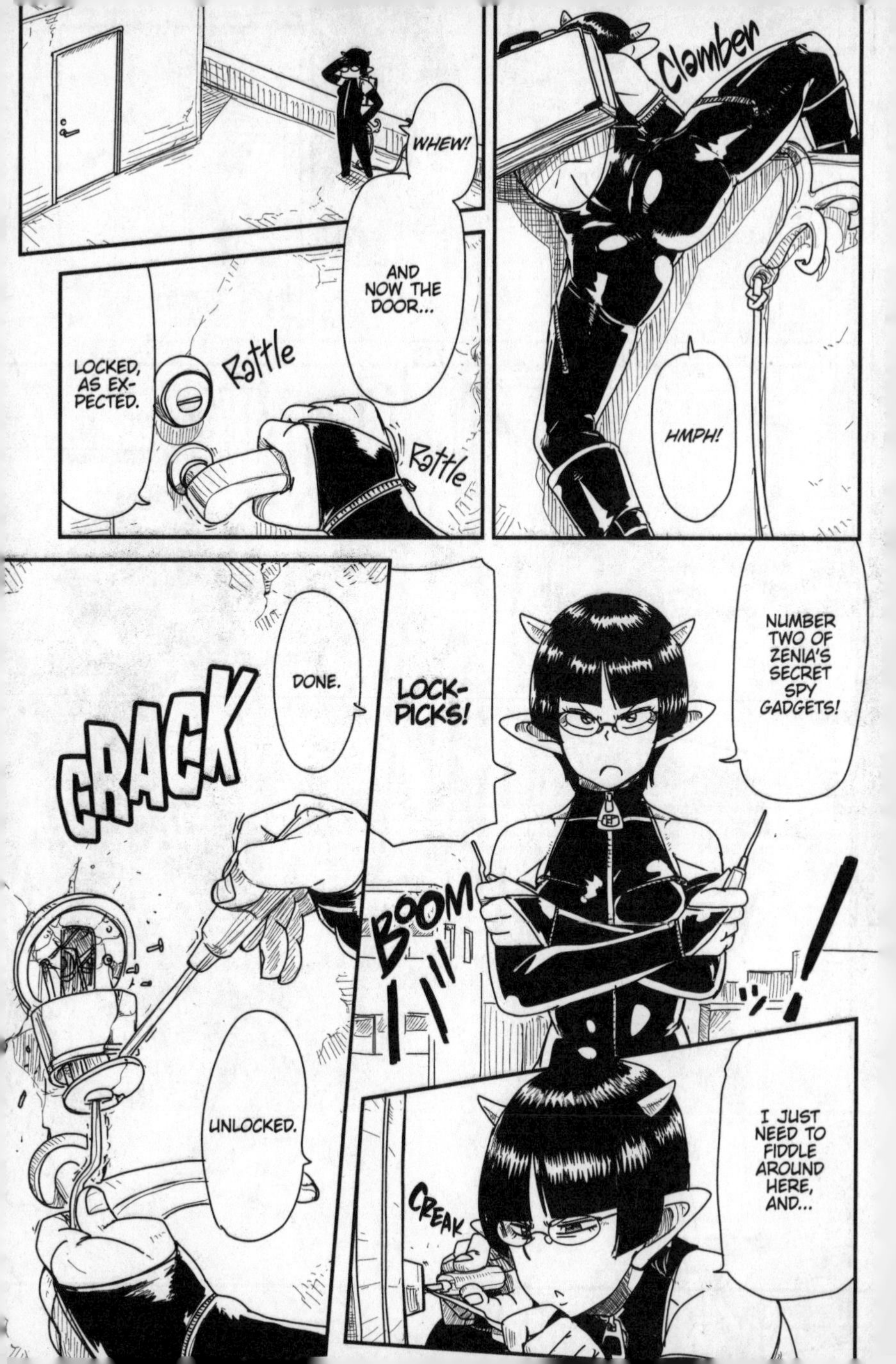
Clamber
HMPH!
WHEW!
AND NOW THE DOOR...
Rattle
Rattle
LOCKED, AS EX-PECTED.
NUMBER TWO OF ZENIA'S SECRET SPY GADGETS!
LOCK-PICKS!
BOOM
I JUST NEED TO FIDDLE AROUND HERE, AND...
CREAK
DONE.
CRACK
UNLOCKED.

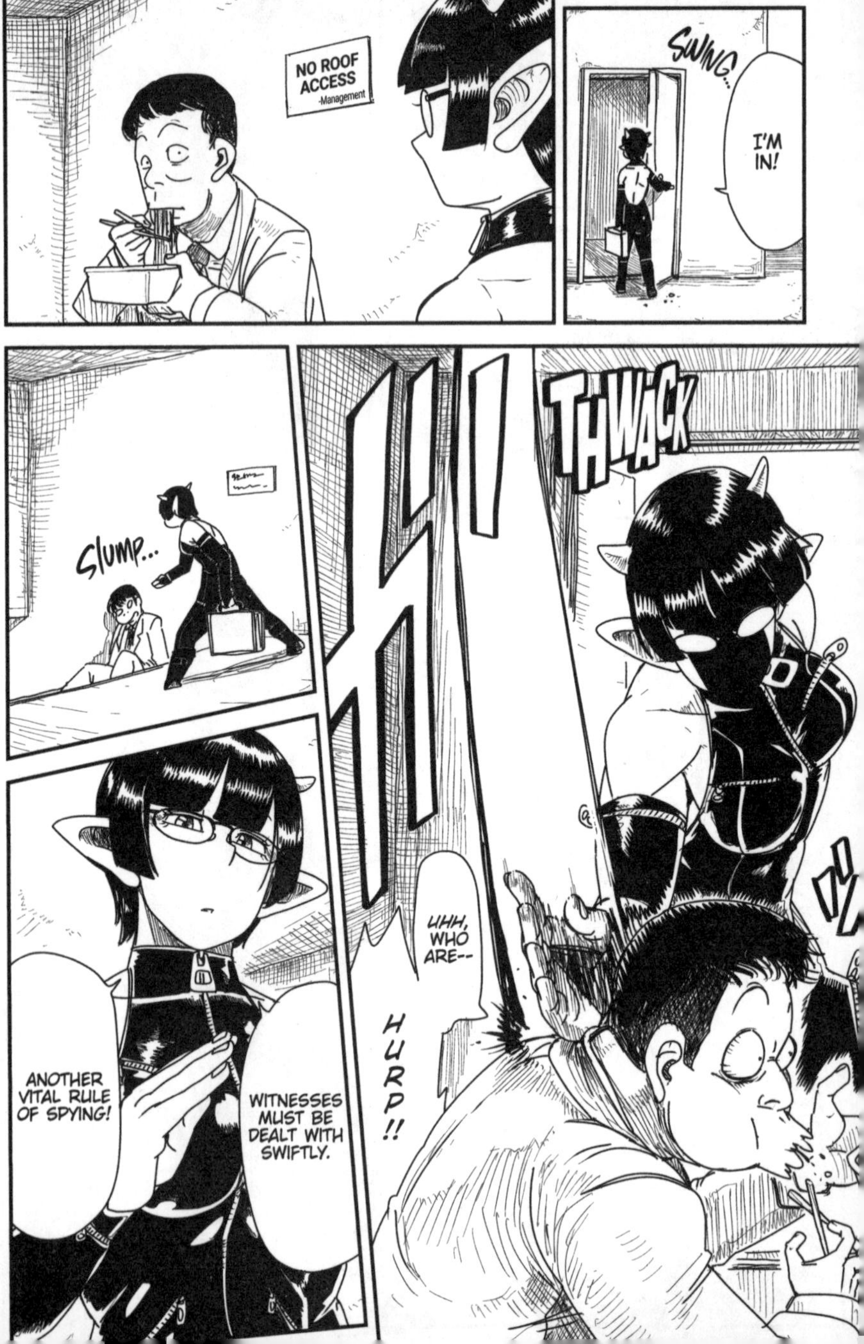
SWING...
I'M IN!
NO ROOF ACCESS -Management
THWACK
UHH, WHO ARE--
HURP!!
Slump...
ANOTHER VITAL RULE OF SPYING!
WITNESSES MUST BE DEALT WITH SWIFTLY.

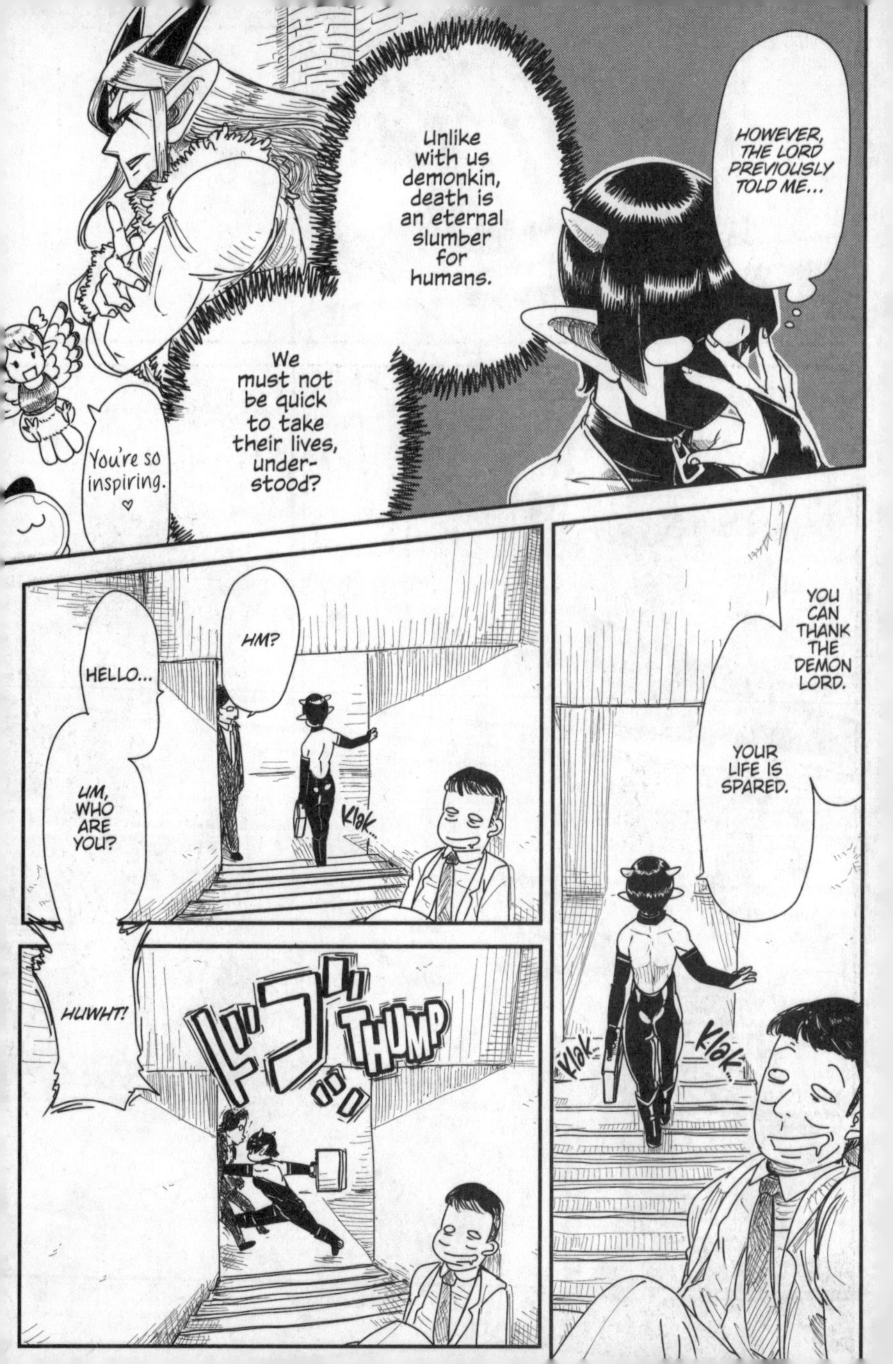
HOWEVER, THE LORD PREVIOUSLY TOLD ME...
Unlike with us demonkin, death is an eternal slumber for humans.
We must not be quick to take their lives, under-stood?
You're so inspiring. ♡
YOU CAN THANK THE DEMON LORD.
YOUR LIFE IS SPARED.
Klak... Klak...
HM?
HELLO...
UM, WHO ARE YOU?
Klak...
HUWHT!
ドゴッ THUMP

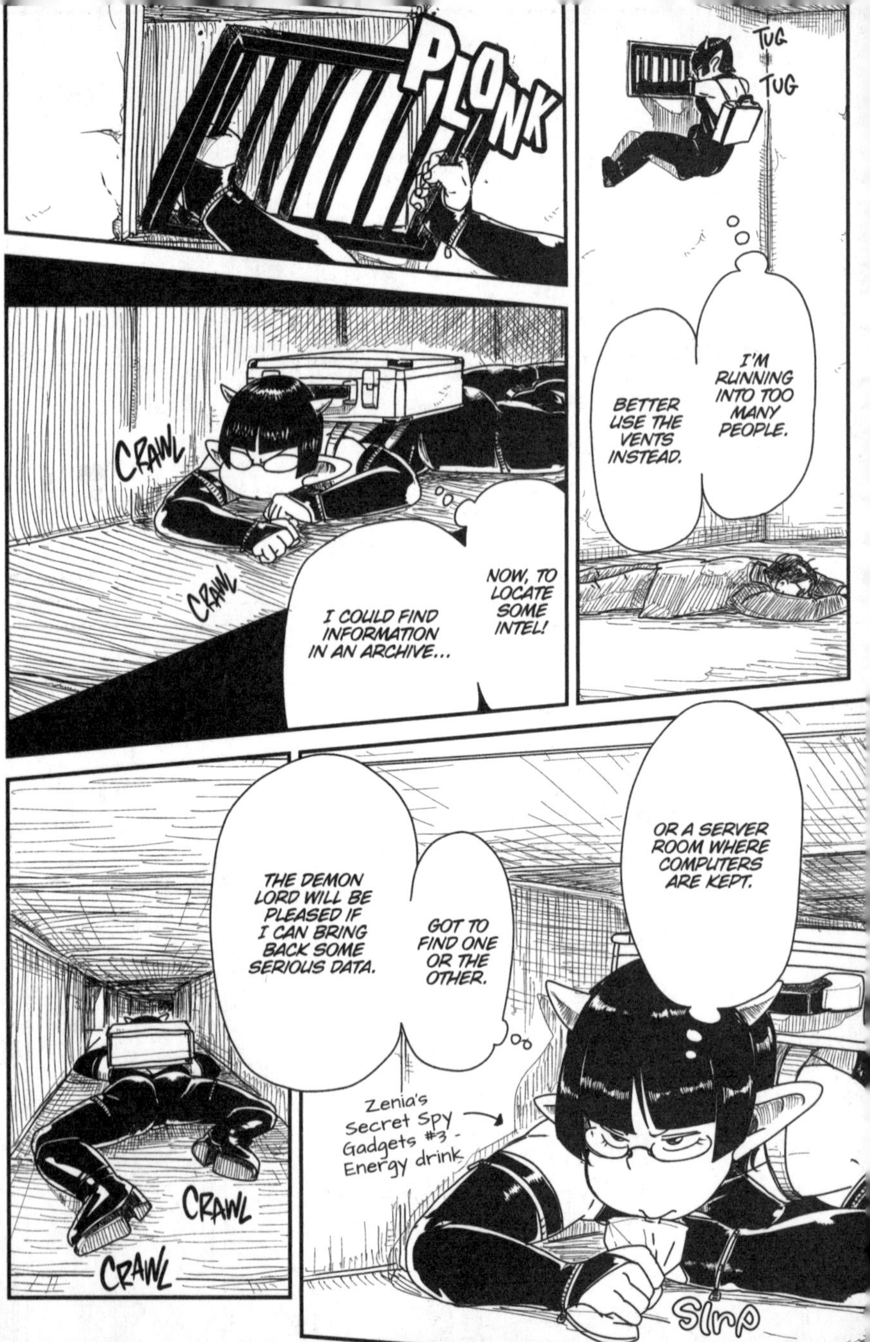
TUG
TUG
I'M RUNNING INTO TOO MANY PEOPLE.
BETTER USE THE VENTS INSTEAD.
PLONK
CRAWL
CRAWL
NOW, TO LOCATE SOME INTEL!
I COULD FIND INFORMATION IN AN ARCHIVE...
OR A SERVER ROOM WHERE COMPUTERS ARE KEPT.
Zenia's Secret Spy Gadgets #3 - Energy drink
Slrp
GOT TO FIND ONE OR THE OTHER.
THE DEMON LORD WILL BE PLEASED IF I CAN BRING BACK SOME SERIOUS DATA.
CRAWL
CRAWL

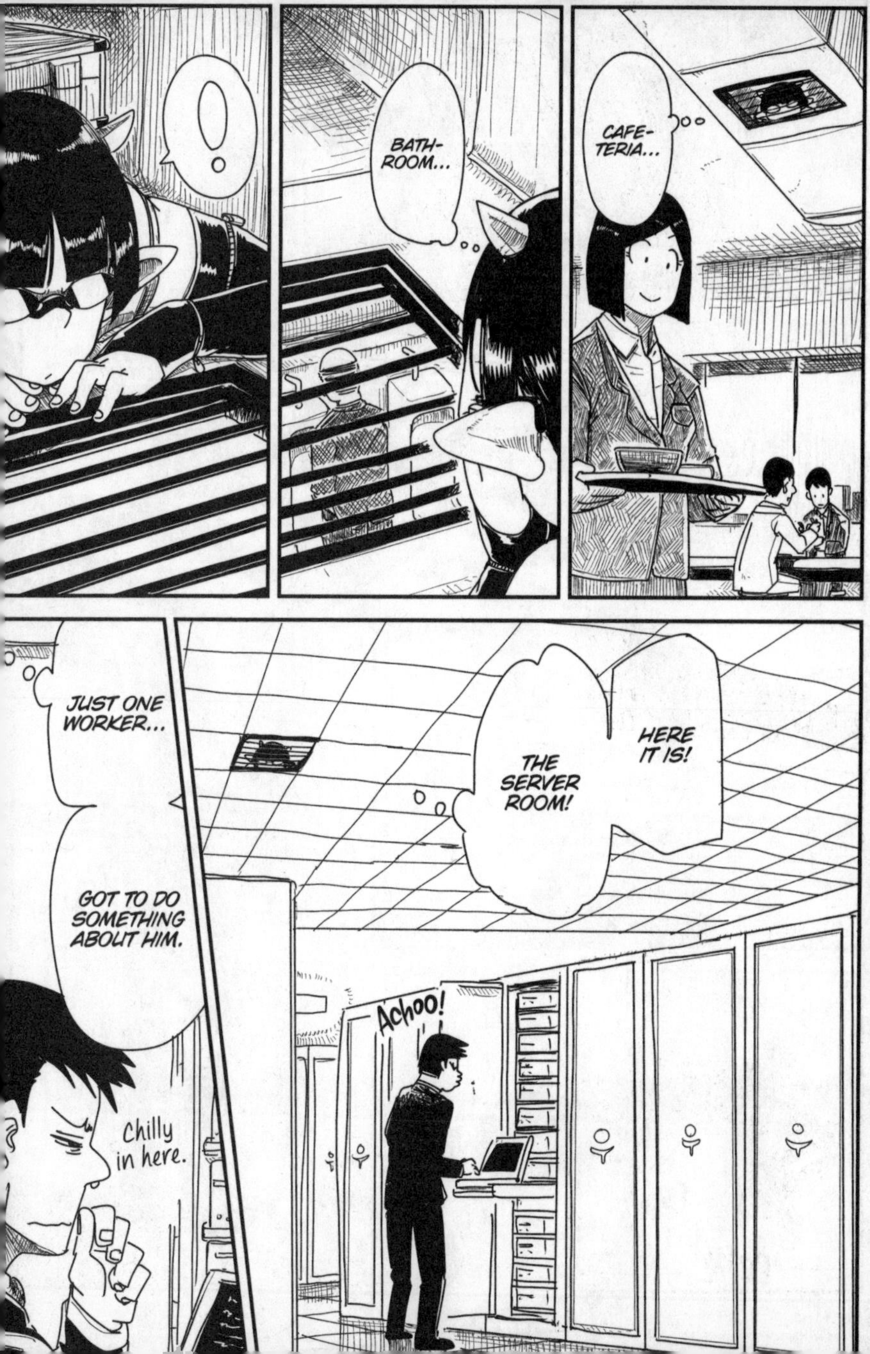
CAFE-TERIA...
BATH-ROOM...
!
HERE IT IS! THE SERVER ROOM!
Achoo!
Chilly in here.
JUST ONE WORKER... GOT TO DO SOMETHING ABOUT HIM.

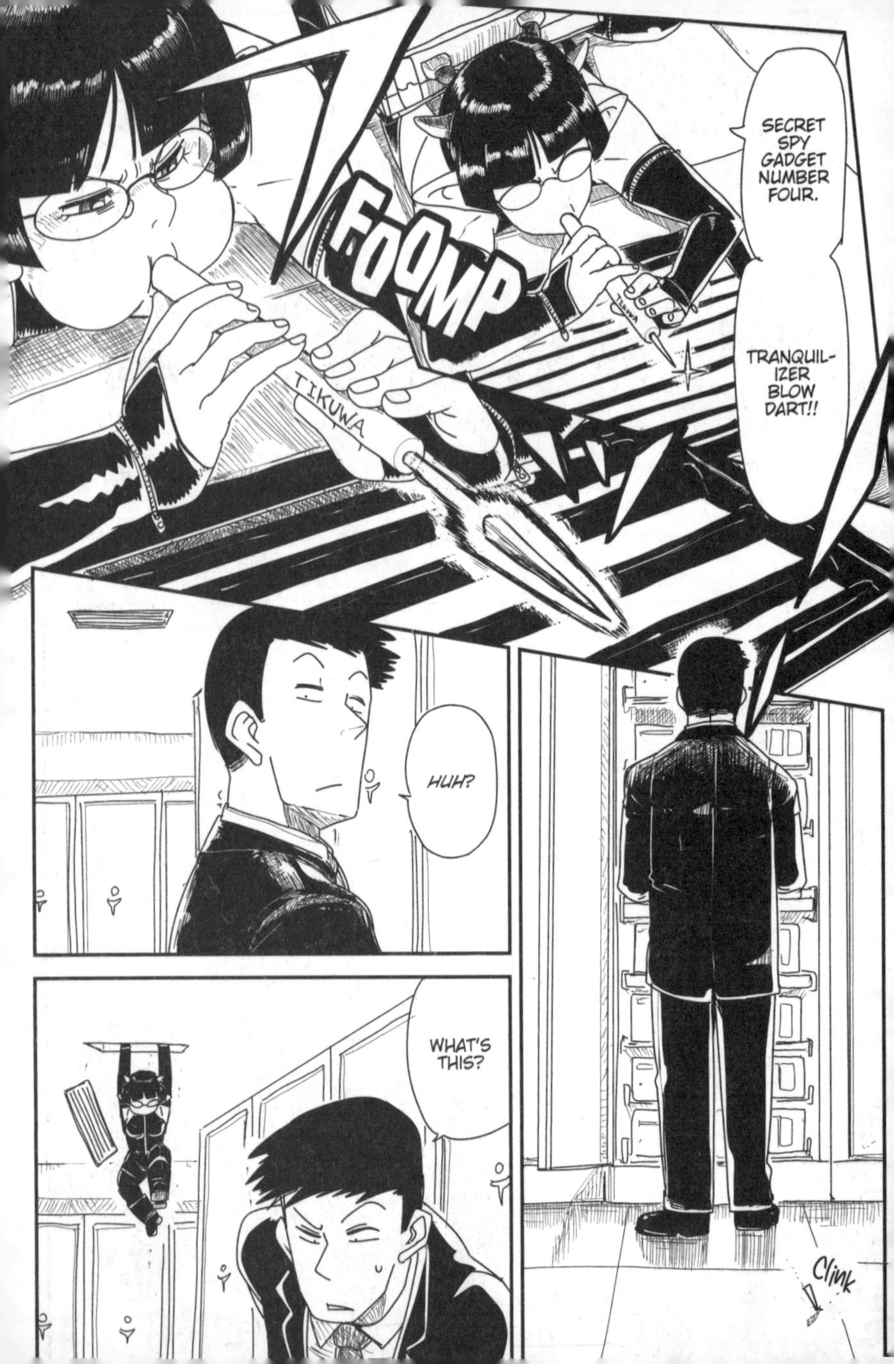
SECRET SPY GADGET NUMBER FOUR.
TRANQUIL-IZER BLOW DART!!
FOOMP
TIKUWA
TIKUWA
Clink
HUH?
WHAT'S THIS?

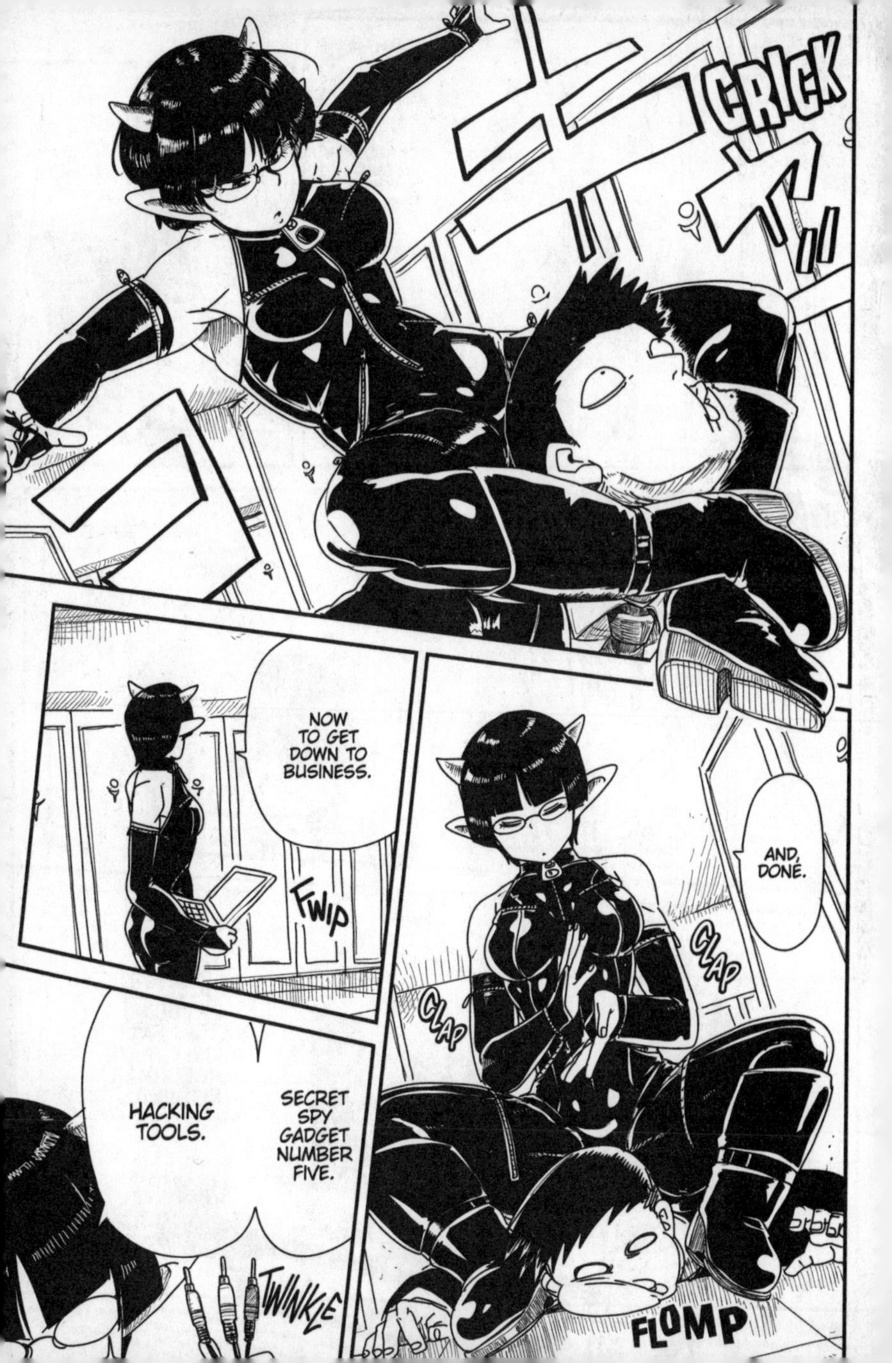
CRICK
AND, DONE.
CLAP
CLAP
FLOMP
NOW TO GET DOWN TO BUSINESS.
FWIP
SECRET SPY GADGET NUMBER FIVE.
HACKING TOOLS.
TWINKLE

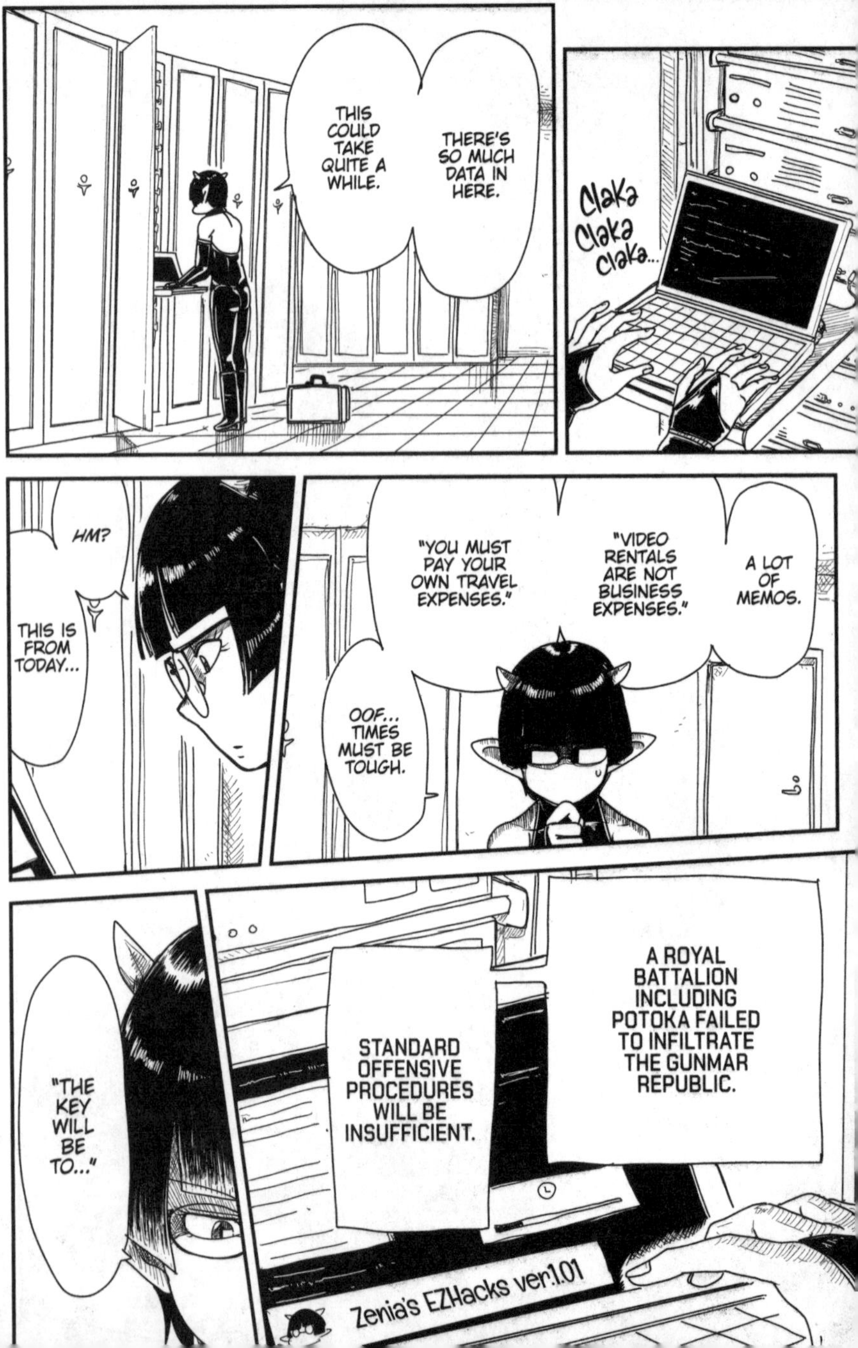
Claka Claka Claka...
THIS COULD TAKE QUITE A WHILE.
THERE'S SO MUCH DATA IN HERE.
A LOT OF MEMOS.
"VIDEO RENTALS ARE NOT BUSINESS EXPENSES."
"YOU MUST PAY YOUR OWN TRAVEL EXPENSES."
OOF... TIMES MUST BE TOUGH.
HM?
THIS IS FROM TODAY...
A ROYAL BATTALION INCLUDING POTOKA FAILED TO INFILTRATE THE GUNMAR REPUBLIC.
STANDARD OFFENSIVE PROCEDURES WILL BE INSUFFICIENT.
Zenia's EZHacks ver.1.01
"THE KEY WILL BE TO..."

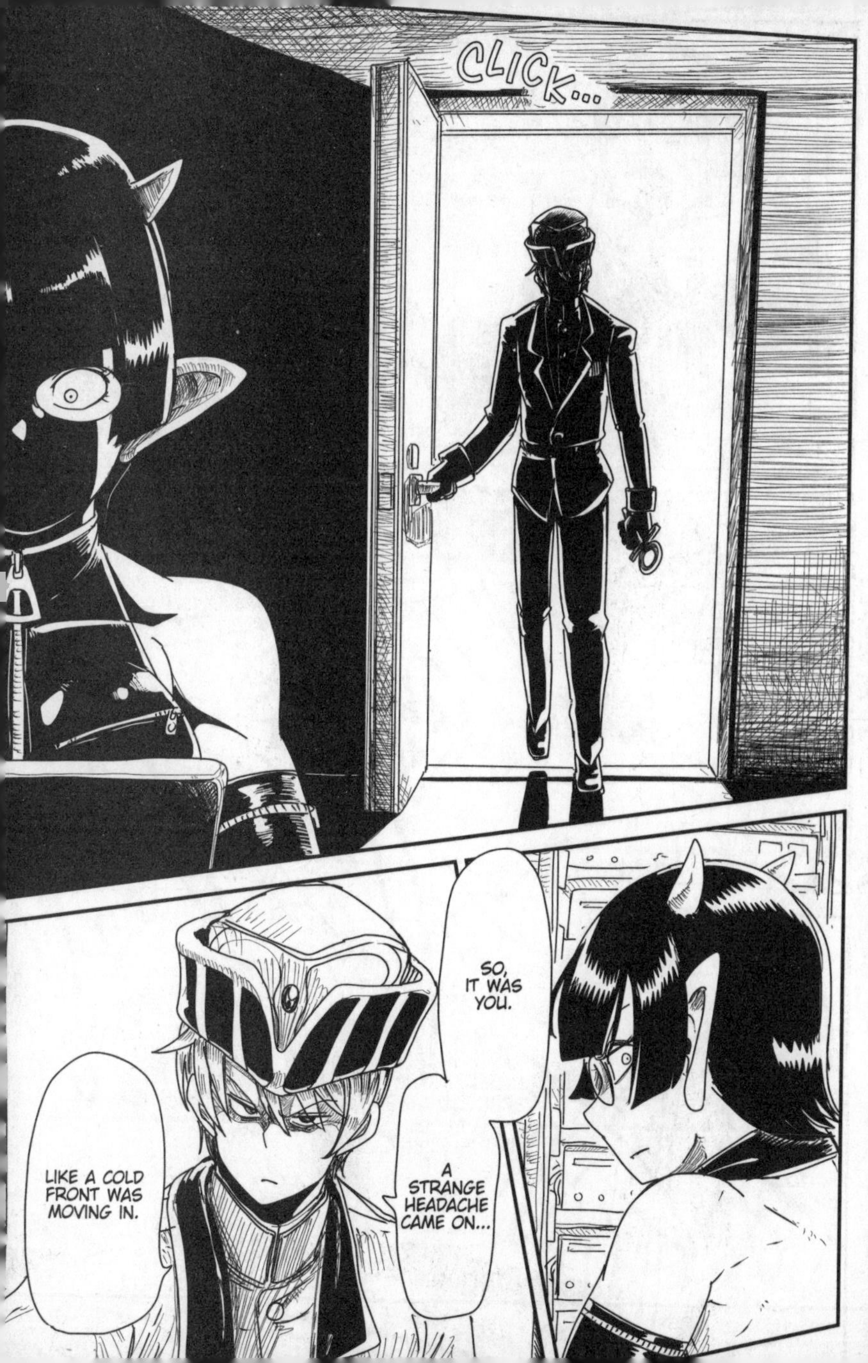
CLICK...
SO, IT WAS YOU.
A STRANGE HEADACHE CAME ON...
LIKE A COLD FRONT WAS MOVING IN.

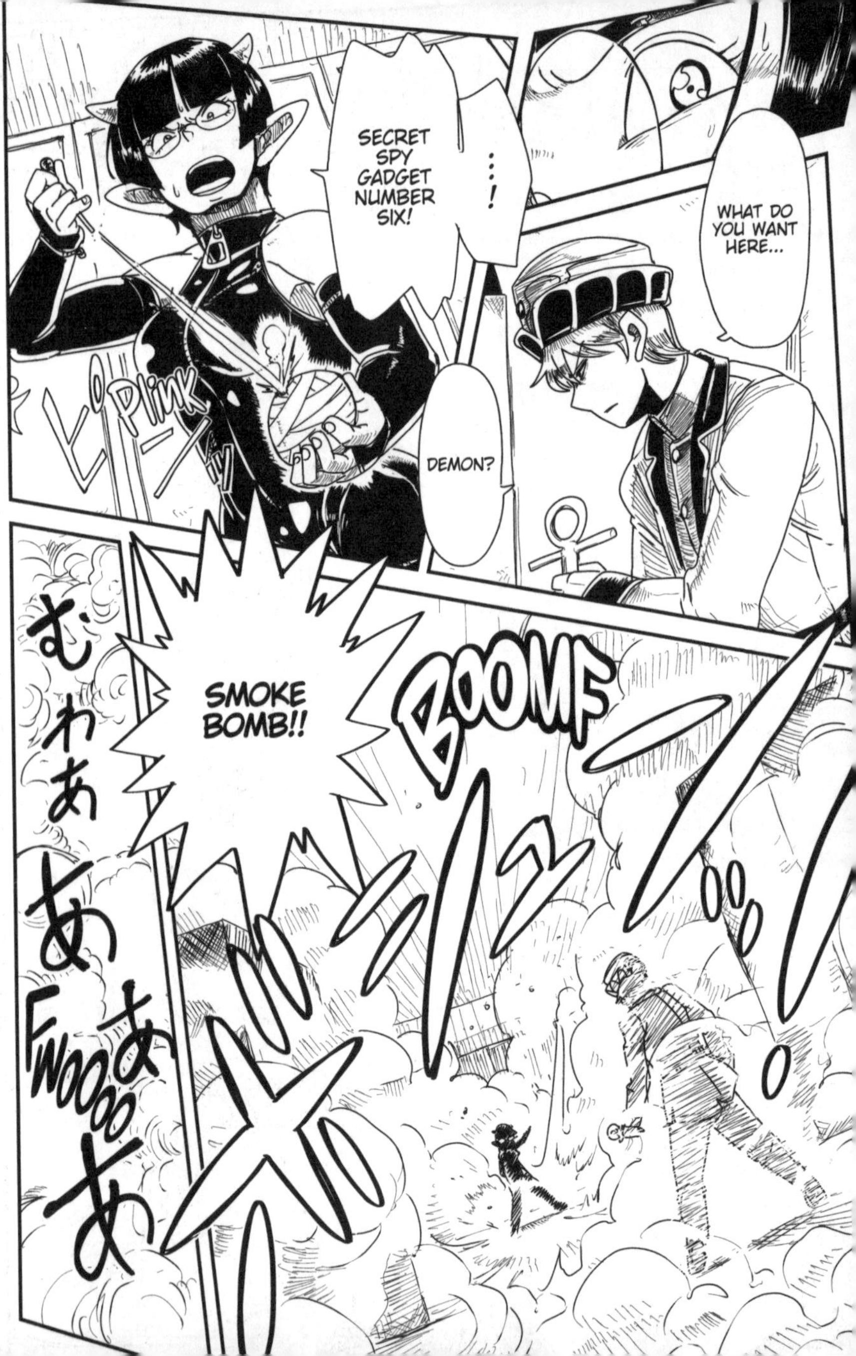
WHAT DO YOU WANT HERE...
DEMON?
...!
SECRET SPY GADGET NUMBER SIX!
PLINK
SMOKE BOMB!!
BOOMF
FWOOOO

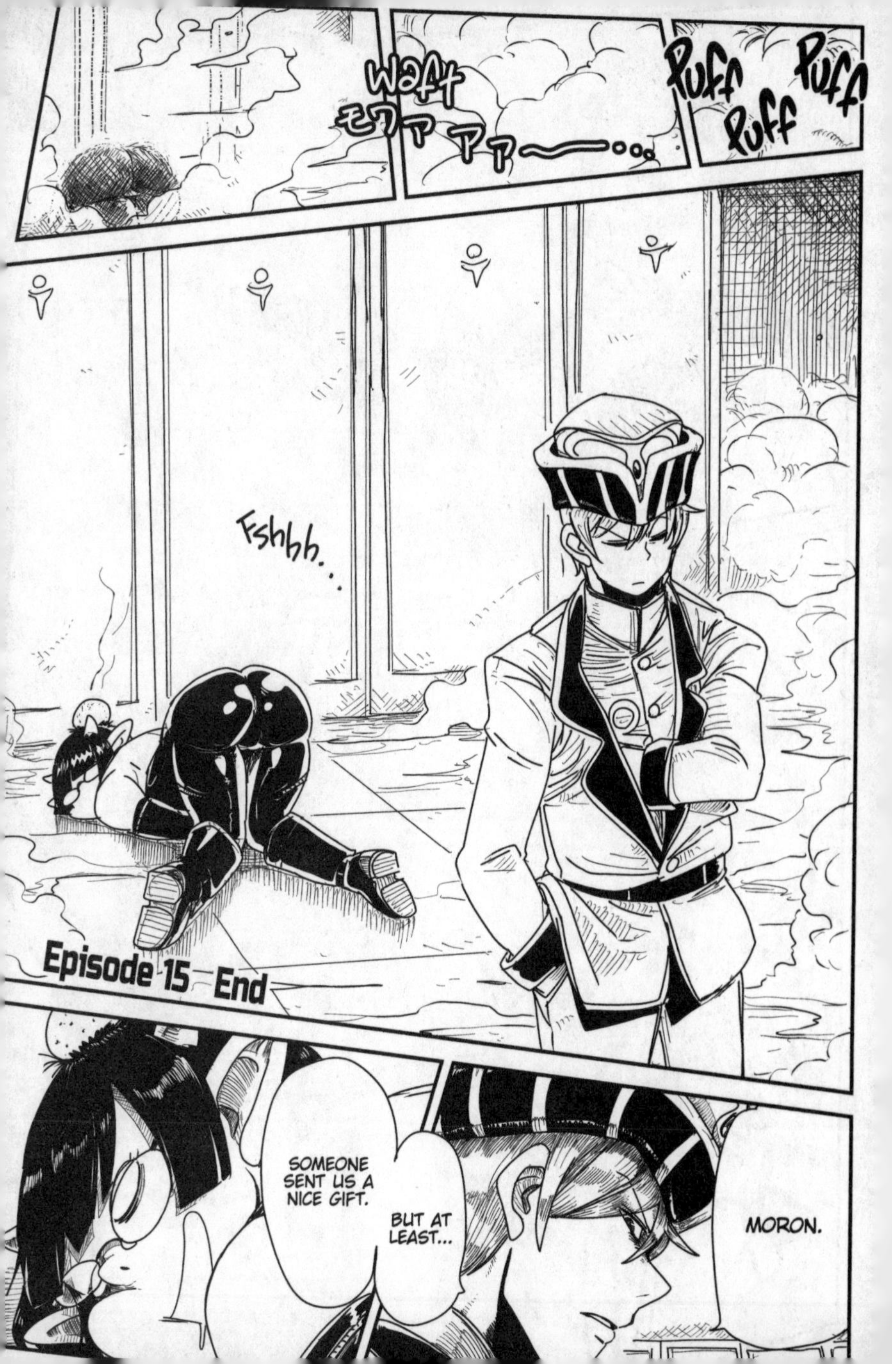

Puff Puff Puff
Waft
モワァァァ〜〜〜。。。
Fshhh...
Episode 15 End
MORON.
BUT AT LEAST...
SOMEONE SENT US A NICE GIFT.

LEVEL 1 DEMON LORD & ONE ROOM HERO

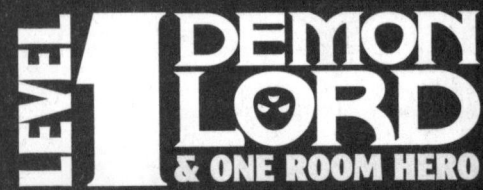

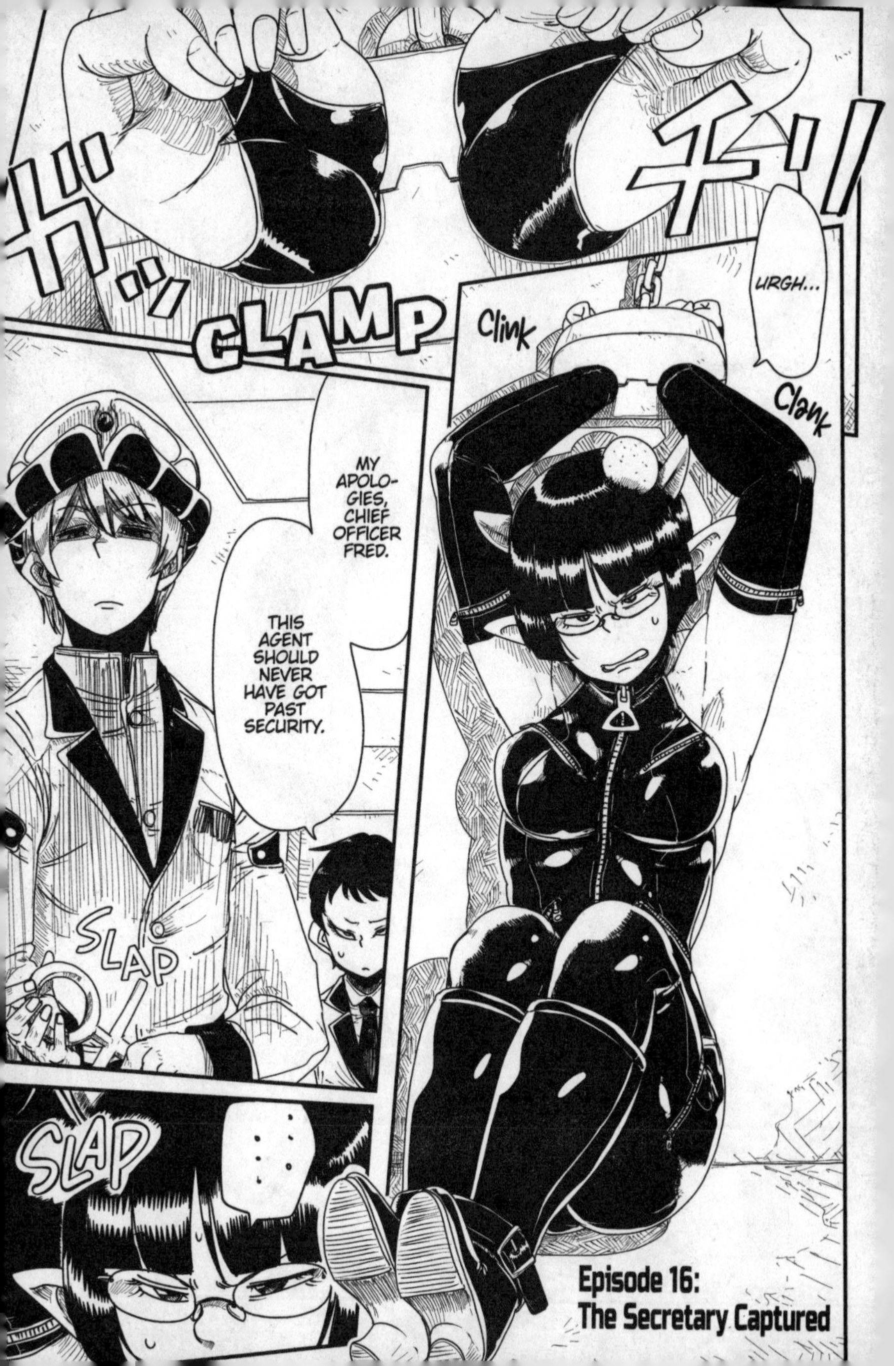
CLAMP
URGH...
Clink
Clank
MY APOLOGIES, CHIEF OFFICER FRED.
THIS AGENT SHOULD NEVER HAVE GOT PAST SECURITY.
SLAP
SLAP
...

Episode 16: The Secretary Captured

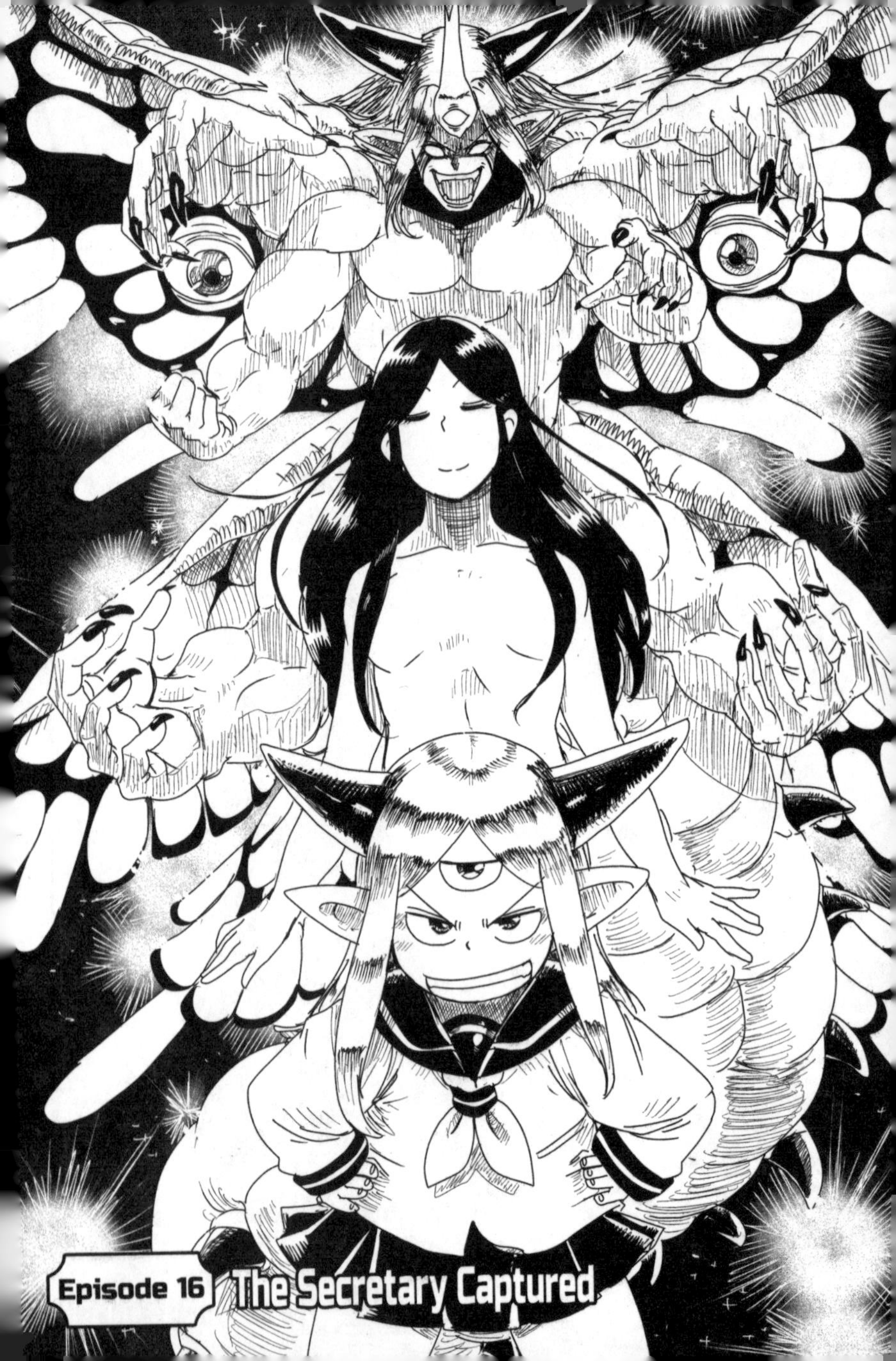
Episode 16
The Secretary Captured

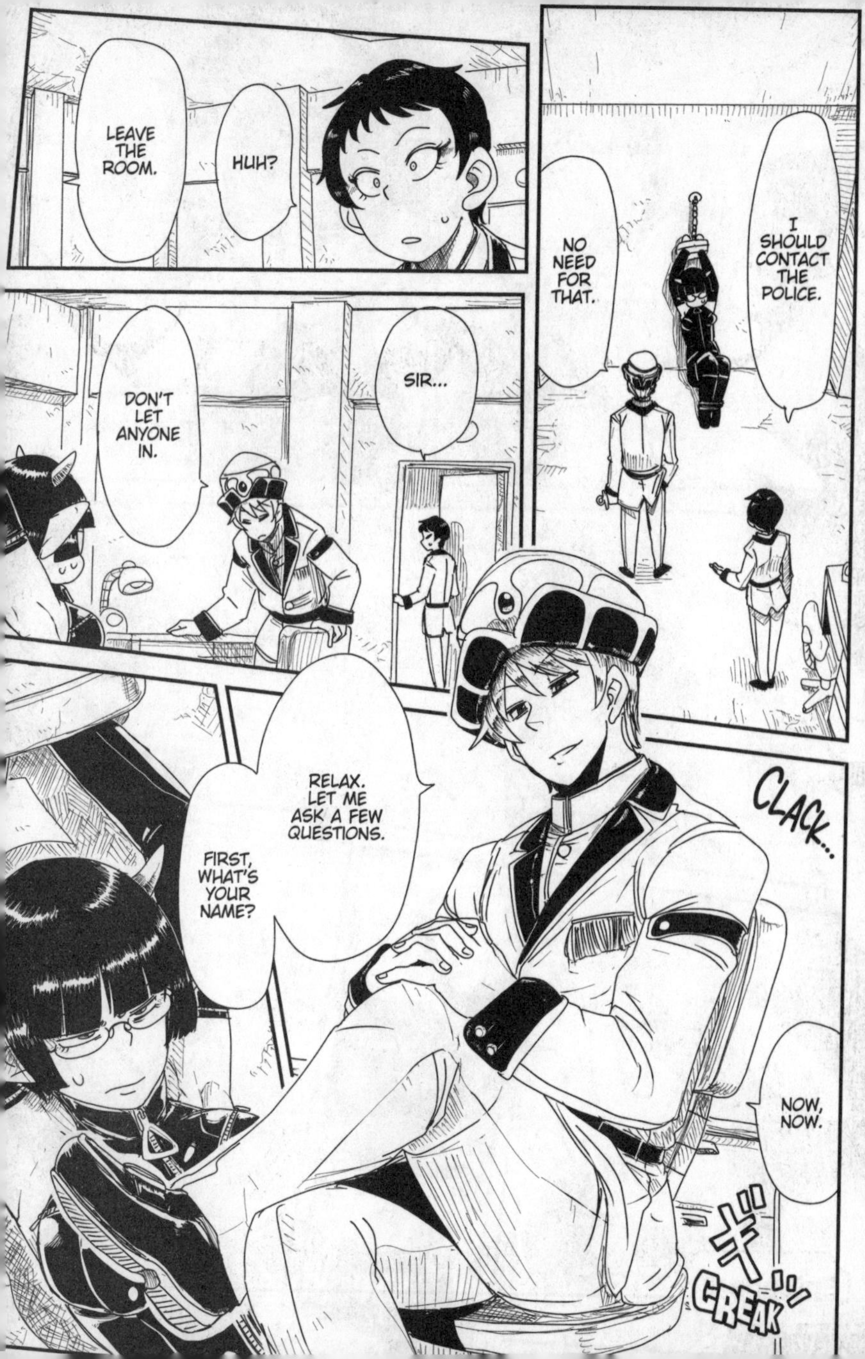
I SHOULD CONTACT THE POLICE.
NO NEED FOR THAT.
LEAVE THE ROOM.
HUH?
SIR...
DON'T LET ANYONE IN.
NOW, NOW.
CLACK...
CREAK
RELAX. LET ME ASK A FEW QUESTIONS.
FIRST, WHAT'S YOUR NAME?

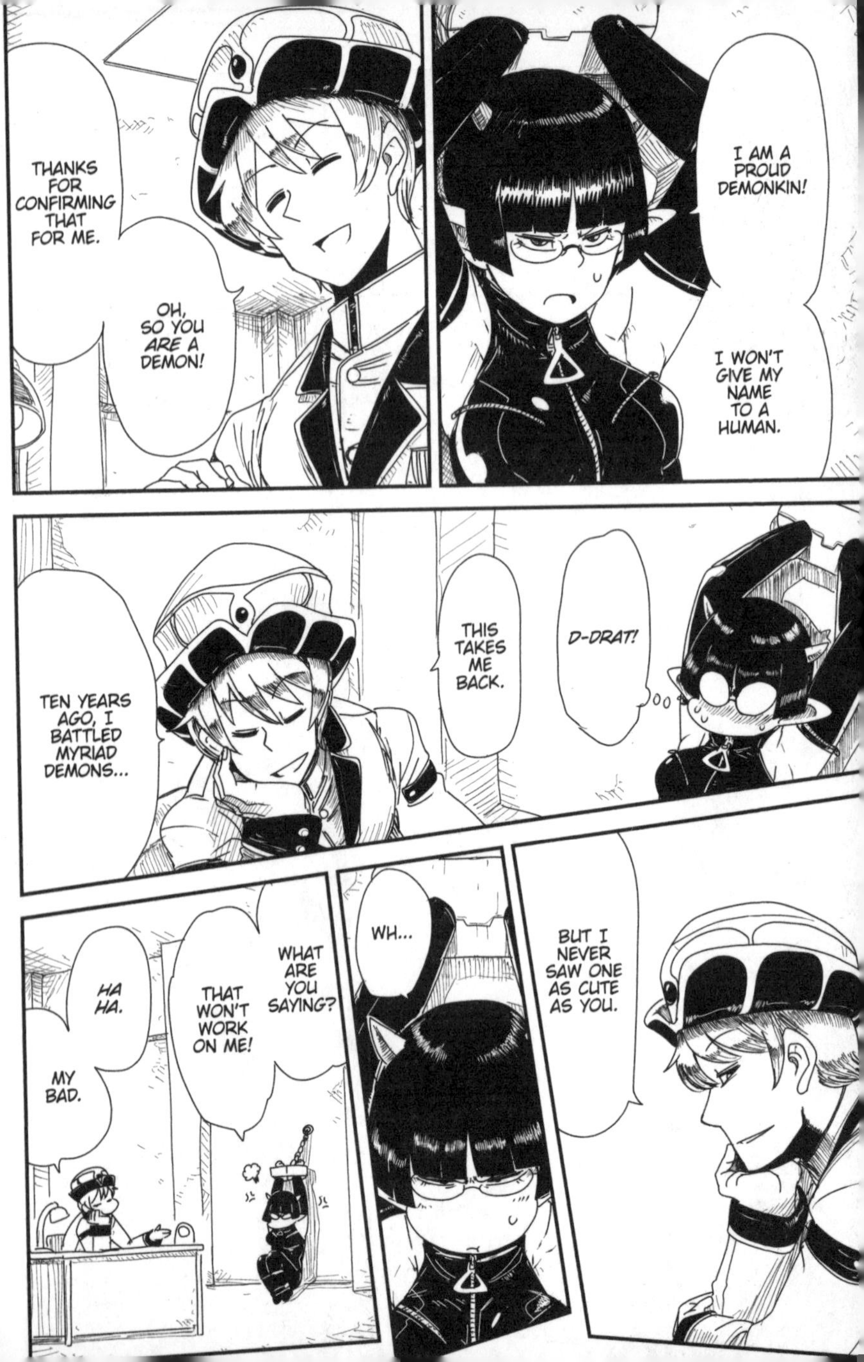
I AM A PROUD DEMONKIN!
I WON'T GIVE MY NAME TO A HUMAN.
OH, SO YOU *ARE* A DEMON!
THANKS FOR CONFIRMING THAT FOR ME.
D-DRAT!
THIS TAKES ME BACK.
TEN YEARS AGO, I BATTLED MYRIAD DEMONS...
BUT I NEVER SAW ONE AS CUTE AS YOU.
WH...
WHAT ARE YOU SAYING?
THAT WON'T WORK ON ME!
HA HA.
MY BAD.

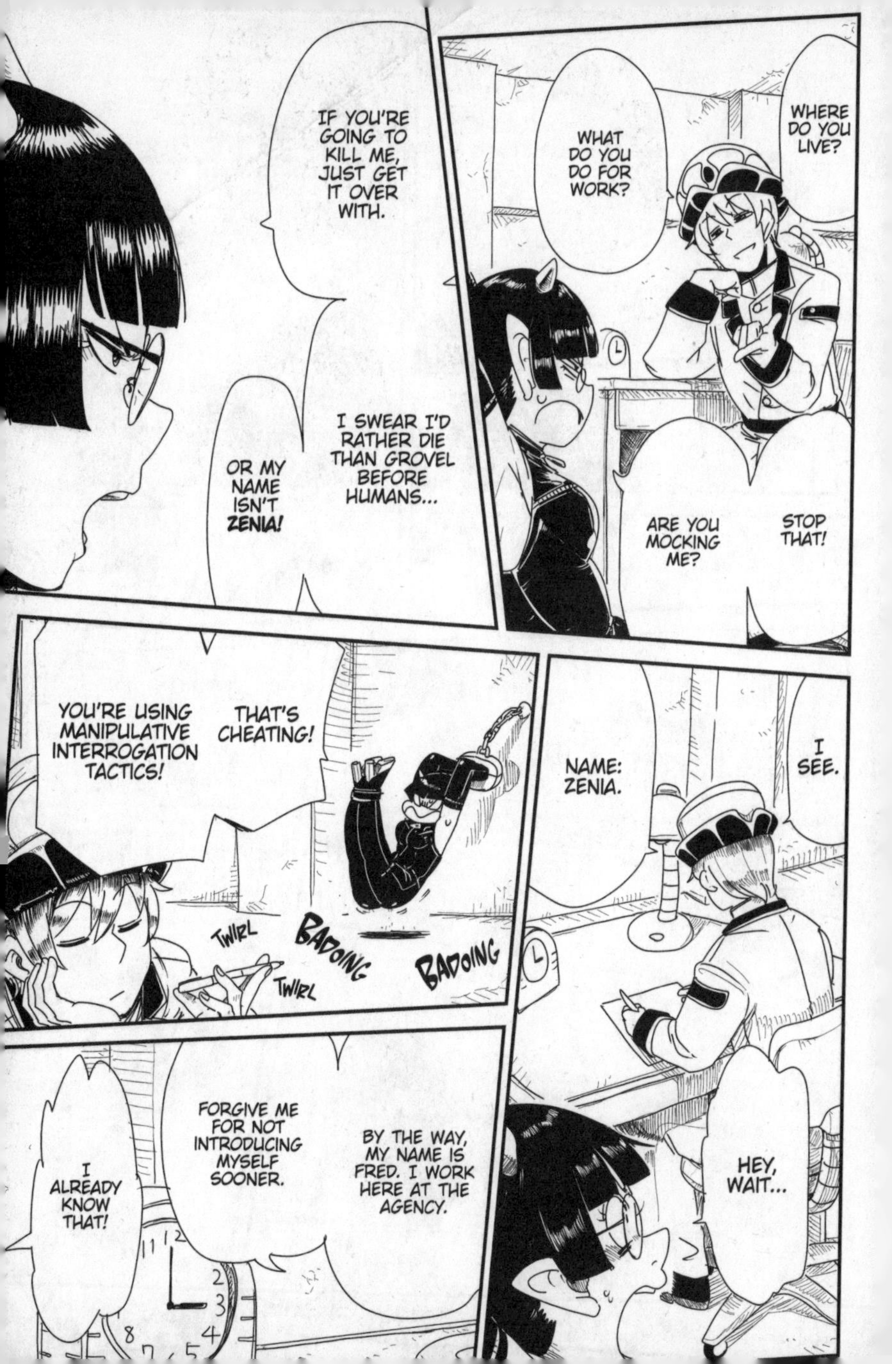
WHERE DO YOU LIVE?
WHAT DO YOU DO FOR WORK?
STOP THAT!
ARE YOU MOCKING ME?
IF YOU'RE GOING TO KILL ME, JUST GET IT OVER WITH.
I SWEAR I'D RATHER DIE THAN GROVEL BEFORE HUMANS...
OR MY NAME ISN'T ZENIA!
I SEE.
NAME: ZENIA.
HEY, WAIT...
THAT'S CHEATING!
YOU'RE USING MANIPULATIVE INTERROGATION TACTICS!
BADOING
BADOING
TWIRL
TWIRL
BY THE WAY, MY NAME IS FRED. I WORK HERE AT THE AGENCY.
FORGIVE ME FOR NOT INTRODUCING MYSELF SOONER.
I ALREADY KNOW THAT!

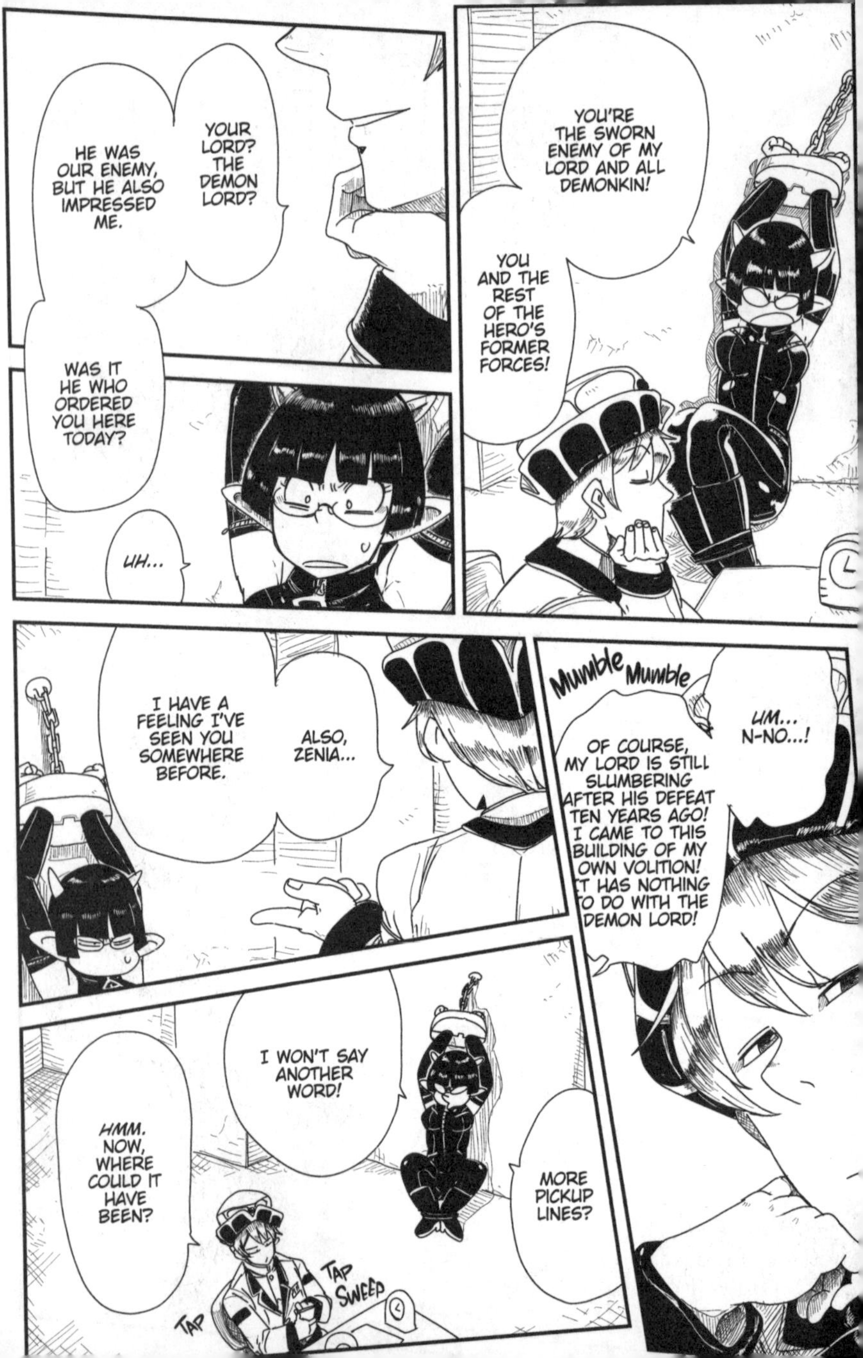
YOU'RE THE SWORN ENEMY OF MY LORD AND ALL DEMONKIN!
YOU AND THE REST OF THE HERO'S FORMER FORCES!
YOUR LORD? THE DEMON LORD?
HE WAS OUR ENEMY, BUT HE ALSO IMPRESSED ME.
WAS IT HE WHO ORDERED YOU HERE TODAY?
UH...
UM... N-NO...!
Mumble Mumble
OF COURSE, MY LORD IS STILL SLUMBERING AFTER HIS DEFEAT TEN YEARS AGO! I CAME TO THIS BUILDING OF MY OWN VOLITION! IT HAS NOTHING TO DO WITH THE DEMON LORD!
ALSO, ZENIA...
I HAVE A FEELING I'VE SEEN YOU SOMEWHERE BEFORE.
MORE PICKUP LINES?
I WON'T SAY ANOTHER WORD!
HMM. NOW, WHERE COULD IT HAVE BEEN?
TAP SWEEP
TAP

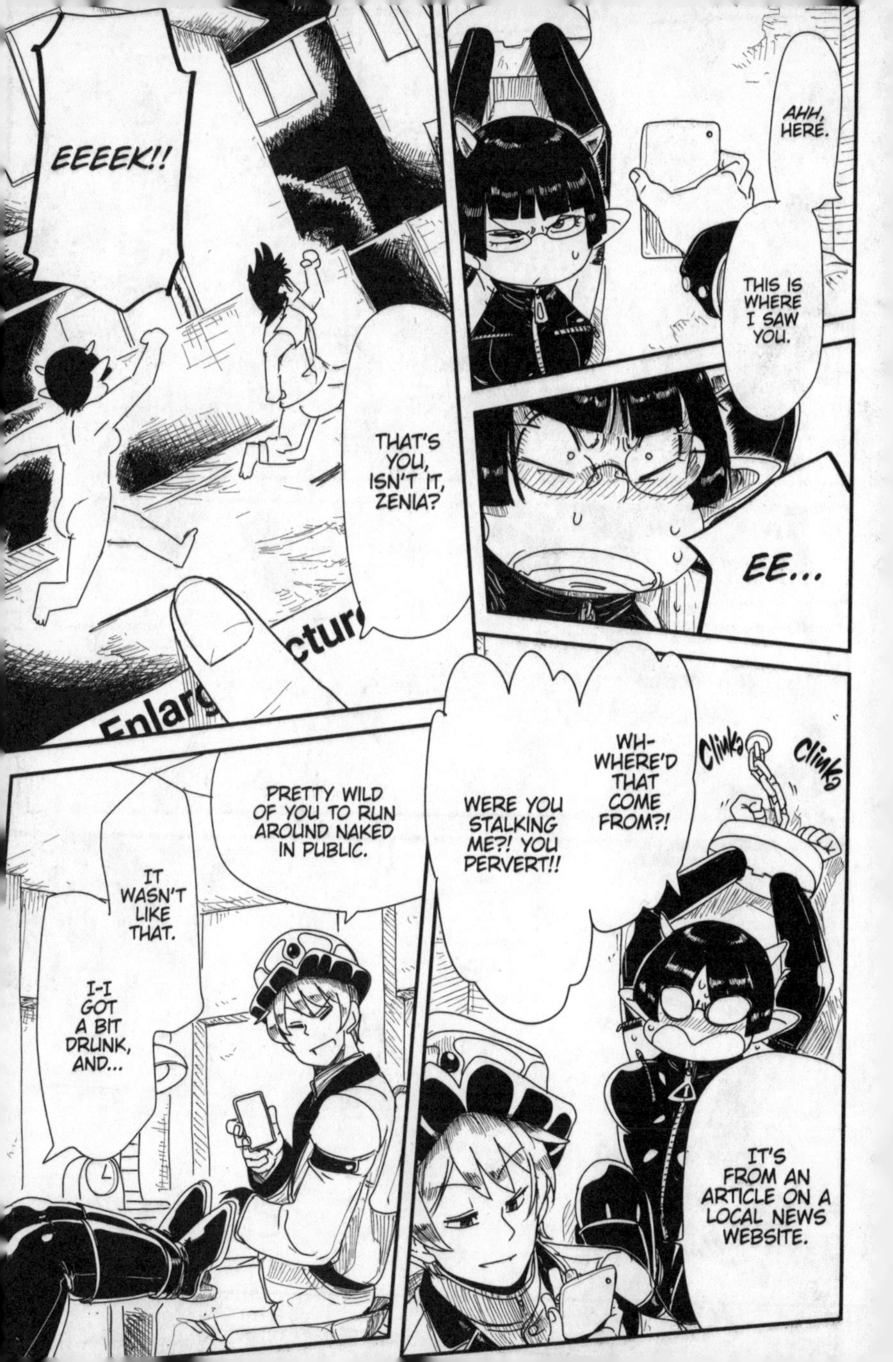
AHH, HERE.
THIS IS WHERE I SAW YOU.
EE...
EEEEK!!
THAT'S YOU, ISN'T IT, ZENIA?
Clinka Clinka
WH- WHERE'D THAT COME FROM?!
WERE YOU STALKING ME?! YOU PERVERT!!
IT'S FROM AN ARTICLE ON A LOCAL NEWS WEBSITE.
PRETTY WILD OF YOU TO RUN AROUND NAKED IN PUBLIC.
IT WASN'T LIKE THAT.
I-I GOT A BIT DRUNK, AND...

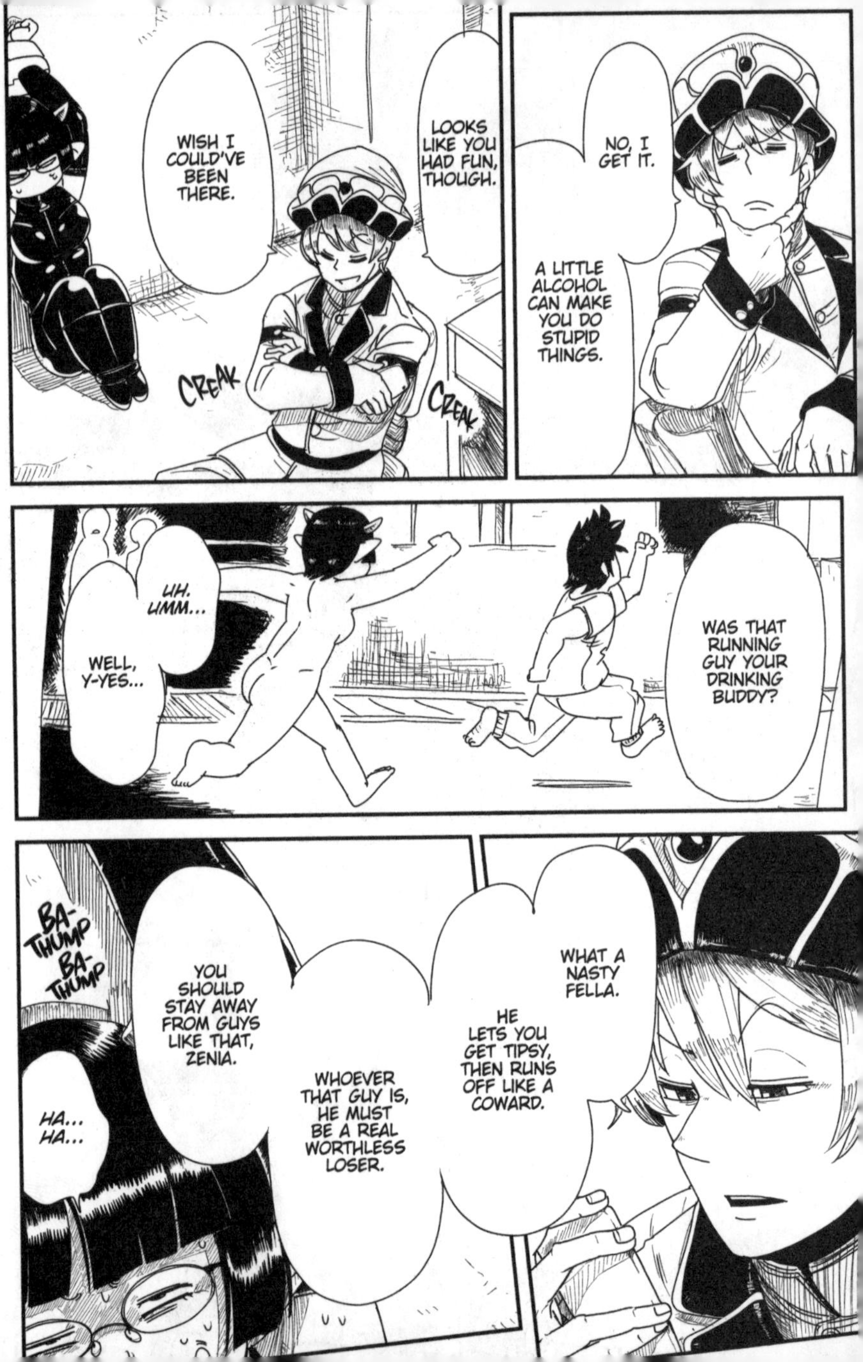
NO, I GET IT.
A LITTLE ALCOHOL CAN MAKE YOU DO STUPID THINGS.
LOOKS LIKE YOU HAD FUN, THOUGH.
WISH I COULD'VE BEEN THERE.
CREAK
CREAK
WAS THAT RUNNING GUY YOUR DRINKING BUDDY?
UH. UMM...
WELL, Y-YES...
WHAT A NASTY FELLA.
HE LETS YOU GET TIPSY, THEN RUNS OFF LIKE A COWARD.
WHOEVER THAT GUY IS, HE MUST BE A REAL WORTHLESS LOSER.
YOU SHOULD STAY AWAY FROM GUYS LIKE THAT, ZENIA.
BA-THUMP BA-THUMP
HA... HA...

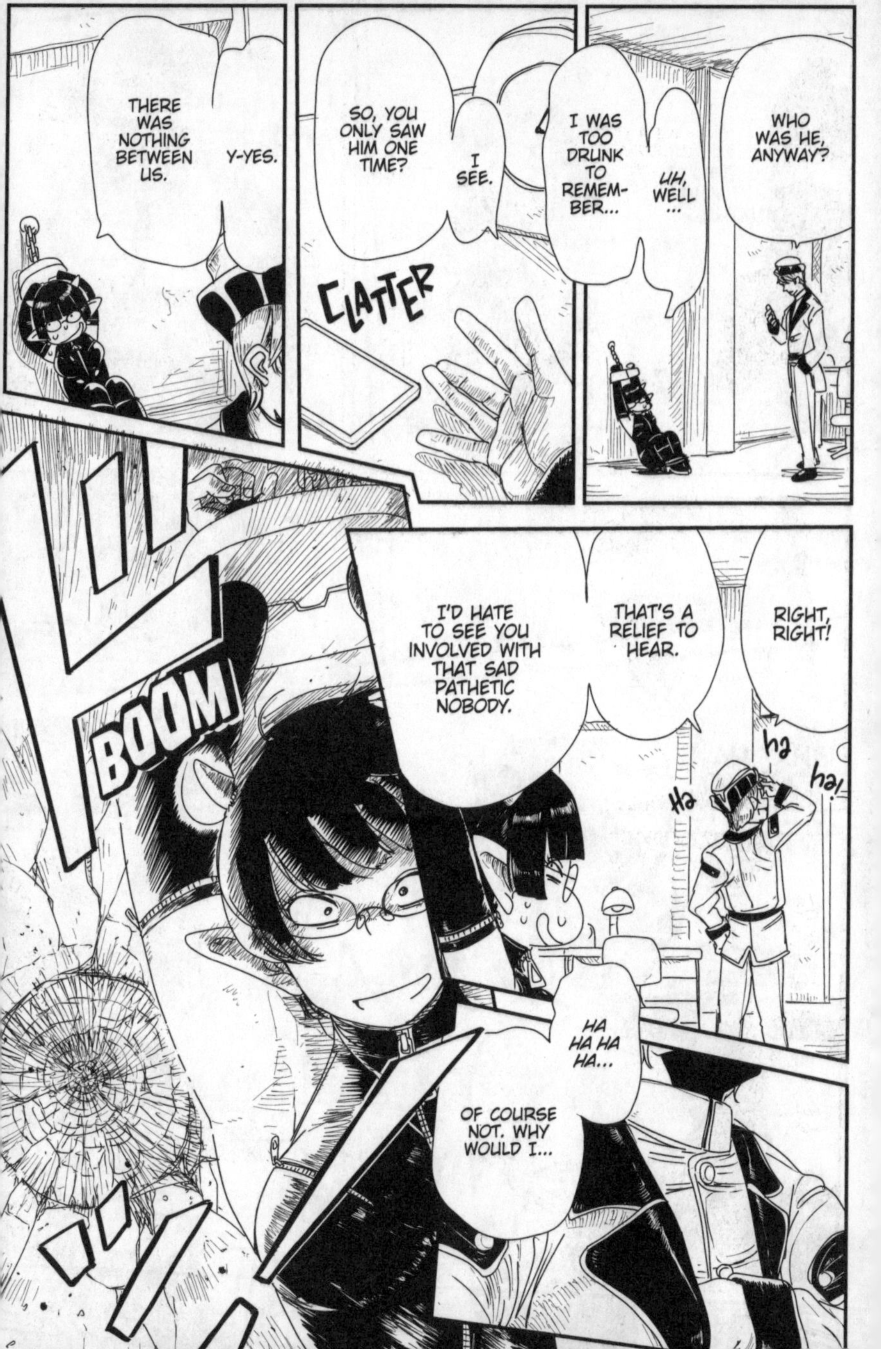
WHO WAS HE, ANYWAY?
UH, WELL...
I WAS TOO DRUNK TO REMEMBER...
I SEE.
SO, YOU ONLY SAW HIM ONE TIME?
CLATTER
Y-YES.
THERE WAS NOTHING BETWEEN US.
RIGHT, RIGHT!
ha ha!
Ha
THAT'S A RELIEF TO HEAR.
I'D HATE TO SEE YOU INVOLVED WITH THAT SAD PATHETIC NOBODY.
HA HA HA HA...
OF COURSE NOT. WHY WOULD I...
BOOM

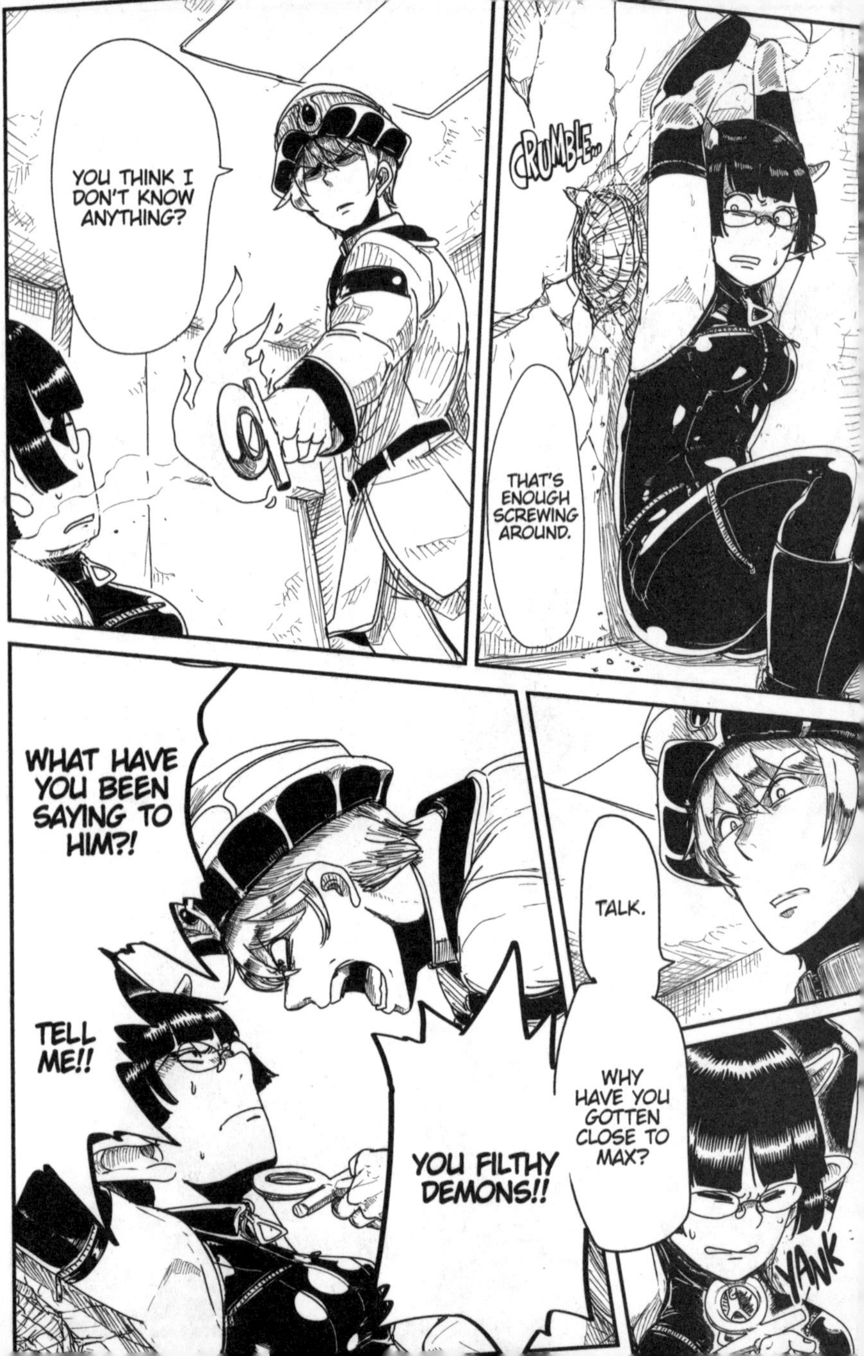
CRUMBLE...
THAT'S ENOUGH SCREWING AROUND.
YOU THINK I DON'T KNOW ANYTHING?
TALK.
WHY HAVE YOU GOTTEN CLOSE TO MAX?
YANK
WHAT HAVE YOU BEEN SAYING TO HIM?!
TELL ME!!
YOU FILTHY DEMONS!!

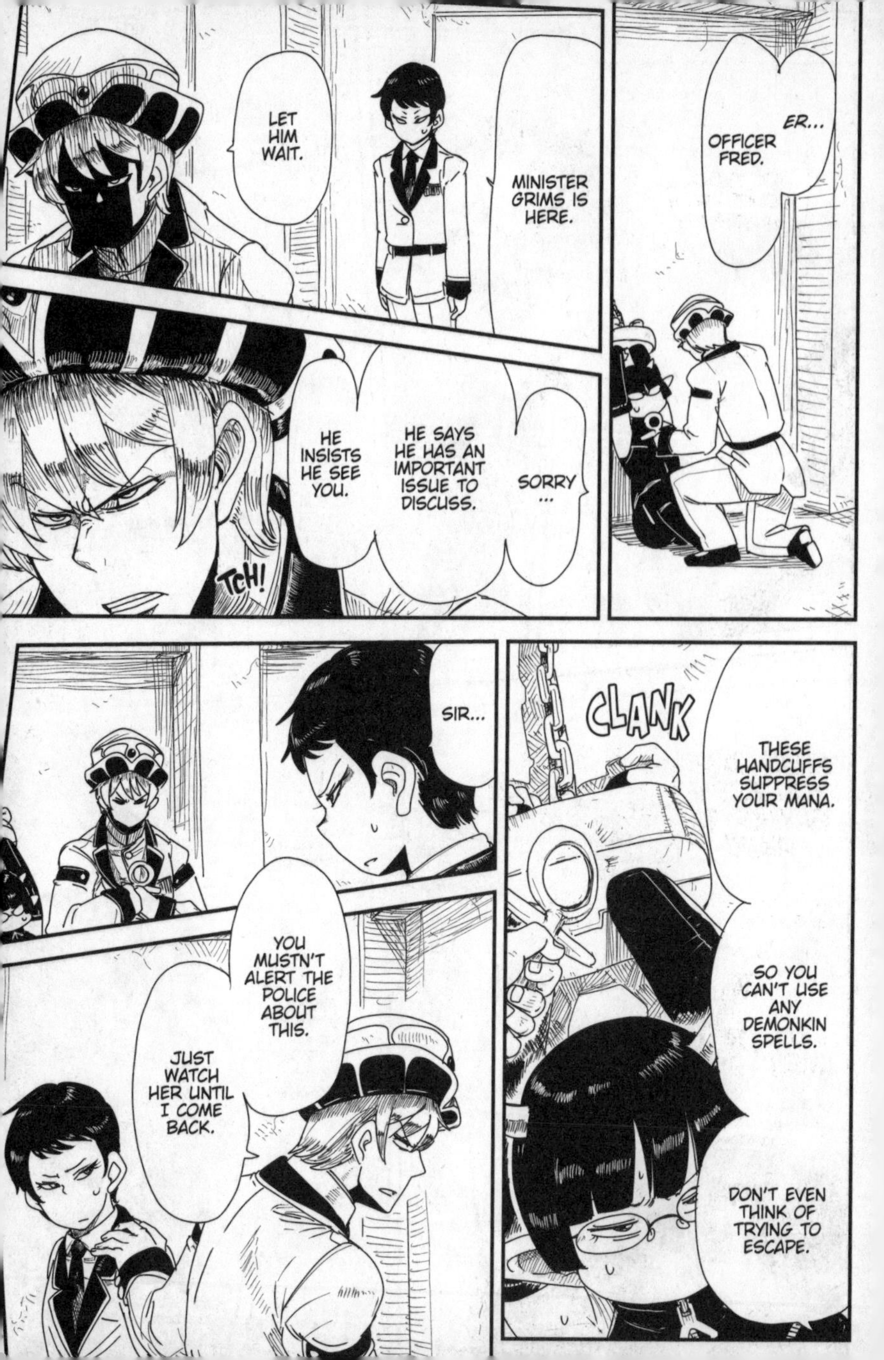
ER... OFFICER FRED.
MINISTER GRIMS IS HERE.
LET HIM WAIT.
SORRY...
HE SAYS HE HAS AN IMPORTANT ISSUE TO DISCUSS.
HE INSISTS HE SEE YOU.
TCH!
CLANK
THESE HANDCUFFS SUPPRESS YOUR MANA.
SO YOU CAN'T USE ANY DEMONKIN SPELLS.
DON'T EVEN THINK OF TRYING TO ESCAPE.
SIR...
YOU MUSTN'T ALERT THE POLICE ABOUT THIS.
JUST WATCH HER UNTIL I COME BACK.

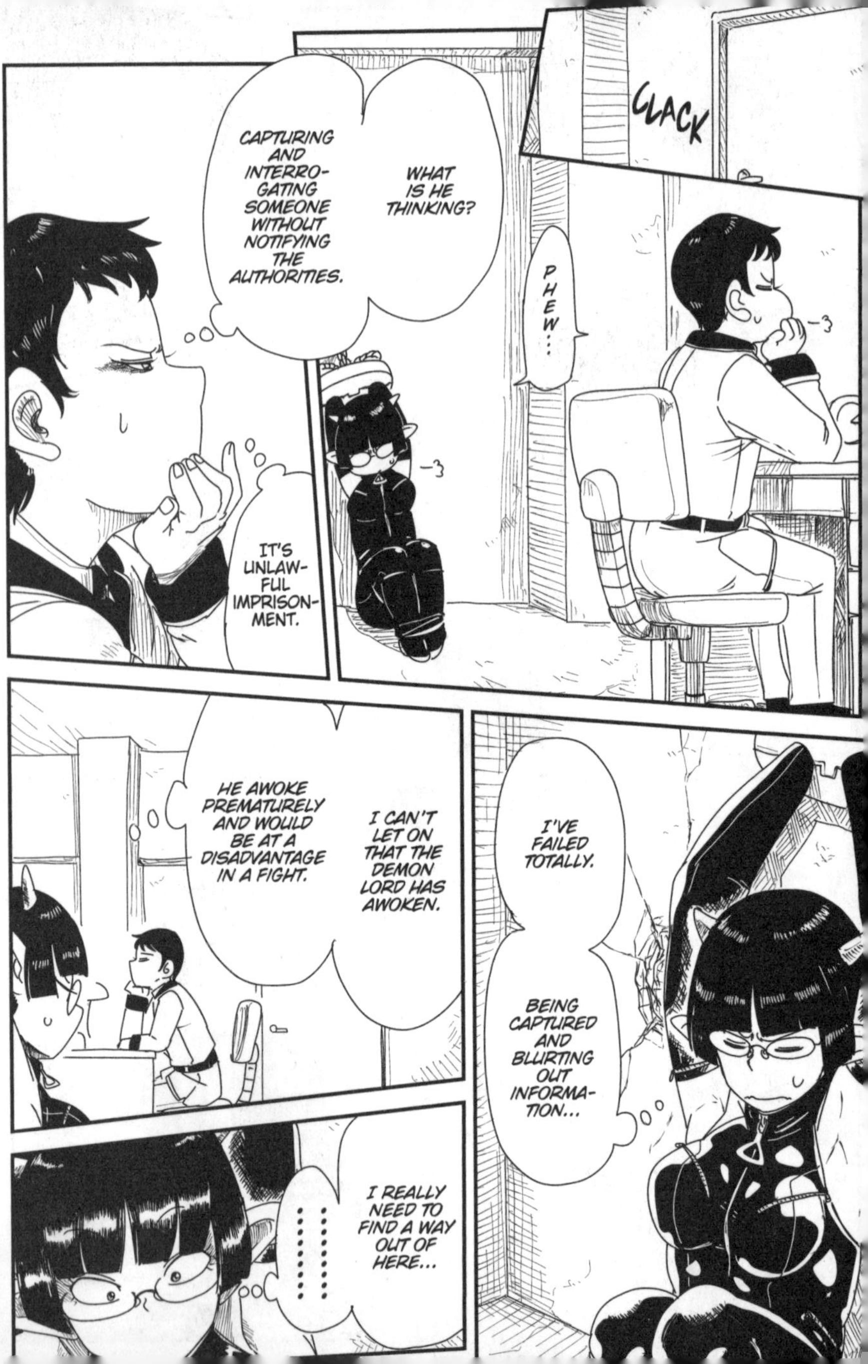
CLACK
PHEW...
WHAT IS HE THINKING?
CAPTURING AND INTERROGATING SOMEONE WITHOUT NOTIFYING THE AUTHORITIES.
IT'S UNLAWFUL IMPRISONMENT.
I'VE FAILED TOTALLY.
BEING CAPTURED AND BLURTING OUT INFORMATION...
I CAN'T LET ON THAT THE DEMON LORD HAS AWOKEN.
HE AWOKE PREMATURELY AND WOULD BE AT A DISADVANTAGE IN A FIGHT.
I REALLY NEED TO FIND A WAY OUT OF HERE...
......

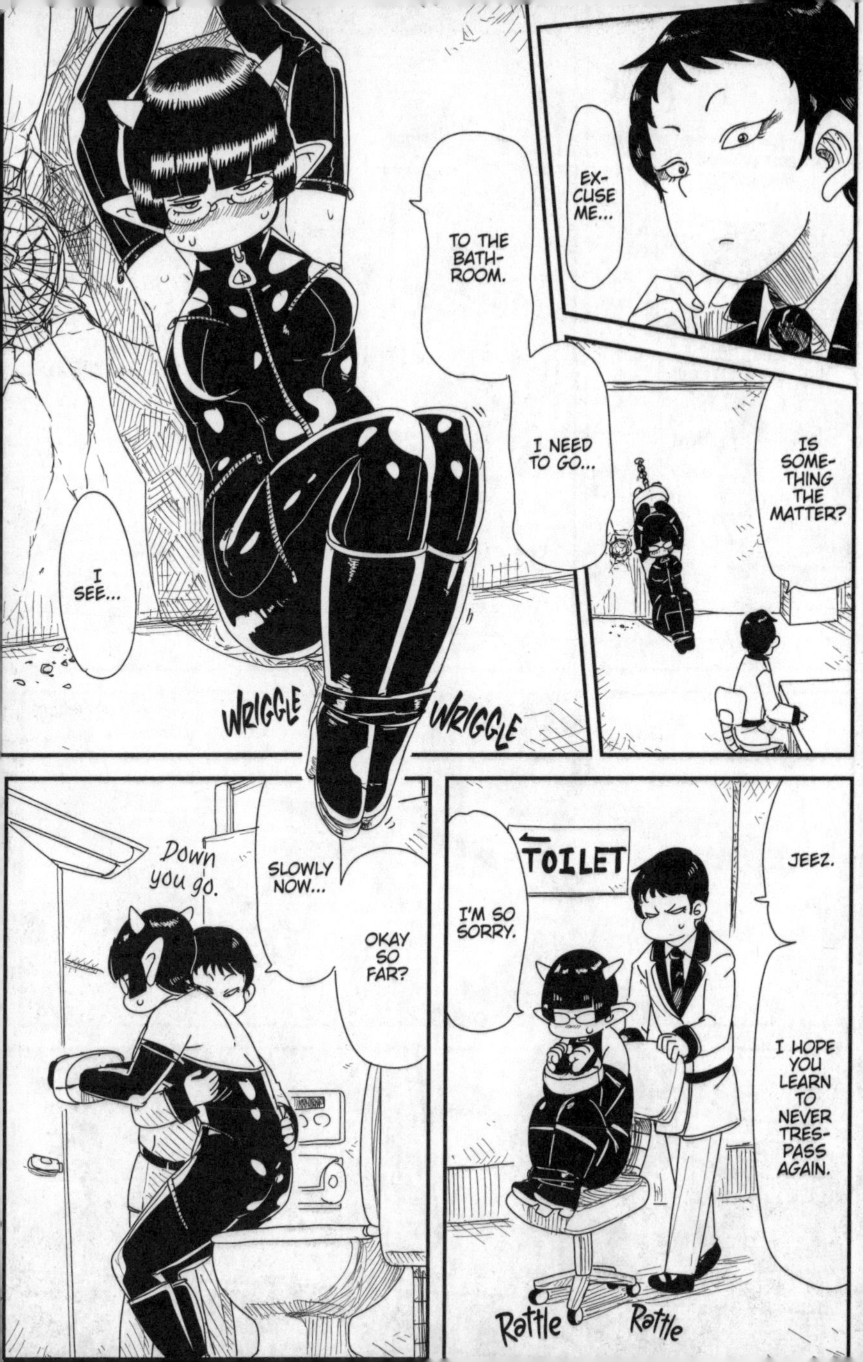
EXCUSE ME...
IS SOMETHING THE MATTER?
I NEED TO GO...
TO THE BATHROOM.
I SEE...
WRIGGLE
WRIGGLE
JEEZ.
I HOPE YOU LEARN TO NEVER TRESPASS AGAIN.
TOILET
I'M SO SORRY.
Rattle
Rattle
SLOWLY NOW...
OKAY SO FAR?
Down you go.

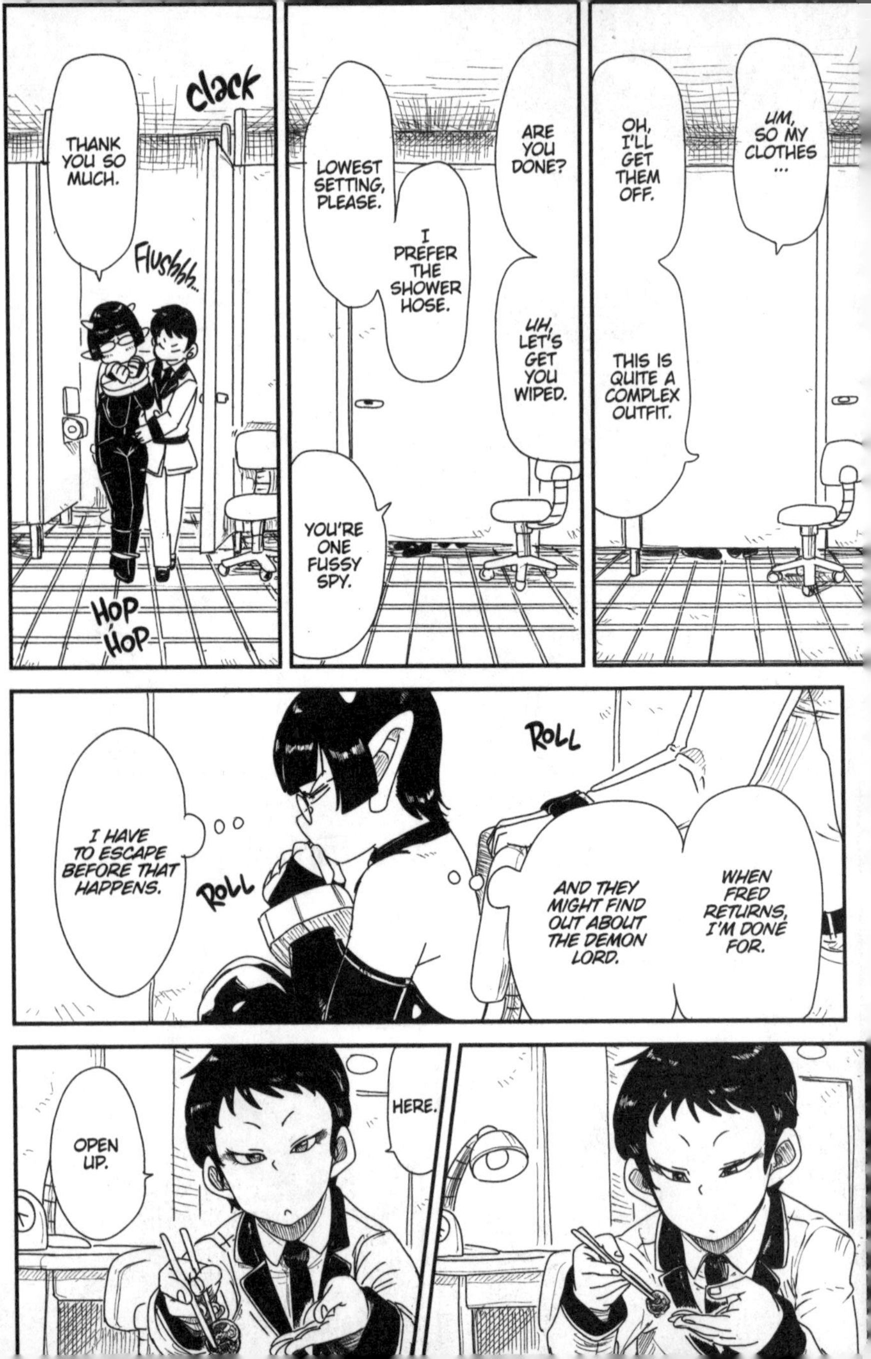
UM, SO MY CLOTHES ...
OH, I'LL GET THEM OFF.
THIS IS QUITE A COMPLEX OUTFIT.
ARE YOU DONE?
UH, LET'S GET YOU WIPED.
LOWEST SETTING, PLEASE.
I PREFER THE SHOWER HOSE.
YOU'RE ONE FUSSY SPY.
Clack
THANK YOU SO MUCH.
Flushhh...
HOP HOP
ROLL
WHEN FRED RETURNS, I'M DONE FOR.
AND THEY MIGHT FIND OUT ABOUT THE DEMON LORD.
I HAVE TO ESCAPE BEFORE THAT HAPPENS.
ROLL
HERE.
OPEN UP.

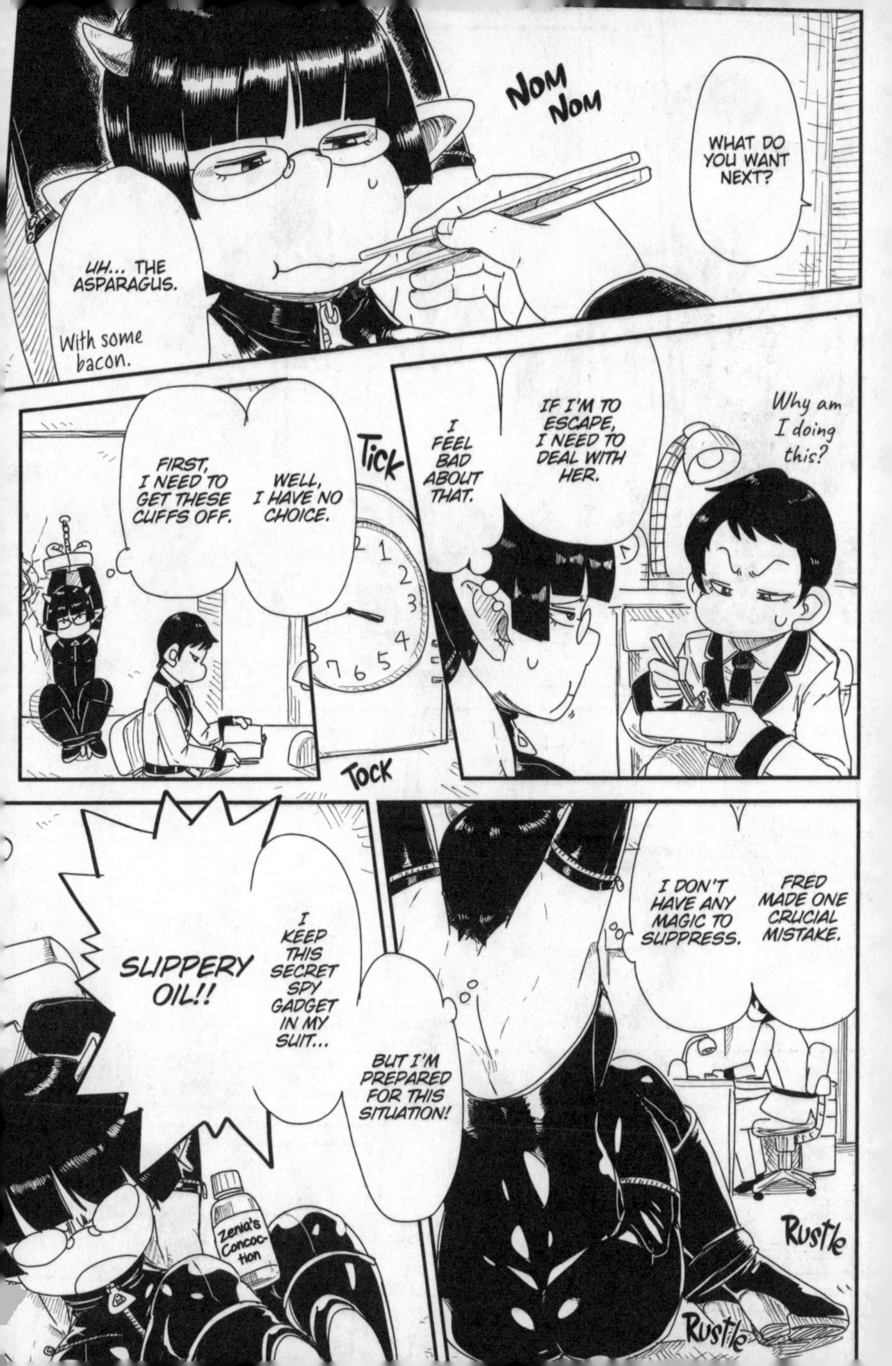
WHAT DO YOU WANT NEXT?
NOM NOM
UH... THE ASPARAGUS.
With some bacon.
Why am I doing this?
IF I'M TO ESCAPE, I NEED TO DEAL WITH HER.
I FEEL BAD ABOUT THAT.
TICK
WELL, I HAVE NO CHOICE.
FIRST, I NEED TO GET THESE CUFFS OFF.
TOCK
FRED MADE ONE CRUCIAL MISTAKE.
I DON'T HAVE ANY MAGIC TO SUPPRESS.
RUSTLE
RUSTLE
BUT I'M PREPARED FOR THIS SITUATION!
I KEEP THIS SECRET SPY GADGET IN MY SUIT...
SLIPPERY OIL!!
Zenia's Concoction

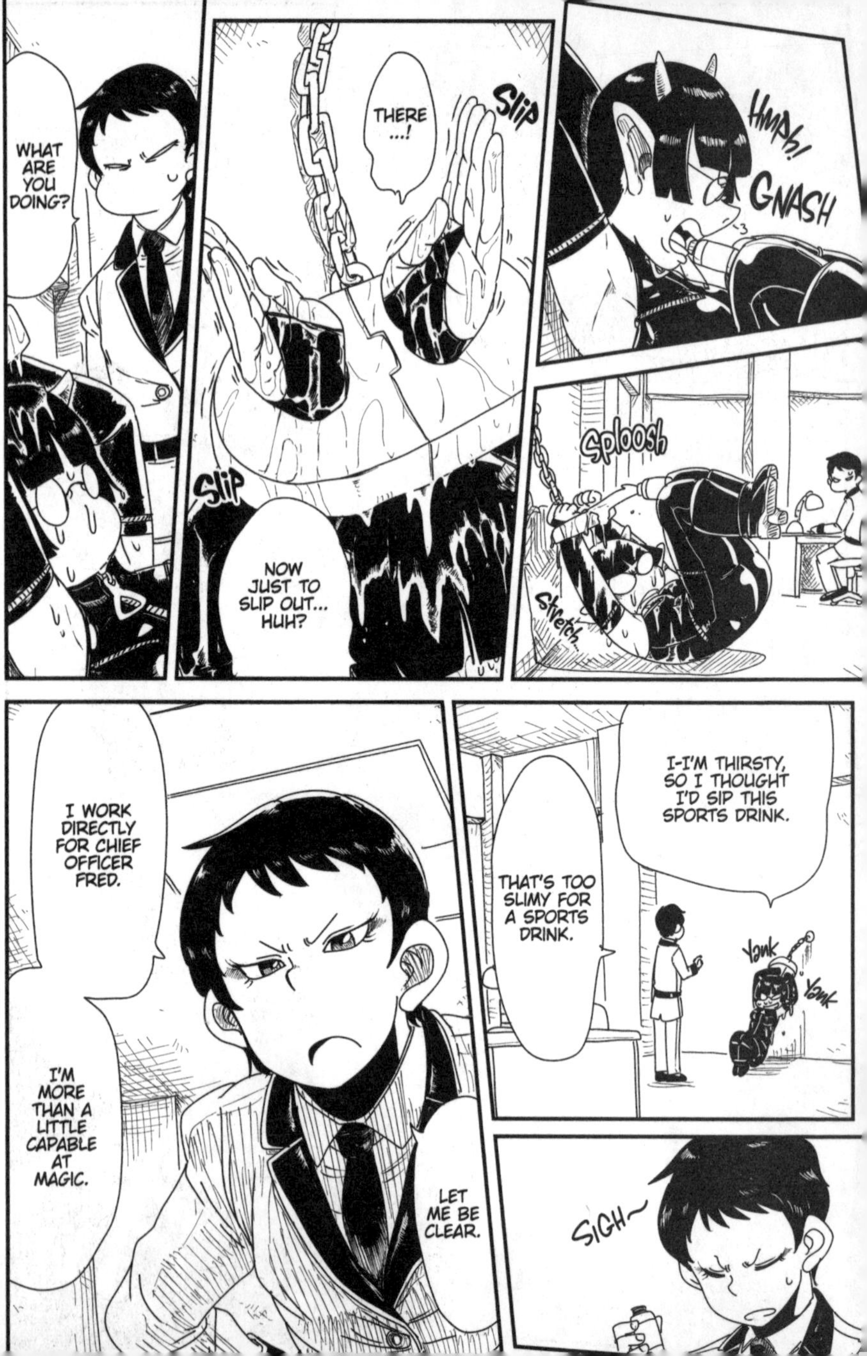
Hmph!
GNASH
Sploosh
Stretch...
THERE ...!
Slip
Slip
NOW JUST TO SLIP OUT... HUH?
WHAT ARE YOU DOING?
I-I'M THIRSTY, SO I THOUGHT I'D SIP THIS SPORTS DRINK.
THAT'S TOO SLIMY FOR A SPORTS DRINK.
Yank
Yank
SIGH~
LET ME BE CLEAR.
I WORK DIRECTLY FOR CHIEF OFFICER FRED.
I'M MORE THAN A LITTLE CAPABLE AT MAGIC.

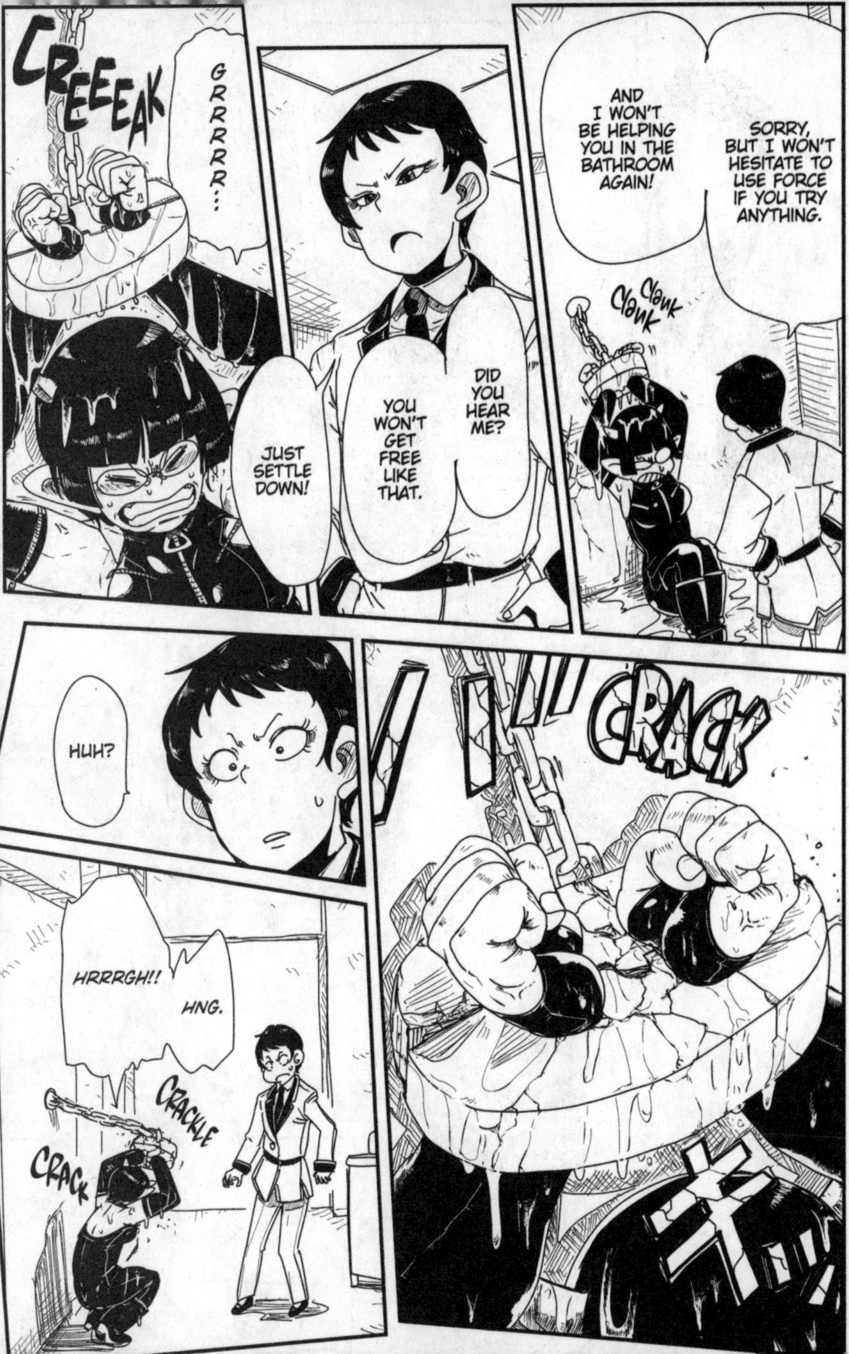
SORRY, BUT I WON'T HESITATE TO USE FORCE IF YOU TRY ANYTHING.
AND I WON'T BE HELPING YOU IN THE BATHROOM AGAIN!
Clank Clank
DID YOU HEAR ME?
YOU WON'T GET FREE LIKE THAT.
JUST SETTLE DOWN!
GRRRRR...
CREEEAK
CRACK
HUH?
HRRRGH!!
HNG.
CRACKLE
CRACK

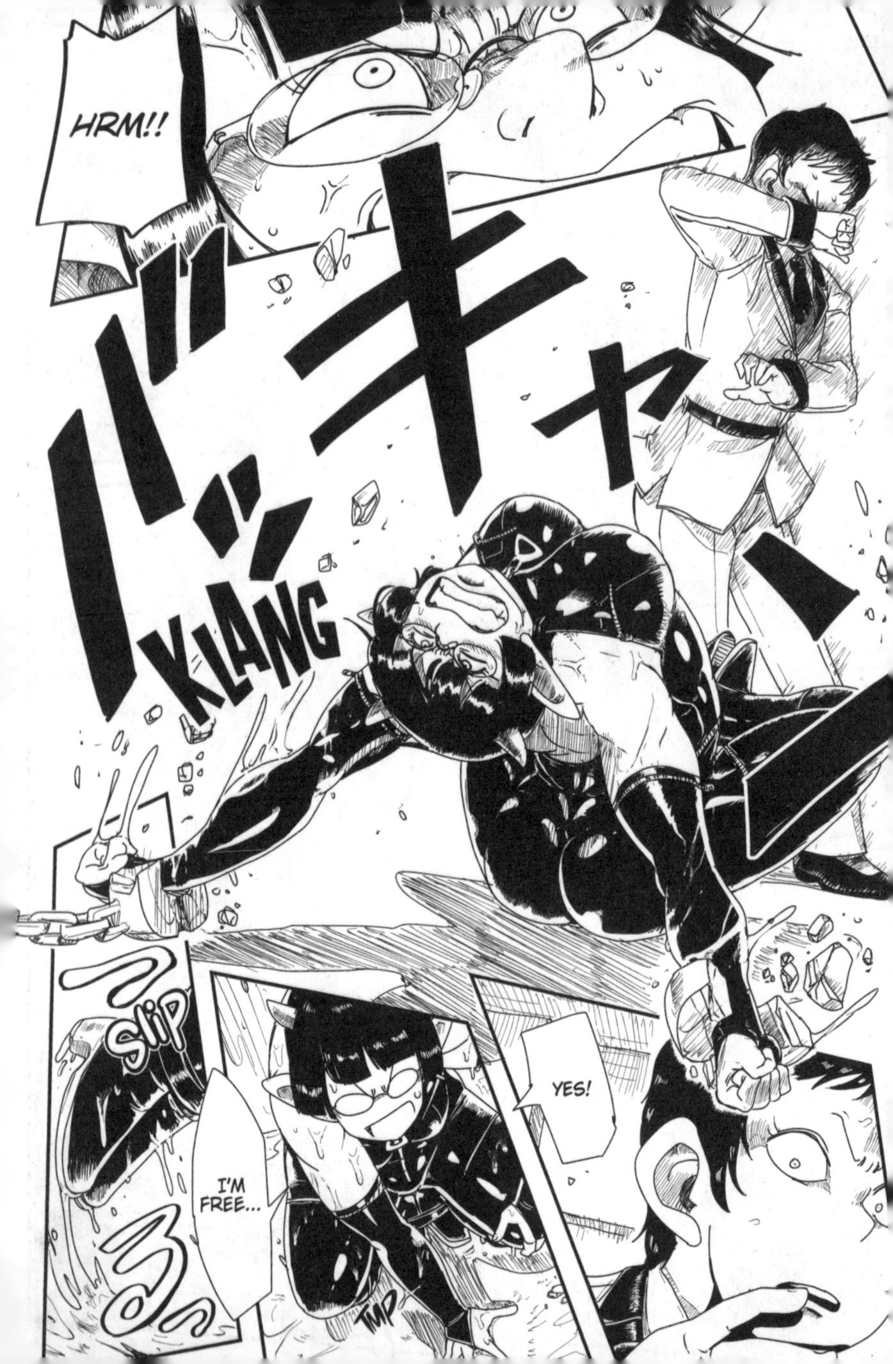
HRM!!
バッキャン
KLANG
YES!
I'M FREE...
SLIP
TMP

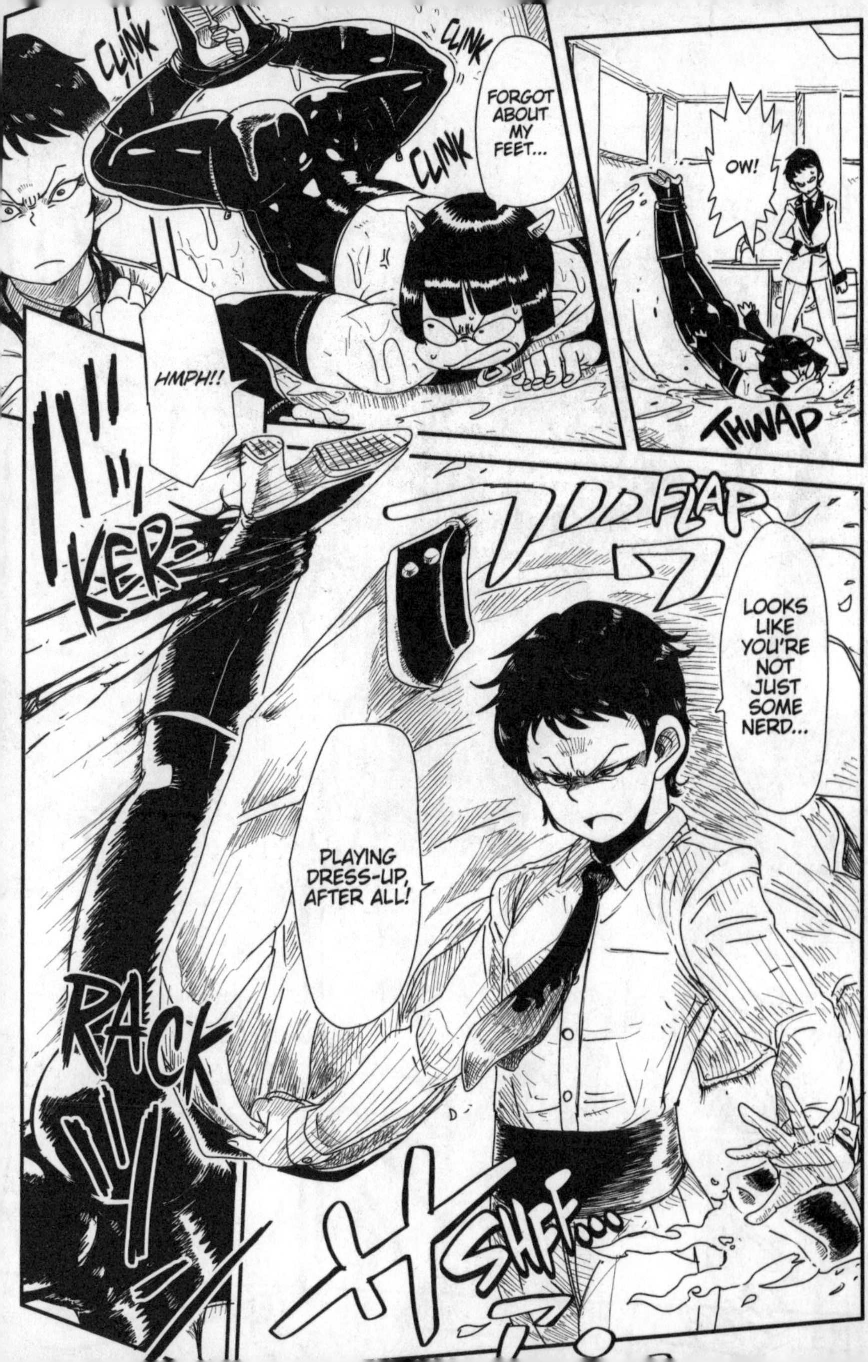
CLINK
CLINK
CLINK
FORGOT ABOUT MY FEET...
OW!
THWAP
HMPH!!
KER
RACK
FLAP
LOOKS LIKE YOU'RE NOT JUST SOME NERD...
PLAYING DRESS-UP, AFTER ALL!

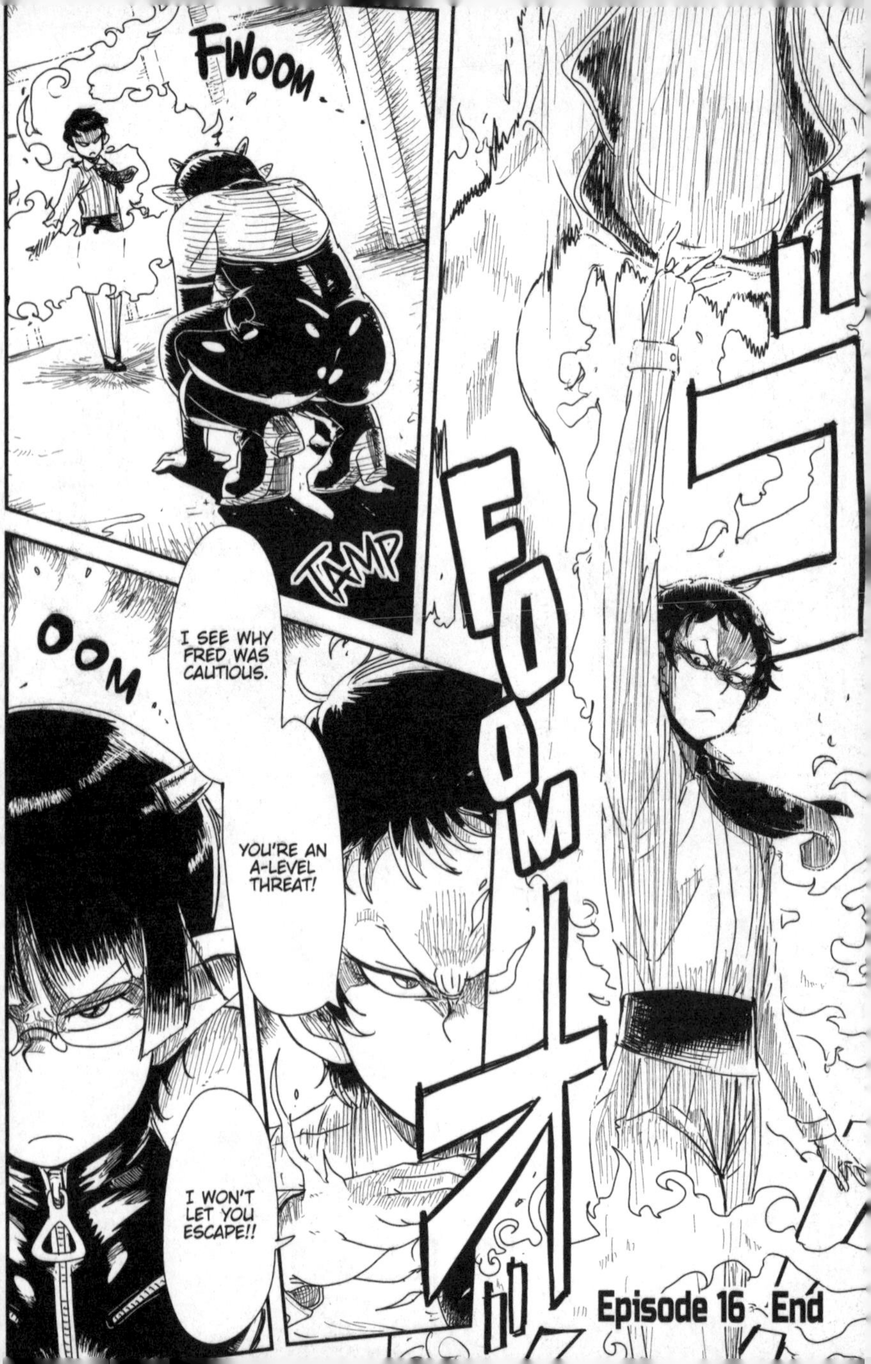
FWOOM
TAMP
FOOM
OOM
I SEE WHY FRED WAS CAUTIOUS.
YOU'RE AN A-LEVEL THREAT!
I WON'T LET YOU ESCAPE!!
Episode 16 End

LEVEL 1 DEMON LORD & ONE ROOM HERO

LEVEL 1 DEMON LORD & ONE ROOM HERO

Episode 17: Sinister Developments

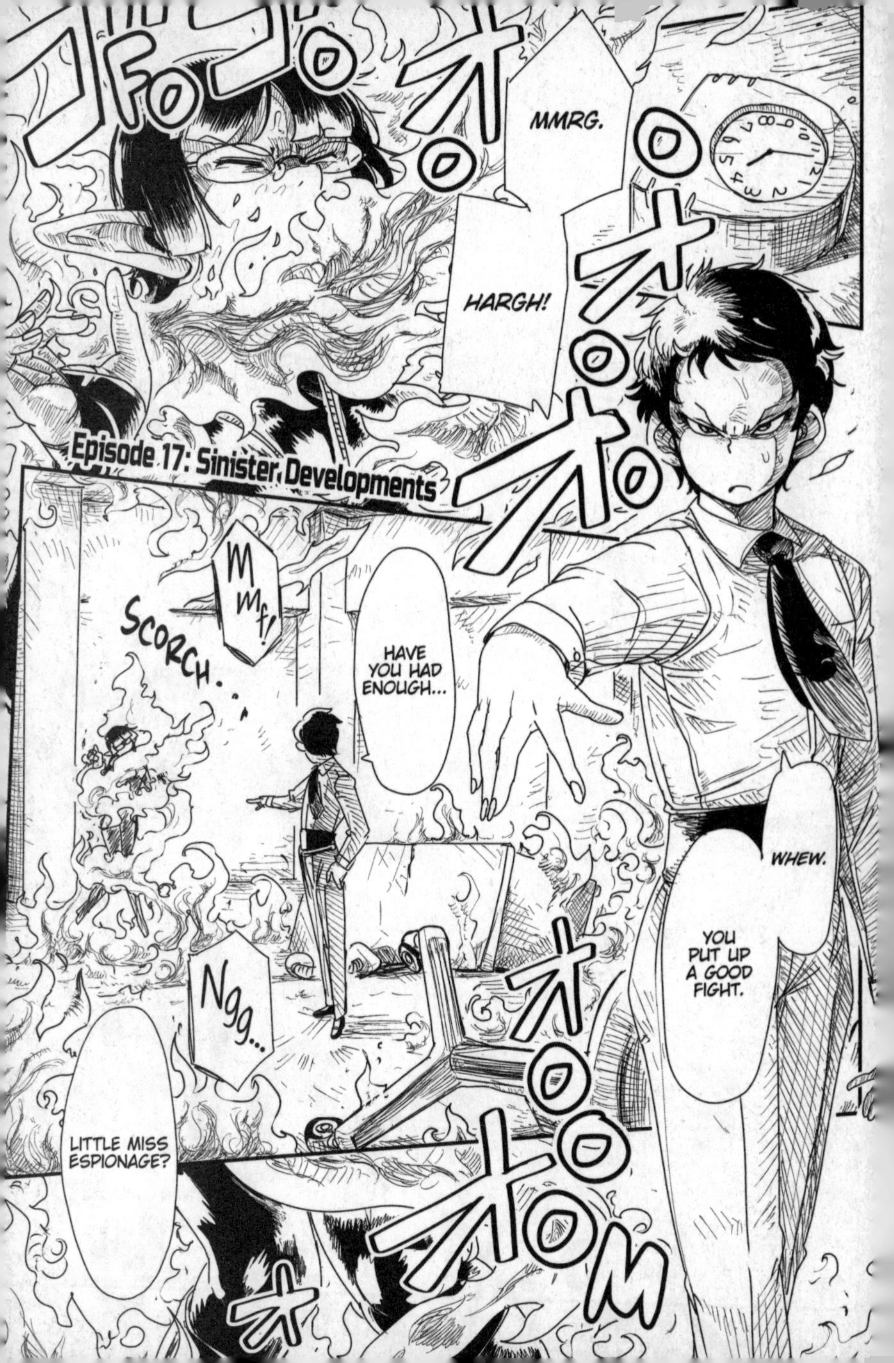
MMRG.
HARGH!
WHEW.
YOU PUT UP A GOOD FIGHT.
HAVE YOU HAD ENOUGH...
LITTLE MISS ESPIONAGE?
Mmf!
SCORCH...
Ngg...

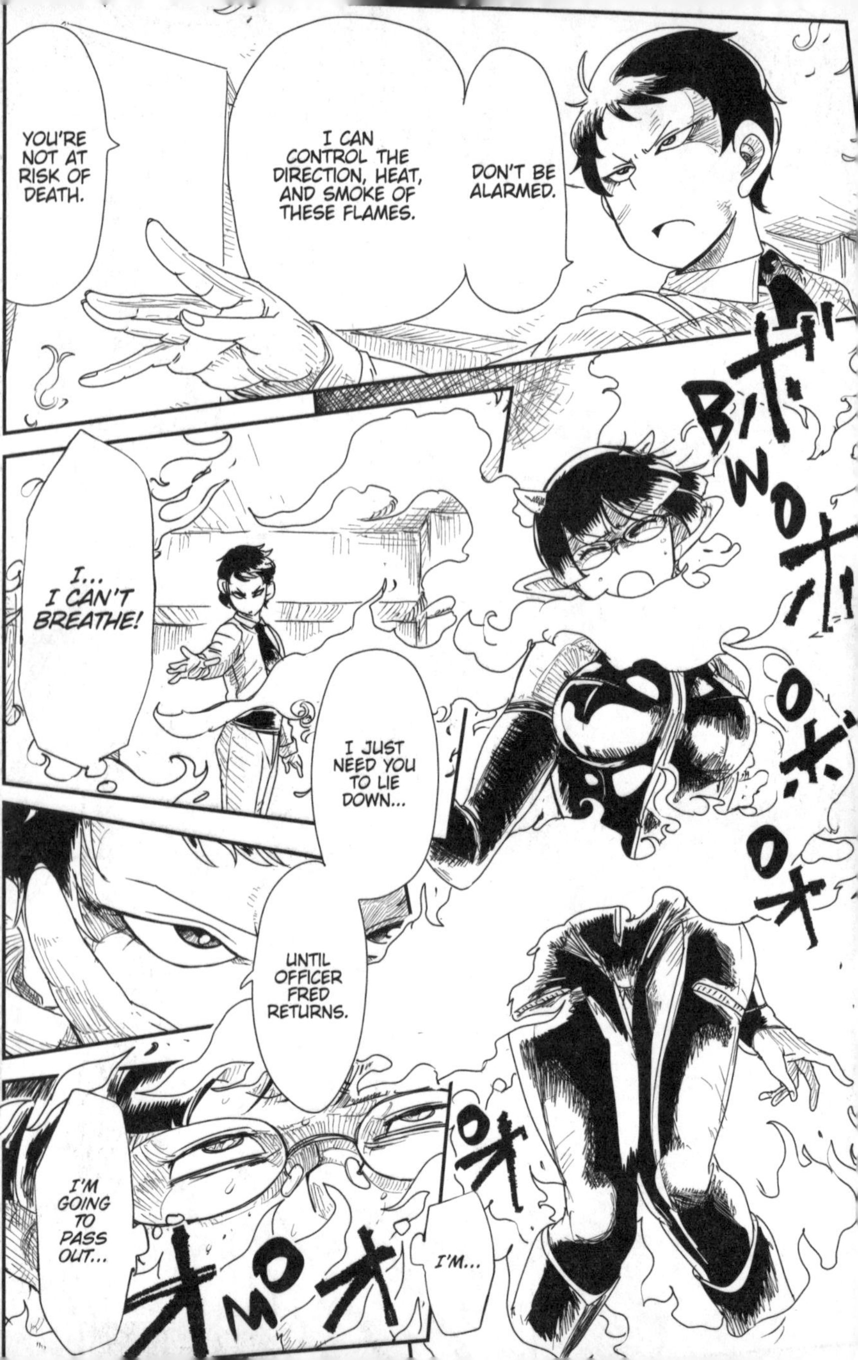
DON'T BE ALARMED.
I CAN CONTROL THE DIRECTION, HEAT, AND SMOKE OF THESE FLAMES.
YOU'RE NOT AT RISK OF DEATH.
BWOOO
I... I CAN'T BREATHE!
I JUST NEED YOU TO LIE DOWN...
UNTIL OFFICER FRED RETURNS.
I'M...
I'M GOING TO PASS OUT...
MO

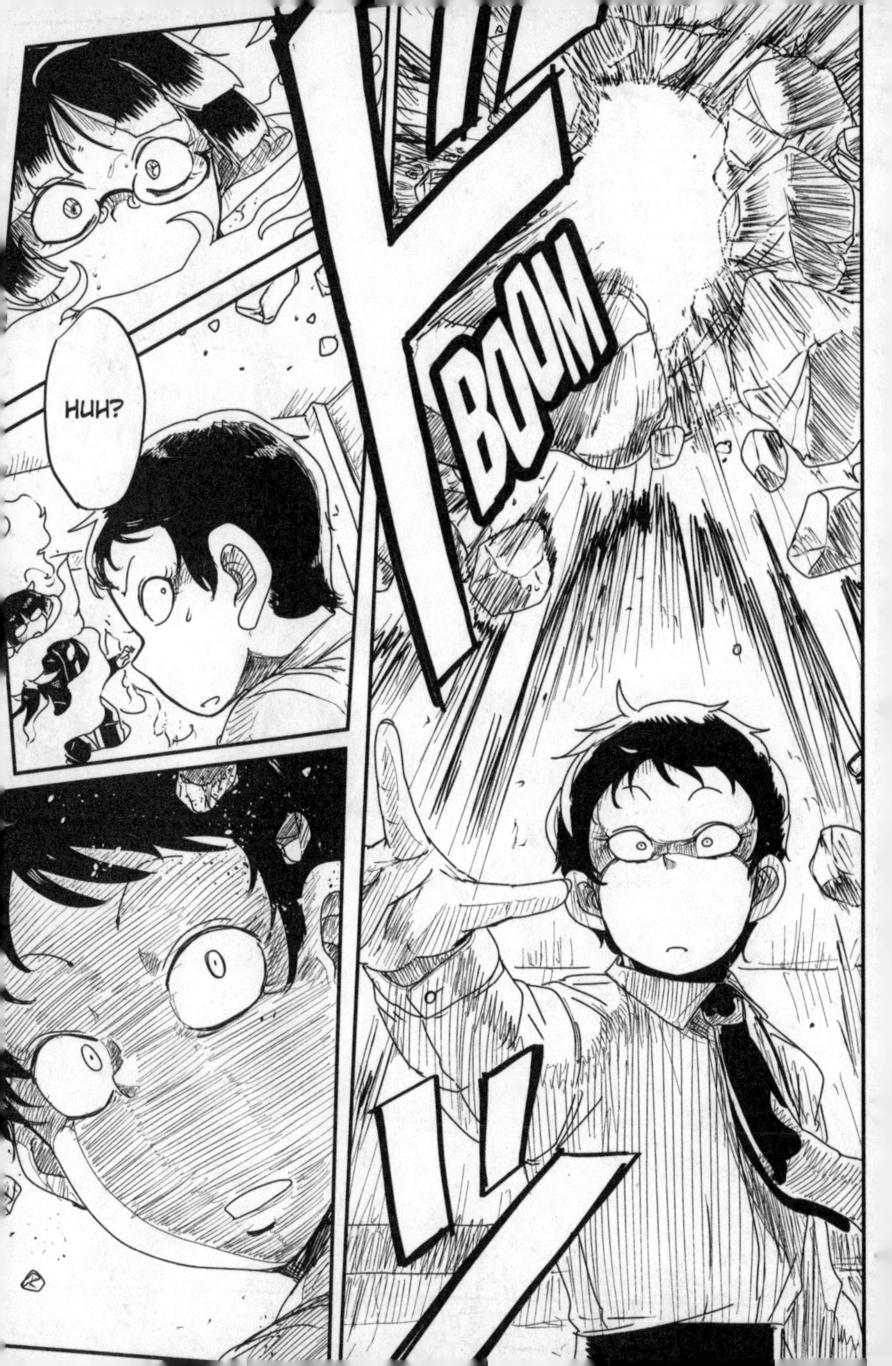
BOOM
HUH?

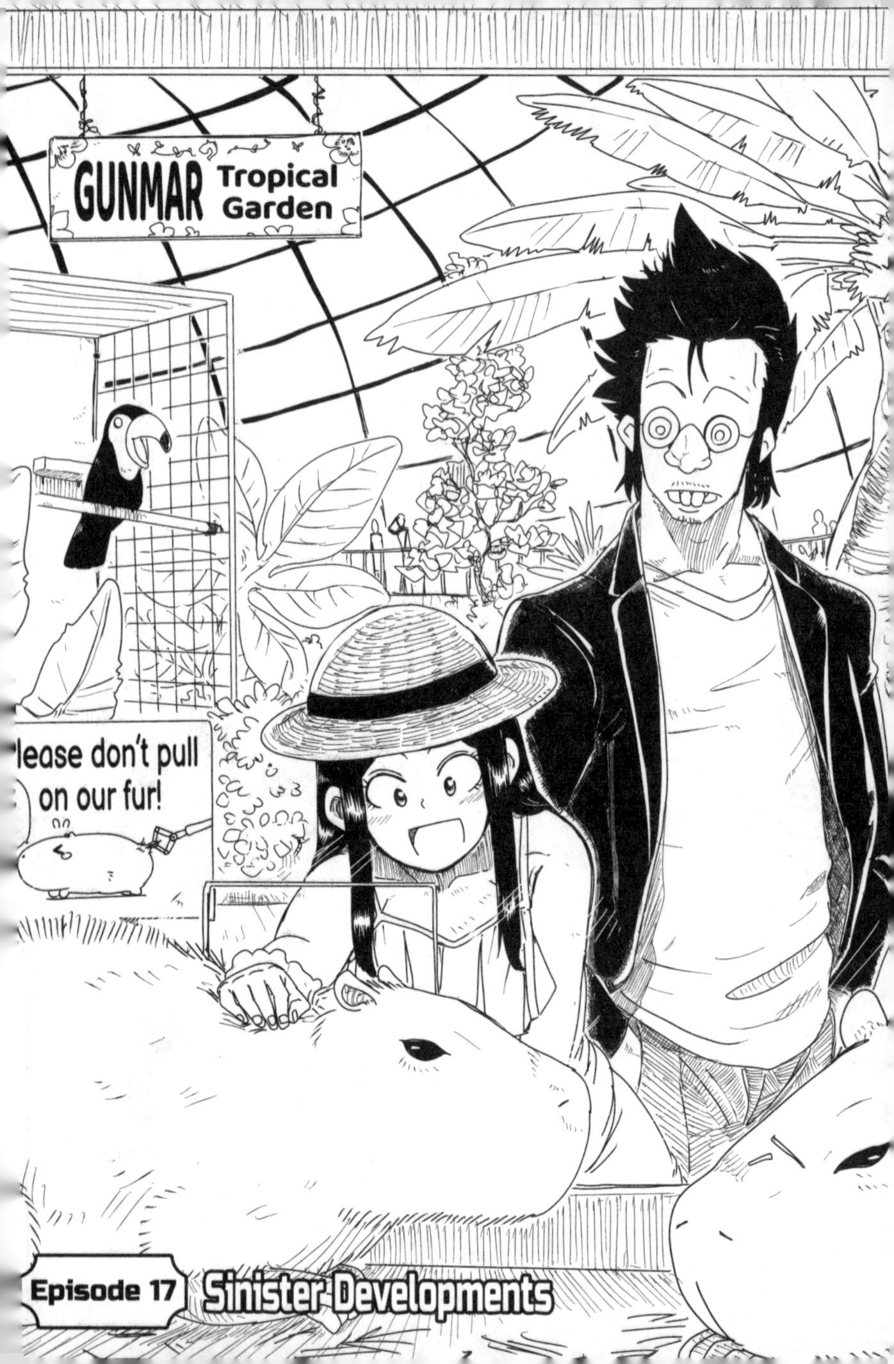

Episode 17 Sinister Developments

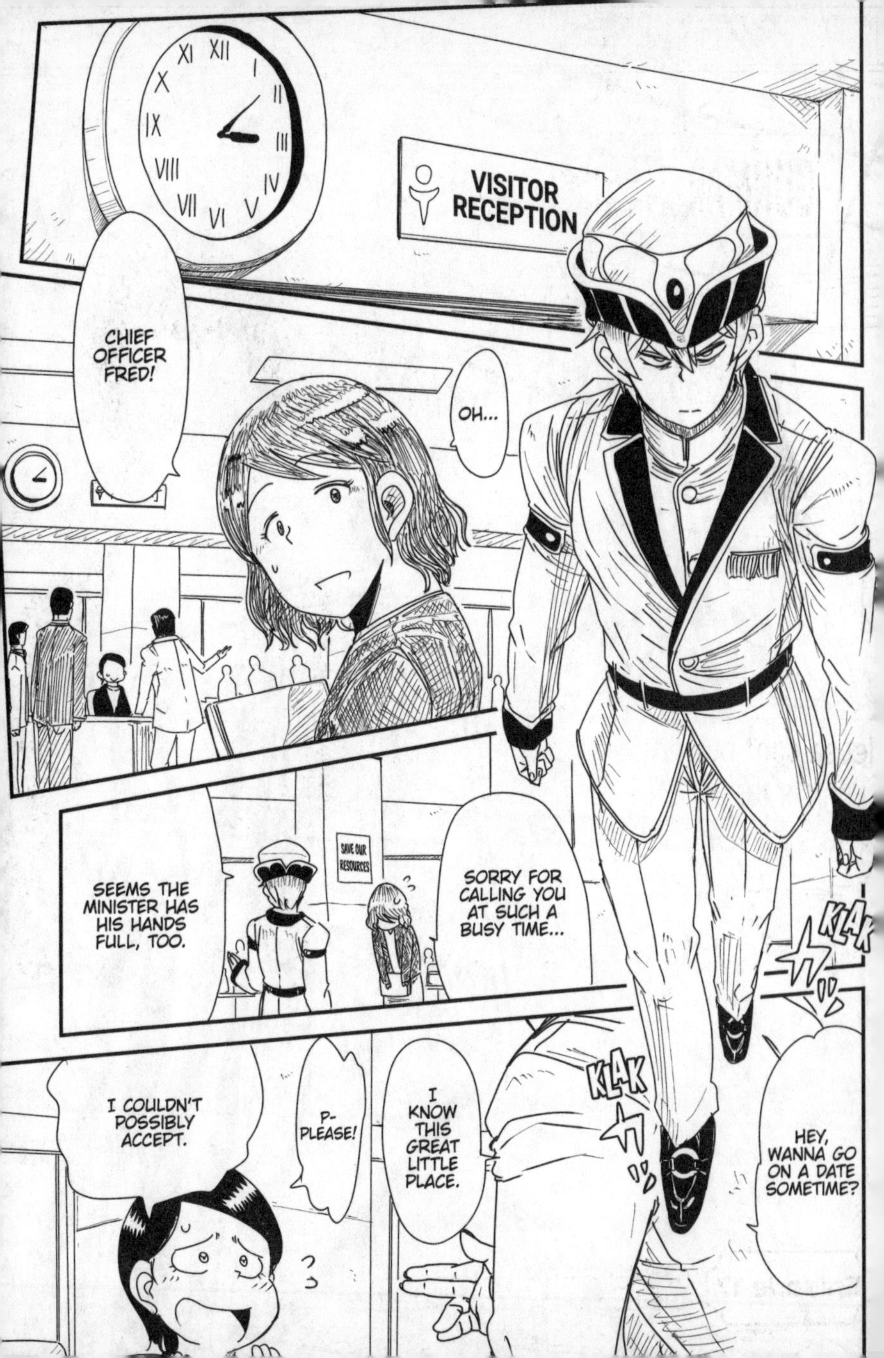
VISITOR RECEPTION
CHIEF OFFICER FRED!
OH...
SORRY FOR CALLING YOU AT SUCH A BUSY TIME...
SAVE OUR RESOURCES
SEEMS THE MINISTER HAS HIS HANDS FULL, TOO.
KLAK
KLAK
HEY, WANNA GO ON A DATE SOMETIME?
I KNOW THIS GREAT LITTLE PLACE.
P-PLEASE!
I COULDN'T POSSIBLY ACCEPT.

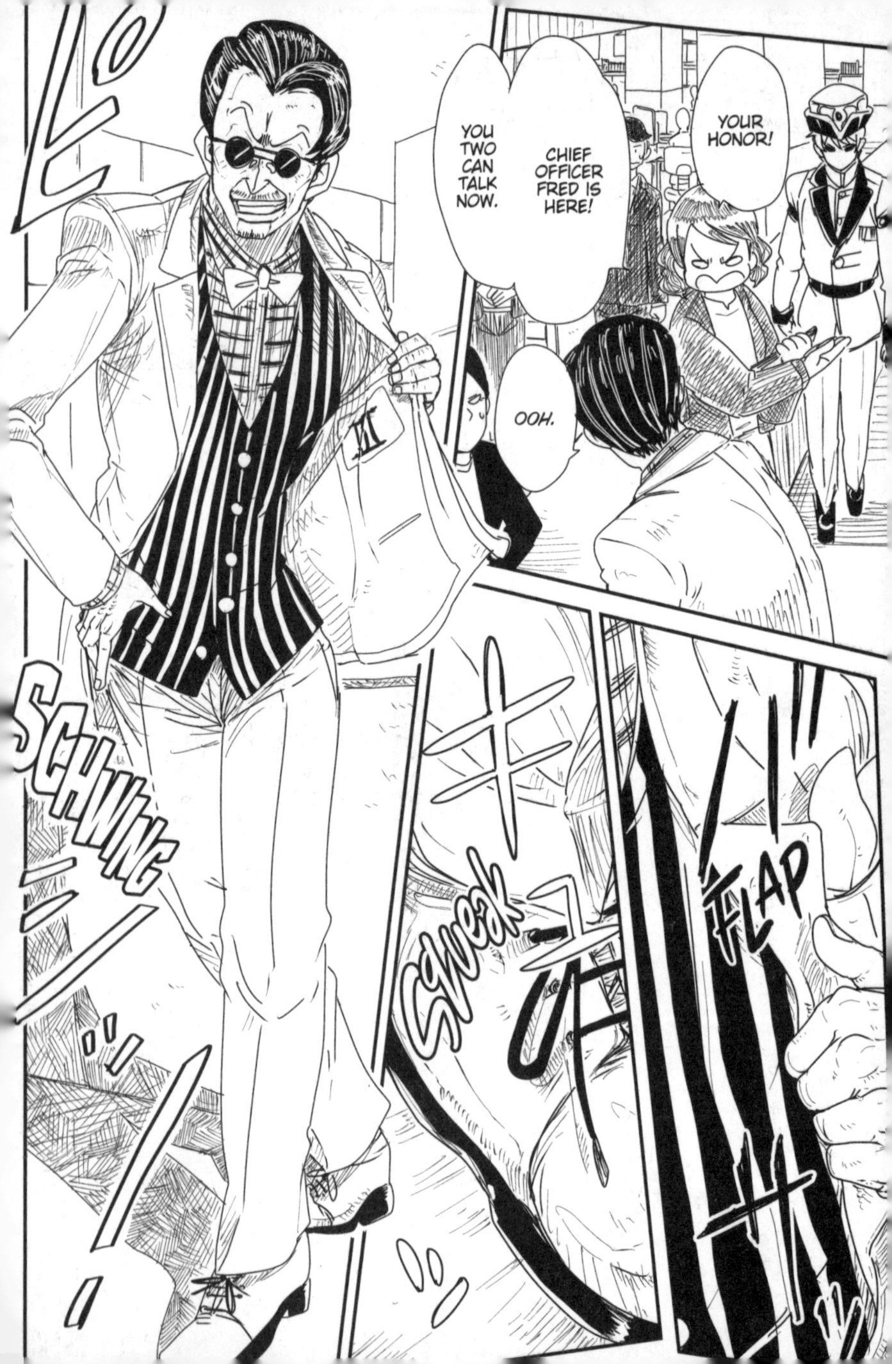
YOUR HONOR!
CHIEF OFFICER FRED IS HERE!
YOU TWO CAN TALK NOW.
OOH.
FLAP
SQUEAK
SCHWING

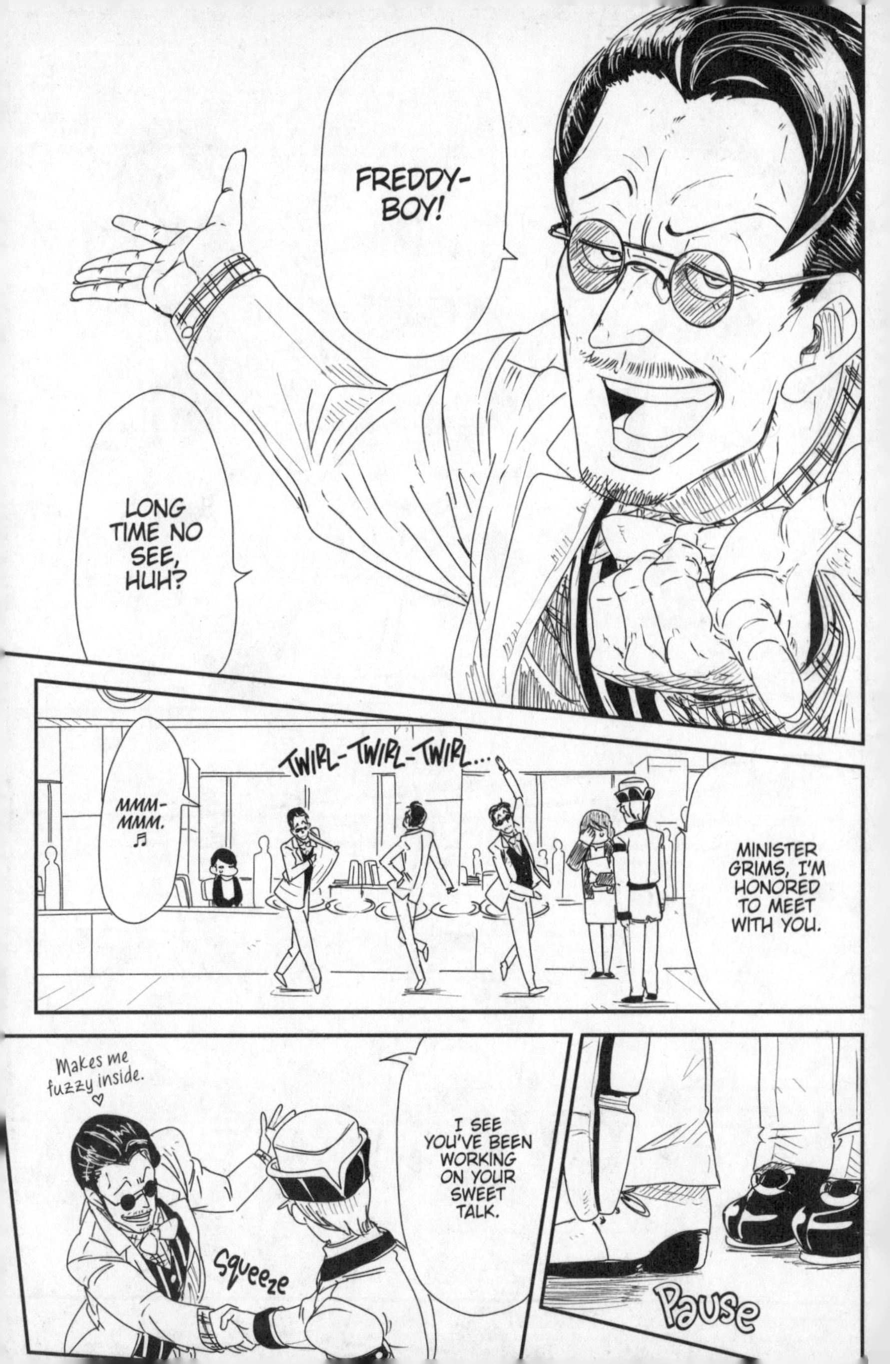
FREDDY-BOY!
LONG TIME NO SEE, HUH?
MINISTER GRIMS, I'M HONORED TO MEET WITH YOU.
TWIRL-TWIRL-TWIRL...
MMM-MMM. ♫
Pause
I SEE YOU'VE BEEN WORKING ON YOUR SWEET TALK.
Squeeze
Makes me fuzzy inside. ♡

SO, HOW'S IT GOING?

Tap Tap Swipe

YOUR HONOR.

PLEASE MAKE THIS BRIEF. THE CHIEF OFFICER IS EXTREMELY BUSY.

SORRY I POPPED IN WITHOUT NOTICE.

Grims · the third
At the Sorcery Agency! Here's the chief and me!

GOT IT! FABULOUS SMILE THERE, CHIEF!

YOUR HONOR, PLEASE!!

SMILE, FREDDY-BOY!

FIRST, NEED A SELFIE!

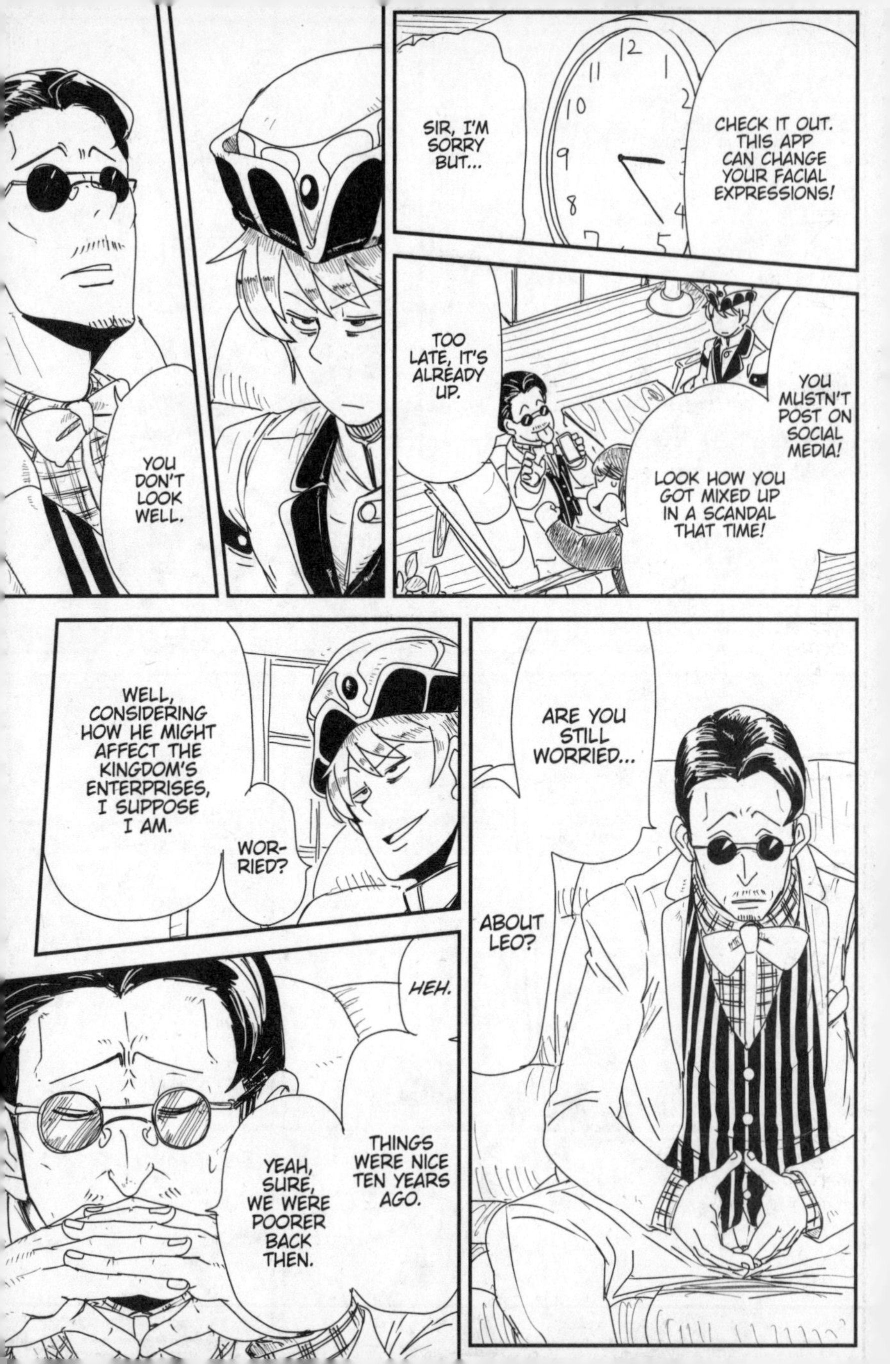
CHECK IT OUT. THIS APP CAN CHANGE YOUR FACIAL EXPRESSIONS!
SIR, I'M SORRY BUT...
YOU MUSTN'T POST ON SOCIAL MEDIA!
LOOK HOW YOU GOT MIXED UP IN A SCANDAL THAT TIME!
TOO LATE, IT'S ALREADY UP.
YOU DON'T LOOK WELL.
ARE YOU STILL WORRIED...
ABOUT LEO?
WOR-RIED?
WELL, CONSIDERING HOW HE MIGHT AFFECT THE KINGDOM'S ENTERPRISES, I SUPPOSE I AM.
HEH.
THINGS WERE NICE TEN YEARS AGO.
YEAH, SURE, WE WERE POORER BACK THEN.

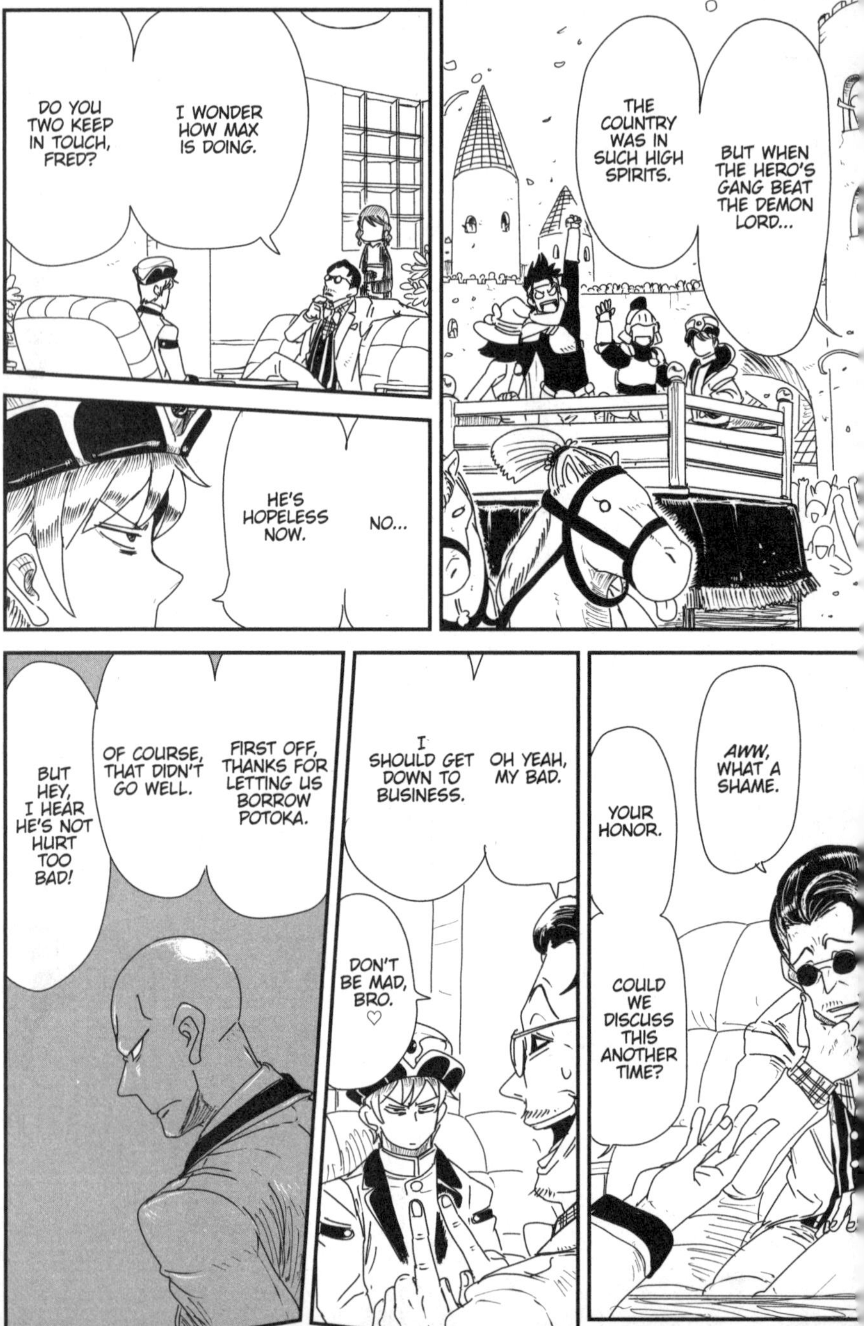
BUT WHEN THE HERO'S GANG BEAT THE DEMON LORD...
THE COUNTRY WAS IN SUCH HIGH SPIRITS.
I WONDER HOW MAX IS DOING.
DO YOU TWO KEEP IN TOUCH, FRED?
NO...
HE'S HOPELESS NOW.
AWW, WHAT A SHAME.
YOUR HONOR.
COULD WE DISCUSS THIS ANOTHER TIME?
OH YEAH, MY BAD.
I SHOULD GET DOWN TO BUSINESS.
DON'T BE MAD, BRO. ♡
FIRST OFF, THANKS FOR LETTING US BORROW POTOKA.
OF COURSE, THAT DIDN'T GO WELL.
BUT HEY, I HEAR HE'S NOT HURT TOO BAD!

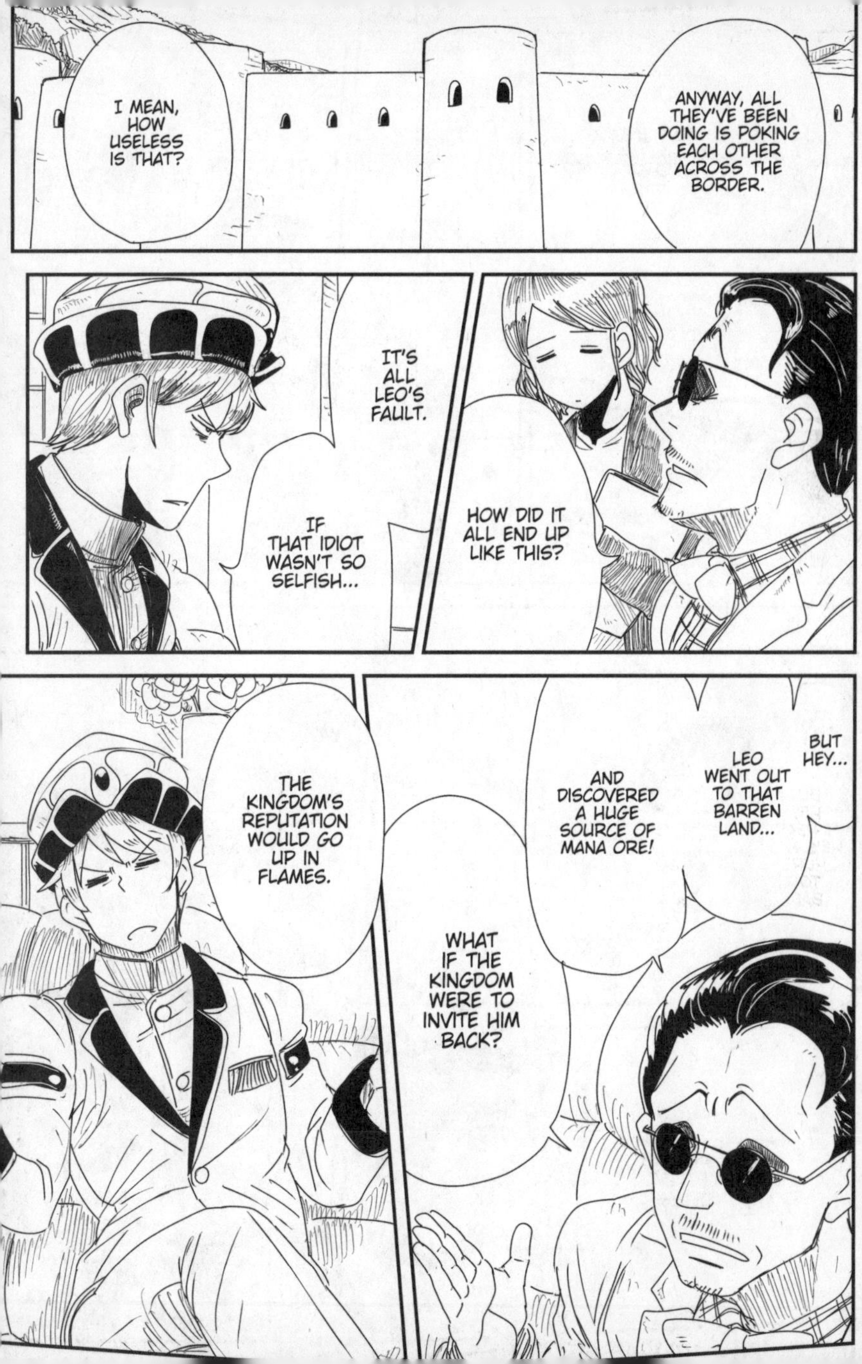
ANYWAY, ALL THEY'VE BEEN DOING IS POKING EACH OTHER ACROSS THE BORDER.
I MEAN, HOW USELESS IS THAT?
HOW DID IT ALL END UP LIKE THIS?
IT'S ALL LEO'S FAULT.
IF THAT IDIOT WASN'T SO SELFISH...
BUT HEY...
LEO WENT OUT TO THAT BARREN LAND...
AND DISCOVERED A HUGE SOURCE OF MANA ORE!
WHAT IF THE KINGDOM WERE TO INVITE HIM BACK?
THE KINGDOM'S REPUTATION WOULD GO UP IN FLAMES.

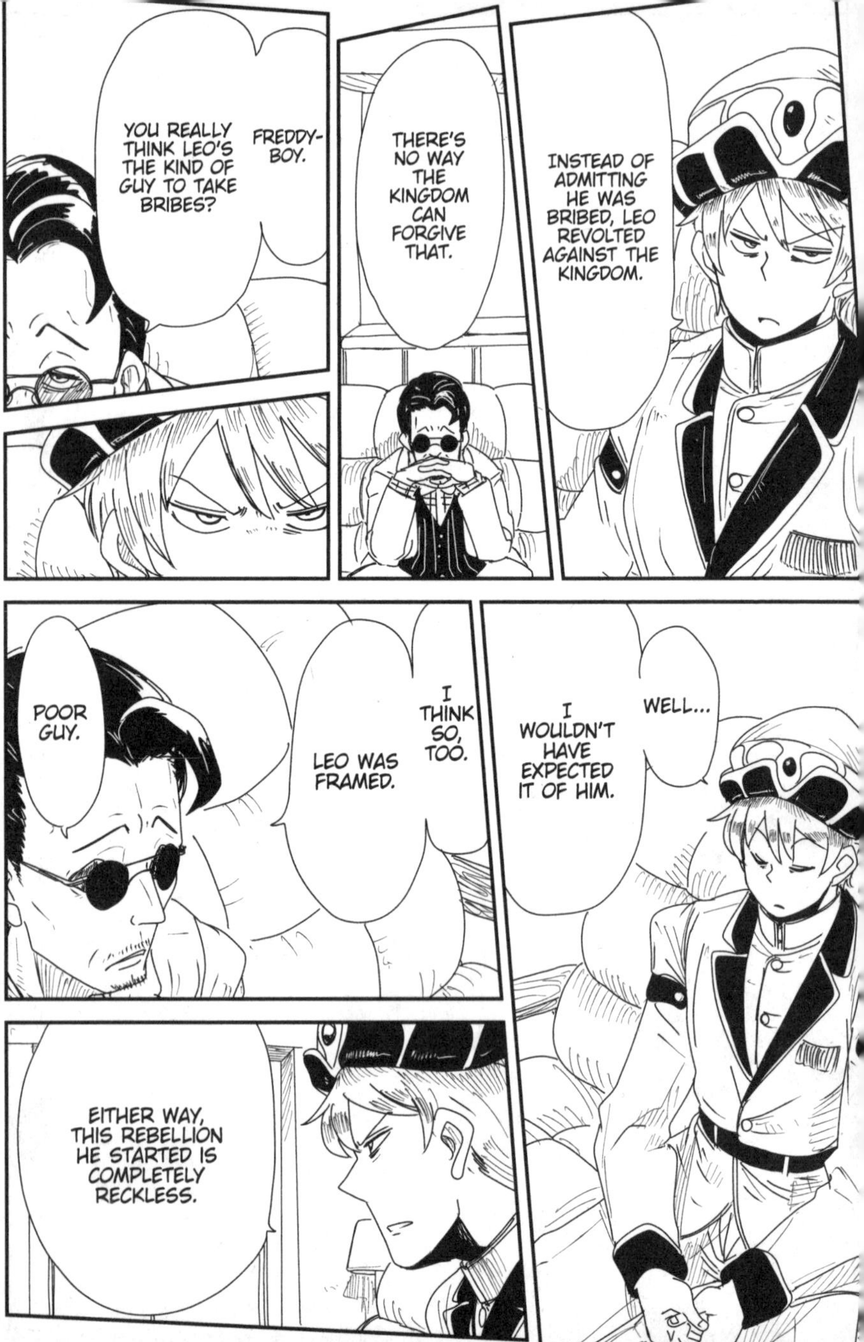
INSTEAD OF ADMITTING HE WAS BRIBED, LEO REVOLTED AGAINST THE KINGDOM.
THERE'S NO WAY THE KINGDOM CAN FORGIVE THAT.
FREDDY-BOY.
YOU REALLY THINK LEO'S THE KIND OF GUY TO TAKE BRIBES?
WELL...
I WOULDN'T HAVE EXPECTED IT OF HIM.
I THINK SO, TOO.
LEO WAS FRAMED.
POOR GUY.
EITHER WAY, THIS REBELLION HE STARTED IS COMPLETELY RECKLESS.

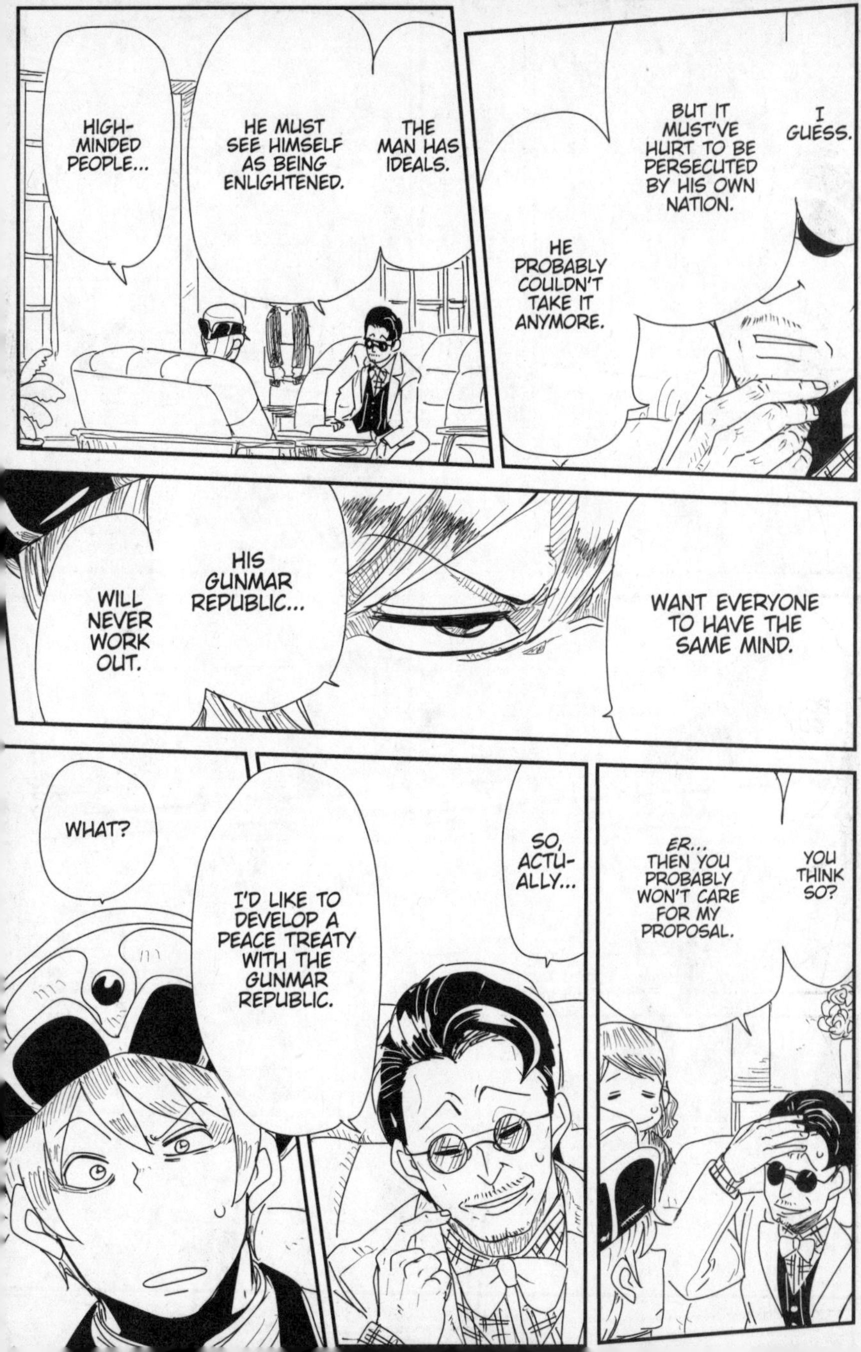
I GUESS.
BUT IT MUST'VE HURT TO BE PERSECUTED BY HIS OWN NATION.
HE PROBABLY COULDN'T TAKE IT ANYMORE.
THE MAN HAS IDEALS.
HE MUST SEE HIMSELF AS BEING ENLIGHTENED.
HIGH-MINDED PEOPLE...
WANT EVERYONE TO HAVE THE SAME MIND.
HIS GUNMAR REPUBLIC...
WILL NEVER WORK OUT.
YOU THINK SO?
ER... THEN YOU PROBABLY WON'T CARE FOR MY PROPOSAL.
SO, ACTU-ALLY...
I'D LIKE TO DEVELOP A PEACE TREATY WITH THE GUNMAR REPUBLIC.
WHAT?

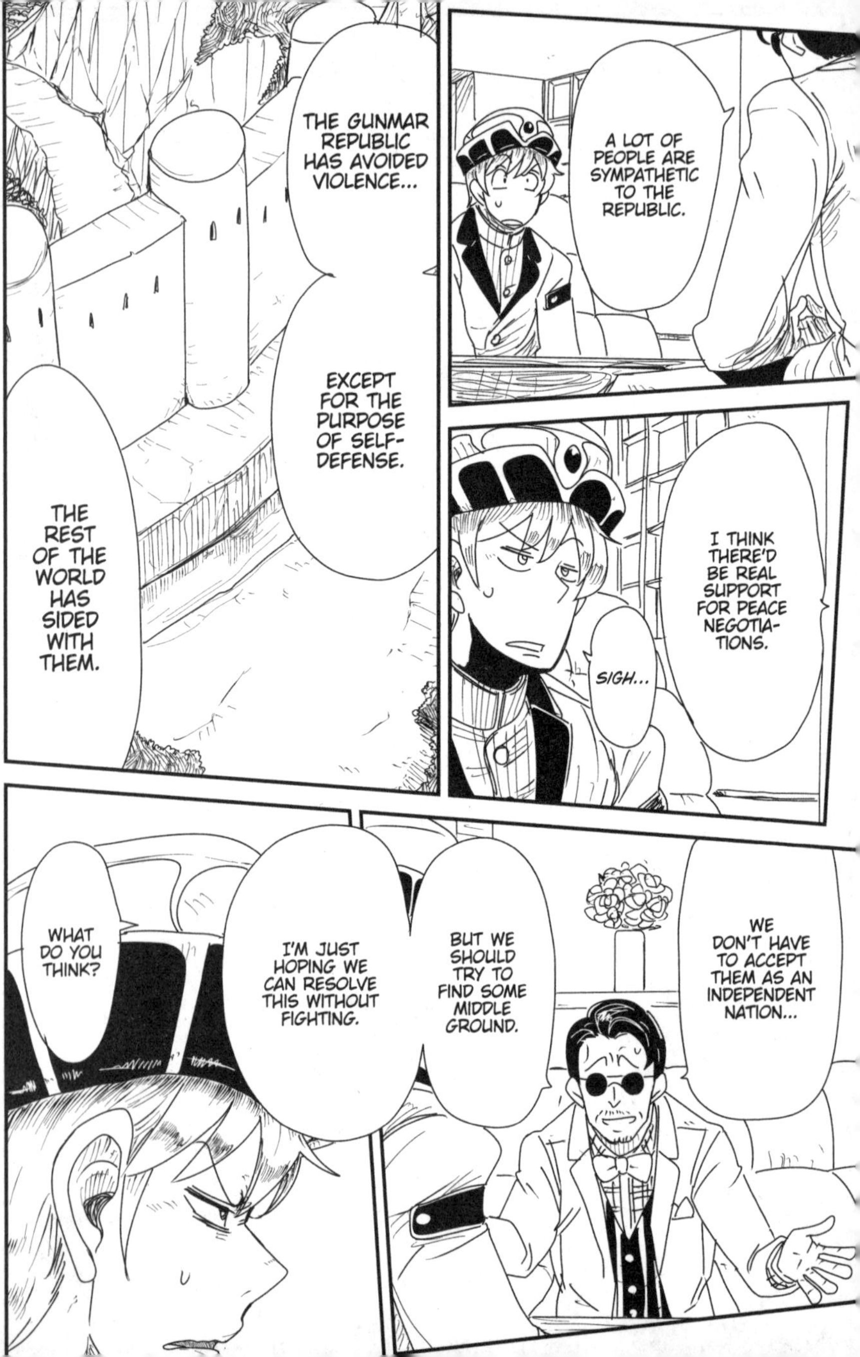
A LOT OF PEOPLE ARE SYMPATHETIC TO THE REPUBLIC.
I THINK THERE'D BE REAL SUPPORT FOR PEACE NEGOTIA-TIONS.
SIGH...
THE GUNMAR REPUBLIC HAS AVOIDED VIOLENCE...
EXCEPT FOR THE PURPOSE OF SELF-DEFENSE.
THE REST OF THE WORLD HAS SIDED WITH THEM.
WE DON'T HAVE TO ACCEPT THEM AS AN INDEPENDENT NATION...
BUT WE SHOULD TRY TO FIND SOME MIDDLE GROUND.
I'M JUST HOPING WE CAN RESOLVE THIS WITHOUT FIGHTING.
WHAT DO YOU THINK?

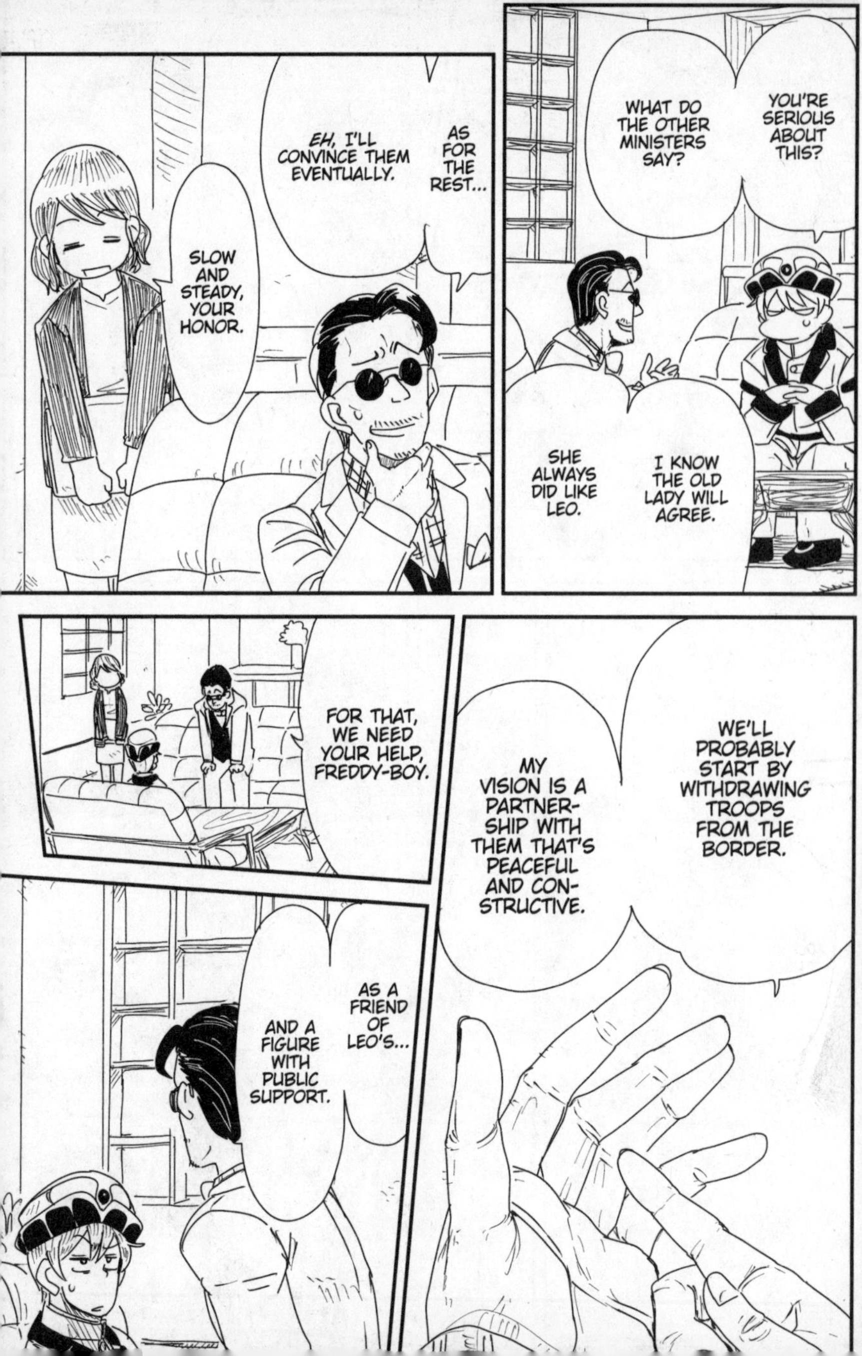
YOU'RE SERIOUS ABOUT THIS?
WHAT DO THE OTHER MINISTERS SAY?
I KNOW THE OLD LADY WILL AGREE.
SHE ALWAYS DID LIKE LEO.
AS FOR THE REST...
EH, I'LL CONVINCE THEM EVENTUALLY.
SLOW AND STEADY, YOUR HONOR.
WE'LL PROBABLY START BY WITHDRAWING TROOPS FROM THE BORDER.
MY VISION IS A PARTNER-SHIP WITH THEM THAT'S PEACEFUL AND CON-STRUCTIVE.
FOR THAT, WE NEED YOUR HELP, FREDDY-BOY.
AS A FRIEND OF LEO'S...
AND A FIGURE WITH PUBLIC SUPPORT.

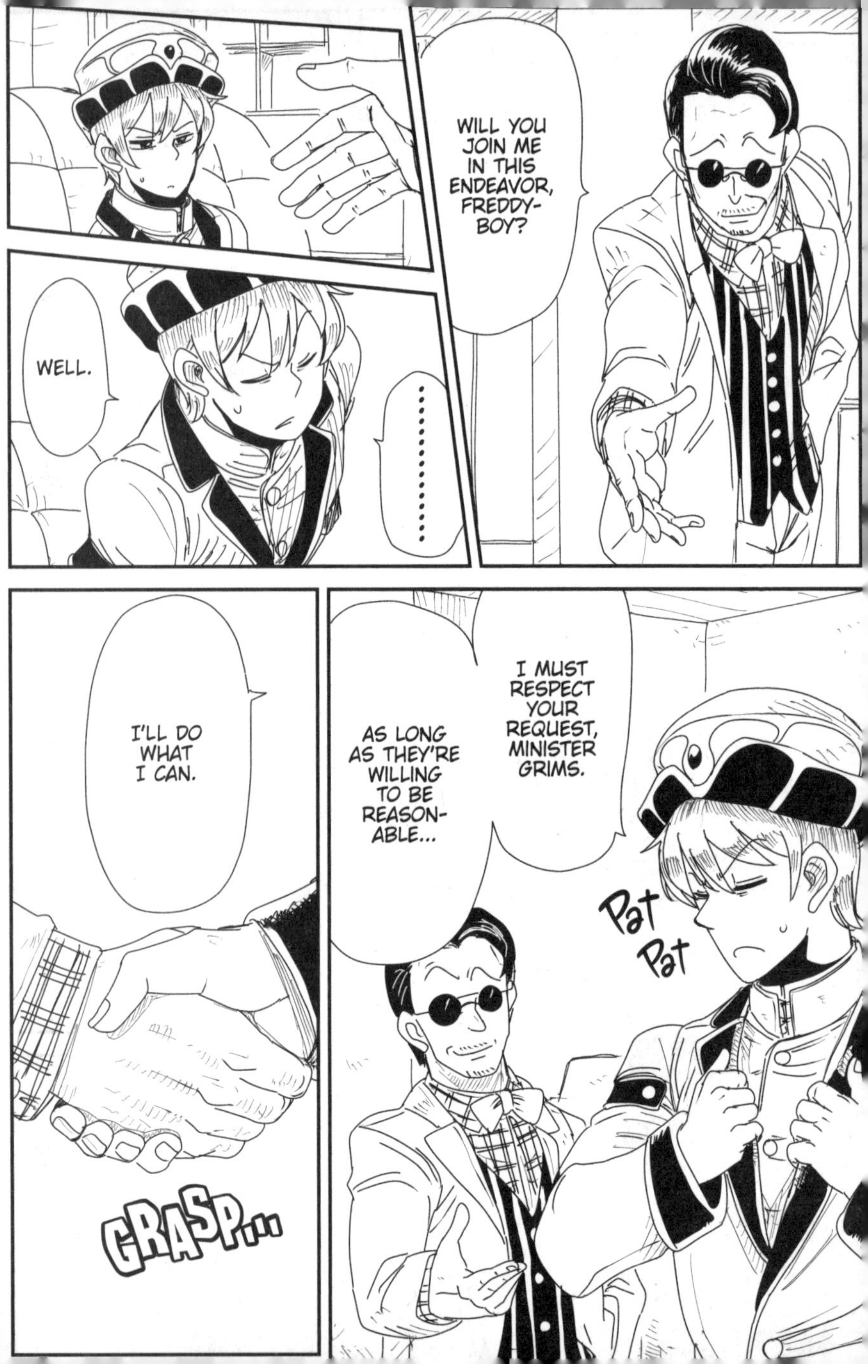
WILL YOU JOIN ME IN THIS ENDEAVOR, FREDDY-BOY?
....
WELL.
I MUST RESPECT YOUR REQUEST, MINISTER GRIMS.
AS LONG AS THEY'RE WILLING TO BE REASONABLE...
Pat Pat
I'LL DO WHAT I CAN.
GRASP...

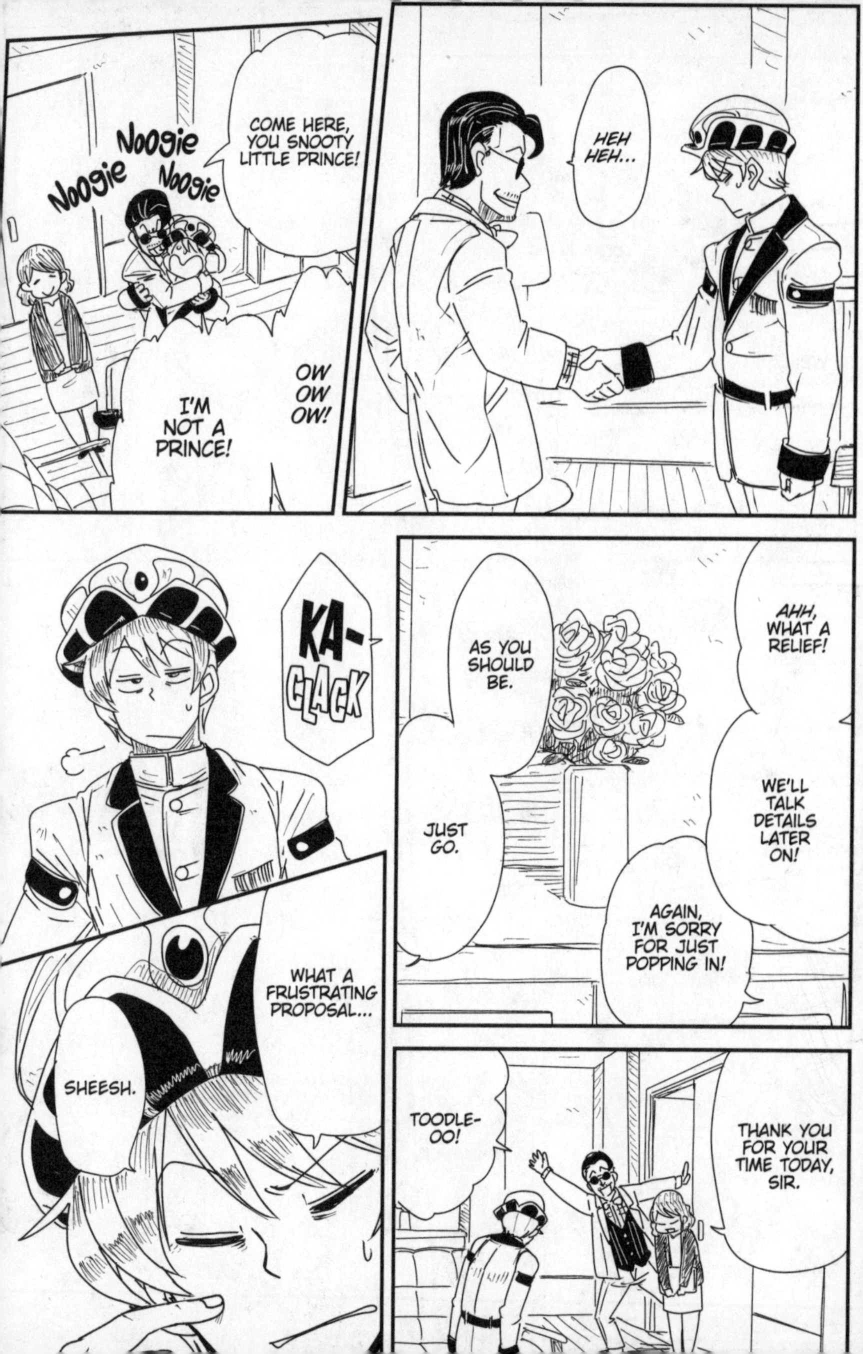
HEH HEH...
COME HERE, YOU SNOOTY LITTLE PRINCE!
Noogie Noogie Noogie
OW OW OW!
I'M NOT A PRINCE!
AHH, WHAT A RELIEF!
WE'LL TALK DETAILS LATER ON!
AGAIN, I'M SORRY FOR JUST POPPING IN!
AS YOU SHOULD BE.
JUST GO.
THANK YOU FOR YOUR TIME TODAY, SIR.
TOODLE-OO!
KA-CLACK
WHAT A FRUSTRATING PROPOSAL...
SHEESH.

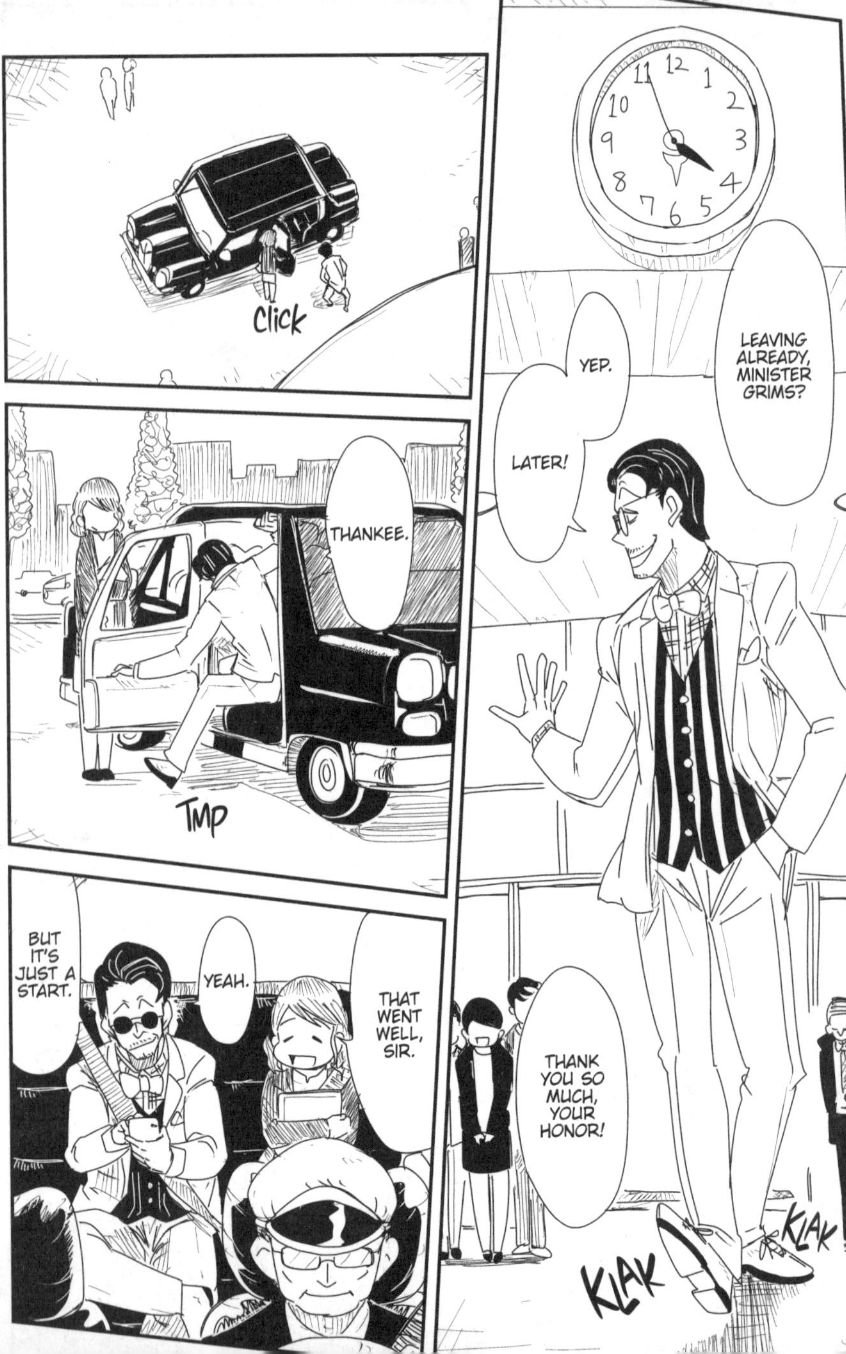
LEAVING ALREADY, MINISTER GRIMS?
YEP.
LATER!
THANK YOU SO MUCH, YOUR HONOR!
KLAK
KLAK
KLAK
CLICK
THANKEE.
TMP
THAT WENT WELL, SIR.
YEAH.
BUT IT'S JUST A START.

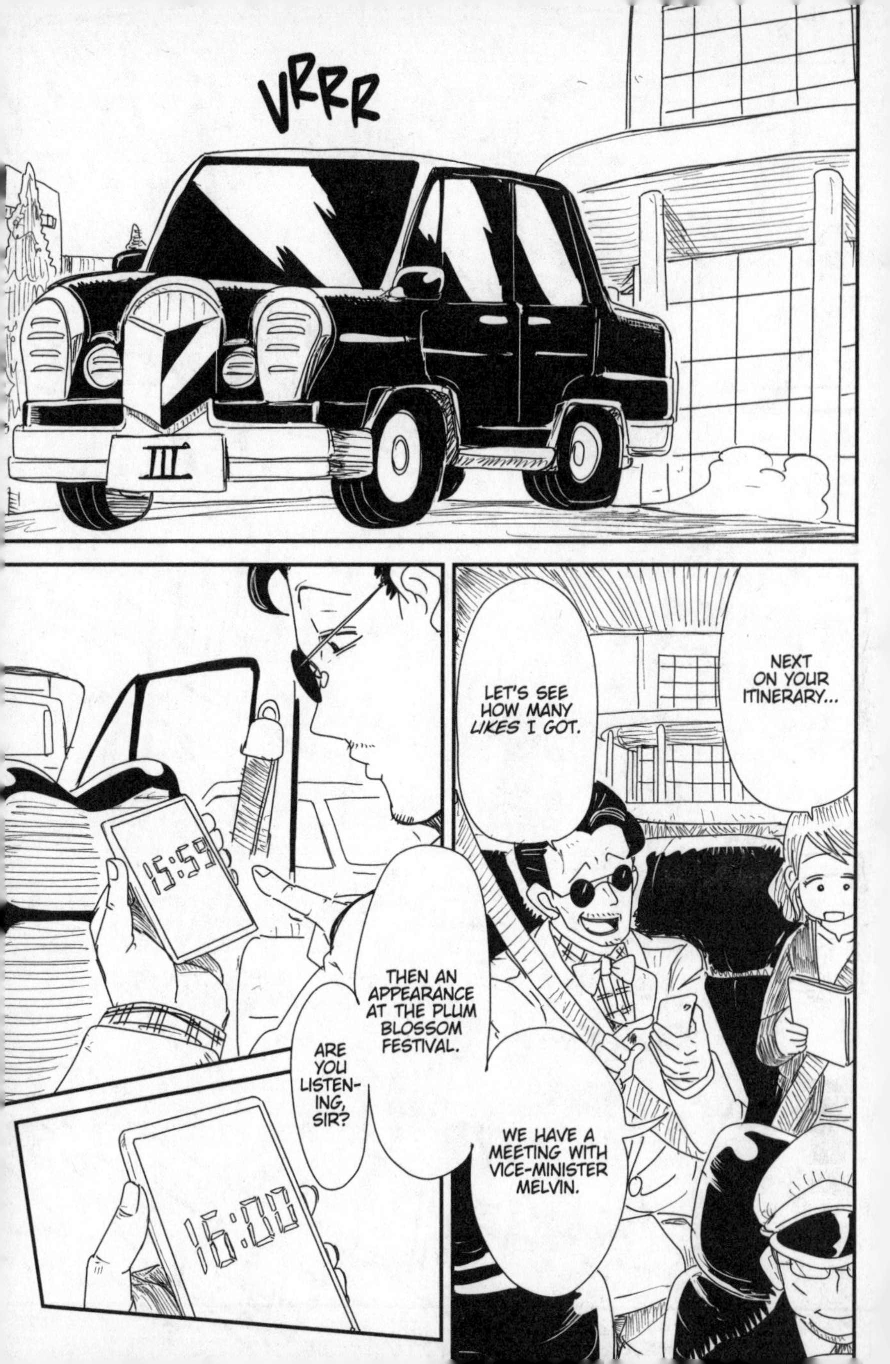
VRRR
NEXT ON YOUR ITINERARY...
LET'S SEE HOW MANY LIKES I GOT.
WE HAVE A MEETING WITH VICE-MINISTER MELVIN.
THEN AN APPEARANCE AT THE PLUM BLOSSOM FESTIVAL.
15:59
ARE YOU LISTENING-ING, SIR?
16:00

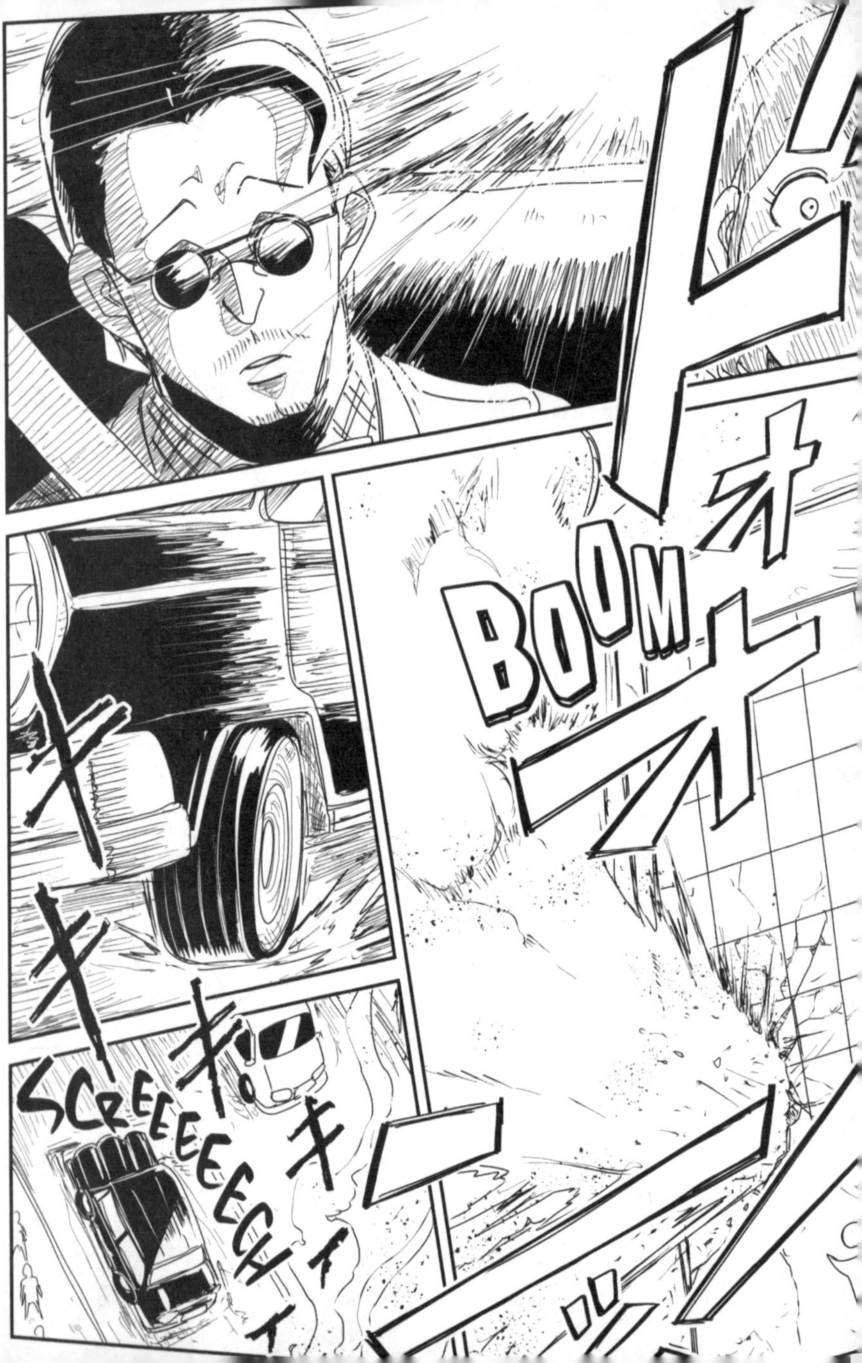
BOOM
SCREEEEEEECH

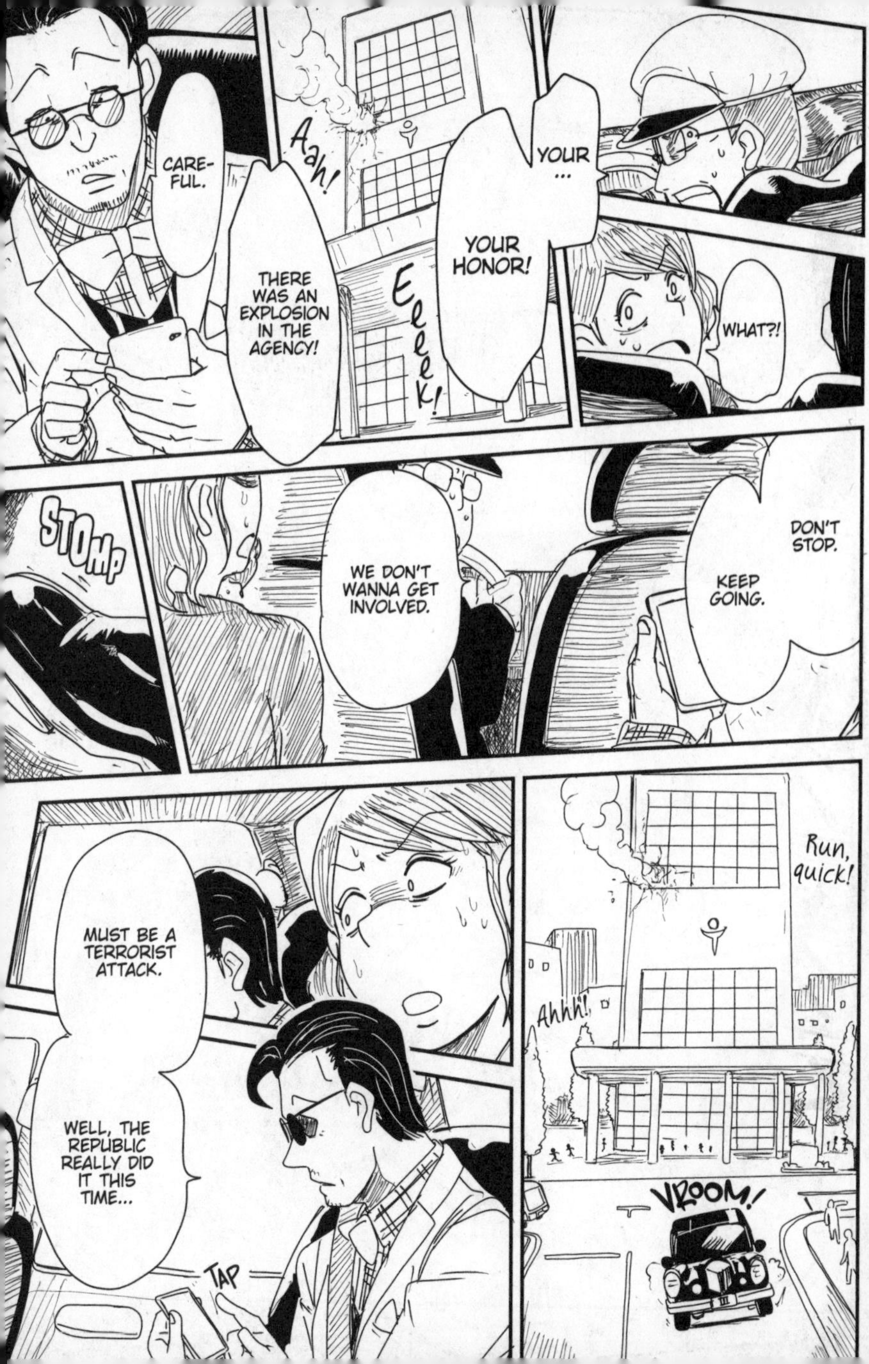
YOUR ...
YOUR HONOR!
WHAT?!
Aah!
Eeeek!
THERE WAS AN EXPLOSION IN THE AGENCY!
CARE-FUL.
DON'T STOP.
KEEP GOING.
WE DON'T WANNA GET INVOLVED.
STOMP
Run, quick!
Ahhh!
VROOM!
MUST BE A TERRORIST ATTACK.
WELL, THE REPUBLIC REALLY DID IT THIS TIME...
TAP

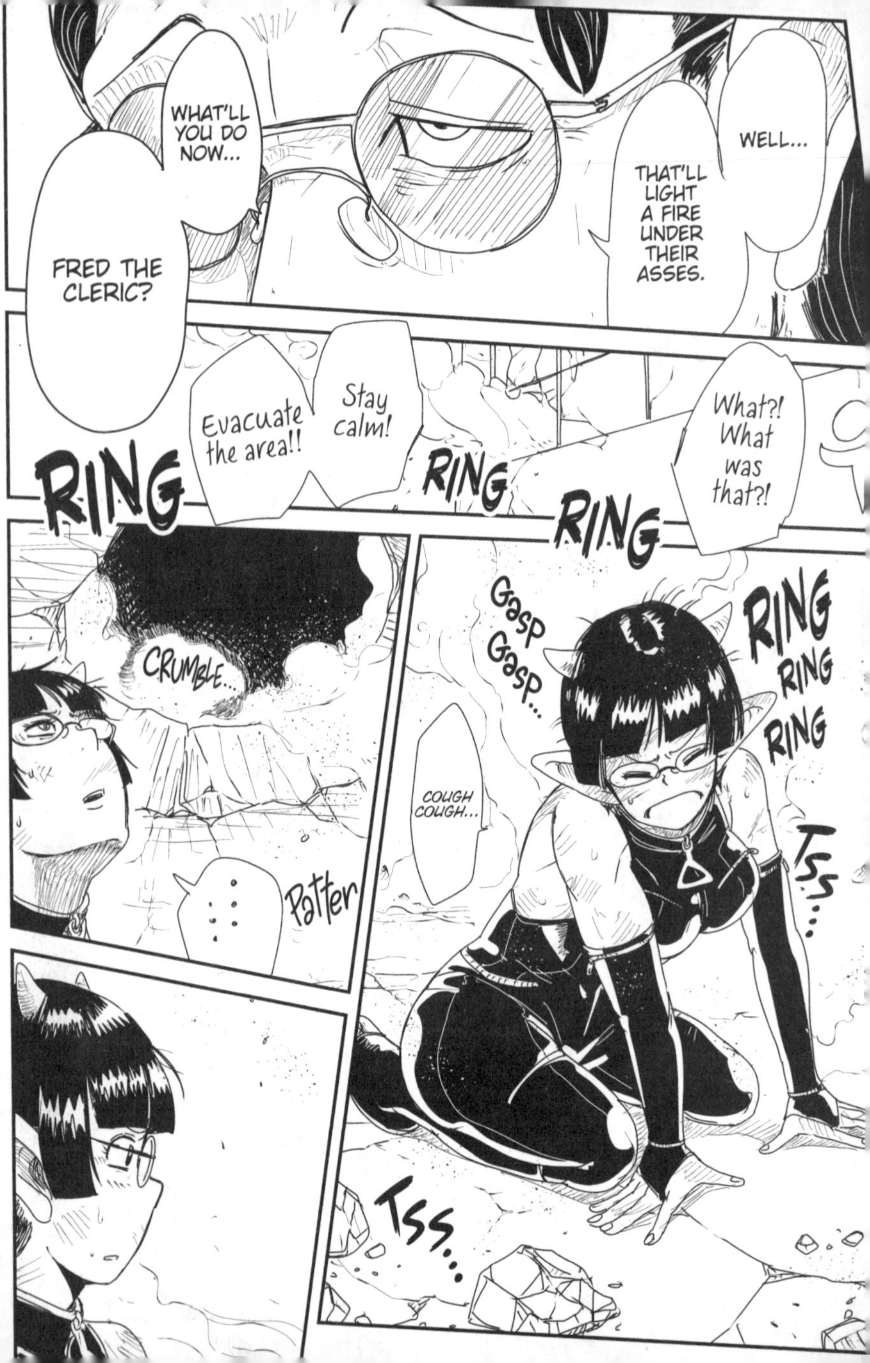
WELL...
THAT'LL LIGHT A FIRE UNDER THEIR ASSES.
WHAT'LL YOU DO NOW...
FRED THE CLERIC?
What?! What was that?!
RING
RING
Stay calm!
Evacuate the area!!
RING
RING RING RING RING
Gasp Gasp...
COUGH COUGH...
Tss...
Tss...
CRUMBLE...
...
Patter

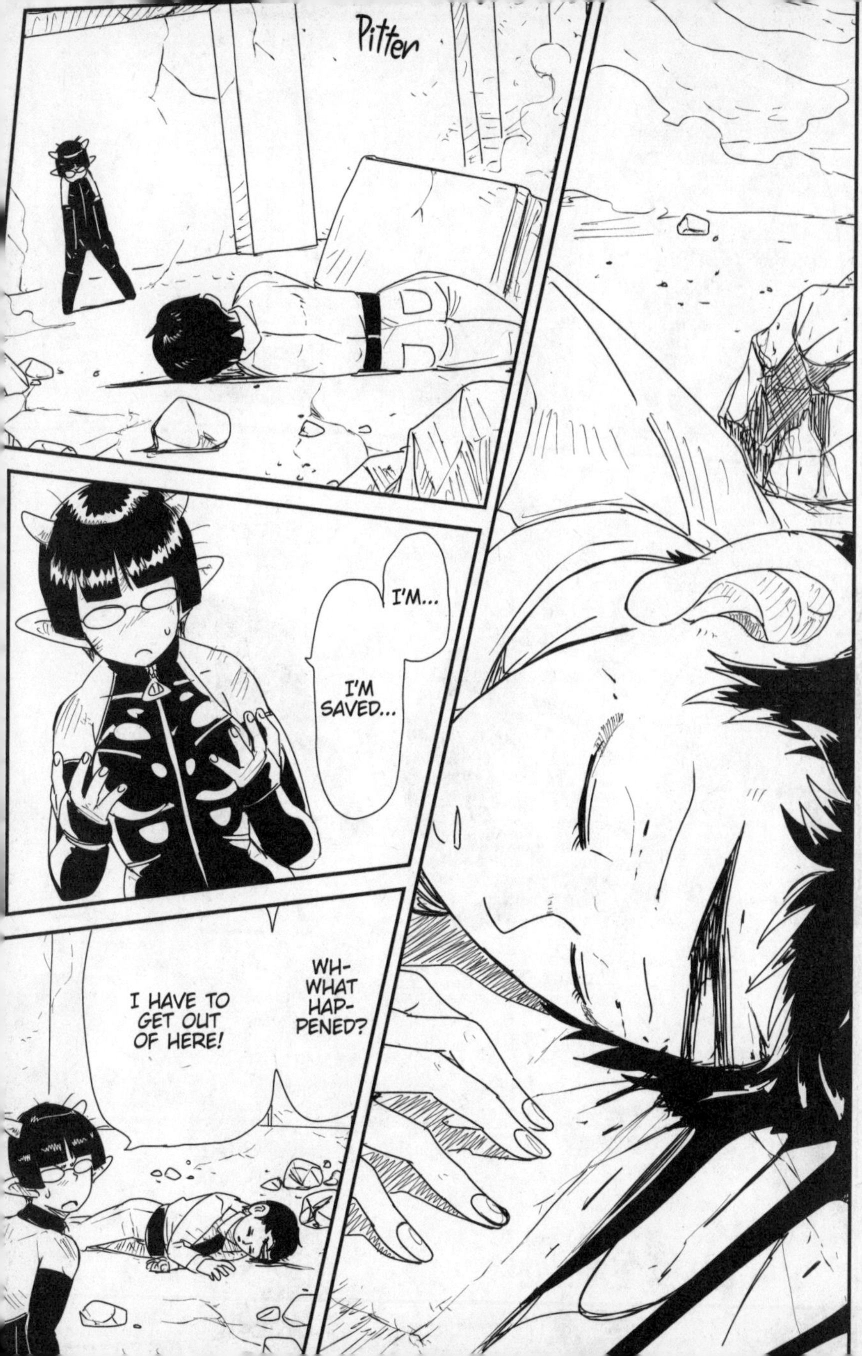
Pitter
I'M...
I'M SAVED...
WH- WHAT HAP- PENED?
I HAVE TO GET OUT OF HERE!

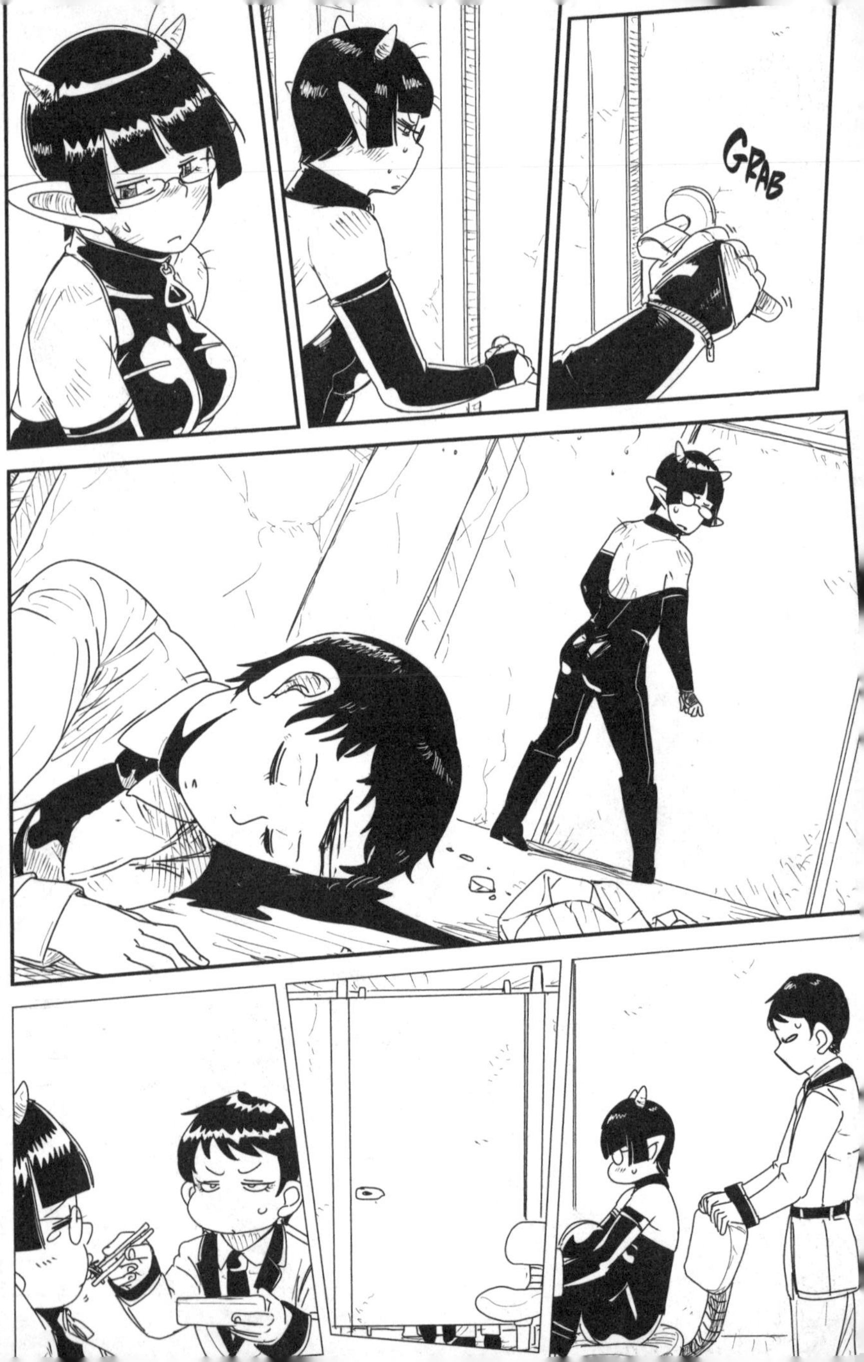
GRAB

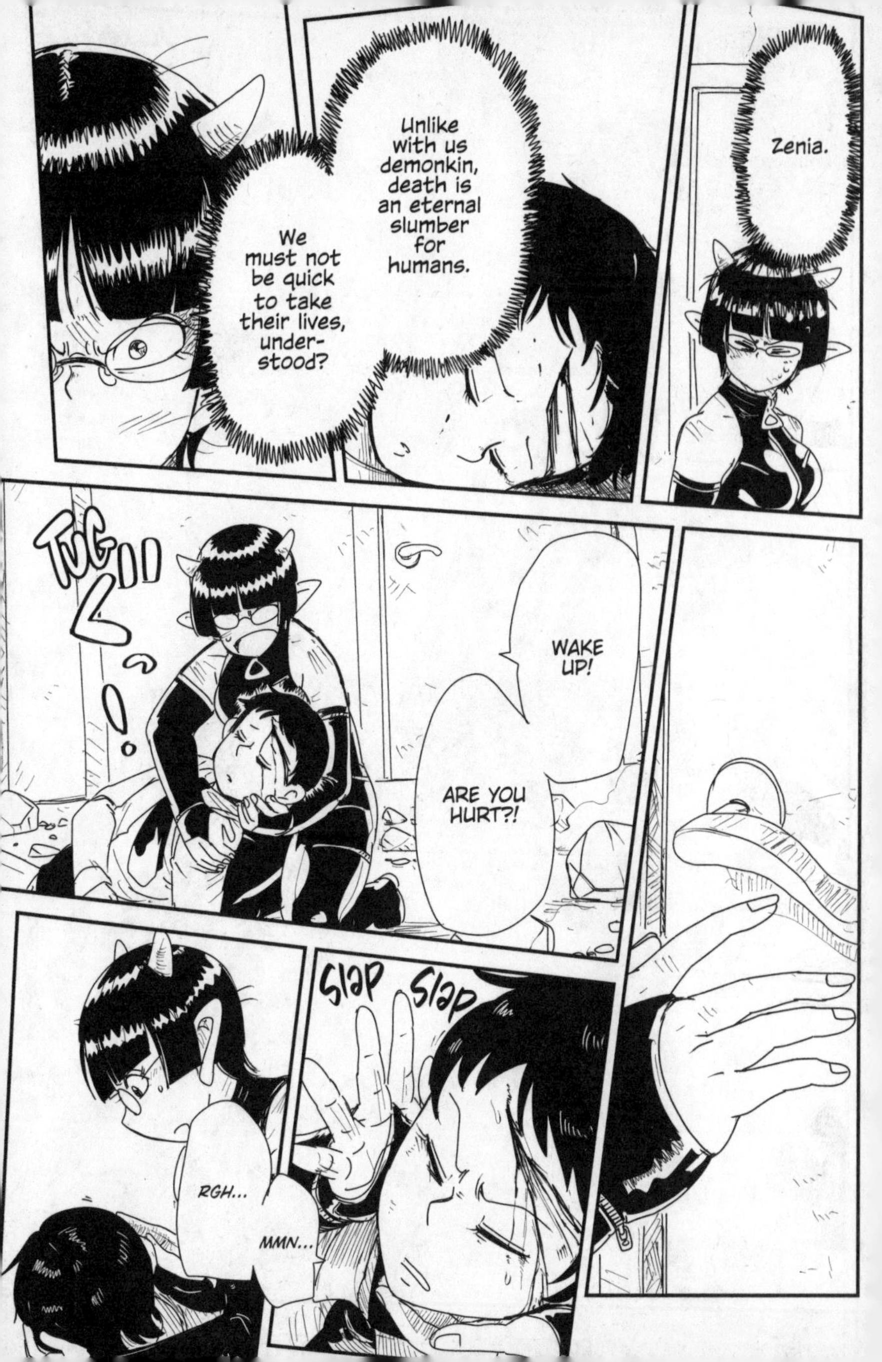
Zenia.
Unlike with us demonkin, death is an eternal slumber for humans.
We must not be quick to take their lives, under-stood?
WAKE UP!
ARE YOU HURT?!
TUG
Slap Slap
RGH...
MMN...

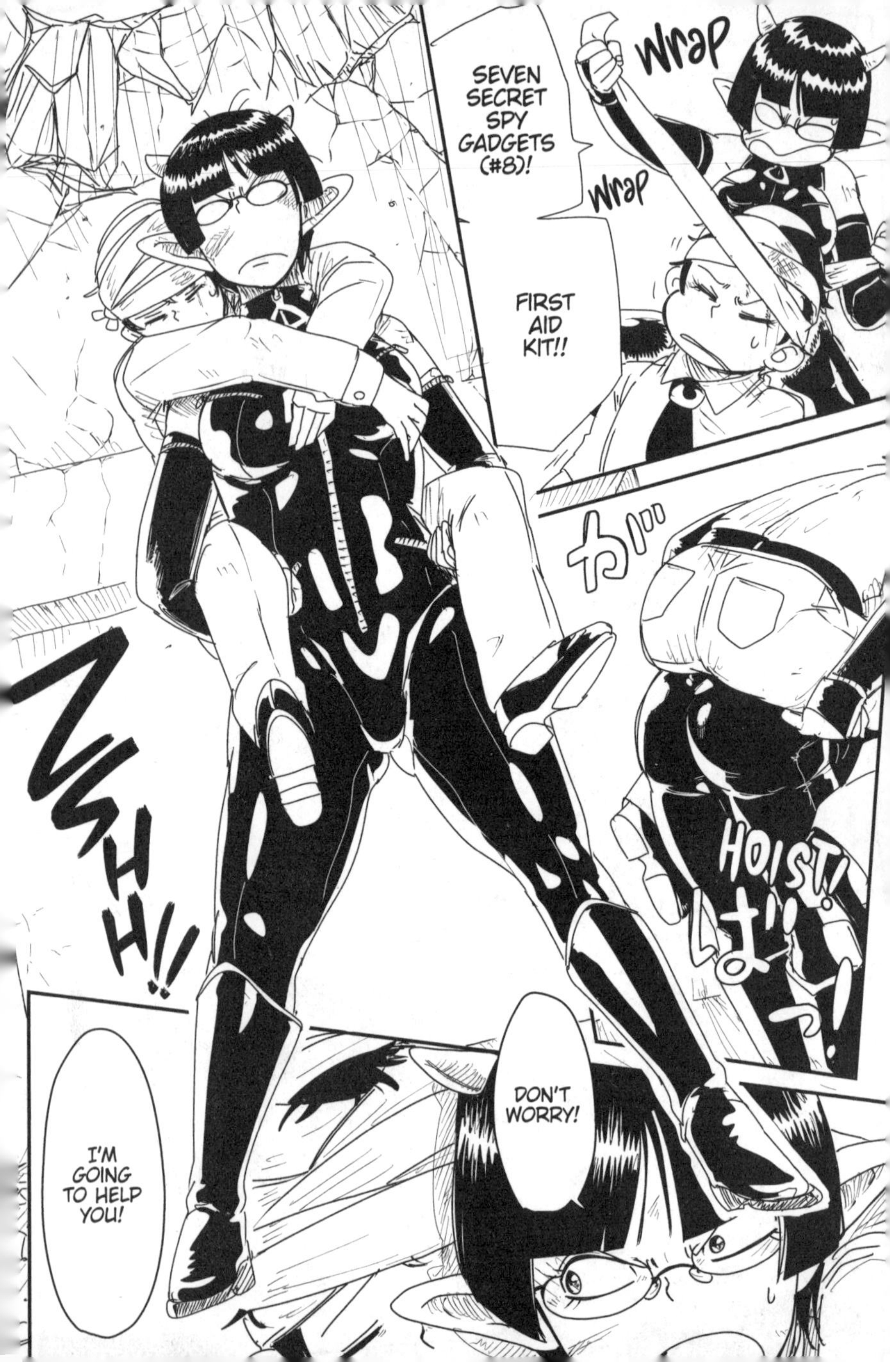
WRAP
WRAP
SEVEN SECRET SPY GADGETS (#8)!
FIRST AID KIT!!
HOIST!
VWSHH!!
DON'T WORRY!
I'M GOING TO HELP YOU!

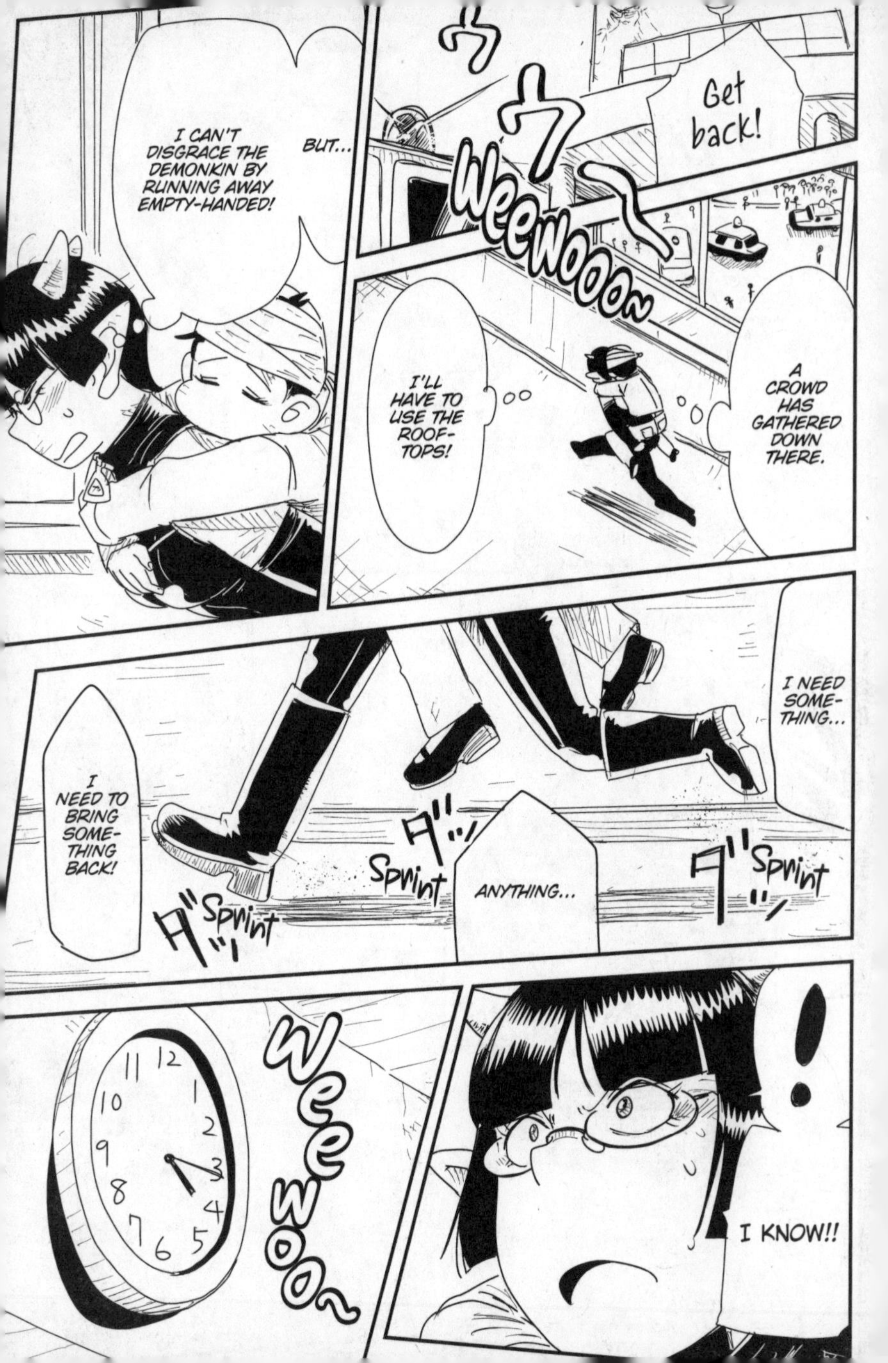
Get back!
ウ ウ
Weewooon~
A CROWD HAS GATHERED DOWN THERE.
I'LL HAVE TO USE THE ROOF-TOPS!
BUT...
I CAN'T DISGRACE THE DEMONKIN BY RUNNING AWAY EMPTY-HANDED!
I NEED SOME-THING...
ダッ Sprint
ANYTHING...
ダッ Sprint
I NEED TO BRING SOME-THING BACK!
ダッ Sprint
!
I KNOW!!
Weewoo~

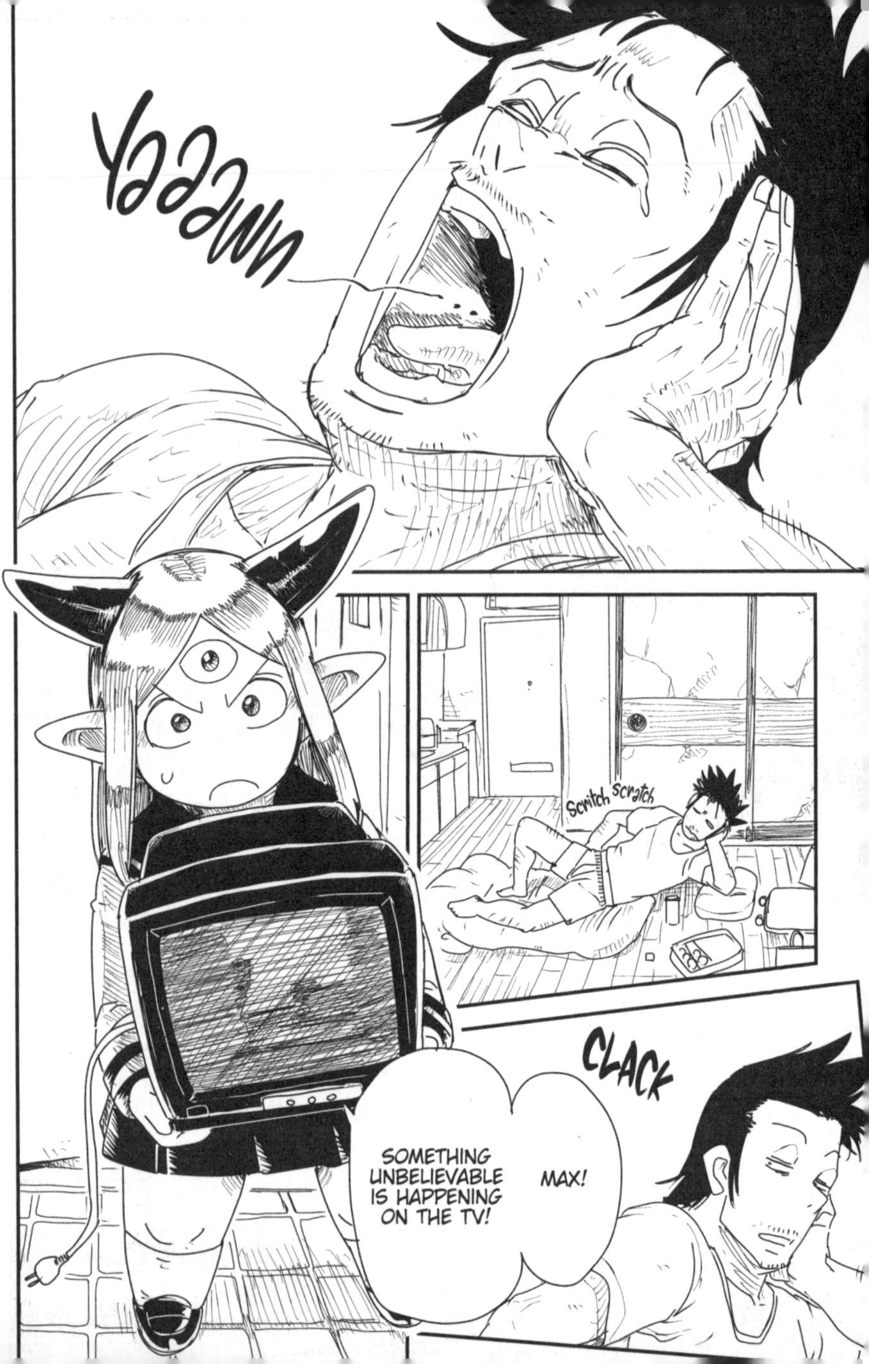
Scritch scratch
CLACK
MAX!
SOMETHING UNBELIEVABLE IS HAPPENING ON THE TV!

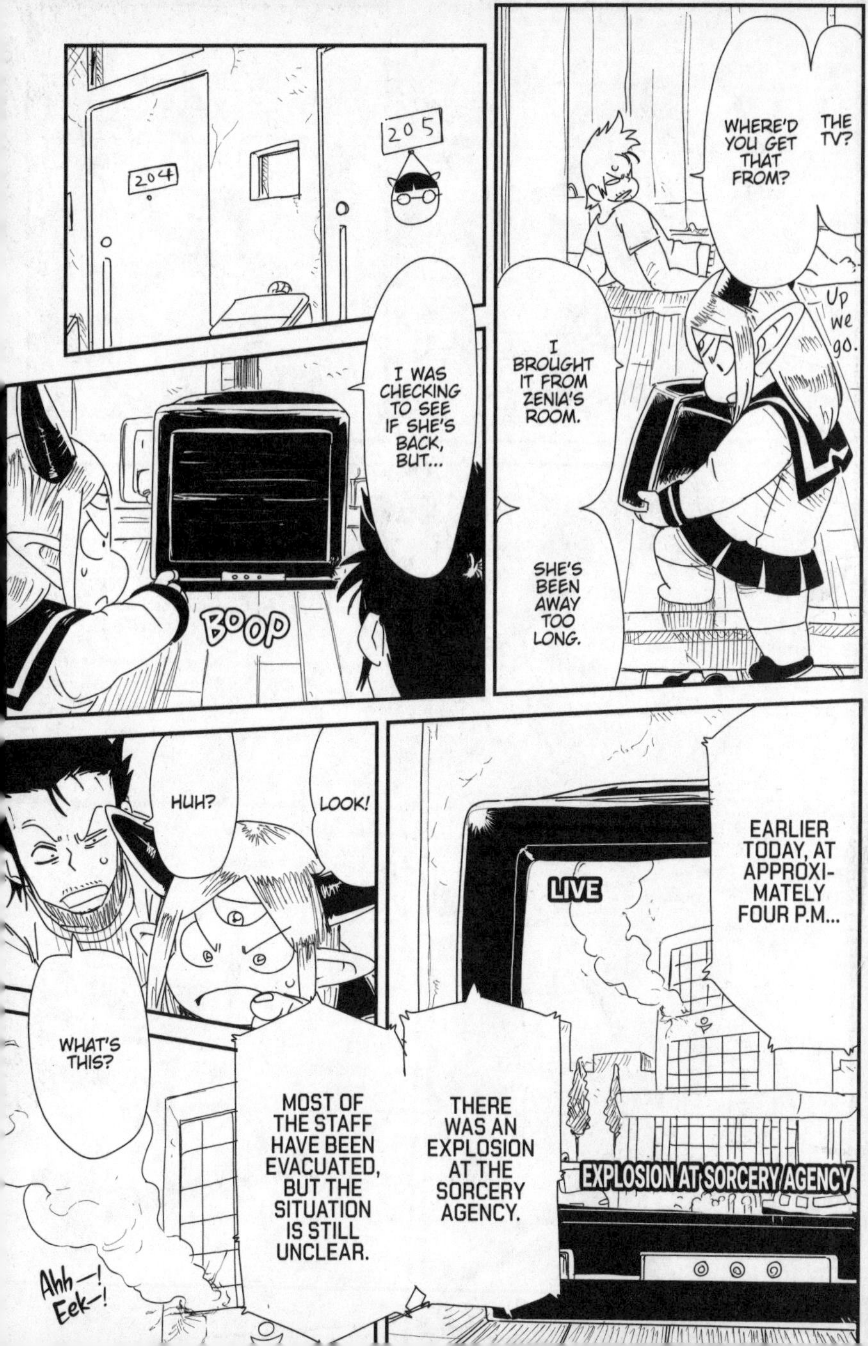
THE TV?
WHERE'D YOU GET THAT FROM?
Up we go.
I BROUGHT IT FROM ZENIA'S ROOM.
SHE'S BEEN AWAY TOO LONG.
205
204
I WAS CHECKING TO SEE IF SHE'S BACK, BUT...
BOOP
EARLIER TODAY, AT APPROXI-MATELY FOUR P.M...
LIVE
EXPLOSION AT SORCERY AGENCY
THERE WAS AN EXPLOSION AT THE SORCERY AGENCY.
MOST OF THE STAFF HAVE BEEN EVACUATED, BUT THE SITUATION IS STILL UNCLEAR.
LOOK!
HUH?
WHAT'S THIS?
Ahh—! Eek—!

YOU THINK SO?	I WOULDN'T WORRY ABOUT HIM. DOESN'T FRED WORK IN THAT PLACE? HE'S TOUGHER THAN SOME EXPLOSION.	WAS IT A TERRORIST ATTACK? MUST BE, HUH?

YOU MEAN, *SHE* DID THIS?

HUH?

RECENTLY I ASKED ZENIA TO DO SOME RESEARCH ON THE SORCERY AGENCY...

I NEVER EXPECTED **THIS** TO HAPPEN.

......

WHY WOULD YOU THINK THAT?

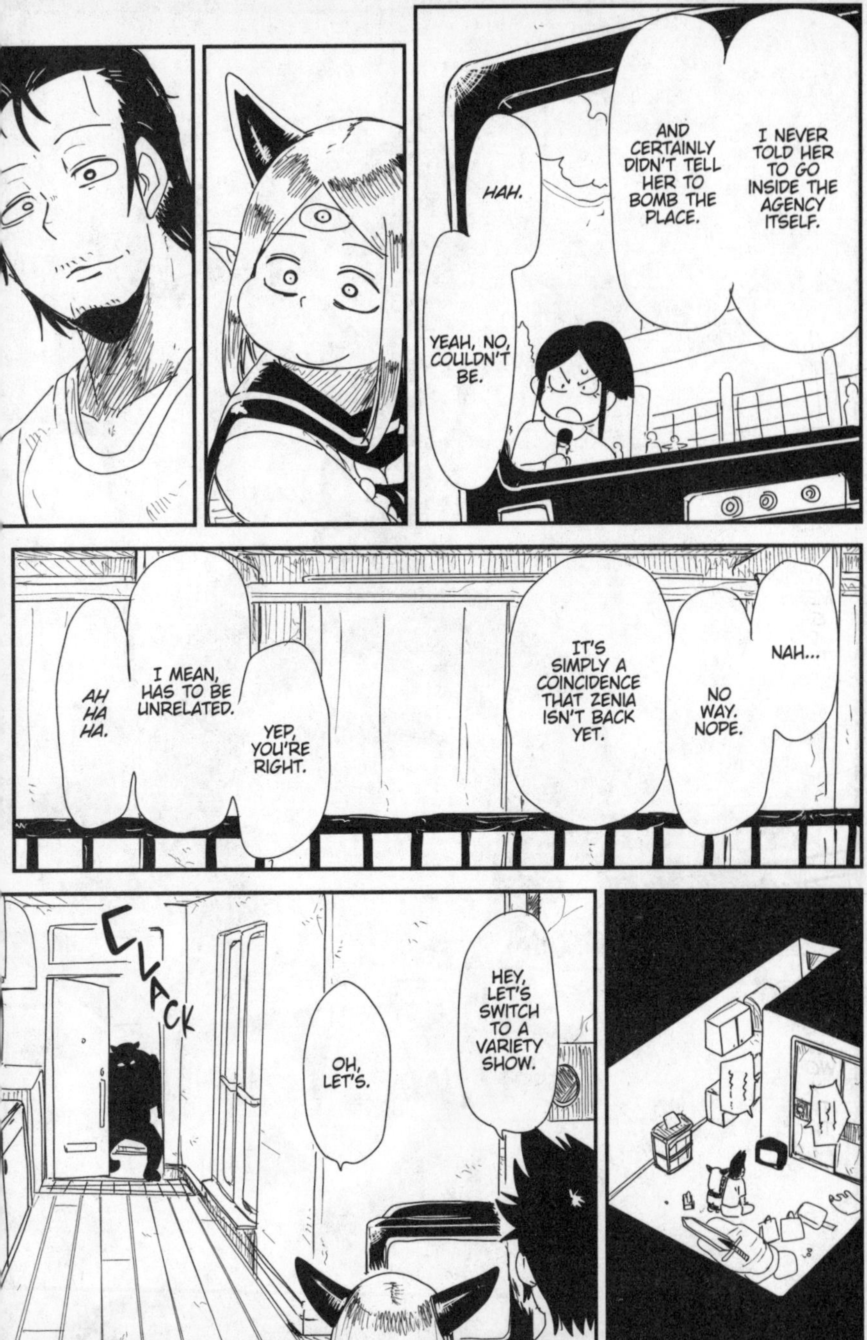
I NEVER TOLD HER TO GO INSIDE THE AGENCY ITSELF.
AND CERTAINLY DIDN'T TELL HER TO BOMB THE PLACE.
HAH.
YEAH, NO, COULDN'T BE.
NAH...
NO WAY. NOPE.
IT'S SIMPLY A COINCIDENCE THAT ZENIA ISN'T BACK YET.
YEP, YOU'RE RIGHT.
I MEAN, HAS TO BE UNRELATED.
AH HA HA.
HEY, LET'S SWITCH TO A VARIETY SHOW.
OH, LET'S.
CLACK

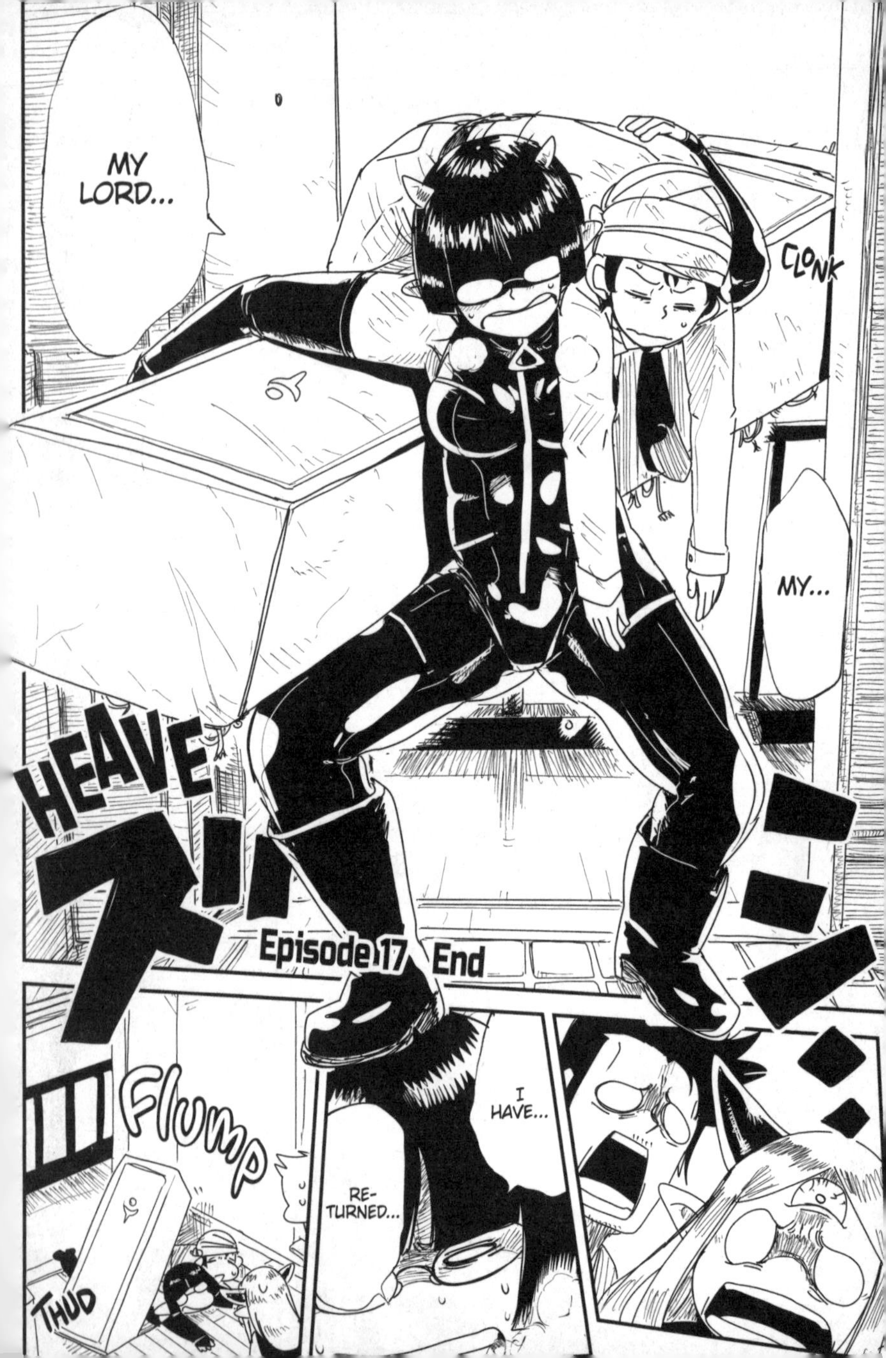
CLONK
MY LORD...
MY...
HEAVE
Episode 17 End
I HAVE...
RE-TURNED...
Flump
THUD

LEVEL 1 DEMON LORD & ONE ROOM HERO

LEVEL 1 DEMON LORD & ONE ROOM HERO

Episode 18: Call of the Eagle

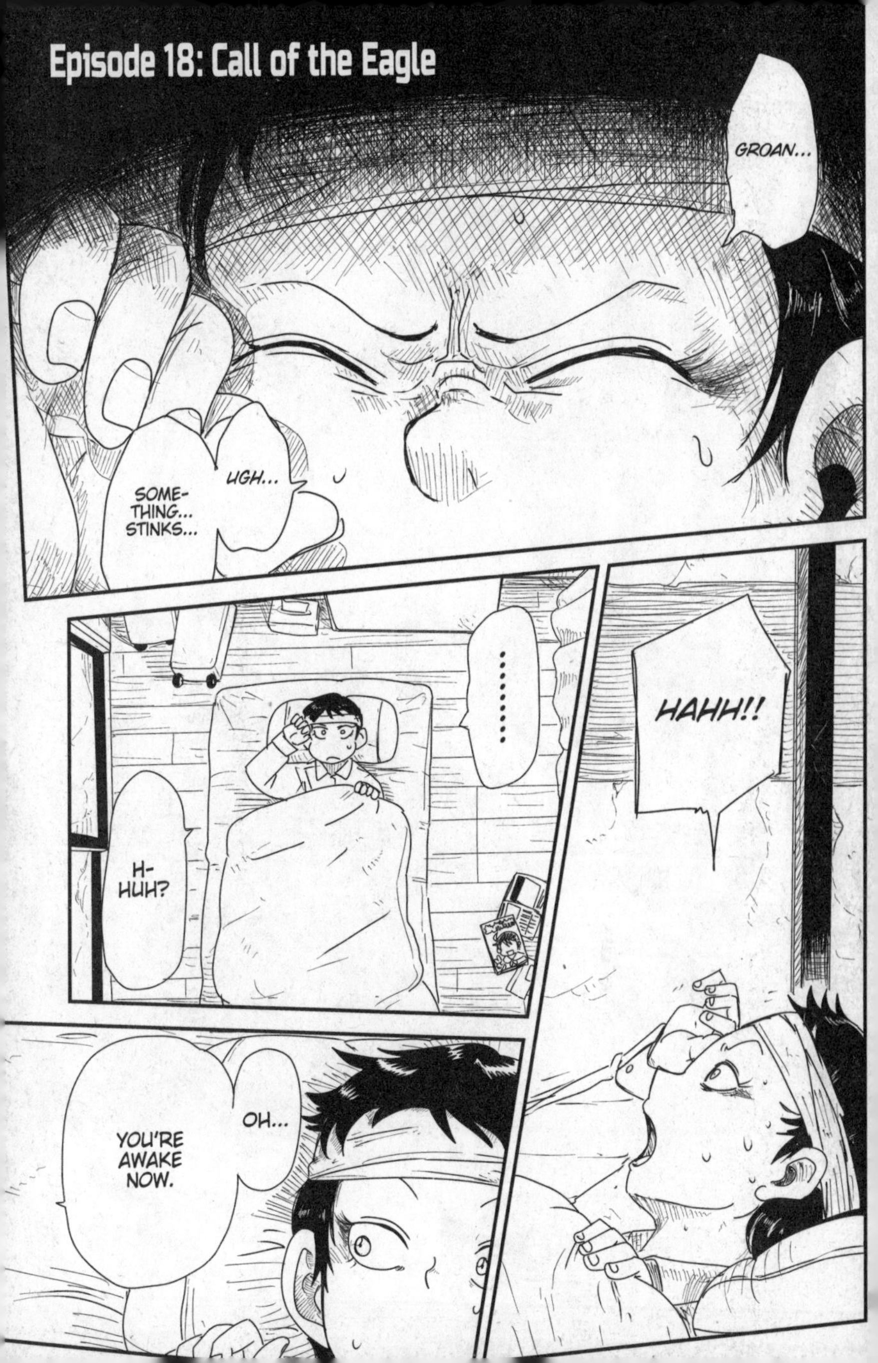
GROAN...
UGH...
SOME-THING... STINKS...
......
H-HUH?
HAHH!!
OH...
YOU'RE AWAKE NOW.

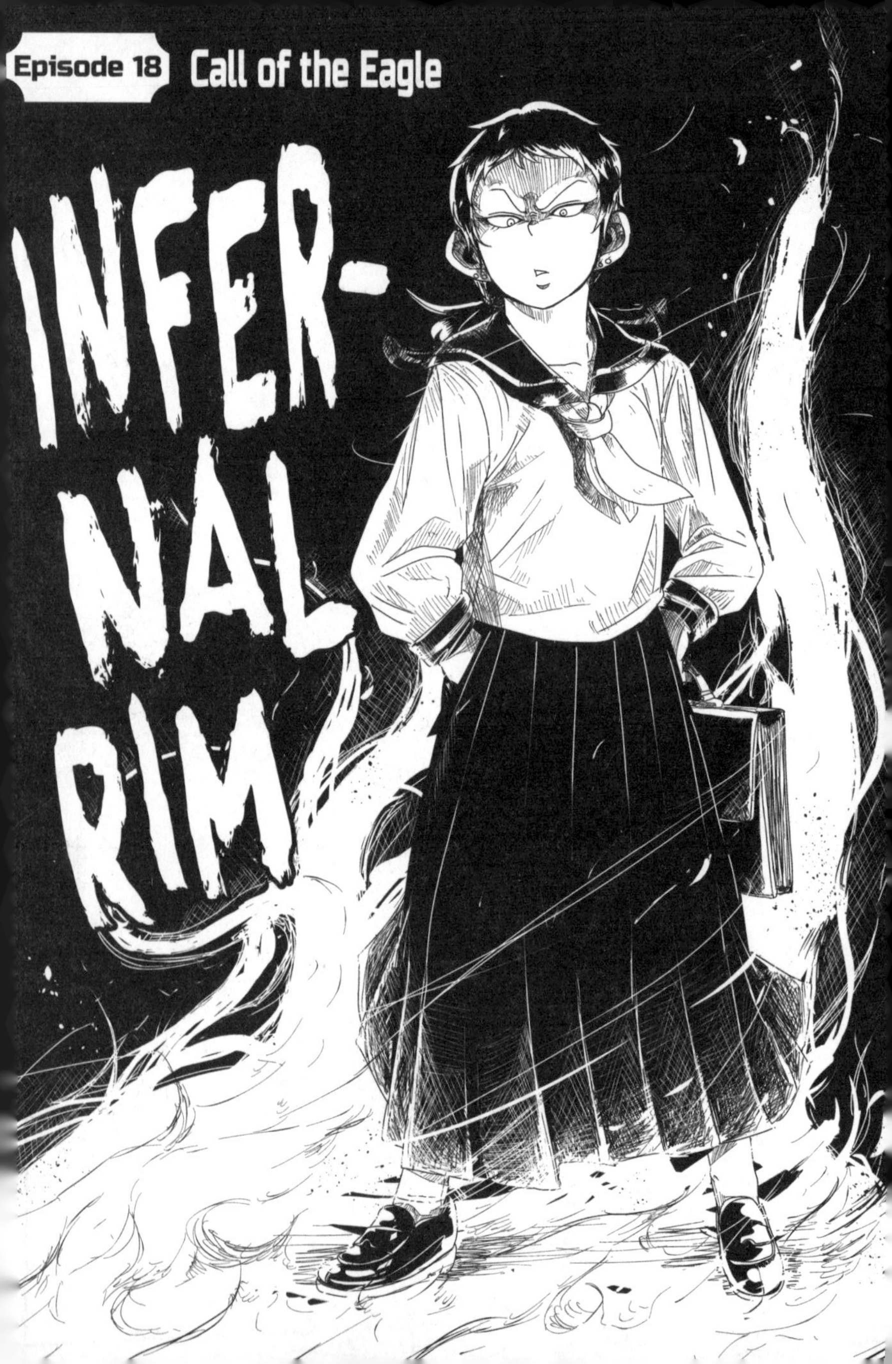
Episode 18
Call of the Eagle
INFER-
NAL
RIM

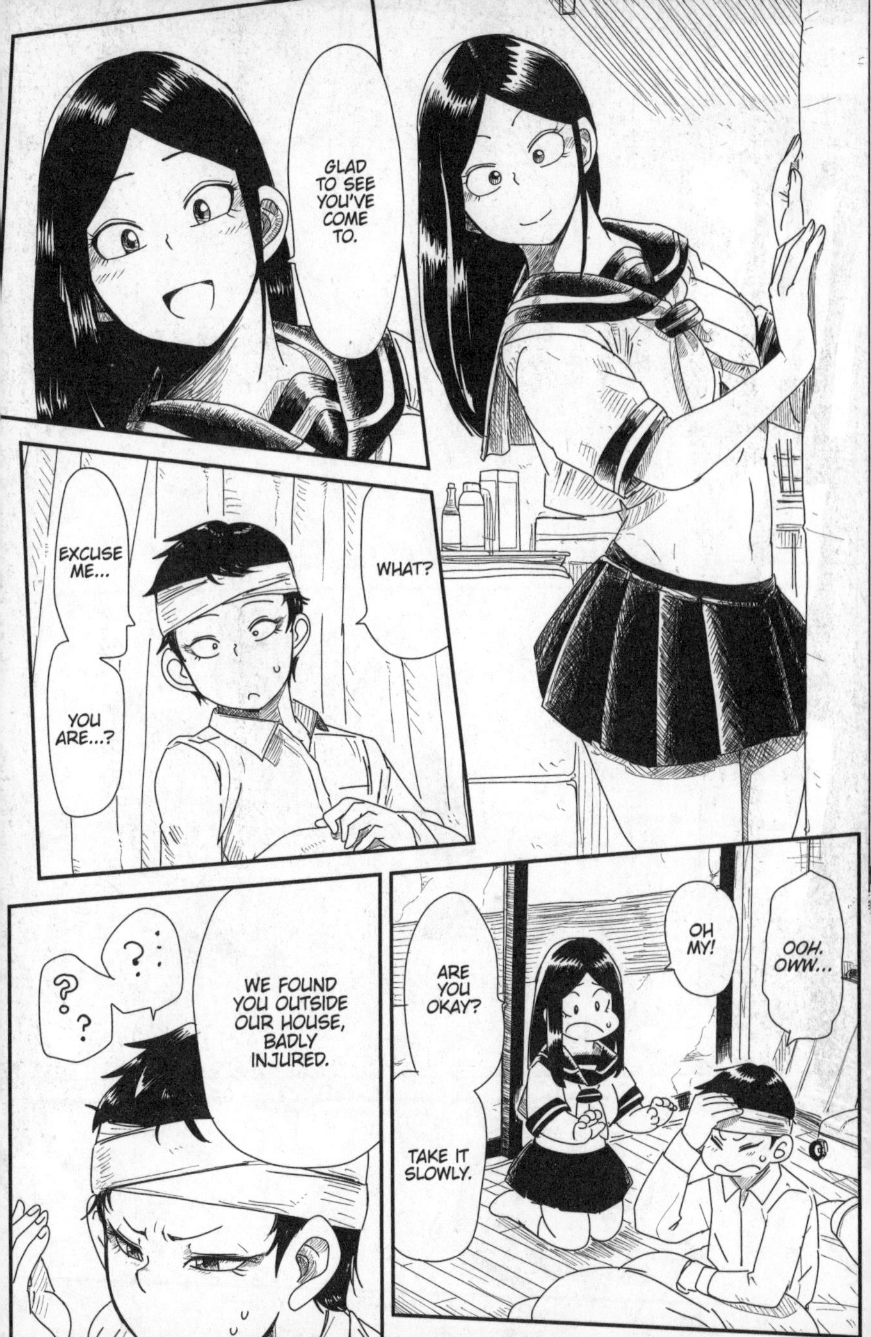
GLAD TO SEE YOU'VE COME TO.
EXCUSE ME...
WHAT?
YOU ARE...?
OOH. OWW...
OH MY!
ARE YOU OKAY?
TAKE IT SLOWLY.
WE FOUND YOU OUTSIDE OUR HOUSE, BADLY INJURED.
? ? ?

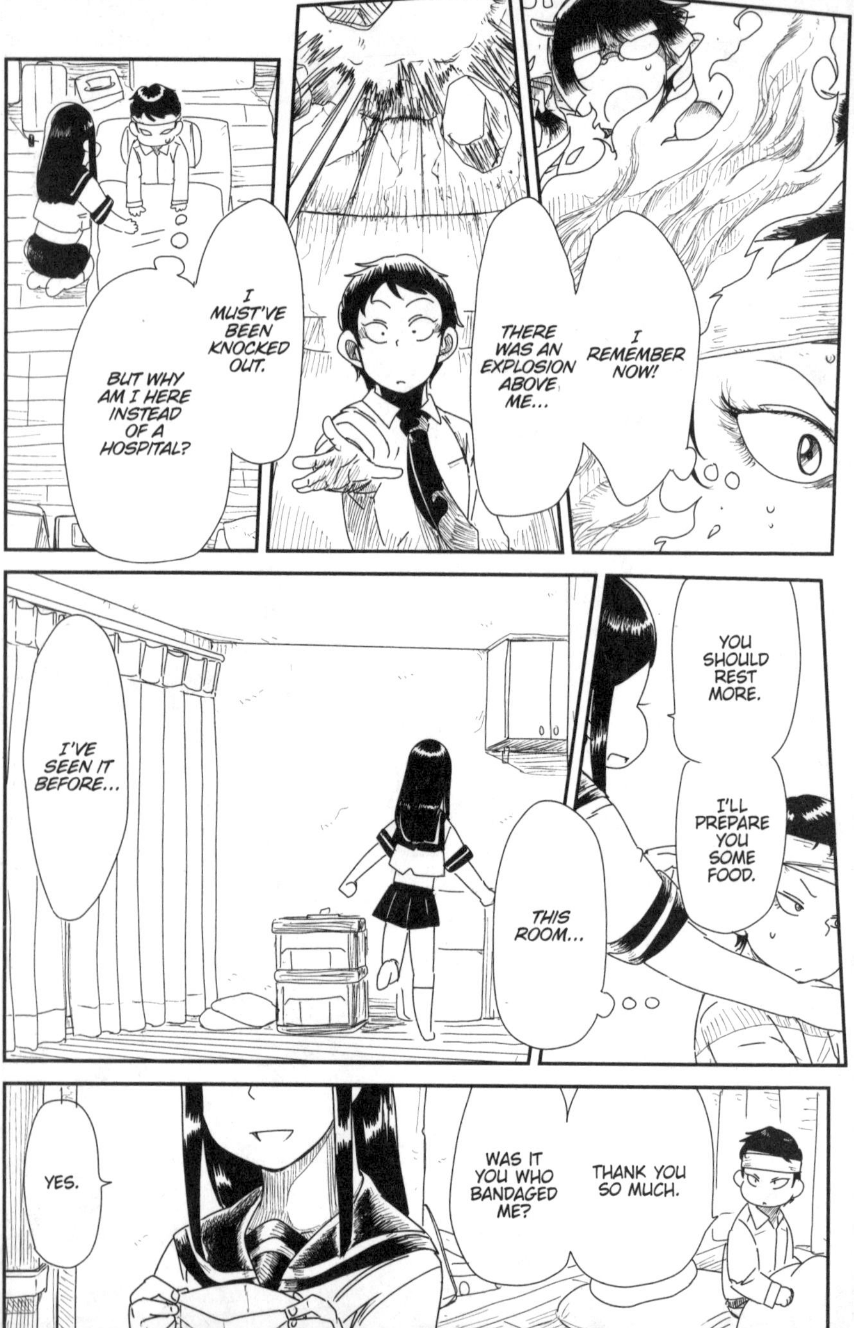
I REMEMBER NOW!
THERE WAS AN EXPLOSION ABOVE ME...
I MUST'VE BEEN KNOCKED OUT.
BUT WHY AM I HERE INSTEAD OF A HOSPITAL?
YOU SHOULD REST MORE.
I'LL PREPARE YOU SOME FOOD.
THIS ROOM...
I'VE SEEN IT BEFORE...
THANK YOU SO MUCH.
WAS IT YOU WHO BANDAGED ME?
YES.

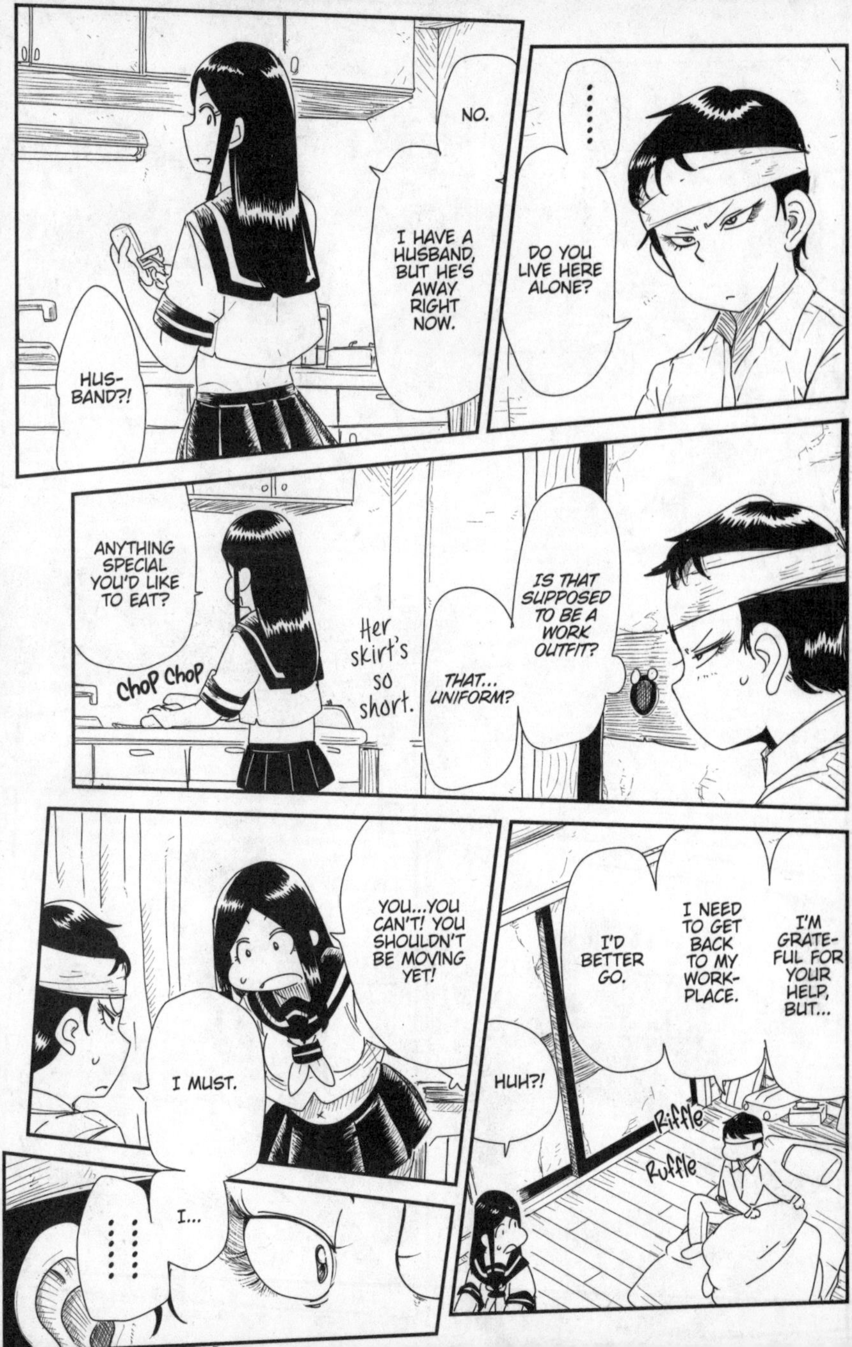
......
DO YOU LIVE HERE ALONE?
NO.
I HAVE A HUSBAND, BUT HE'S AWAY RIGHT NOW.
HUS-BAND?!
IS THAT SUPPOSED TO BE A WORK OUTFIT?
THAT... UNIFORM?
Her skirt's so short.
ANYTHING SPECIAL YOU'D LIKE TO EAT?
Chop Chop
I'M GRATE-FUL FOR YOUR HELP, BUT...
I NEED TO GET BACK TO MY WORK-PLACE.
I'D BETTER GO.
HUH?!
Riffle
Ruffle
YOU...YOU CAN'T! YOU SHOULDN'T BE MOVING YET!
I MUST.
I...
......

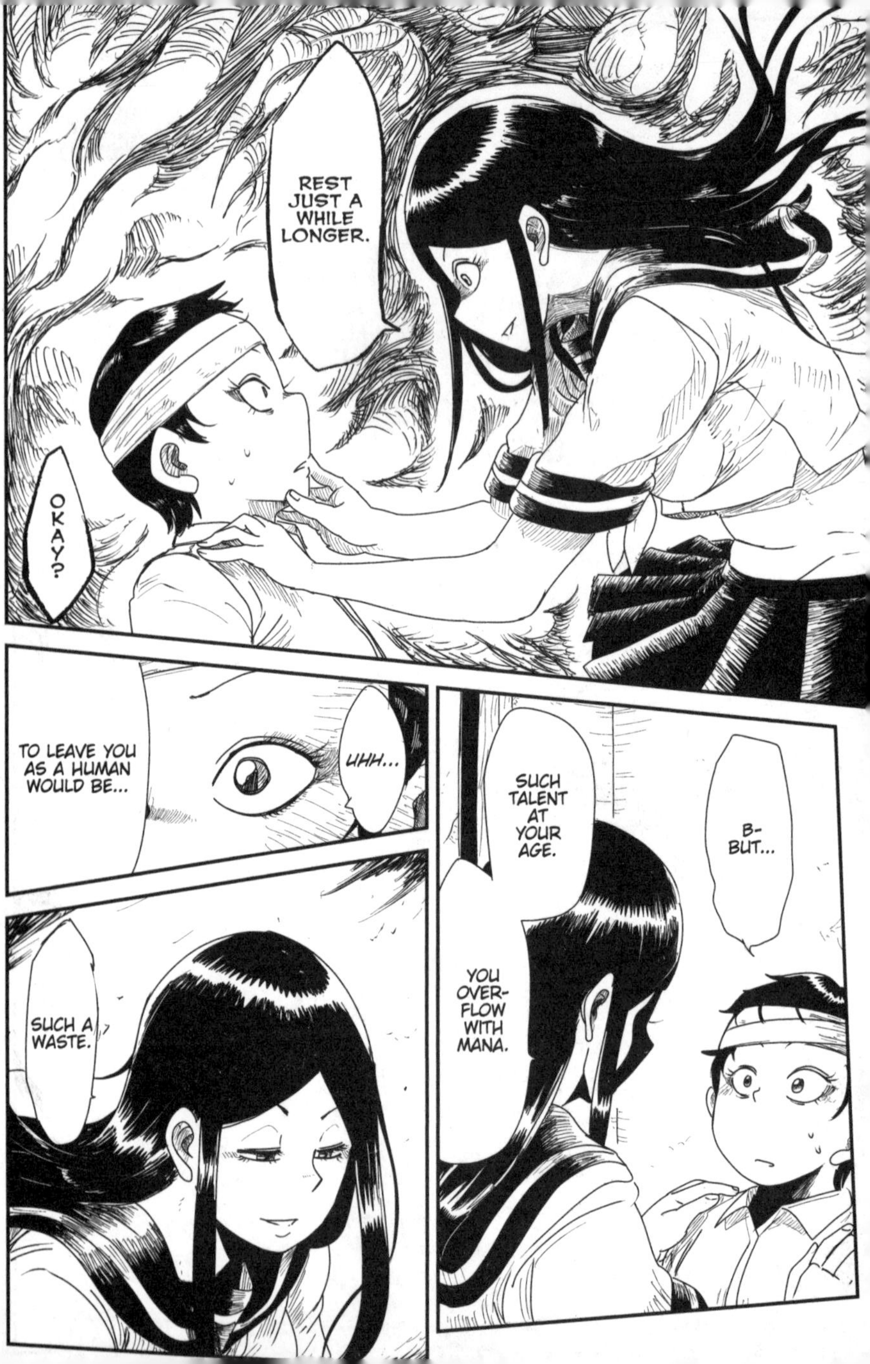
REST JUST A WHILE LONGER.
OKAY?
B-BUT...
SUCH TALENT AT YOUR AGE.
YOU OVERFLOW WITH MANA.
UHH...
TO LEAVE YOU AS A HUMAN WOULD BE...
SUCH A WASTE.

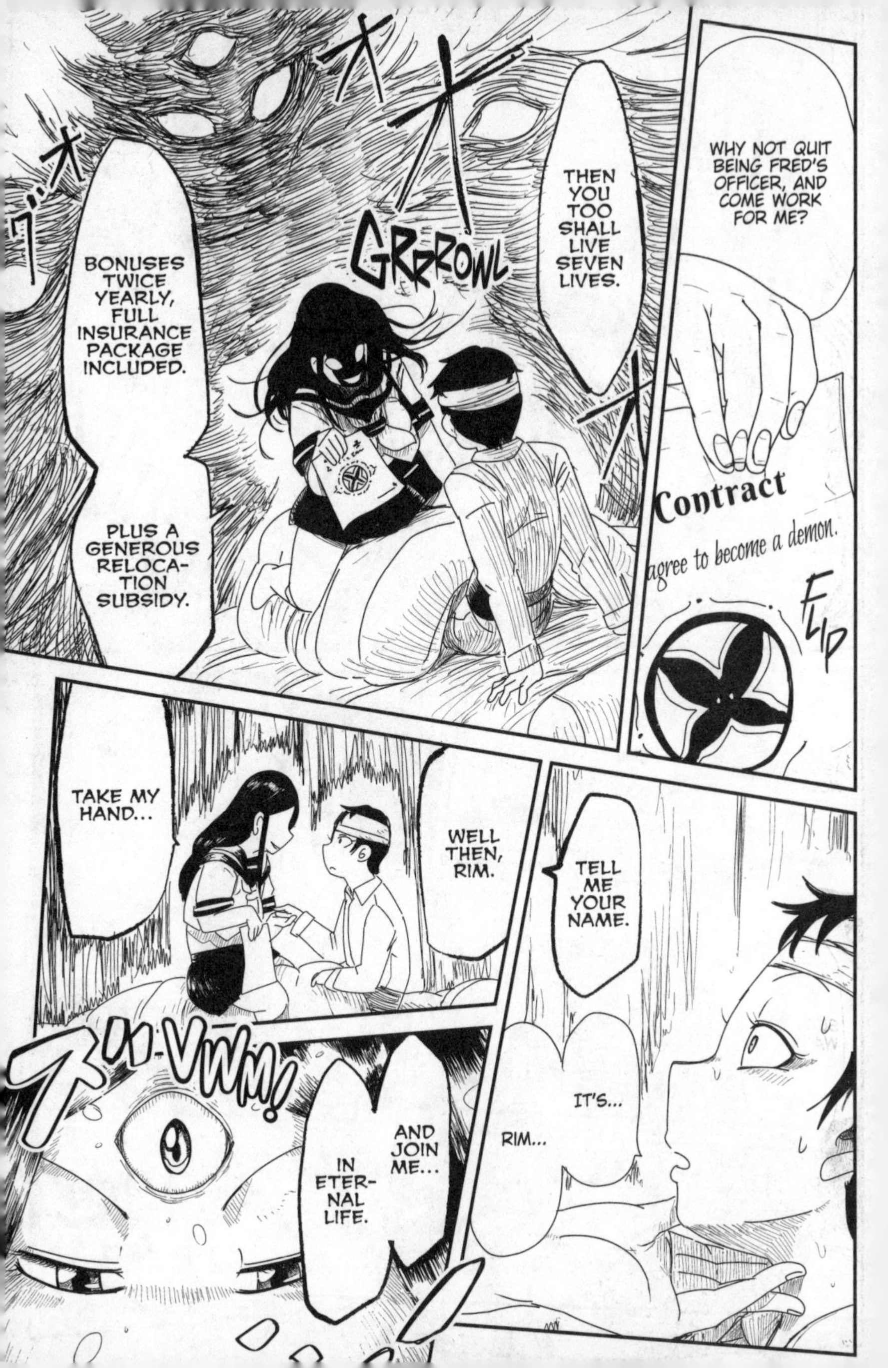
WHY NOT QUIT BEING FRED'S OFFICER, AND COME WORK FOR ME?
Contract
agree to become a demon.
FLIP
THEN YOU TOO SHALL LIVE SEVEN LIVES.
GRRROWL
BONUSES TWICE YEARLY, FULL INSURANCE PACKAGE INCLUDED.
PLUS A GENEROUS RELOCATION SUBSIDY.
TELL ME YOUR NAME.
IT'S...
RIM...
WELL THEN, RIM.
TAKE MY HAND...
VWM!
AND JOIN ME...
IN ETERNAL LIFE.

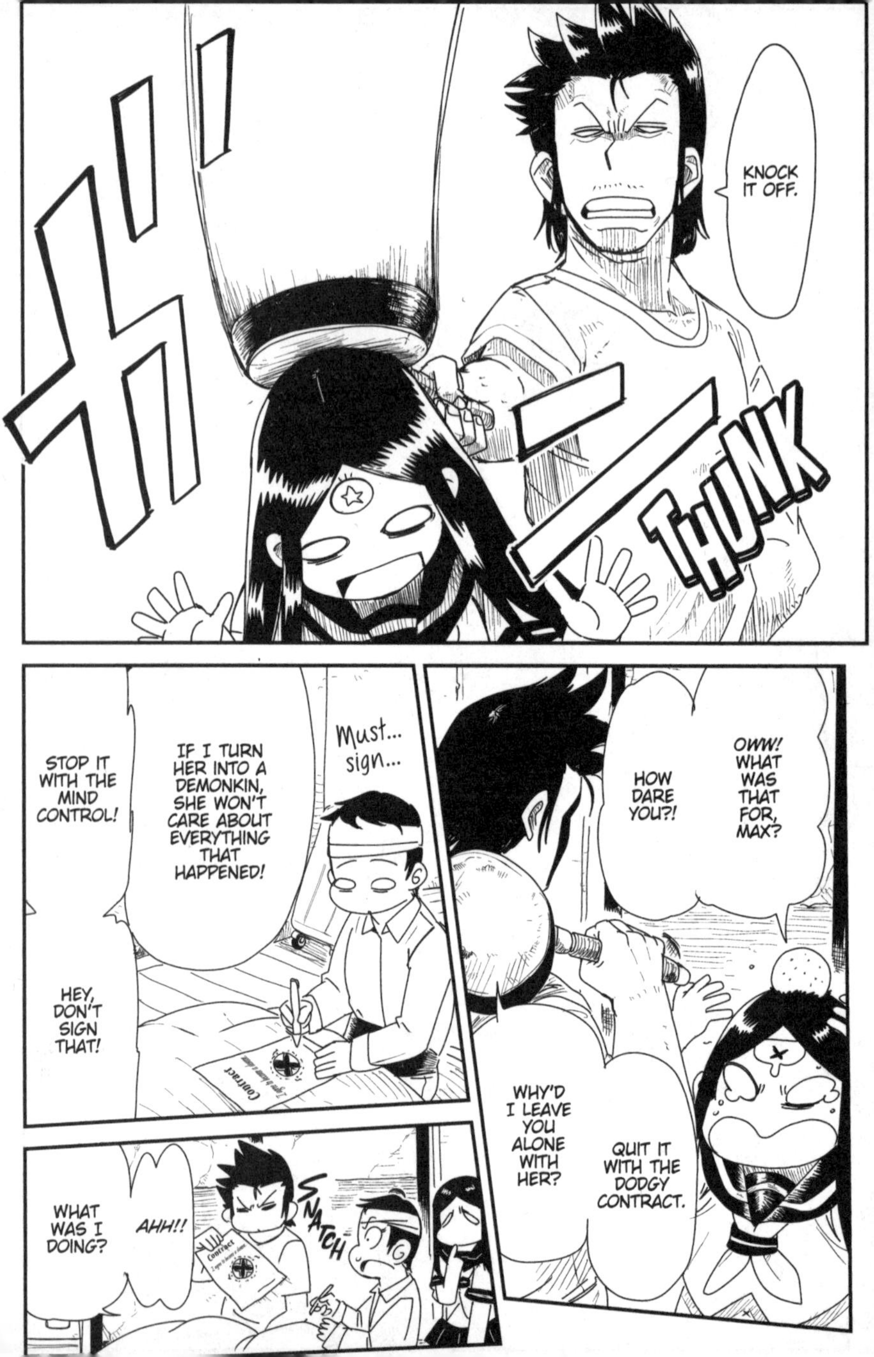
KNOCK IT OFF.
THUNK
OWW! WHAT WAS THAT FOR, MAX?
HOW DARE YOU?!
WHY'D I LEAVE YOU ALONE WITH HER?
QUIT IT WITH THE DODGY CONTRACT.
Must... sign...
IF I TURN HER INTO A DEMONKIN, SHE WON'T CARE ABOUT EVERYTHING THAT HAPPENED!
STOP IT WITH THE MIND CONTROL!
HEY, DON'T SIGN THAT!
Contract
SNATCH
AHH!!
WHAT WAS I DOING?
Contract

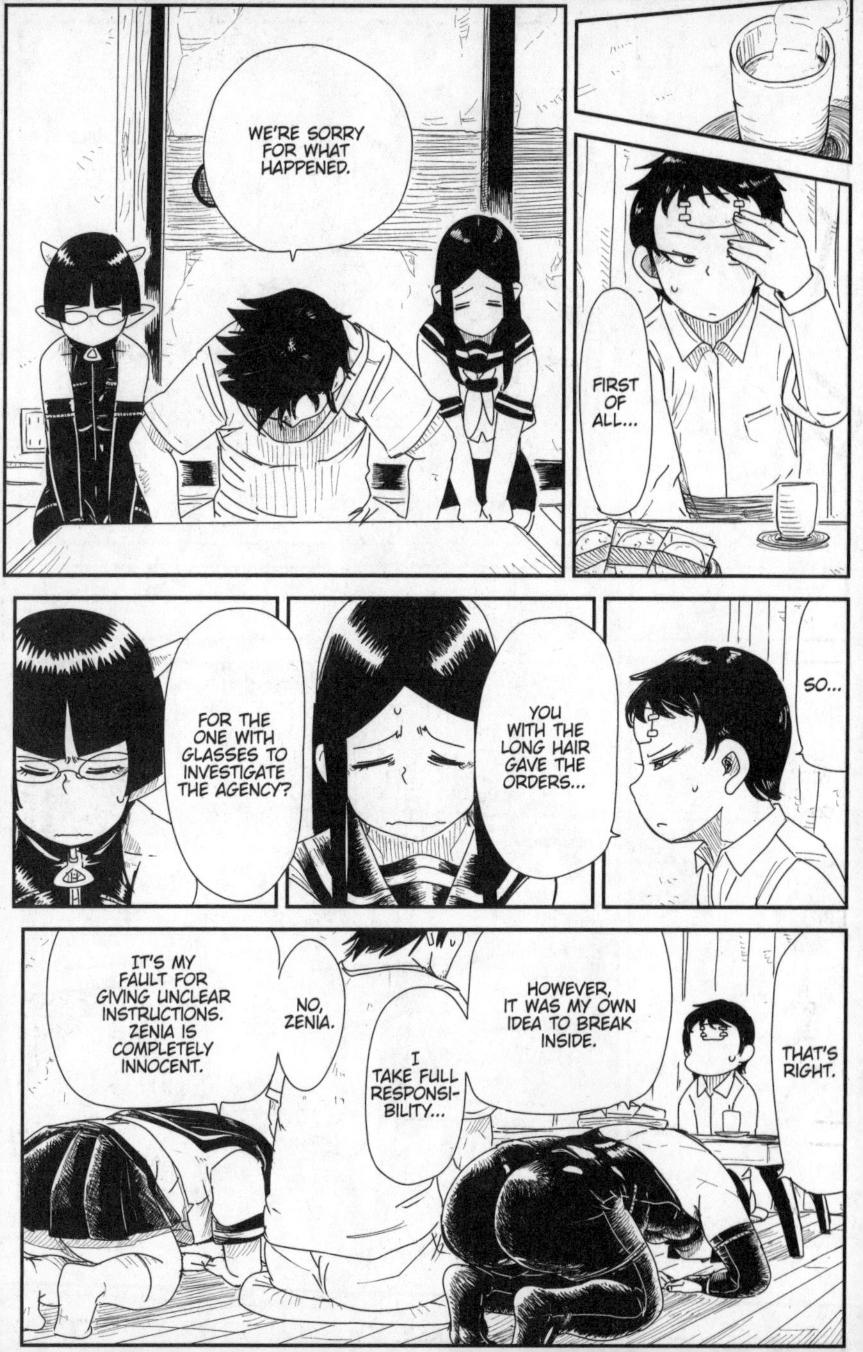
WE'RE SORRY FOR WHAT HAPPENED.
FIRST OF ALL...
SO...
YOU WITH THE LONG HAIR GAVE THE ORDERS...
FOR THE ONE WITH GLASSES TO INVESTIGATE THE AGENCY?
THAT'S RIGHT.
HOWEVER, IT WAS MY OWN IDEA TO BREAK INSIDE.
I TAKE FULL RESPONSI- BILITY...
NO, ZENIA.
IT'S MY FAULT FOR GIVING UNCLEAR INSTRUCTIONS. ZENIA IS COMPLETELY INNOCENT.

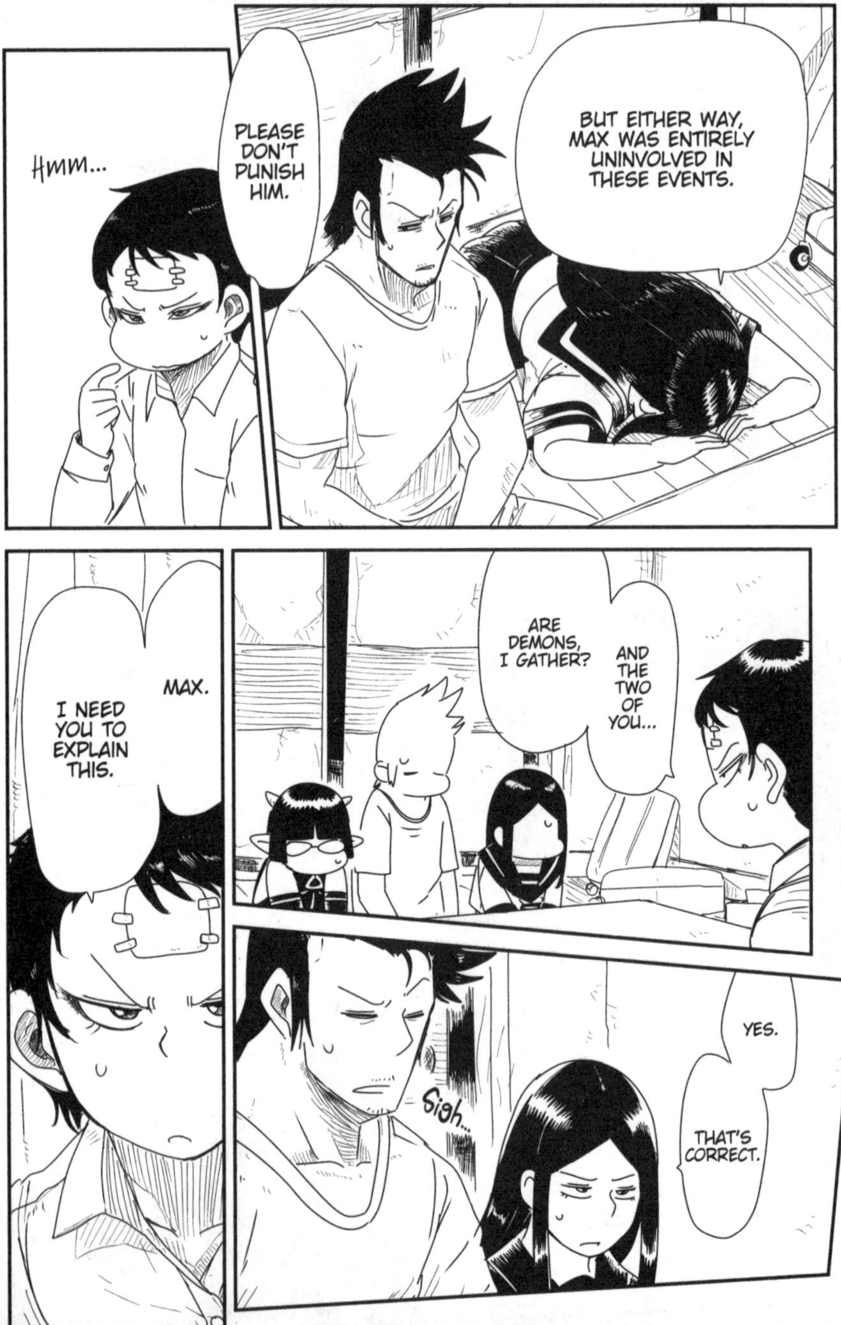
BUT EITHER WAY, MAX WAS ENTIRELY UNINVOLVED IN THESE EVENTS.
PLEASE DON'T PUNISH HIM.
Hmm...
AND THE TWO OF YOU...
ARE DEMONS, I GATHER?
YES.
THAT'S CORRECT.
Sigh...
MAX.
I NEED YOU TO EXPLAIN THIS.

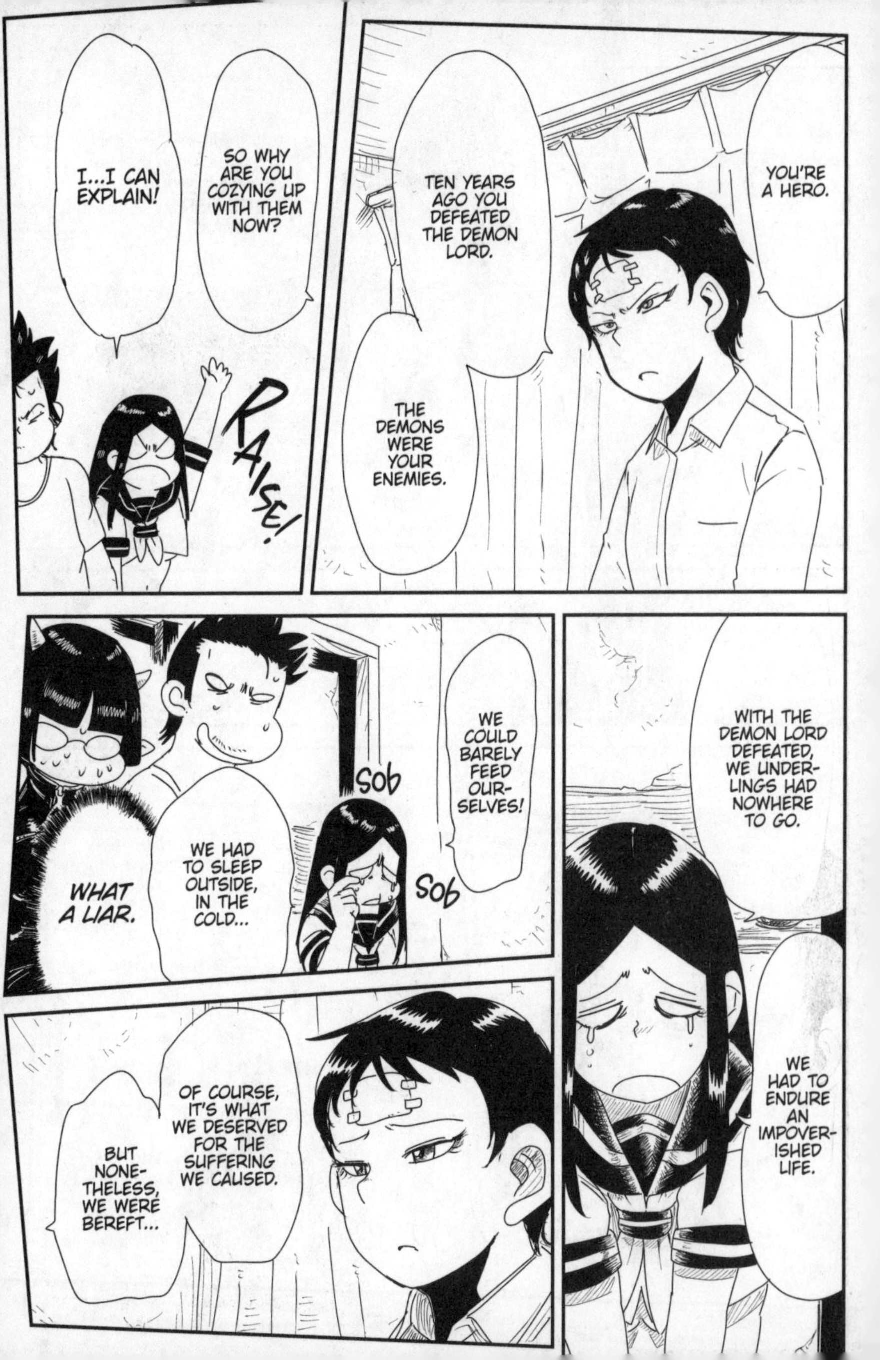
YOU'RE A HERO.
TEN YEARS AGO YOU DEFEATED THE DEMON LORD.
THE DEMONS WERE YOUR ENEMIES.
SO WHY ARE YOU COZYING UP WITH THEM NOW?
I...I CAN EXPLAIN!
RAISE!
WITH THE DEMON LORD DEFEATED, WE UNDER-LINGS HAD NOWHERE TO GO.
WE HAD TO ENDURE AN IMPOVER-ISHED LIFE.
WE COULD BARELY FEED OUR-SELVES!
SOB
SOB
WE HAD TO SLEEP OUTSIDE, IN THE COLD...
WHAT A LIAR.
OF COURSE, IT'S WHAT WE DESERVED FOR THE SUFFERING WE CAUSED.
BUT NONE-THELESS, WE WERE BEREFT...

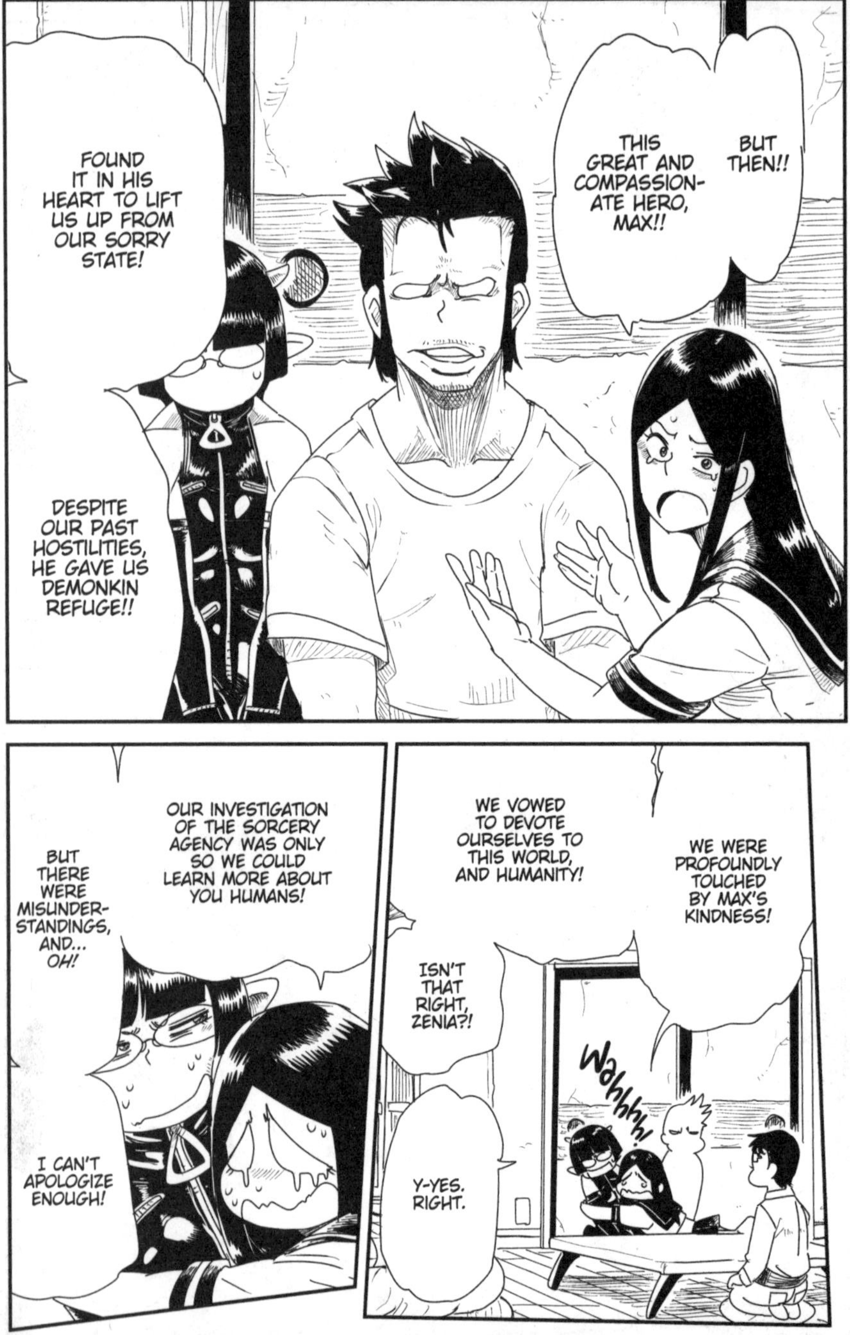
BUT THEN!!
THIS GREAT AND COMPASSION-ATE HERO, MAX!!
FOUND IT IN HIS HEART TO LIFT US UP FROM OUR SORRY STATE!
DESPITE OUR PAST HOSTILITIES, HE GAVE US DEMONKIN REFUGE!!
WE WERE PROFOUNDLY TOUCHED BY MAX'S KINDNESS!
WE VOWED TO DEVOTE OURSELVES TO THIS WORLD, AND HUMANITY!
ISN'T THAT RIGHT, ZENIA?!
Wahhhh!
Y-YES. RIGHT.
OUR INVESTIGATION OF THE SORCERY AGENCY WAS ONLY SO WE COULD LEARN MORE ABOUT YOU HUMANS!
BUT THERE WERE MISUNDER-STANDINGS, AND... OH!
I CAN'T APOLOGIZE ENOUGH!

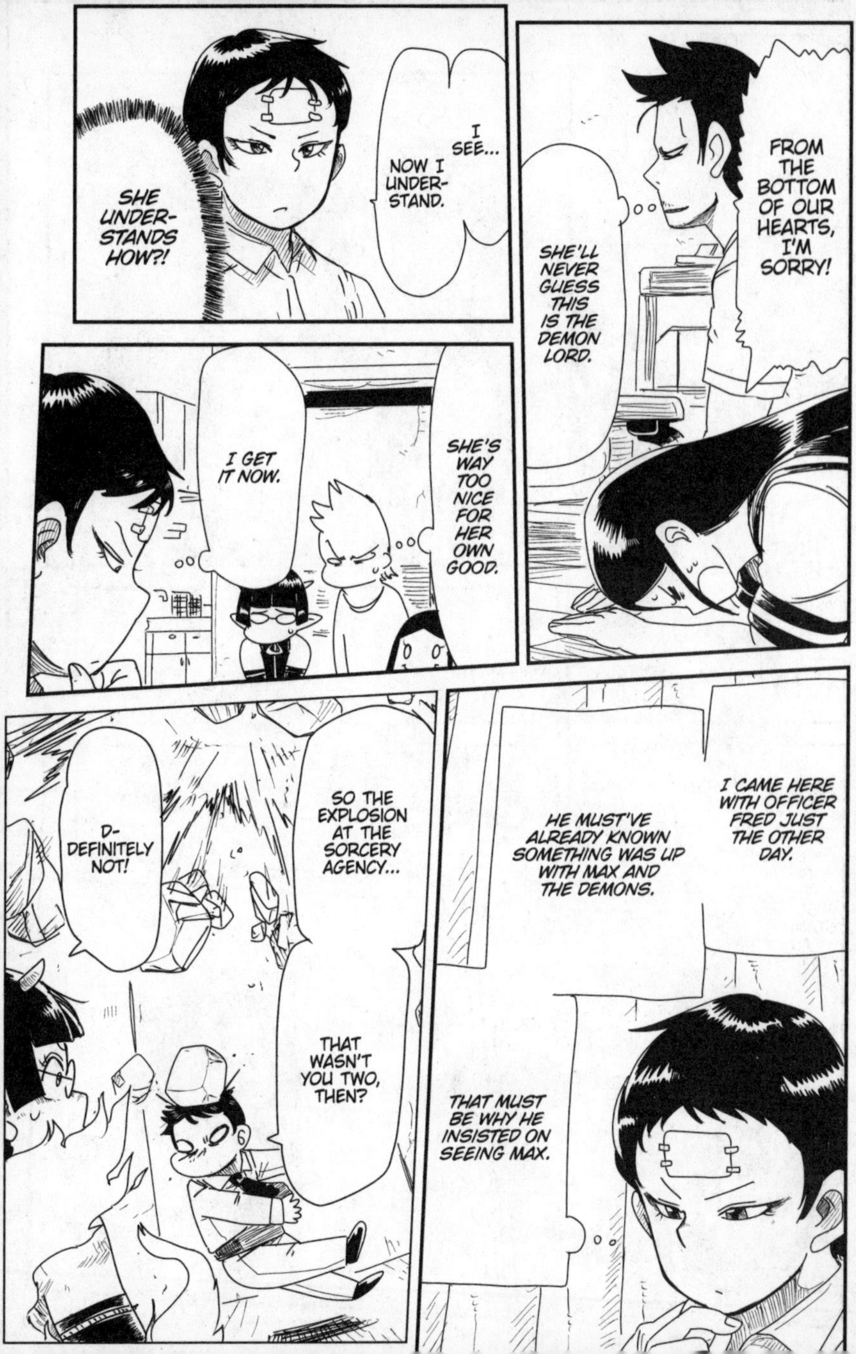
FROM THE BOTTOM OF OUR HEARTS, I'M SORRY!
SHE'LL NEVER GUESS THIS IS THE DEMON LORD.
I SEE...
NOW I UNDERSTAND.
SHE UNDERSTANDS HOW?!
SHE'S WAY TOO NICE FOR HER OWN GOOD.
I GET IT NOW.
I CAME HERE WITH OFFICER FRED JUST THE OTHER DAY.
HE MUST'VE ALREADY KNOWN SOMETHING WAS UP WITH MAX AND THE DEMONS.
THAT MUST BE WHY HE INSISTED ON SEEING MAX.
SO THE EXPLOSION AT THE SORCERY AGENCY...
THAT WASN'T YOU TWO, THEN?
D-DEFINITELY NOT!

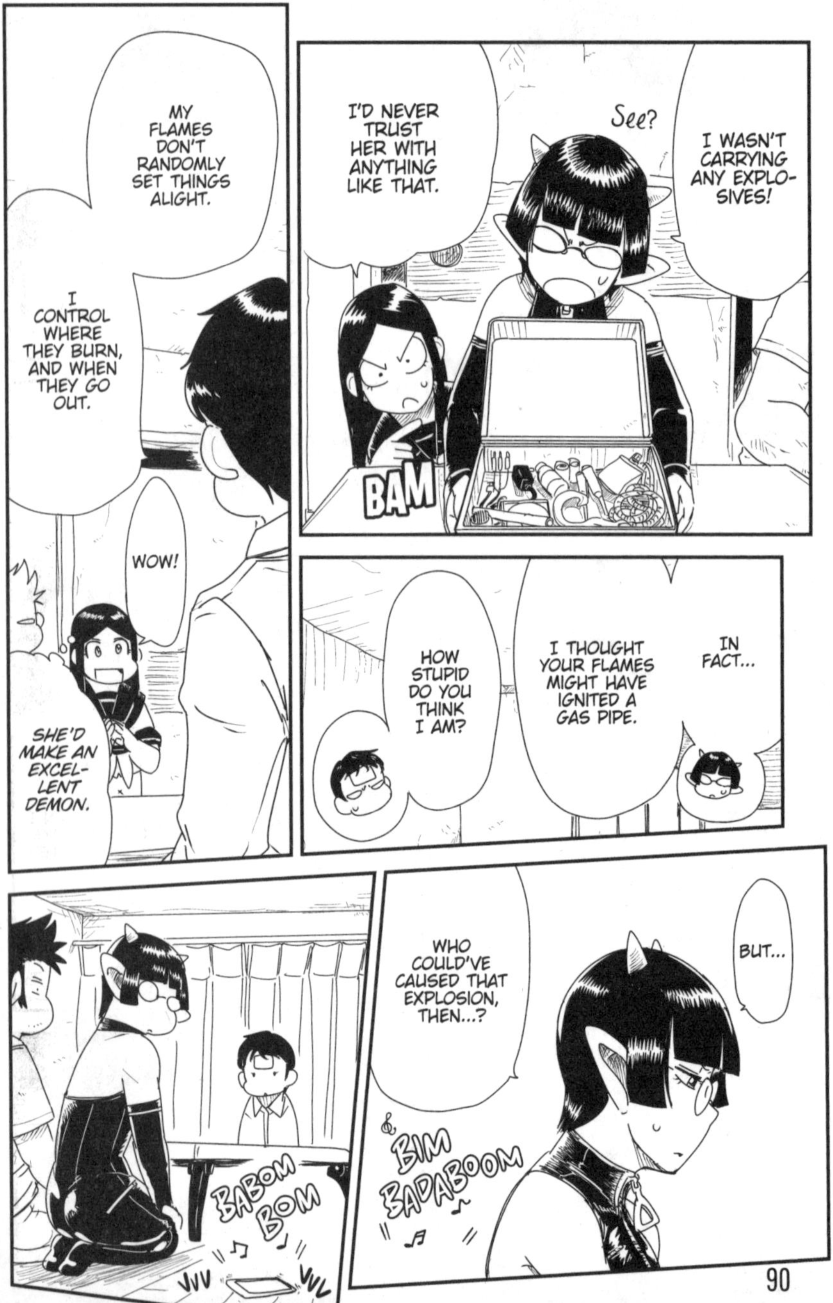
See?
I WASN'T CARRYING ANY EXPLOSIVES!
I'D NEVER TRUST HER WITH ANYTHING LIKE THAT.
BAM
IN FACT...
I THOUGHT YOUR FLAMES MIGHT HAVE IGNITED A GAS PIPE.
HOW STUPID DO YOU THINK I AM?
MY FLAMES DON'T RANDOMLY SET THINGS ALIGHT.
I CONTROL WHERE THEY BURN, AND WHEN THEY GO OUT.
WOW!
SHE'D MAKE AN EXCELLENT DEMON.
BUT...
WHO COULD'VE CAUSED THAT EXPLOSION, THEN...?
BIM BADABOOM
BABOM BOM

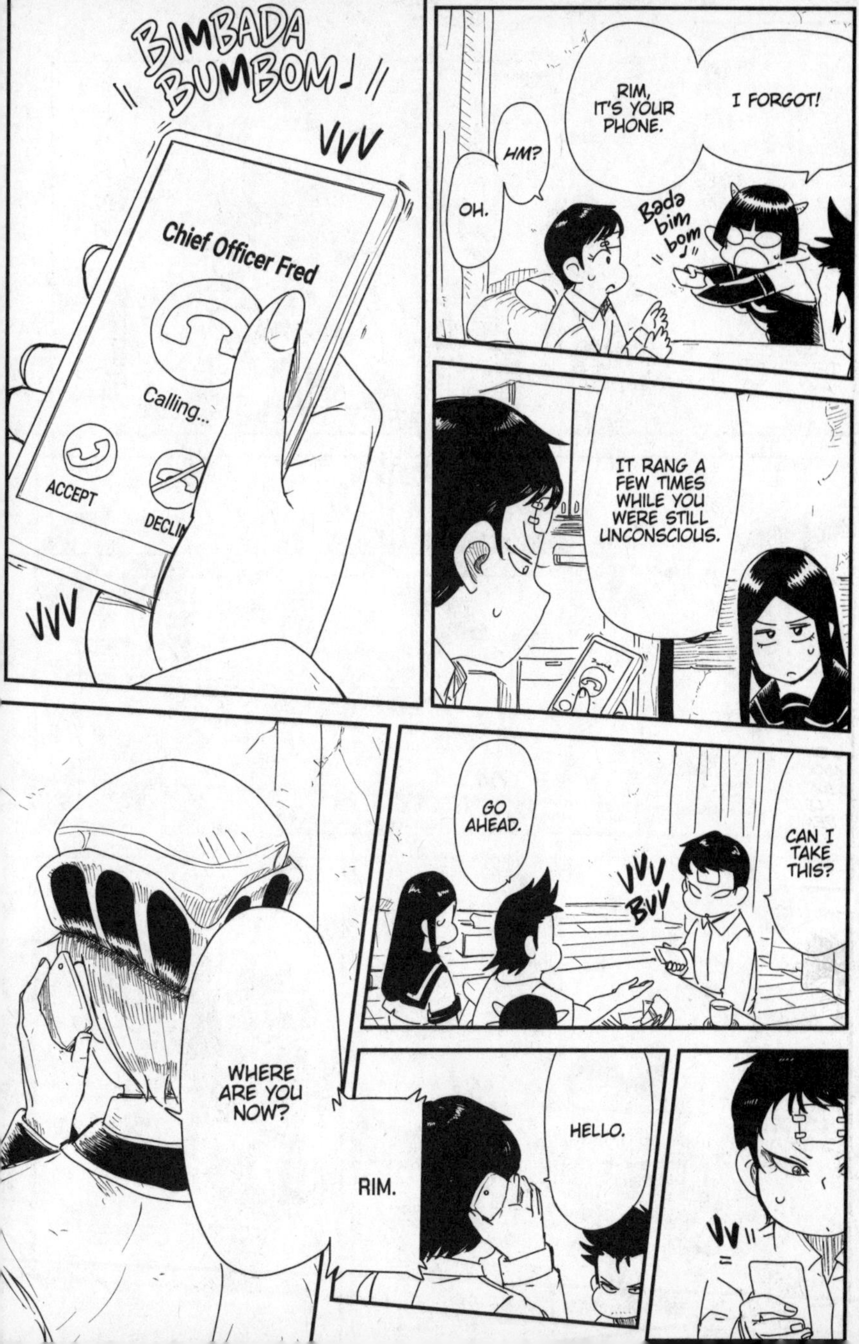
I FORGOT!
RIM, IT'S YOUR PHONE.
Bada bim bom
HM?
OH.
IT RANG A FEW TIMES WHILE YOU WERE STILL UNCONSCIOUS.
BIMBADA BUMBOM
VVV
Chief Officer Fred
Calling...
ACCEPT
DECLIN
VVV
CAN I TAKE THIS?
VVV BVV
GO AHEAD.
VV
HELLO.
RIM.
WHERE ARE YOU NOW?

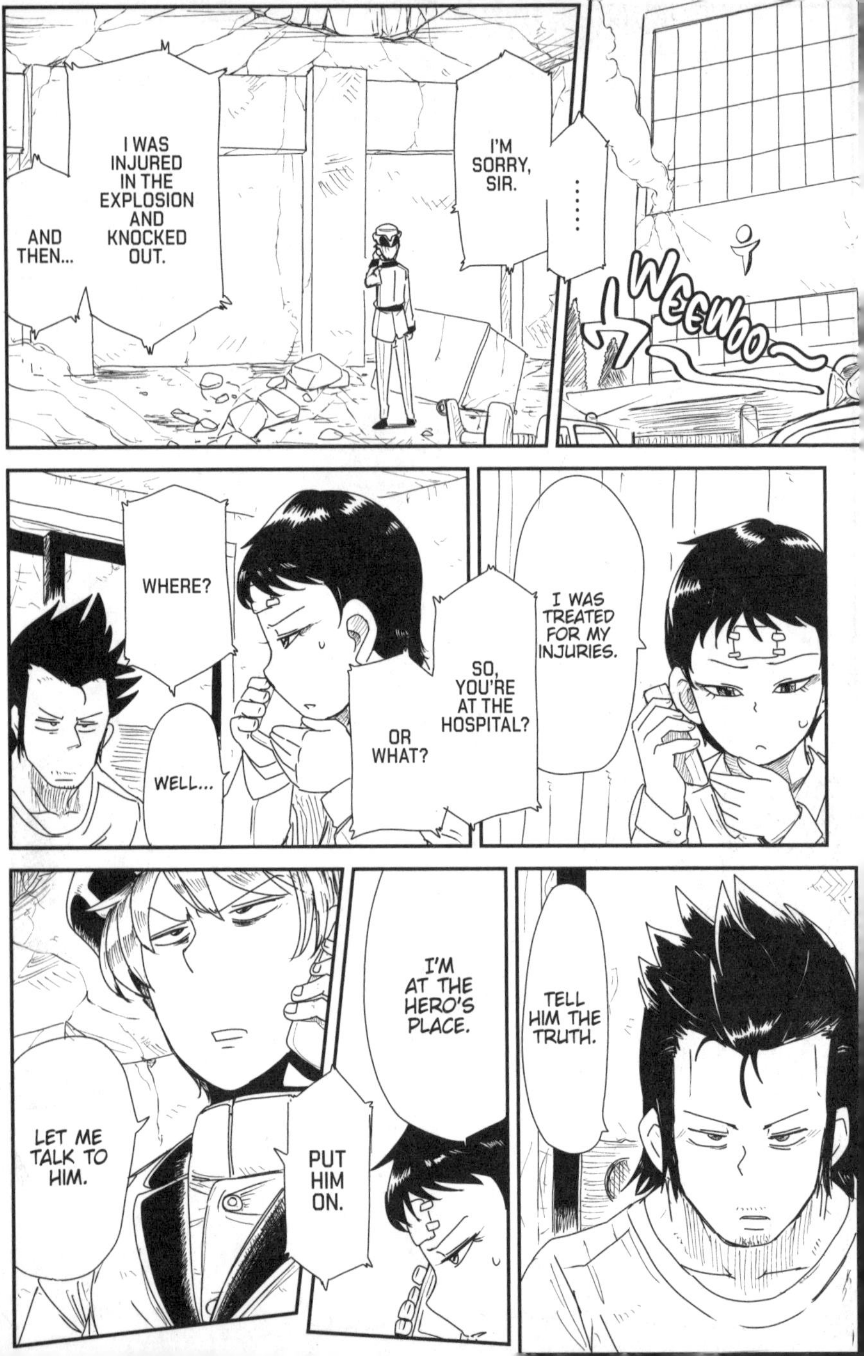
WEEWOO~
......
I'M SORRY, SIR.
I WAS INJURED IN THE EXPLOSION AND KNOCKED OUT.
AND THEN...
I WAS TREATED FOR MY INJURIES.
SO, YOU'RE AT THE HOSPITAL?
OR WHAT?
WHERE?
WELL...
TELL HIM THE TRUTH.
I'M AT THE HERO'S PLACE.
PUT HIM ON.
LET ME TALK TO HIM.

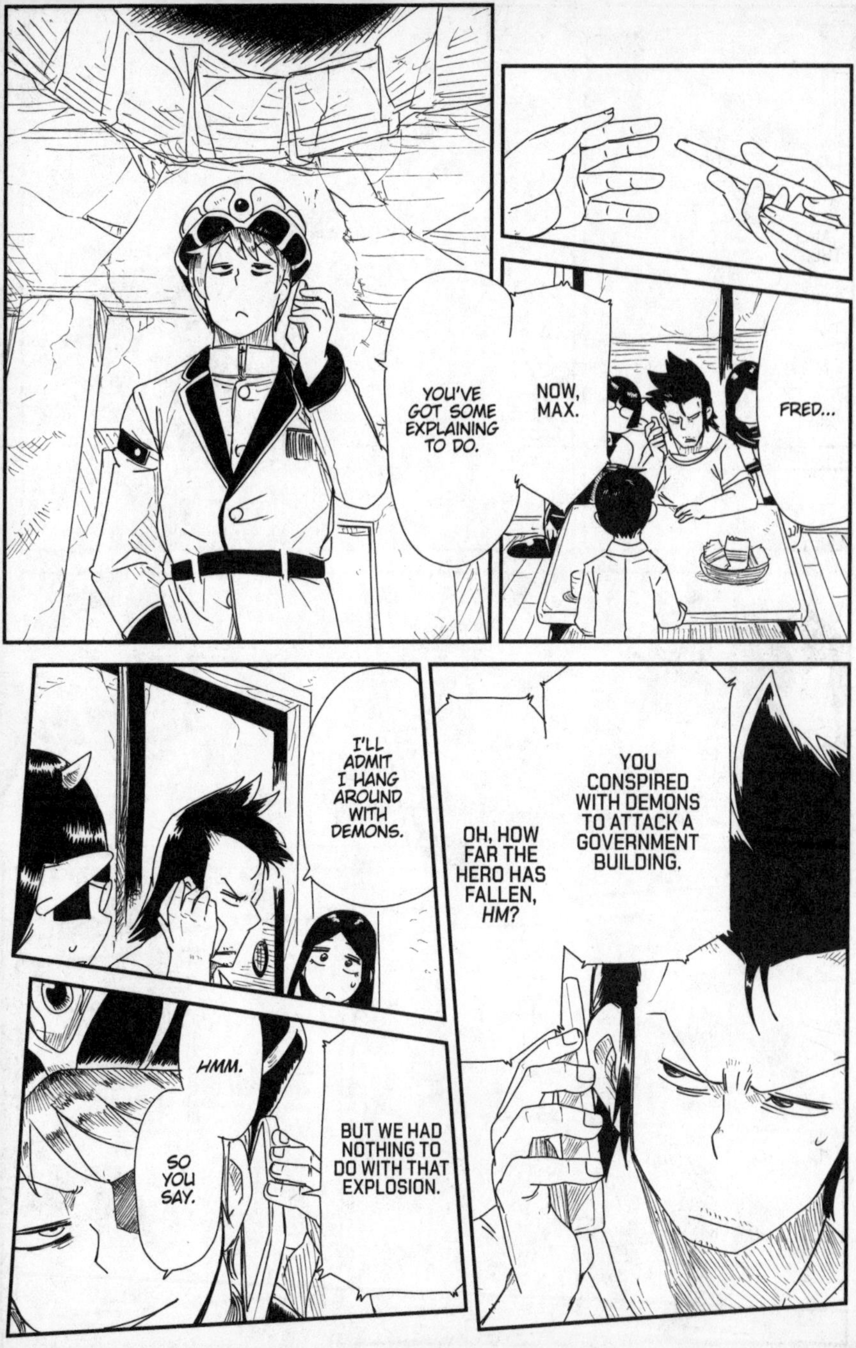
NOW, MAX.
YOU'VE GOT SOME EXPLAINING TO DO.
FRED...
YOU CONSPIRED WITH DEMONS TO ATTACK A GOVERNMENT BUILDING.
OH, HOW FAR THE HERO HAS FALLEN, *HM?*
I'LL ADMIT I HANG AROUND WITH DEMONS.
BUT WE HAD NOTHING TO DO WITH THAT EXPLOSION.
HMM.
SO YOU SAY.

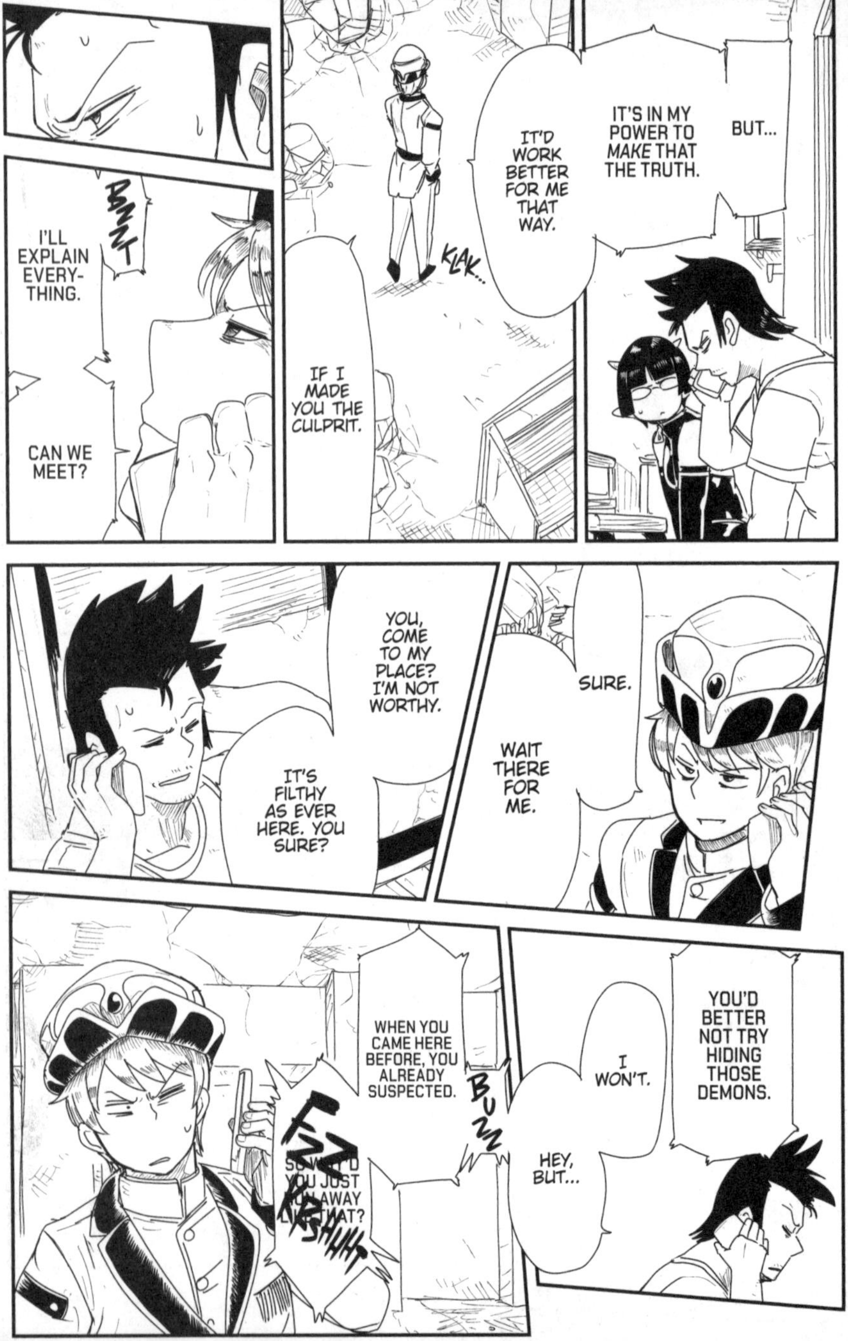
I'LL EXPLAIN EVERY-THING.
BZZZT
CAN WE MEET?
IF I MADE YOU THE CULPRIT.
KLAK...
IT'D WORK BETTER FOR ME THAT WAY.
IT'S IN MY POWER TO *MAKE* THAT THE TRUTH.
BUT...
YOU, COME TO MY PLACE? I'M NOT WORTHY.
IT'S FILTHY AS EVER HERE. YOU SURE?
SURE.
WAIT THERE FOR ME.
WHEN YOU CAME HERE BEFORE, YOU ALREADY SUSPECTED.
SO WHY'D YOU JUST RUN AWAY LIKE THAT?
BUZZ
YOU'D BETTER NOT TRY HIDING THOSE DEMONS.
I WON'T.
HEY, BUT...

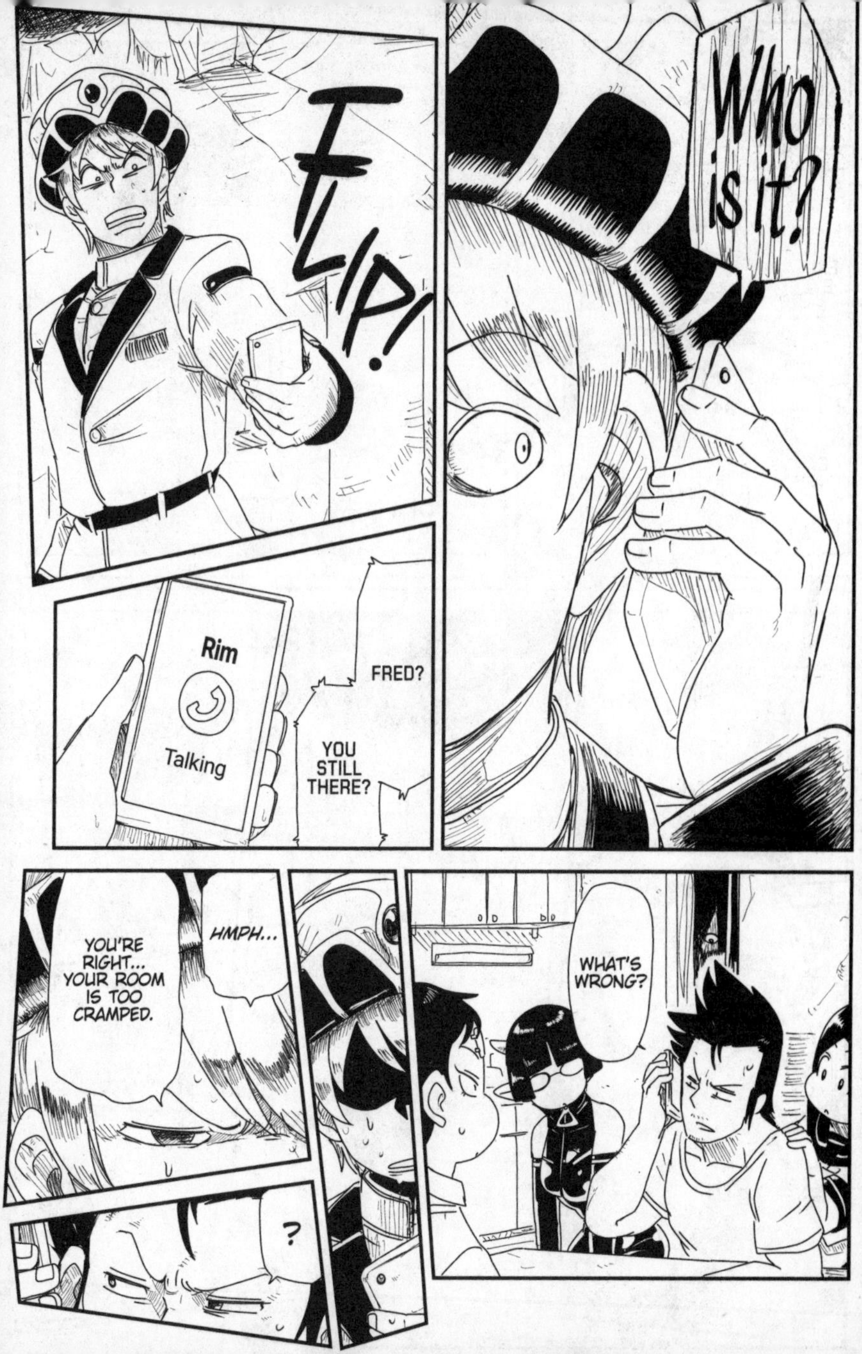

FLIP!
Who is it?
Rim
Talking
FRED?
YOU STILL THERE?
YOU'RE RIGHT... YOUR ROOM IS TOO CRAMPED.
HMPH...
WHAT'S WRONG?
?

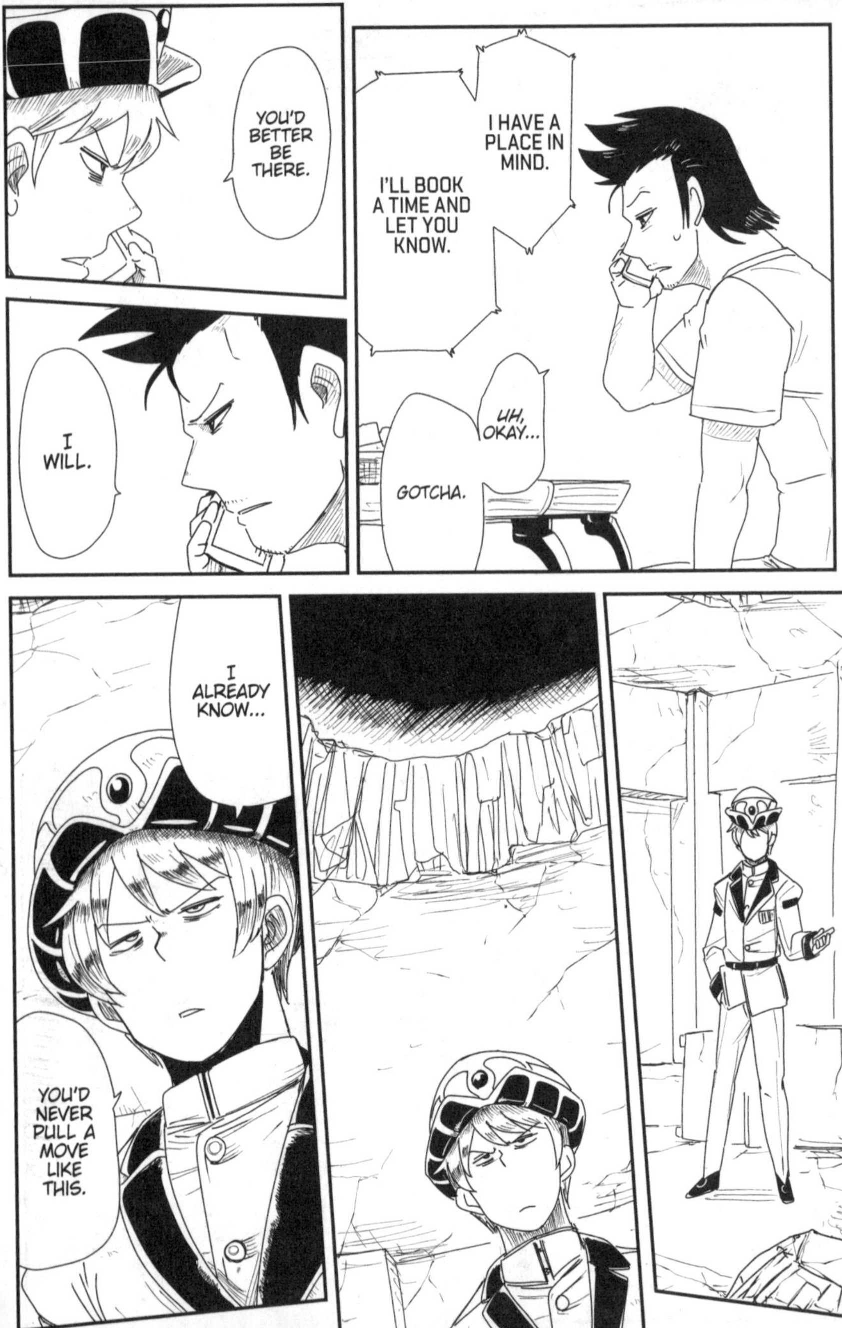
I HAVE A PLACE IN MIND.
I'LL BOOK A TIME AND LET YOU KNOW.
UH, OKAY...
GOTCHA.
YOU'D BETTER BE THERE.
I WILL.
I ALREADY KNOW...
YOU'D NEVER PULL A MOVE LIKE THIS.

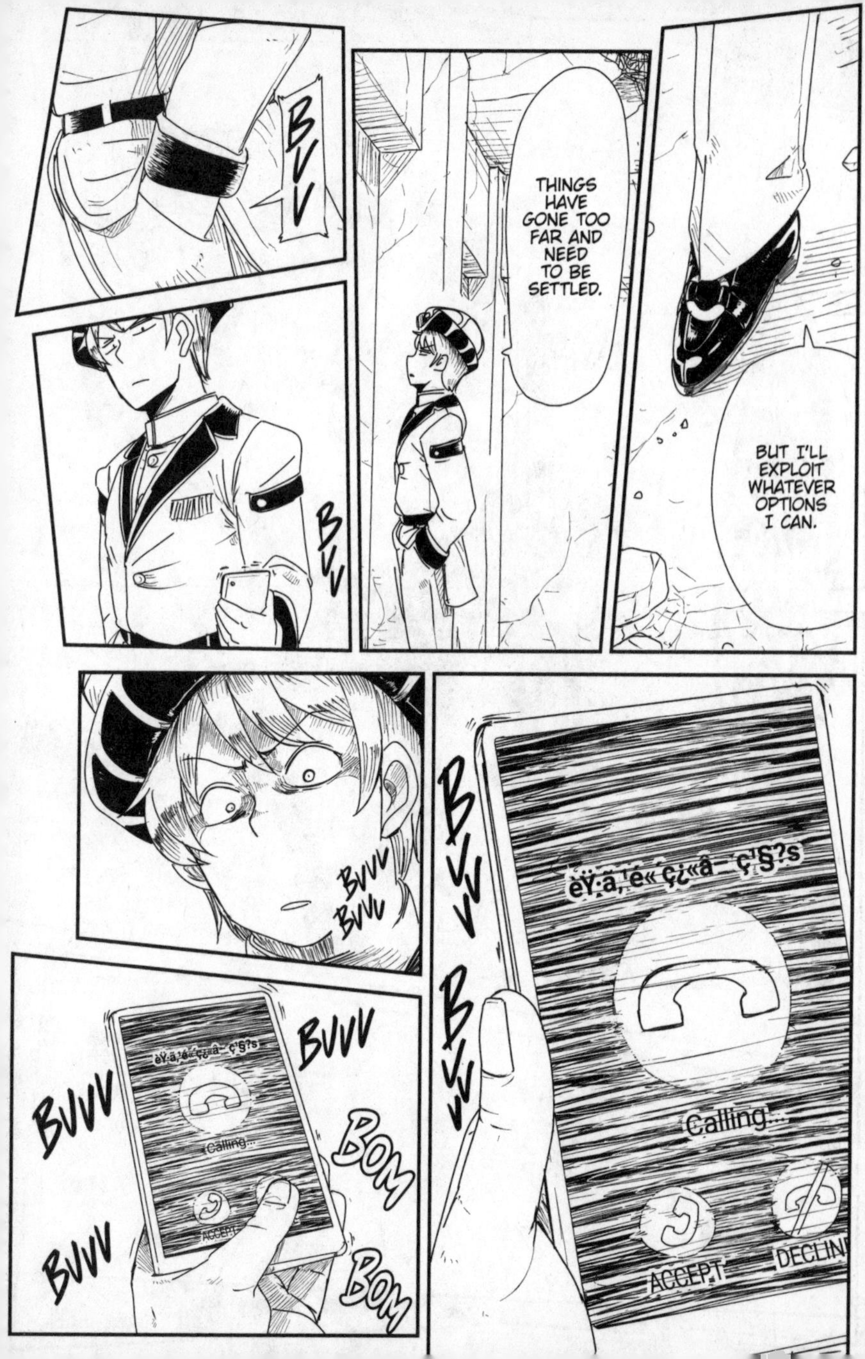
BVVV
BVVV
THINGS HAVE GONE TOO FAR AND NEED TO BE SETTLED.
BUT I'LL EXPLOIT WHATEVER OPTIONS I CAN.
BVVV BVVV
BVVV
BVVV
Calling...
ACCEPT
DECLIN
BVVV
BVVV
BVVV
Calling...
ACCEPT
BOM
BOM

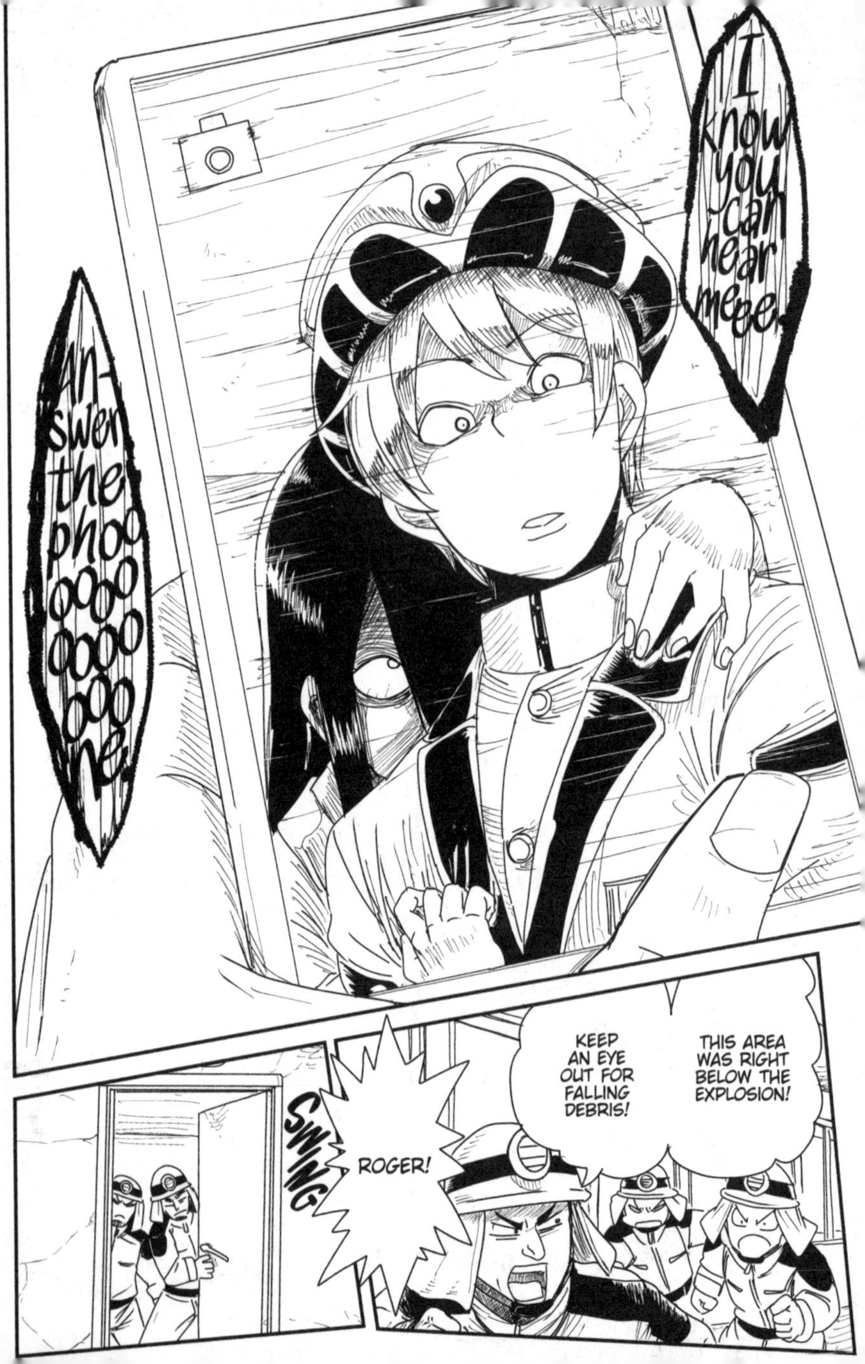

I know you can hear meee
An-swer the phoooooooooooooone
THIS AREA WAS RIGHT BELOW THE EXPLOSION!
KEEP AN EYE OUT FOR FALLING DEBRIS!
ROGER!
SWING

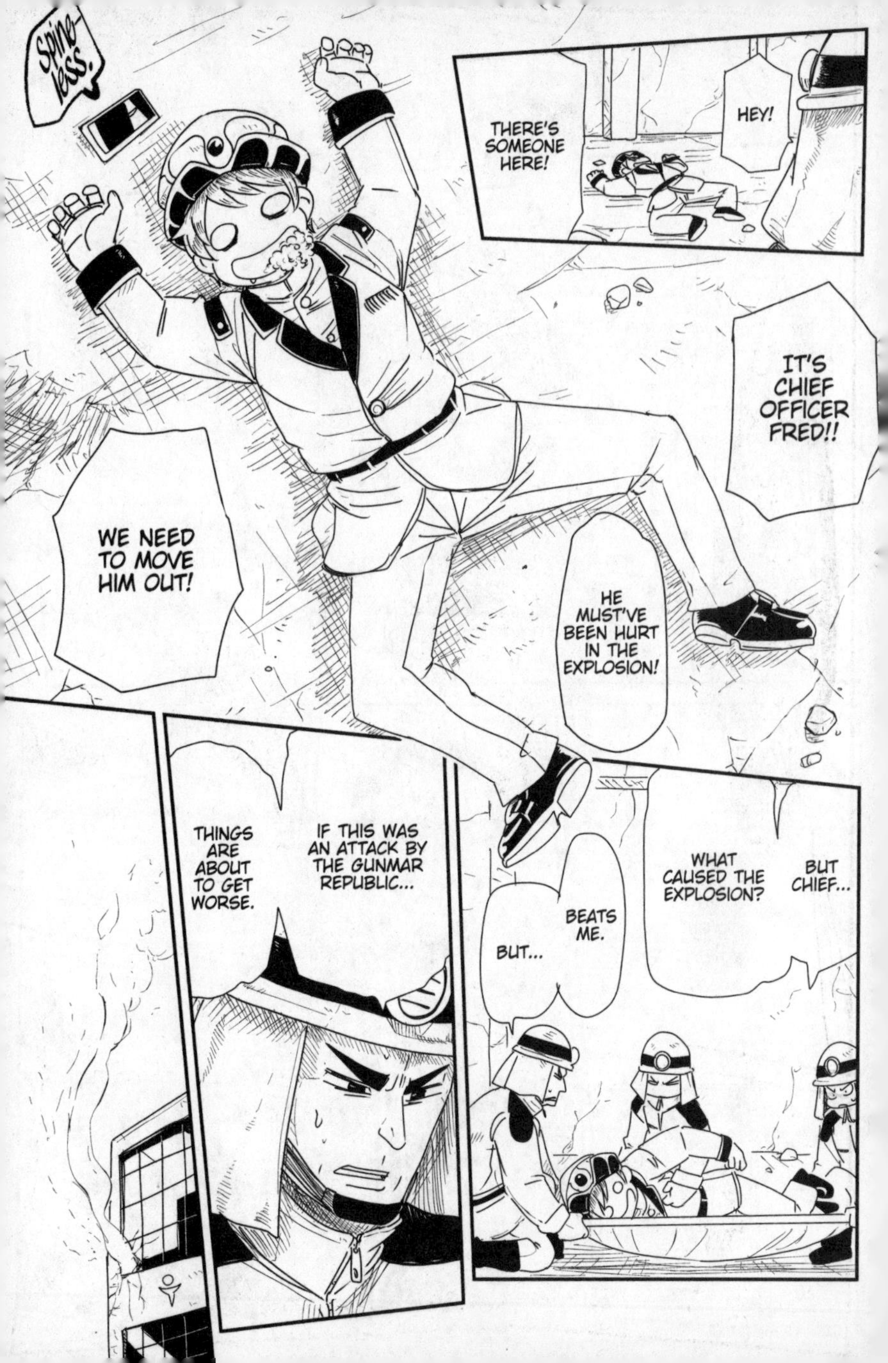
HEY!
THERE'S SOMEONE HERE!
IT'S CHIEF OFFICER FRED!!
HE MUST'VE BEEN HURT IN THE EXPLOSION!
WE NEED TO MOVE HIM OUT!
Spineless.
BUT CHIEF...
WHAT CAUSED THE EXPLOSION?
BEATS ME.
BUT...
IF THIS WAS AN ATTACK BY THE GUNMAR REPUBLIC...
THINGS ARE ABOUT TO GET WORSE.

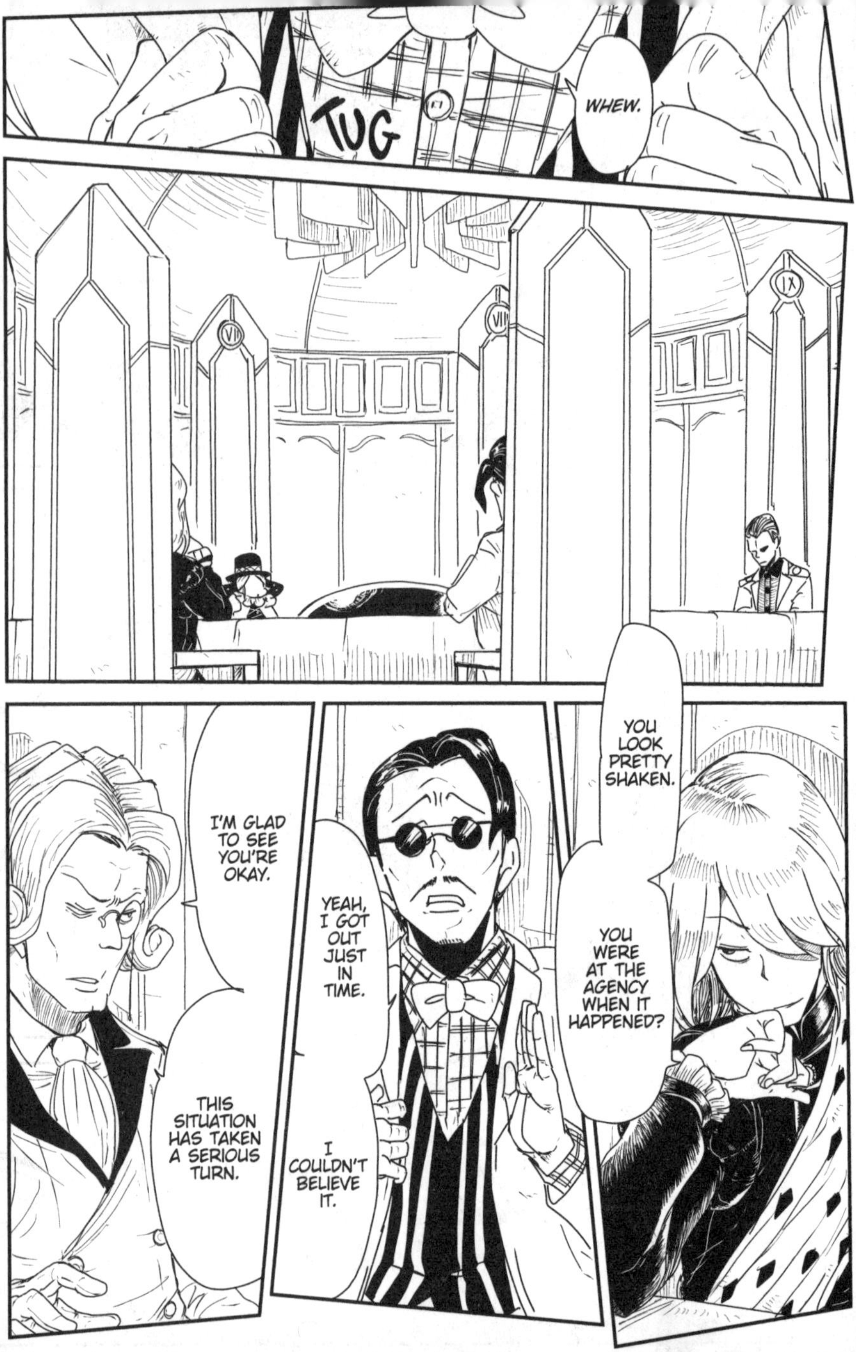
WHEW.
TUG
YOU LOOK PRETTY SHAKEN.
YOU WERE AT THE AGENCY WHEN IT HAPPENED?
YEAH, I GOT OUT JUST IN TIME.
I COULDN'T BELIEVE IT.
I'M GLAD TO SEE YOU'RE OKAY.
THIS SITUATION HAS TAKEN A SERIOUS TURN.

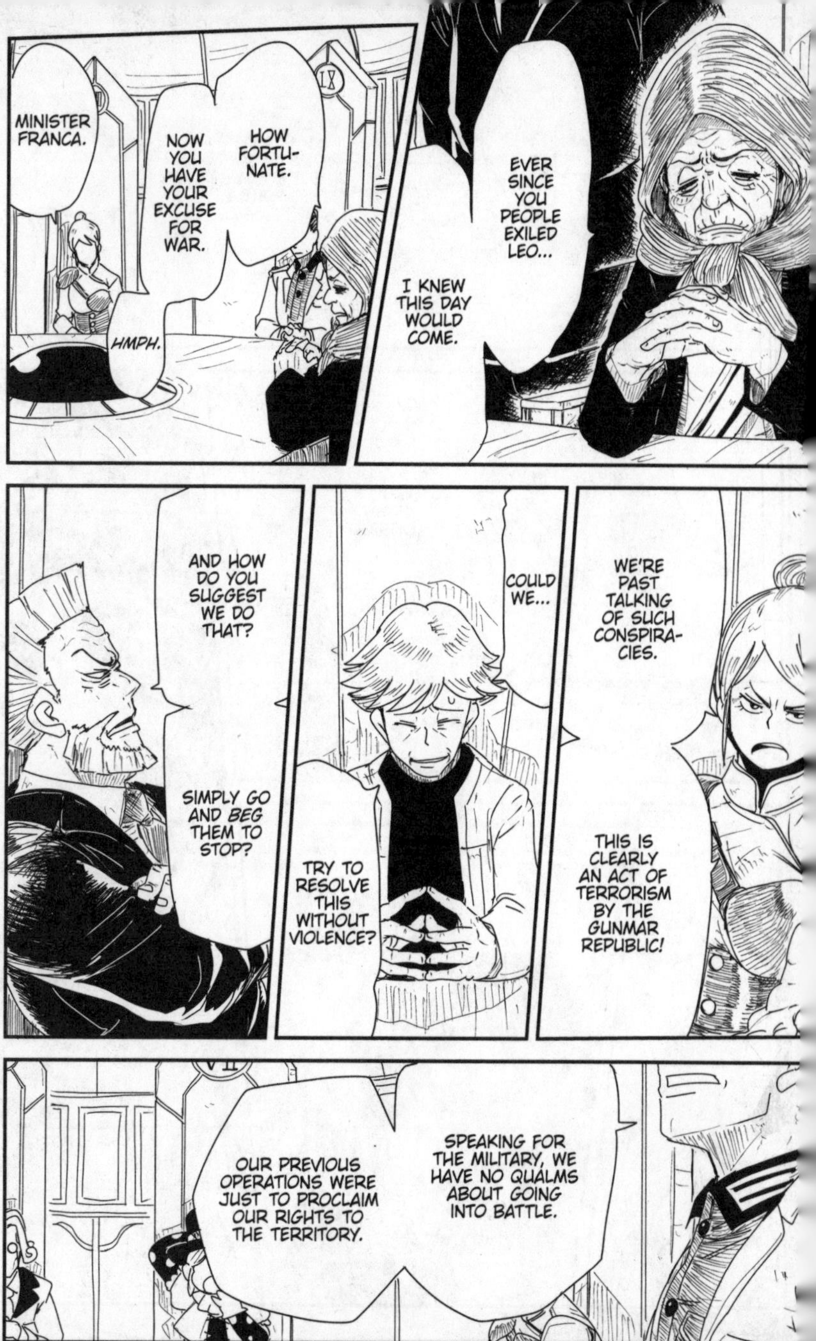
EVER SINCE YOU PEOPLE EXILED LEO...
I KNEW THIS DAY WOULD COME.
HOW FORTUNATE.
NOW YOU HAVE YOUR EXCUSE FOR WAR.
MINISTER FRANCA.
HMPH.
WE'RE PAST TALKING OF SUCH CONSPIRACIES.
THIS IS CLEARLY AN ACT OF TERRORISM BY THE GUNMAR REPUBLIC!
COULD WE...
TRY TO RESOLVE THIS WITHOUT VIOLENCE?
AND HOW DO YOU SUGGEST WE DO THAT?
SIMPLY GO AND *BEG* THEM TO STOP?
SPEAKING FOR THE MILITARY, WE HAVE NO QUALMS ABOUT GOING INTO BATTLE.
OUR PREVIOUS OPERATIONS WERE JUST TO PROCLAIM OUR RIGHTS TO THE TERRITORY.

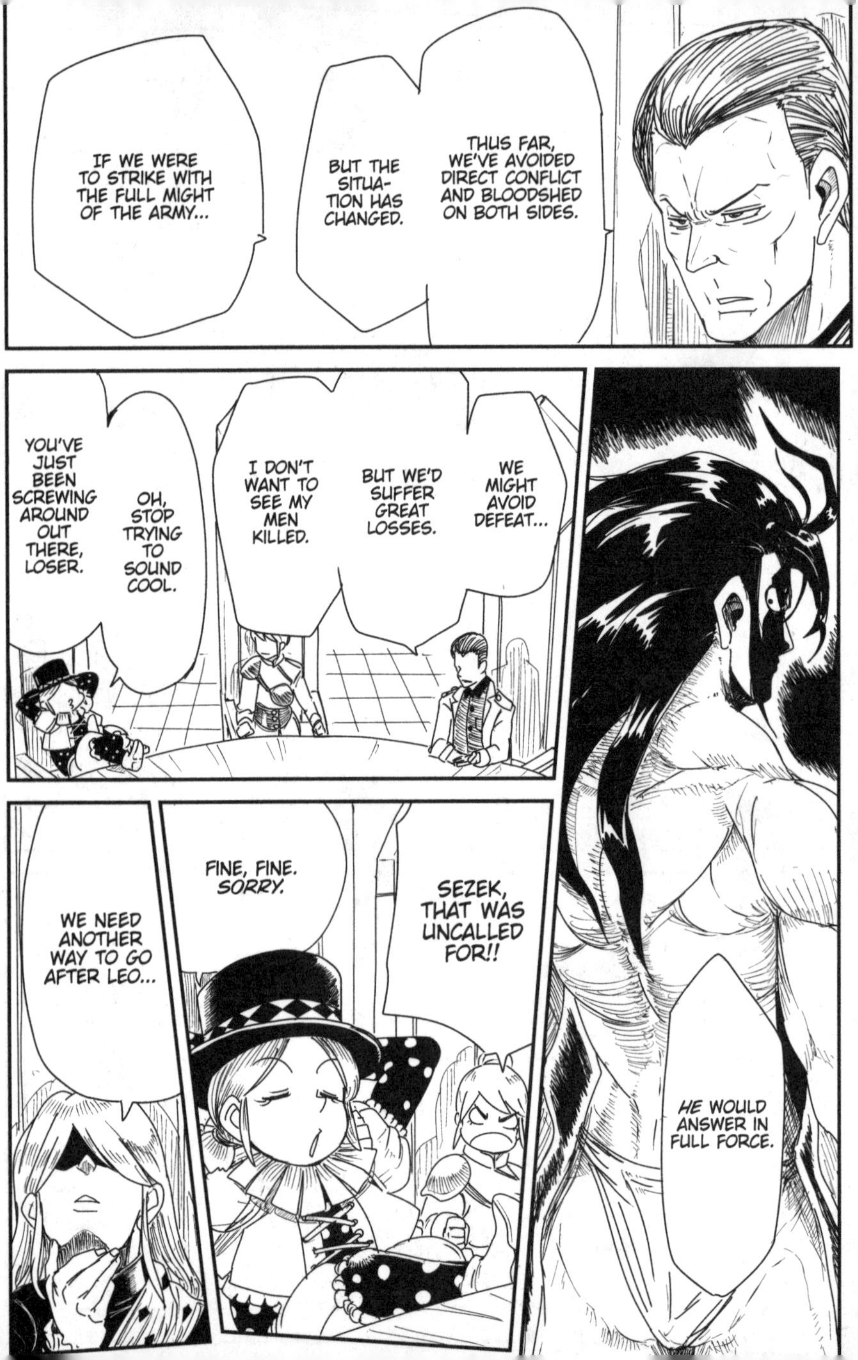
THUS FAR, WE'VE AVOIDED DIRECT CONFLICT AND BLOODSHED ON BOTH SIDES.
BUT THE SITUATION HAS CHANGED.
IF WE WERE TO STRIKE WITH THE FULL MIGHT OF THE ARMY...
HE WOULD ANSWER IN FULL FORCE.
WE MIGHT AVOID DEFEAT...
BUT WE'D SUFFER GREAT LOSSES.
I DON'T WANT TO SEE MY MEN KILLED.
OH, STOP TRYING TO SOUND COOL.
YOU'VE JUST BEEN SCREWING AROUND OUT THERE, LOSER.
SEZEK, THAT WAS UNCALLED FOR!!
FINE, FINE. *SORRY.*
WE NEED ANOTHER WAY TO GO AFTER LEO...

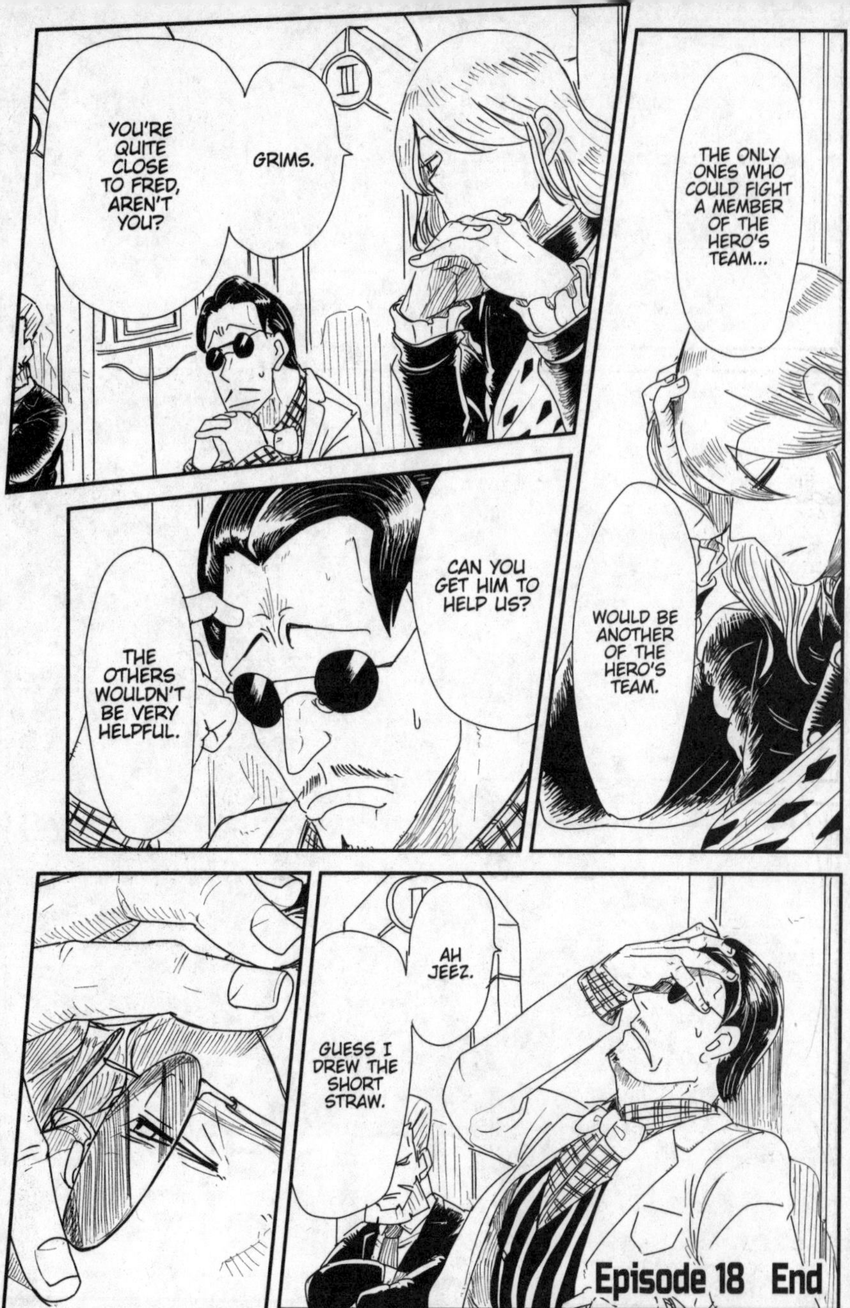
THE ONLY ONES WHO COULD FIGHT A MEMBER OF THE HERO'S TEAM...
WOULD BE ANOTHER OF THE HERO'S TEAM.
GRIMS.
YOU'RE QUITE CLOSE TO FRED, AREN'T YOU?
CAN YOU GET HIM TO HELP US?
THE OTHERS WOULDN'T BE VERY HELPFUL.
AH JEEZ.
GUESS I DREW THE SHORT STRAW.
Episode 18 End

LEVEL 1 DEMON LORD & ONE ROOM HERO

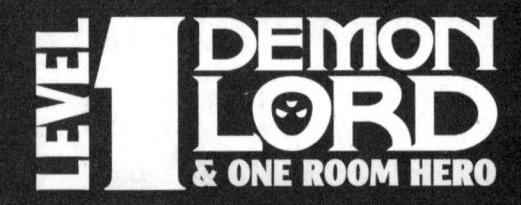

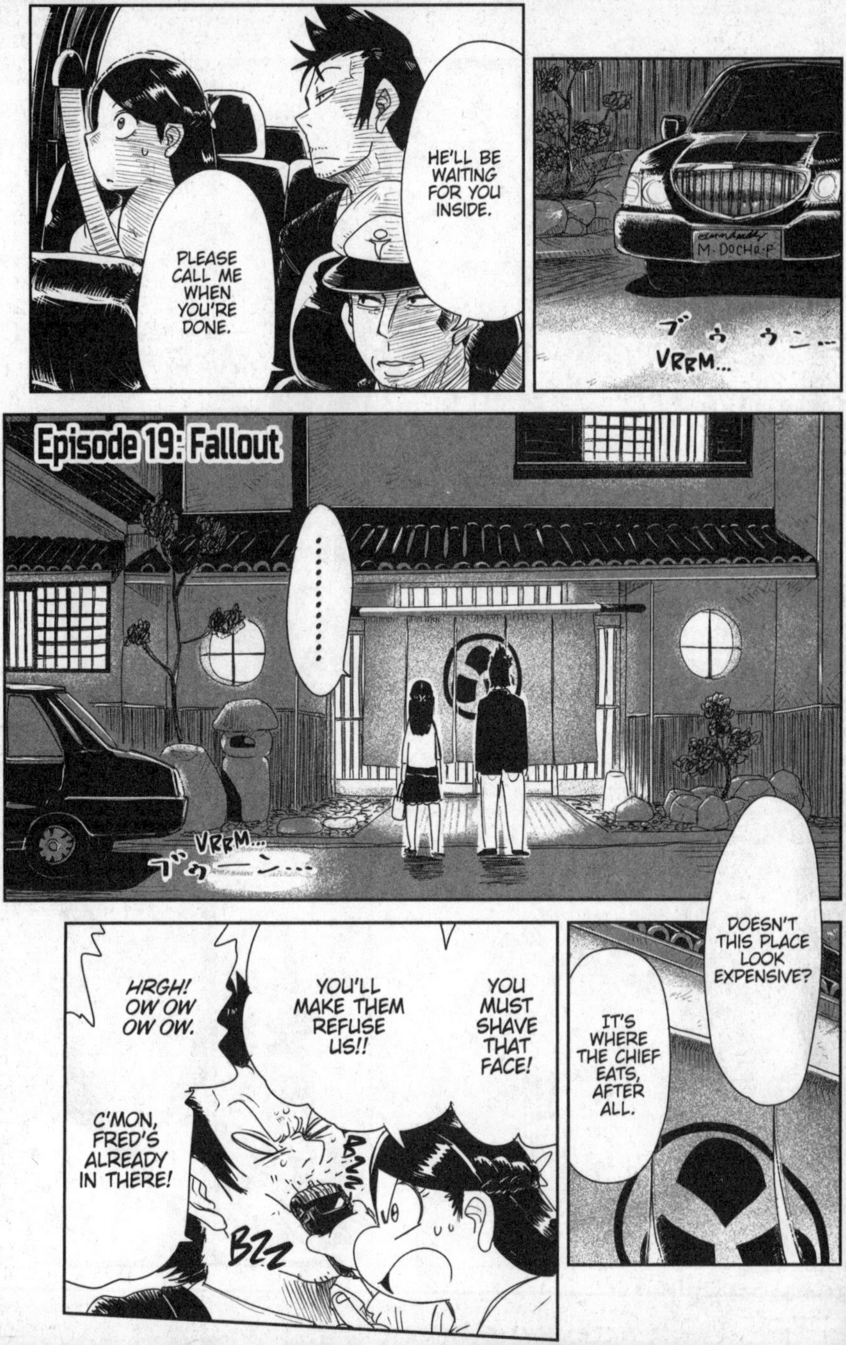
ブゥゥン…
VRRM...
HE'LL BE WAITING FOR YOU INSIDE.
PLEASE CALL ME WHEN YOU'RE DONE.
Episode 19: Fallout
......
VRRM...
ブゥーン…
DOESN'T THIS PLACE LOOK EXPENSIVE?
IT'S WHERE THE CHIEF EATS, AFTER ALL.
YOU MUST SHAVE THAT FACE!
YOU'LL MAKE THEM REFUSE US!!
HRGH! OW OW OW OW.
C'MON, FRED'S ALREADY IN THERE!
BZZ
BZZ

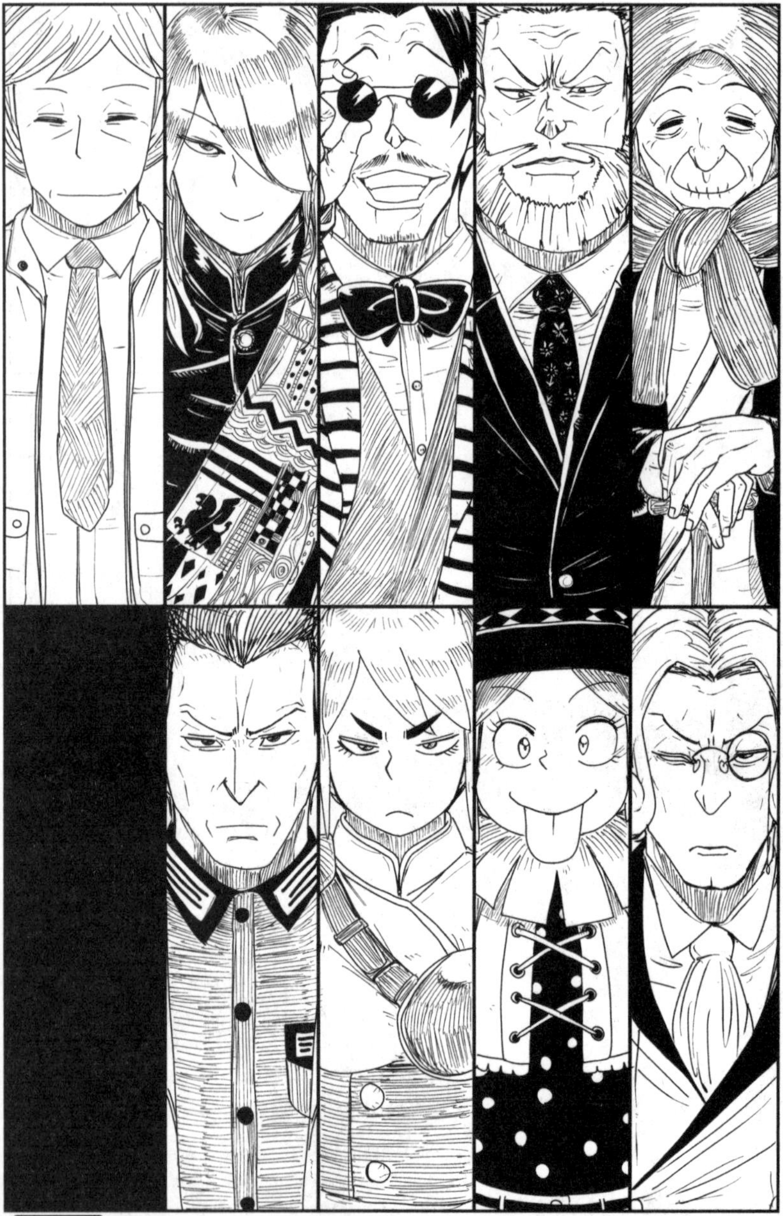

Episode 19 Fallout

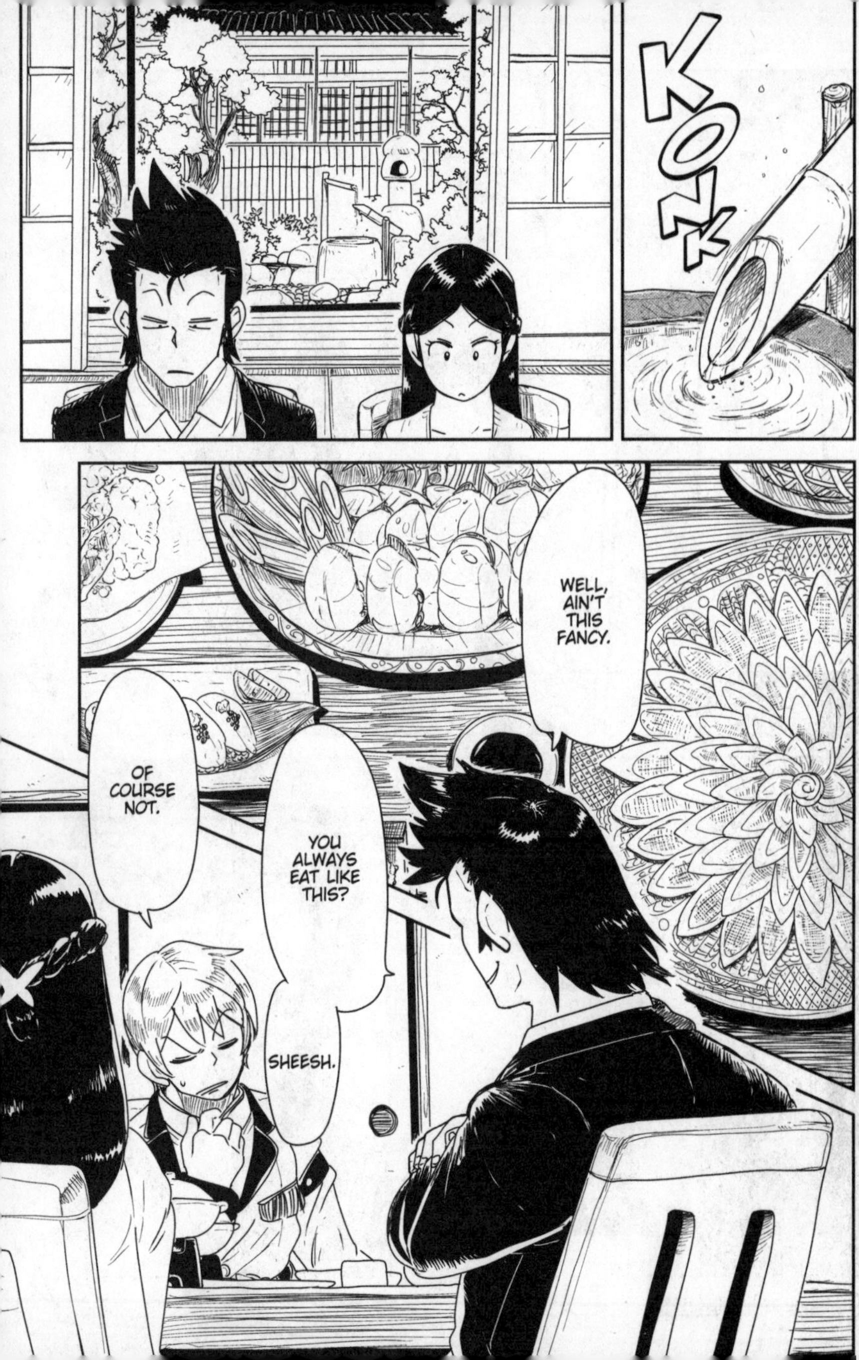
KONK
WELL, AIN'T THIS FANCY.
YOU ALWAYS EAT LIKE THIS?
OF COURSE NOT.
SHEESH.

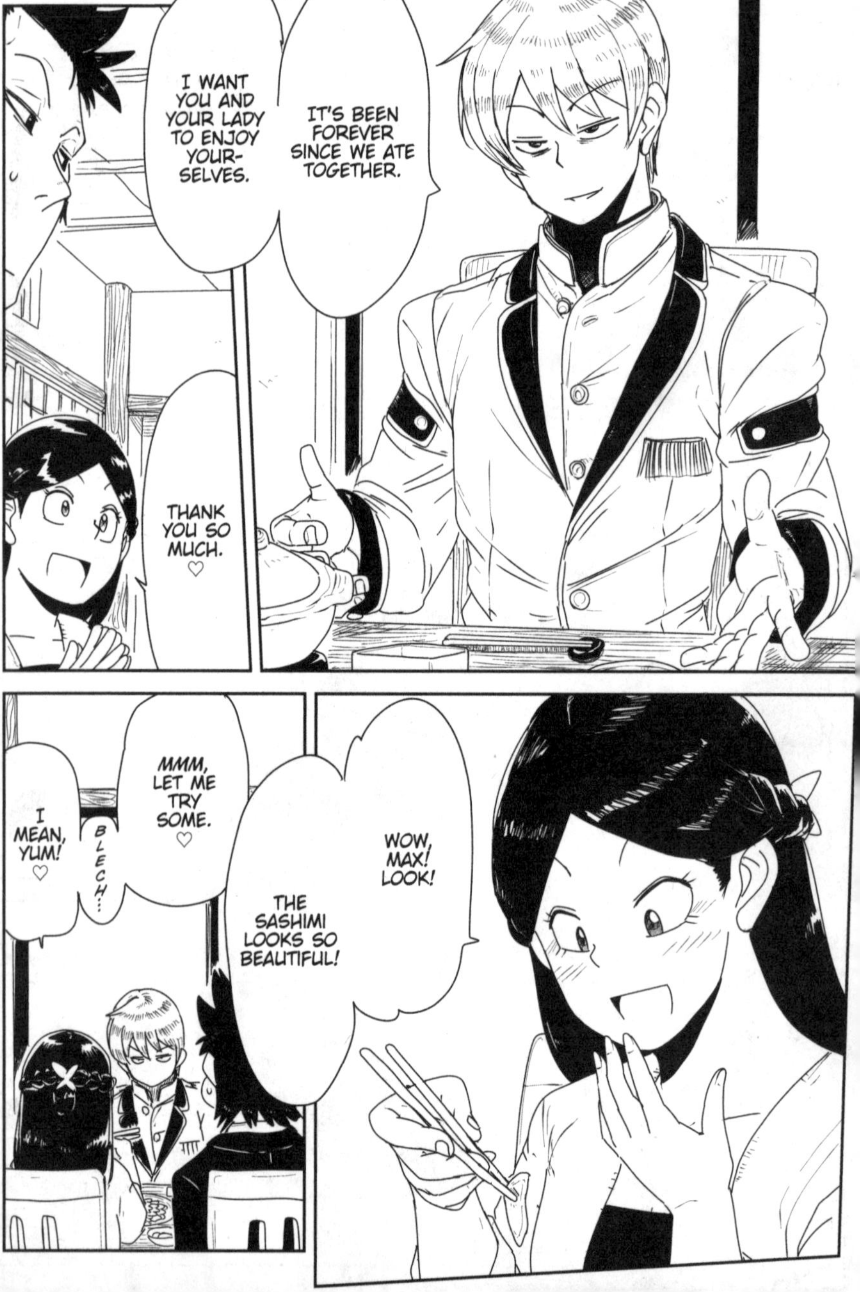
IT'S BEEN FOREVER SINCE WE ATE TOGETHER.
I WANT YOU AND YOUR LADY TO ENJOY YOUR-SELVES.
THANK YOU SO MUCH. ♡
WOW, MAX! LOOK!
THE SASHIMI LOOKS SO BEAUTIFUL!
MMM, LET ME TRY SOME. ♡
BLECH...
I MEAN, YUM! ♡

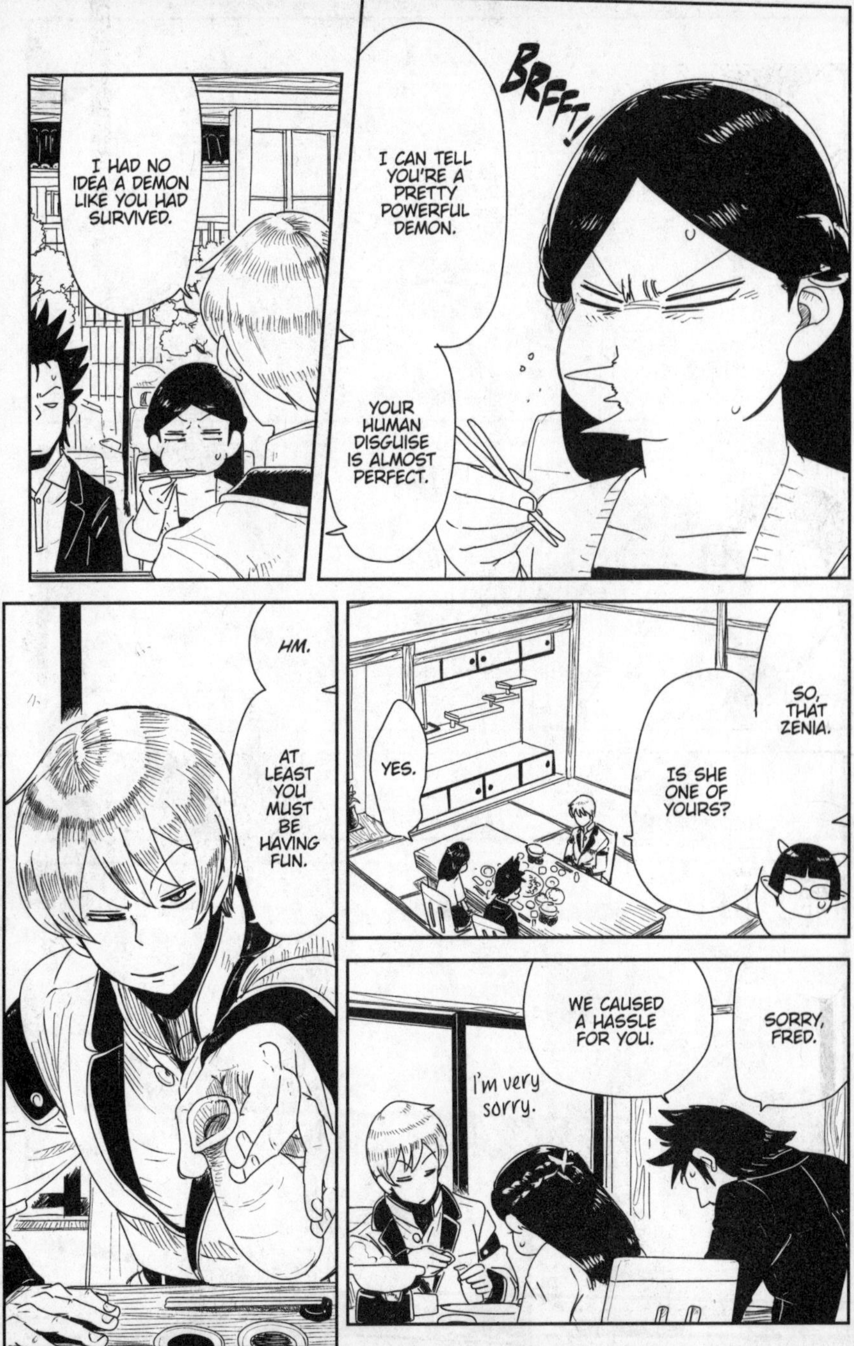
BRFFT!
I CAN TELL YOU'RE A PRETTY POWERFUL DEMON.
YOUR HUMAN DISGUISE IS ALMOST PERFECT.
I HAD NO IDEA A DEMON LIKE YOU HAD SURVIVED.
SO, THAT ZENIA.
IS SHE ONE OF YOURS?
YES.
SORRY, FRED.
WE CAUSED A HASSLE FOR YOU.
I'm very sorry.
HM.
AT LEAST YOU MUST BE HAVING FUN.

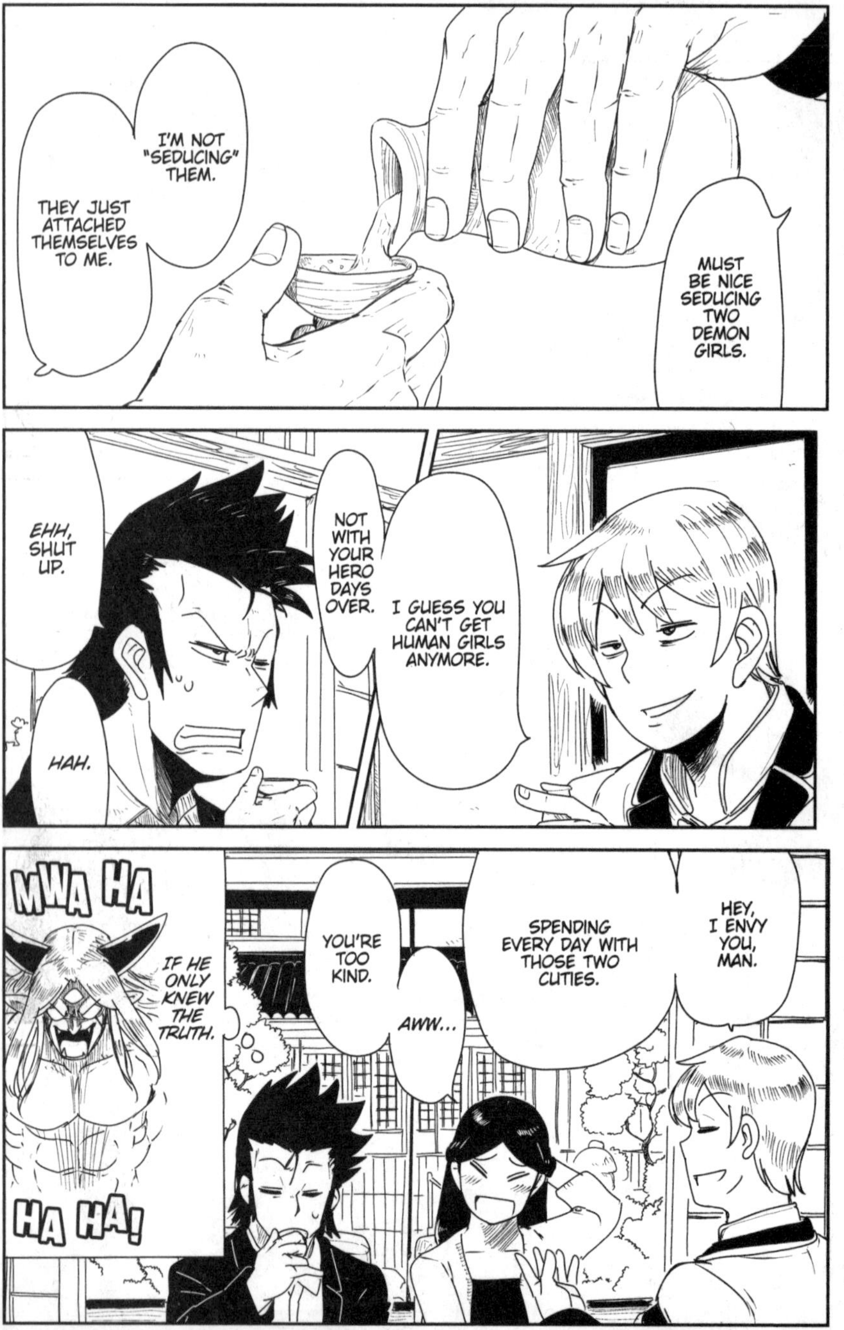
MUST BE NICE SEDUCING TWO DEMON GIRLS.
I'M NOT "SEDUCING" THEM.
THEY JUST ATTACHED THEMSELVES TO ME.
I GUESS YOU CAN'T GET HUMAN GIRLS ANYMORE.
NOT WITH YOUR HERO DAYS OVER.
EHH, SHUT UP.
HAH.
HEY, I ENVY YOU, MAN.
SPENDING EVERY DAY WITH THOSE TWO CUTIES.
YOU'RE TOO KIND.
AWW...
MWA HA
HA HA!
IF HE ONLY KNEW THE TRUTH.

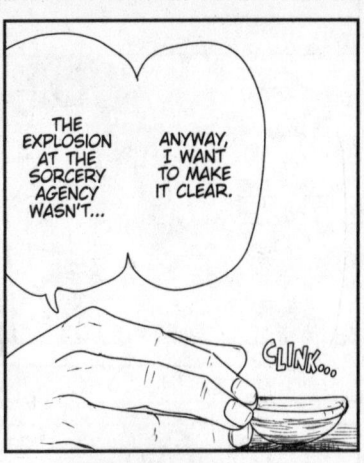

ANYWAY, I WANT TO MAKE IT CLEAR.

THE EXPLOSION AT THE SORCERY AGENCY WASN'T...

I ALREADY KNOW IT WASN'T YOU WHO DID IT.

CLINK...

IF SHE HAD SET THE BOMB, SHE WOULDN'T HAVE STUCK AROUND, WOULD SHE?

NO MATTER HOW DUMB SHE IS.

Y-- YEAH!

ZENIA LEFT SIGNS OF ACTIVITY ALL THROUGHOUT THE BUILDING.

BOY, AM I GLAD TO HAVE YOU AS A FRIEND!

COME ON NOW.

I KNEW YOU'D UNDERSTAND, FRED!

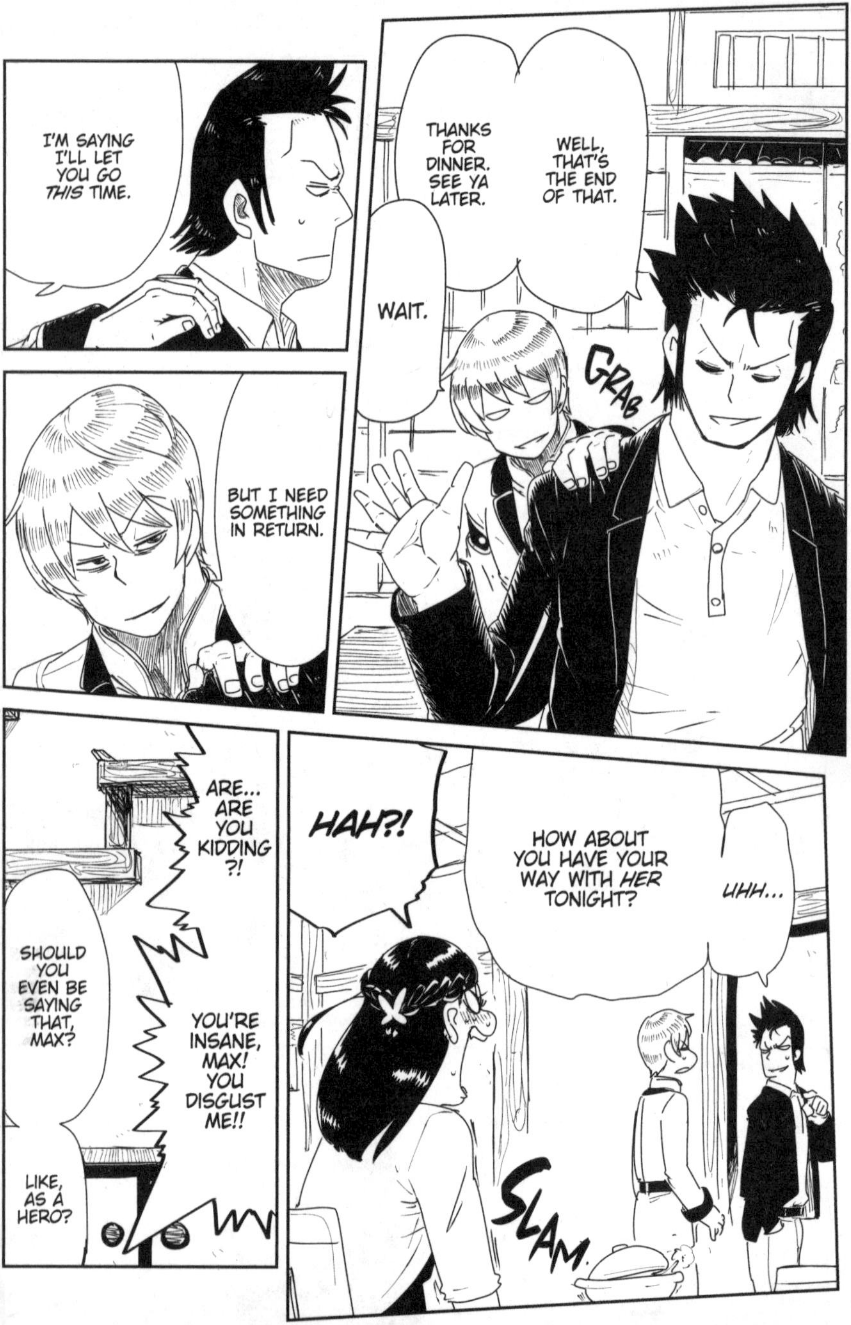
WELL, THAT'S THE END OF THAT.
THANKS FOR DINNER. SEE YA LATER.
WAIT.
GRAB
I'M SAYING I'LL LET YOU GO *THIS* TIME.
BUT I NEED SOMETHING IN RETURN.
HOW ABOUT YOU HAVE YOUR WAY WITH *HER* TONIGHT?
UHH...
HAH?!
SLAM.
ARE... ARE YOU KIDDING?!
YOU'RE INSANE, MAX! YOU DISGUST ME!!
SHOULD YOU EVEN BE SAYING THAT, MAX?
LIKE, AS A HERO?

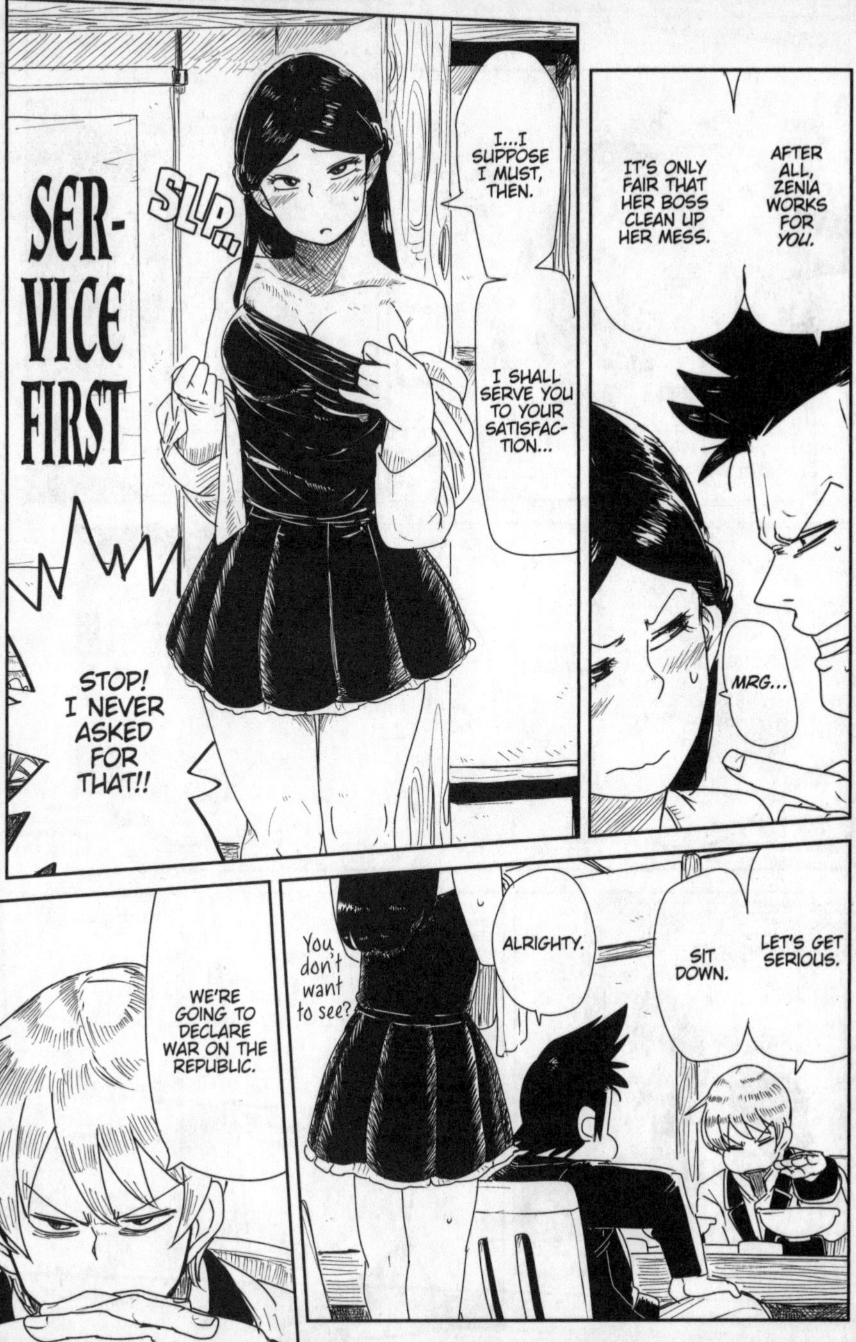
AFTER ALL, ZENIA WORKS FOR YOU.
IT'S ONLY FAIR THAT HER BOSS CLEAN UP HER MESS.
MRG...
I...I SUPPOSE I MUST, THEN.
I SHALL SERVE YOU TO YOUR SATISFACTION...
SLIP...
SER-VICE FIRST
STOP! I NEVER ASKED FOR THAT!!
LET'S GET SERIOUS.
SIT DOWN.
ALRIGHTY.
You don't want to see?
WE'RE GOING TO DECLARE WAR ON THE REPUBLIC.

WHO ELSE? OF COURSE.

BUT WAS IT REALLY THE GUNMAR REPUBLIC?

ALL BECAUSE THEY WENT AND BLEW UP THE SORCERY AGENCY.

IT WAS WEAK SAUCE AS EXPLOSIONS GO, AFTER ALL.

JUST SAYING...

WHO KNOWS?

NUFFIN'.

WHAT ARE YOU TRYING TO SAY...

MAX?

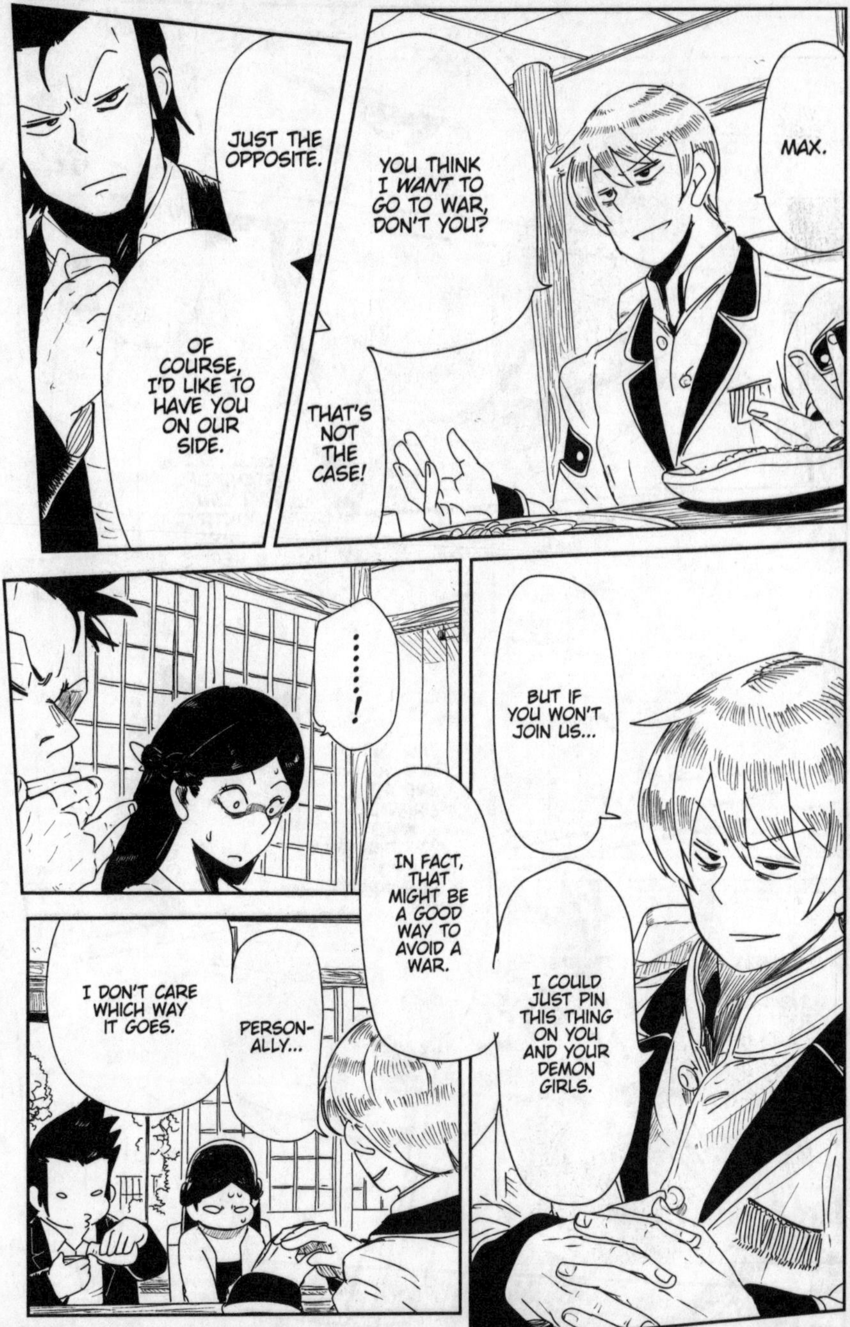
MAX.
YOU THINK I *WANT* TO GO TO WAR, DON'T YOU?
THAT'S NOT THE CASE!
JUST THE OPPOSITE.
OF COURSE, I'D LIKE TO HAVE YOU ON OUR SIDE.
BUT IF YOU WON'T JOIN US...
I COULD JUST PIN THIS THING ON YOU AND YOUR DEMON GIRLS.
IN FACT, THAT MIGHT BE A GOOD WAY TO AVOID A WAR.
......!
PERSON-ALLY...
I DON'T CARE WHICH WAY IT GOES.

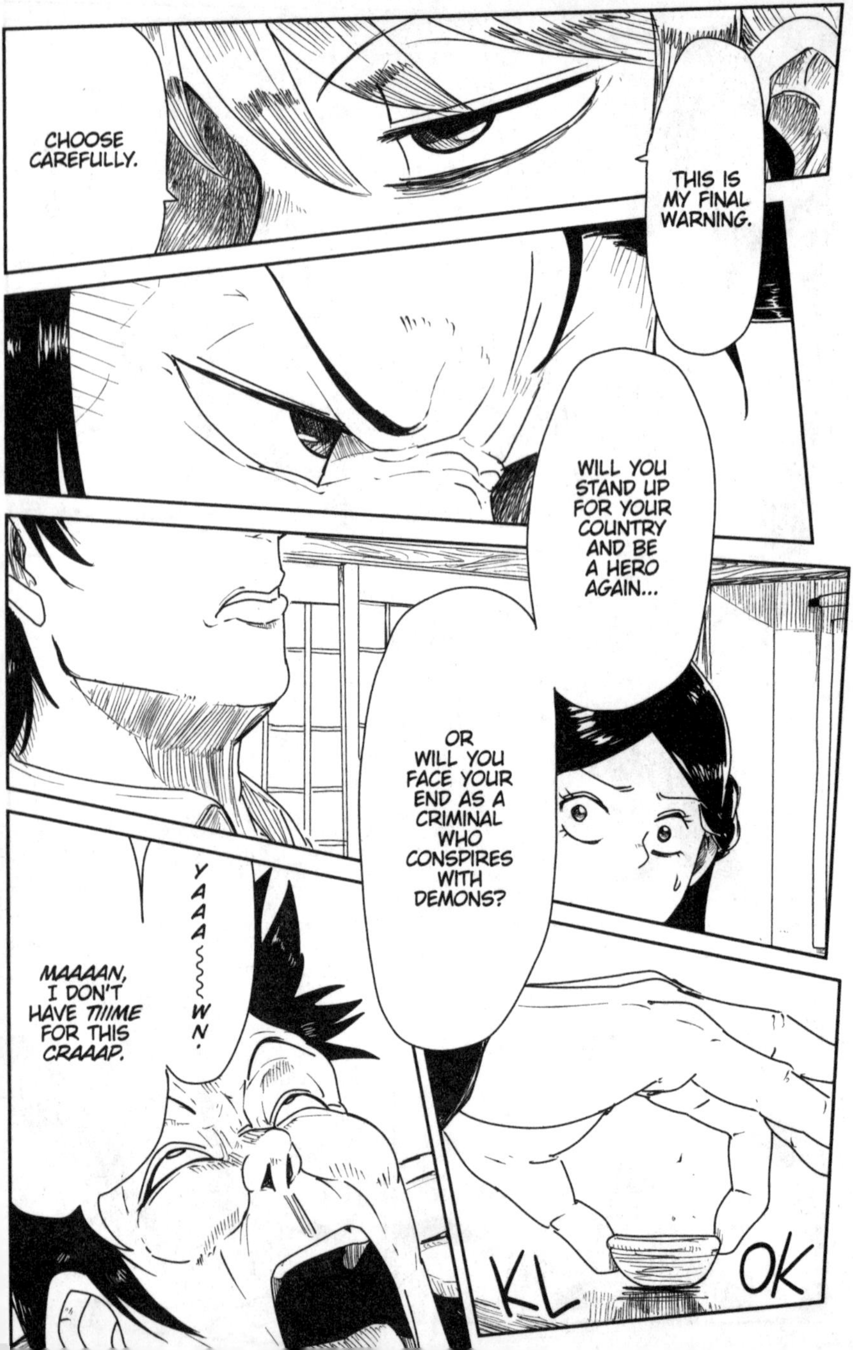
THIS IS MY FINAL WARNING.
CHOOSE CAREFULLY.
WILL YOU STAND UP FOR YOUR COUNTRY AND BE A HERO AGAIN...
OR WILL YOU FACE YOUR END AS A CRIMINAL WHO CONSPIRES WITH DEMONS?
KL OK
YAAAA~WN.
MAAAAN, I DON'T HAVE TIIIME FOR THIS CRAAAP.

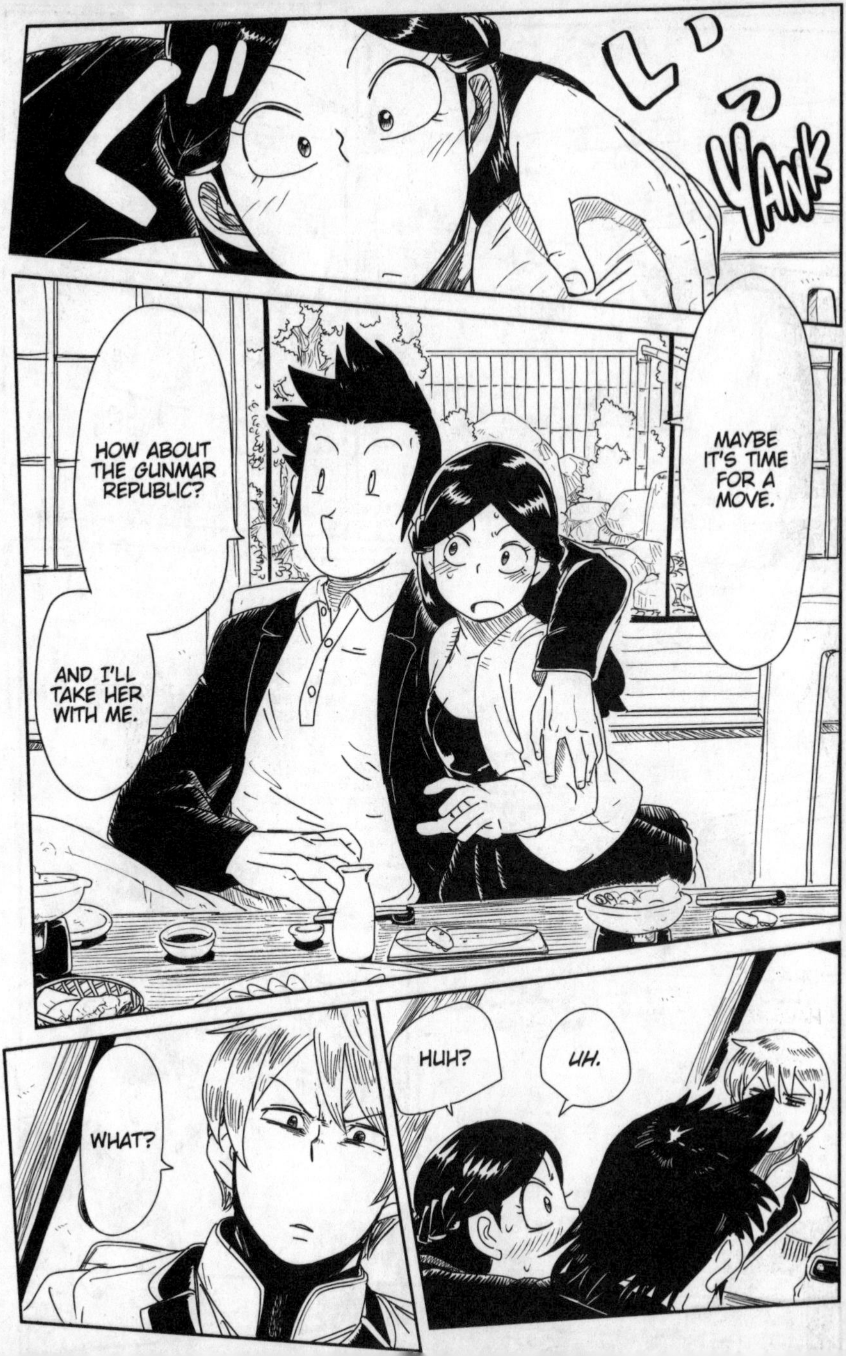
YANK
MAYBE IT'S TIME FOR A MOVE.
HOW ABOUT THE GUNMAR REPUBLIC?
AND I'LL TAKE HER WITH ME.
UH.
HUH?
WHAT?

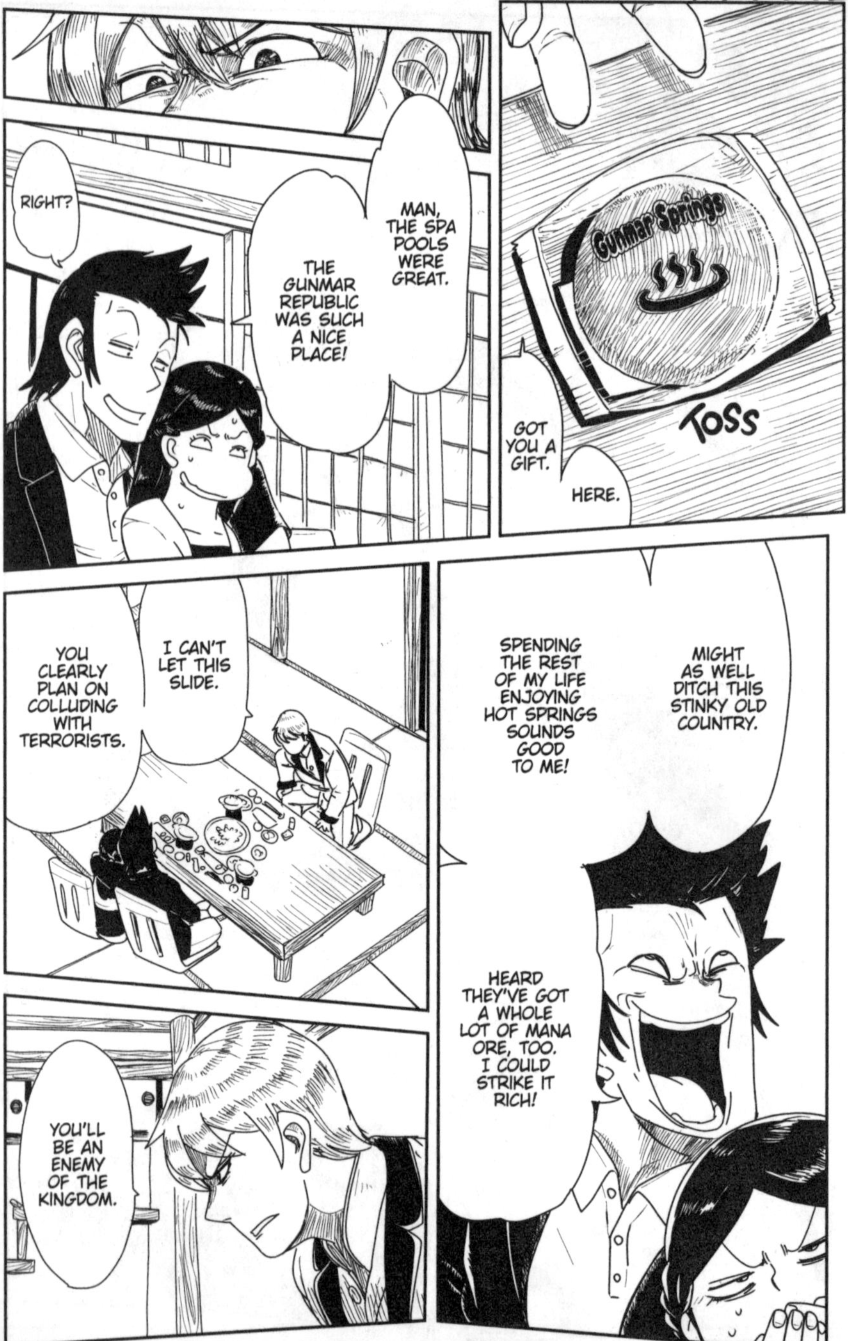
Gunmar Springs
TOSS
GOT YOU A GIFT.
HERE.
MAN, THE SPA POOLS WERE GREAT.
THE GUNMAR REPUBLIC WAS SUCH A NICE PLACE!
RIGHT?
MIGHT AS WELL DITCH THIS STINKY OLD COUNTRY.
SPENDING THE REST OF MY LIFE ENJOYING HOT SPRINGS SOUNDS GOOD TO ME!
HEARD THEY'VE GOT A WHOLE LOT OF MANA ORE, TOO. I COULD STRIKE IT RICH!
I CAN'T LET THIS SLIDE.
YOU CLEARLY PLAN ON COLLUDING WITH TERRORISTS.
YOU'LL BE AN ENEMY OF THE KINGDOM.

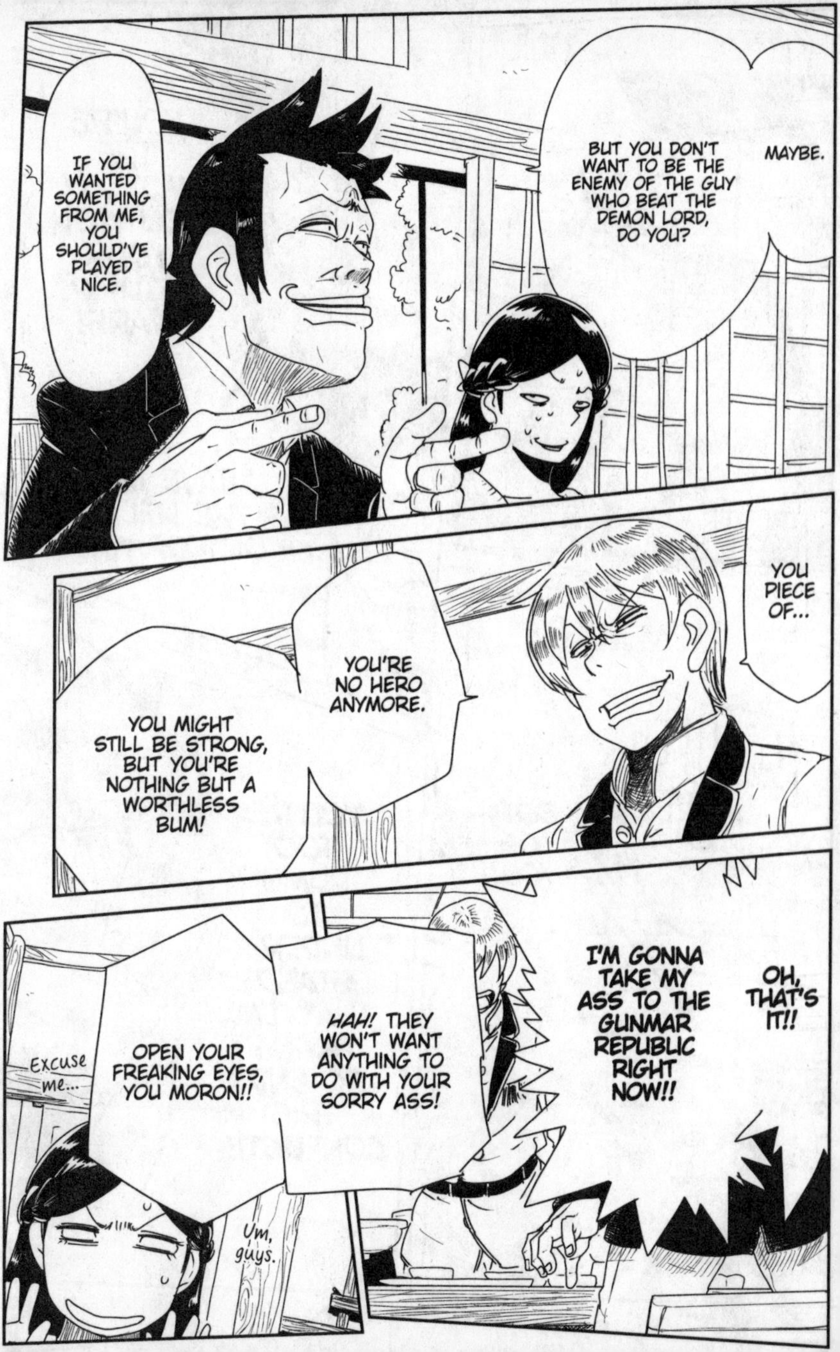
MAYBE.
BUT YOU DON'T WANT TO BE THE ENEMY OF THE GUY WHO BEAT THE DEMON LORD, DO YOU?
IF YOU WANTED SOMETHING FROM ME, YOU SHOULD'VE PLAYED NICE.
YOU PIECE OF...
YOU'RE NO HERO ANYMORE.
YOU MIGHT STILL BE STRONG, BUT YOU'RE NOTHING BUT A WORTHLESS BUM!
OH, THAT'S IT!!
I'M GONNA TAKE MY ASS TO THE GUNMAR REPUBLIC RIGHT NOW!!
HAH! THEY WON'T WANT ANYTHING TO DO WITH YOUR SORRY ASS!
OPEN YOUR FREAKING EYES, YOU MORON!!
Um, guys.
Excuse me...

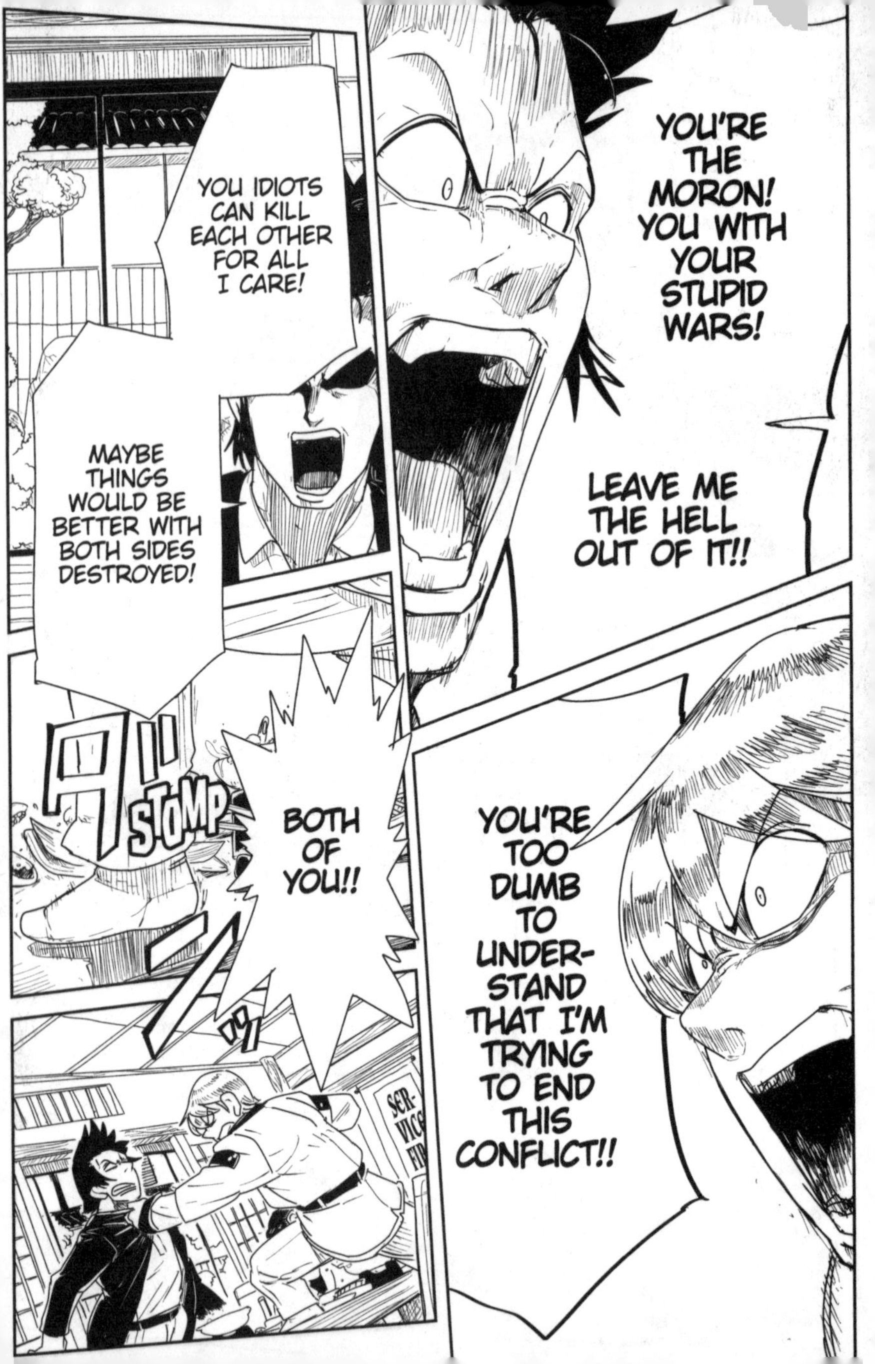
YOU'RE THE MORON! YOU WITH YOUR STUPID WARS!
LEAVE ME THE HELL OUT OF IT!!
YOU IDIOTS CAN KILL EACH OTHER FOR ALL I CARE!
MAYBE THINGS WOULD BE BETTER WITH BOTH SIDES DESTROYED!
YOU'RE TOO DUMB TO UNDER-STAND THAT I'M TRYING TO END THIS CONFLICT!!
BOTH OF YOU!!
STOMP
SER-VICE

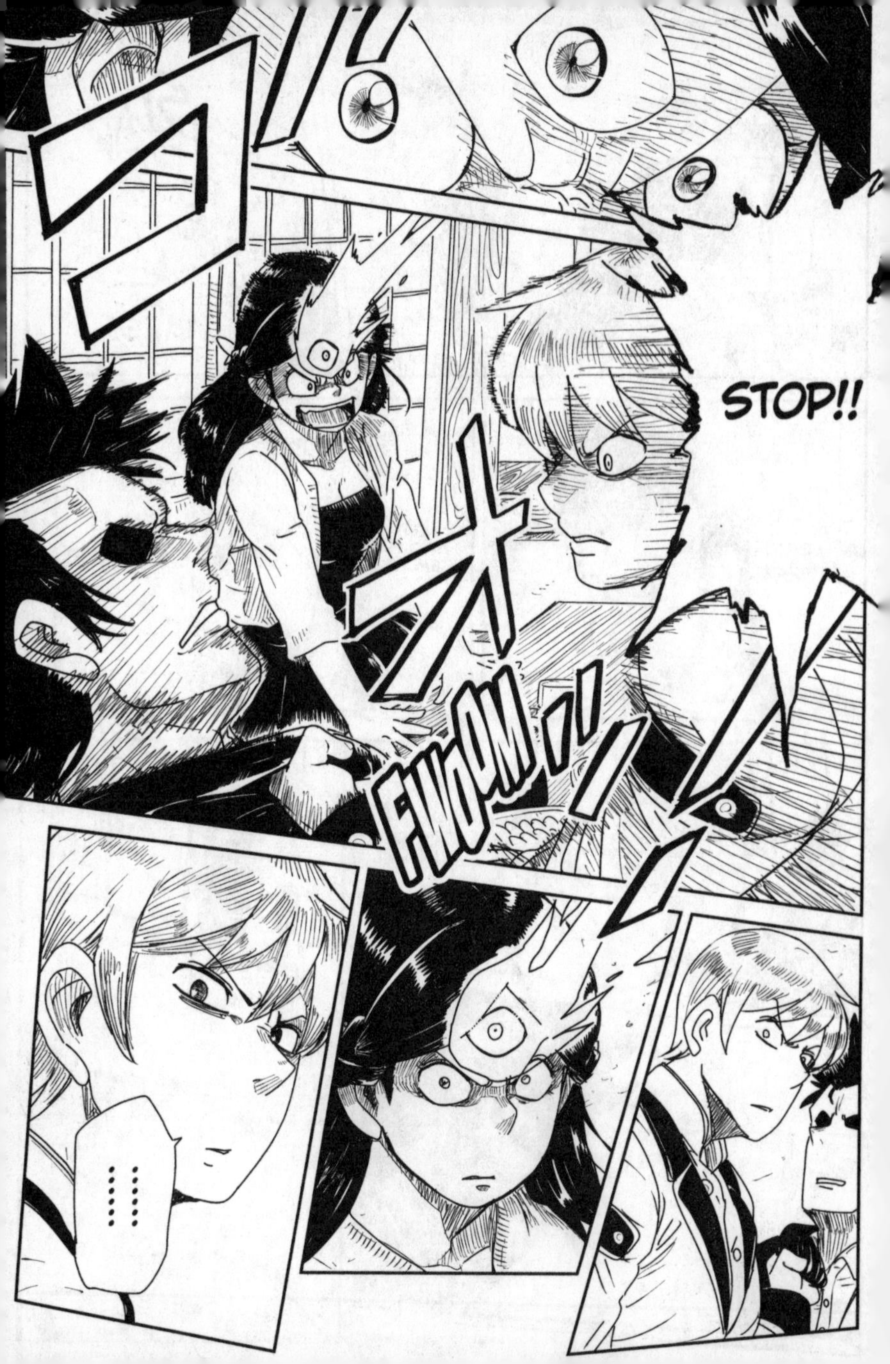
STOP!!
FWOOM!!
......

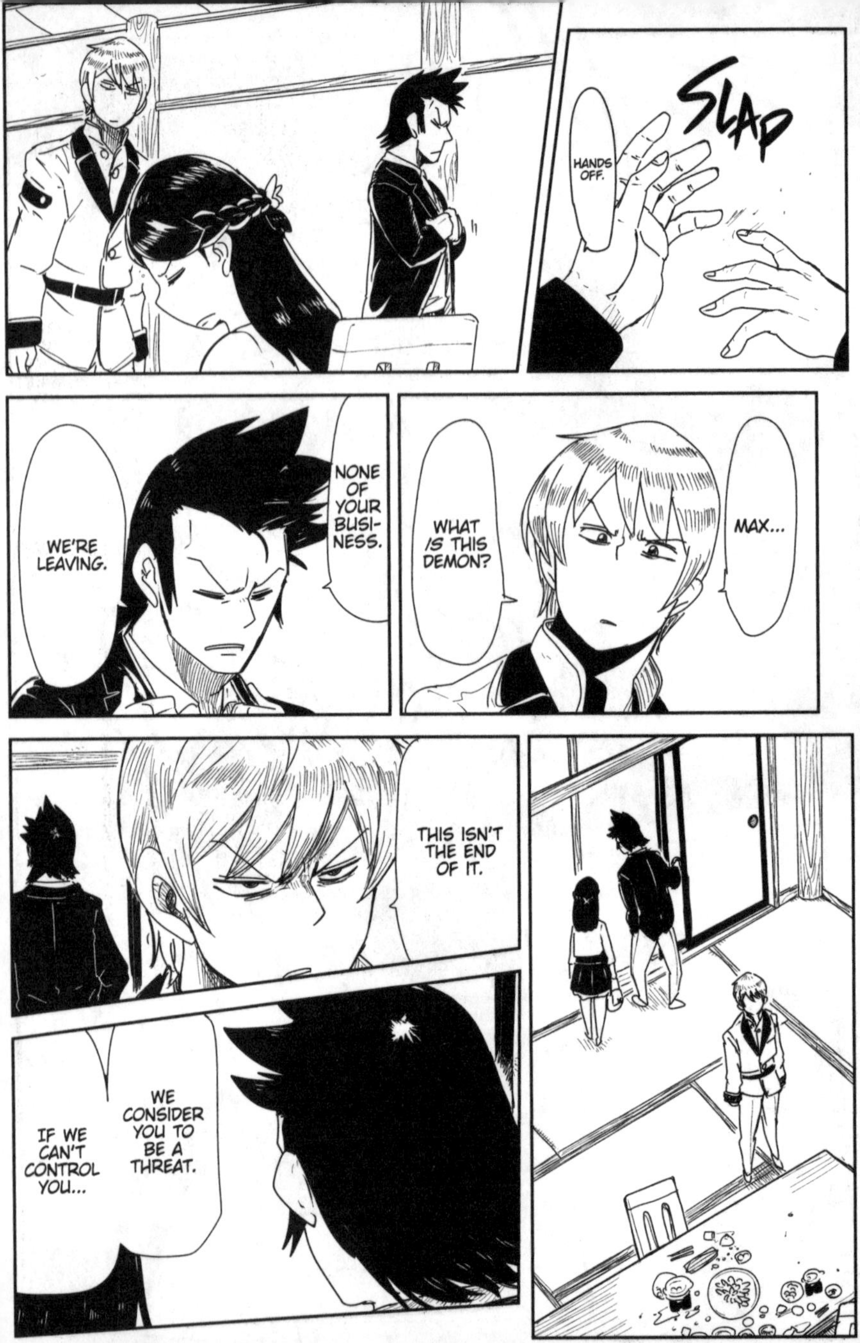
SLAP
HANDS OFF.
MAX...
WHAT IS THIS DEMON?
NONE OF YOUR BUSI-NESS.
WE'RE LEAVING.
THIS ISN'T THE END OF IT.
WE CONSIDER YOU TO BE A THREAT.
IF WE CAN'T CONTROL YOU...

OH YEAH. SORRY I'M SHORT ON CASH TODAY.

OUR TAX MONEY WILL COVER IT, RIGHT? I'LL GET IT NEXT TIME.

I SHOULD'VE PUT SOME POISON IN THERE.

Schwip

KLAK

FINALLY HOME.

THAT'S YOUR BEST OUTFIT.

DON'T LEAVE YOUR CLOTHES LYING AROUND, MAX.

EHH.

Sigh

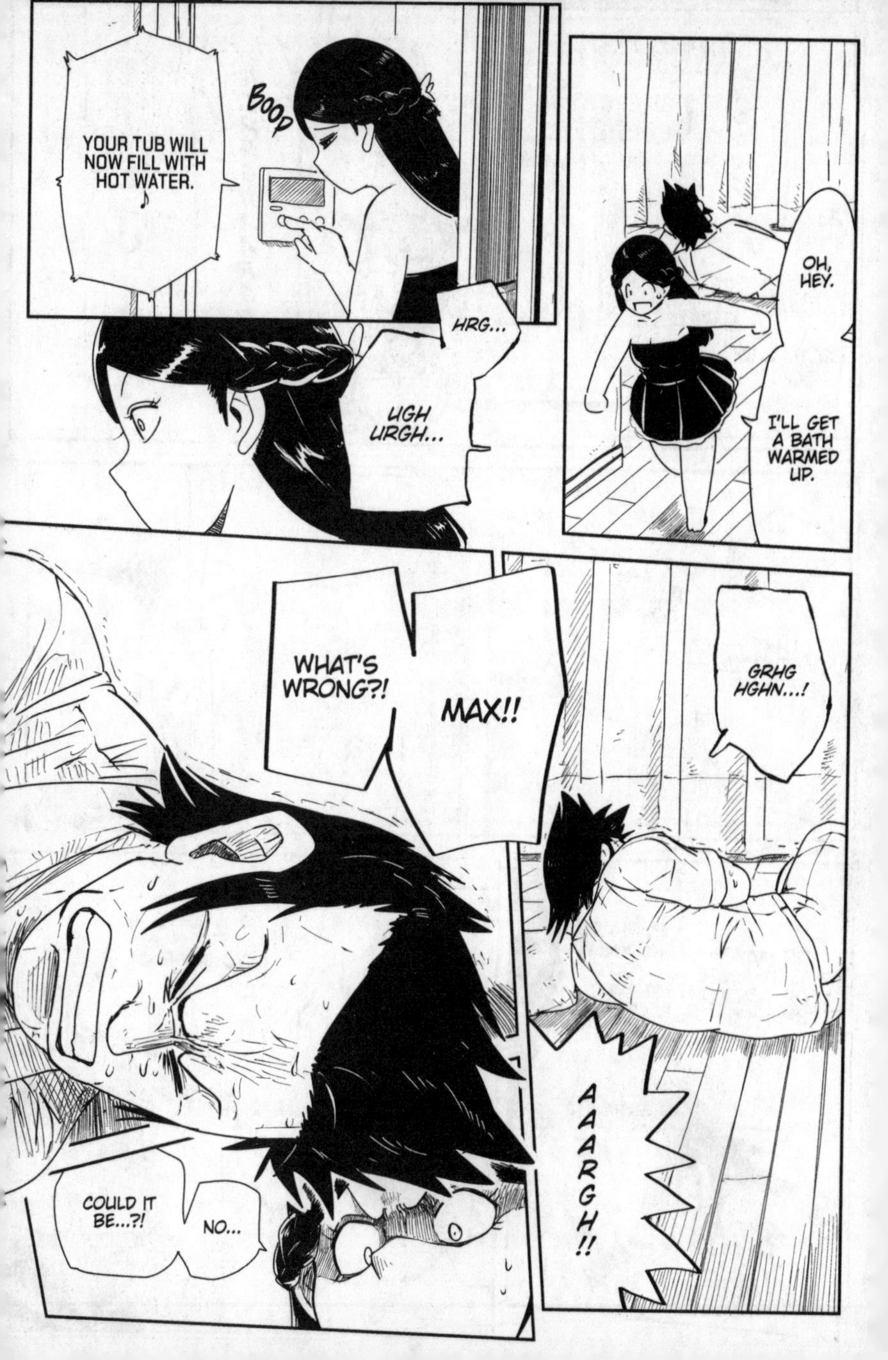
OH, HEY.
I'LL GET A BATH WARMED UP.
BOOP
YOUR TUB WILL NOW FILL WITH HOT WATER. ♪
HRG...
UGH URGH...
GRHG HGHN...!
AAARGH!!
MAX!!
WHAT'S WRONG?!
NO...
COULD IT BE...?!

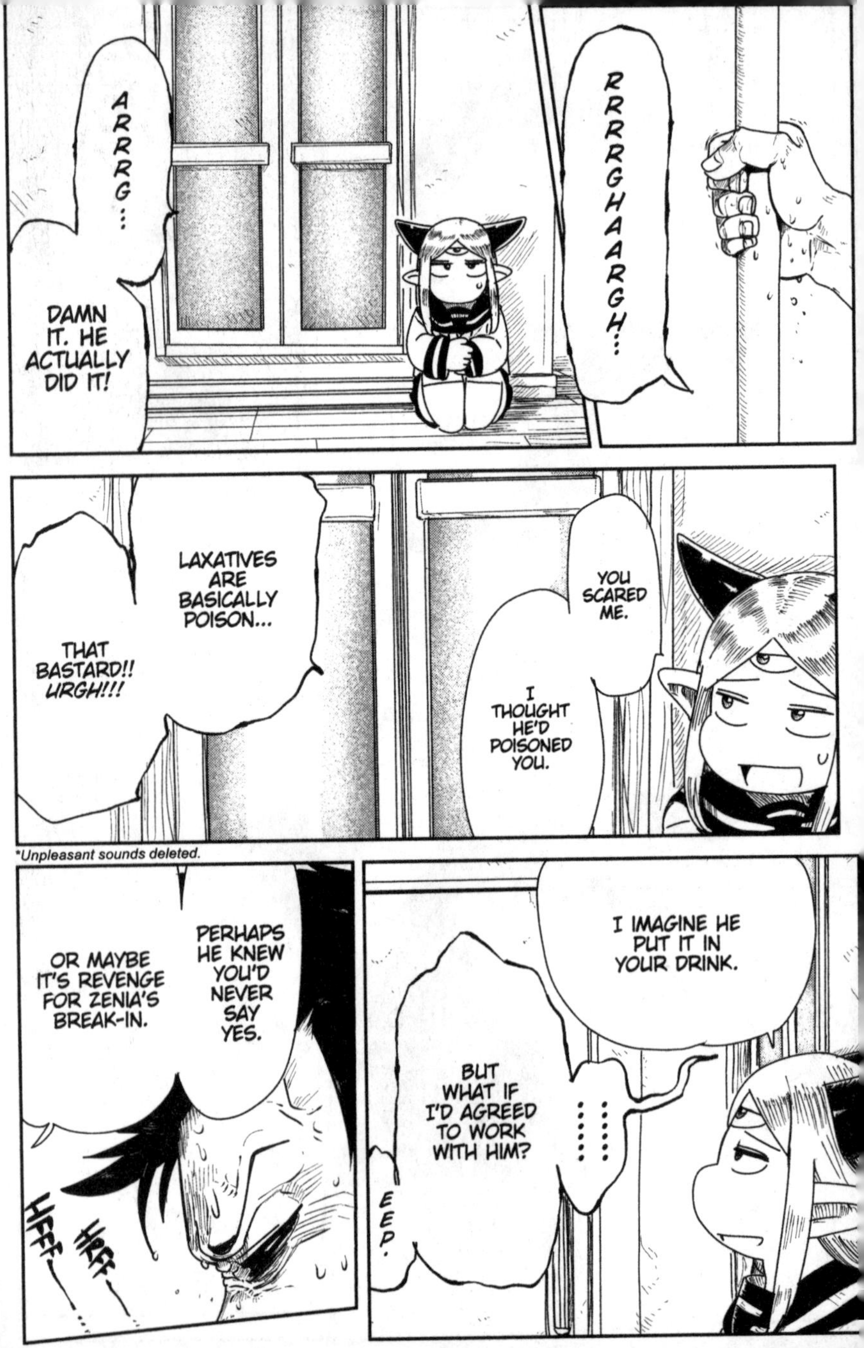
RRRRGHAAARGH...
ARRRG...
DAMN IT. HE ACTUALLY DID IT!
YOU SCARED ME.
I THOUGHT HE'D POISONED YOU.
LAXATIVES ARE BASICALLY POISON...
THAT BASTARD!! URGH!!!
I IMAGINE HE PUT IT IN YOUR DRINK.
BUT WHAT IF I'D AGREED TO WORK WITH HIM?
......
EEP.
PERHAPS HE KNEW YOU'D NEVER SAY YES.
OR MAYBE IT'S REVENGE FOR ZENIA'S BREAK-IN.
HFFF...
HFFF...

*Unpleasant sounds deleted.

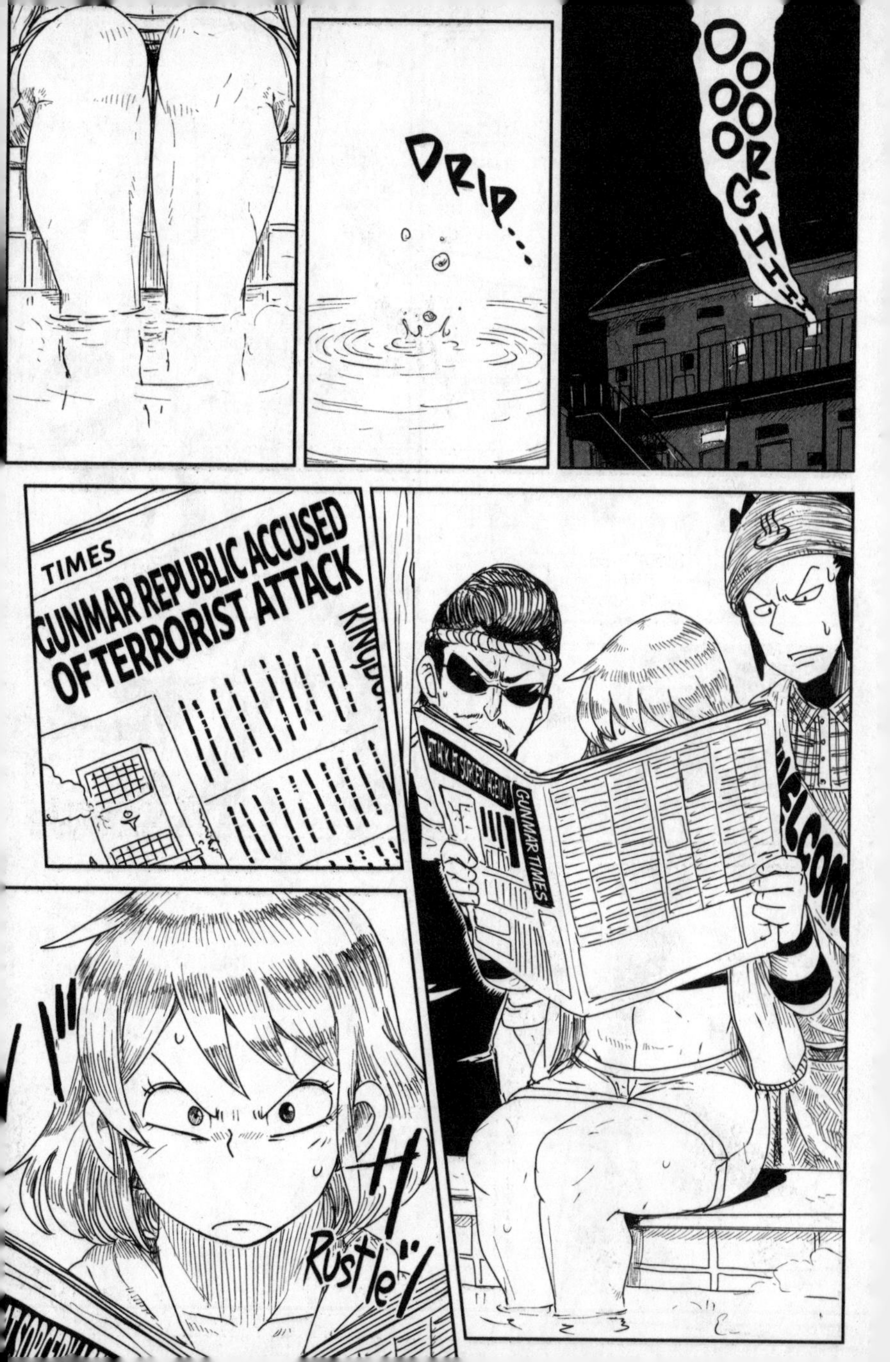
OOOOORGHHH
DRIP...
TIMES
GUNMAR REPUBLIC ACCUSED OF TERRORIST ATTACK
GUNMAR TIMES
!!
Rustle

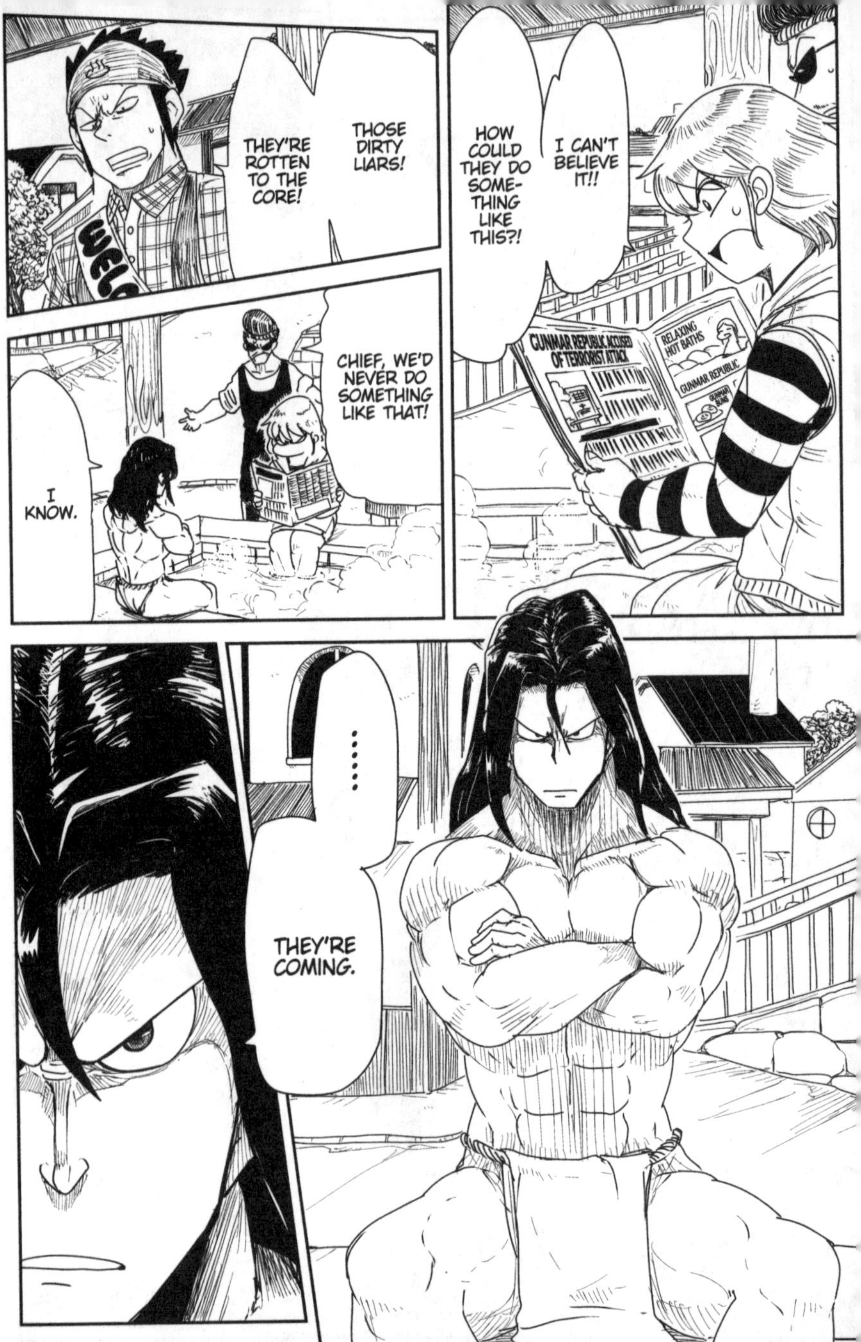
I CAN'T BELIEVE IT!!
HOW COULD THEY DO SOME-THING LIKE THIS?!
GUNMAR REPUBLIC ACCUSED OF TERRORIST ATTACK
RELAXING HOT BATHS
GUNMAR REPUBLIC
THOSE DIRTY LIARS!
THEY'RE ROTTEN TO THE CORE!
CHIEF, WE'D NEVER DO SOMETHING LIKE THAT!
I KNOW.
......
THEY'RE COMING.

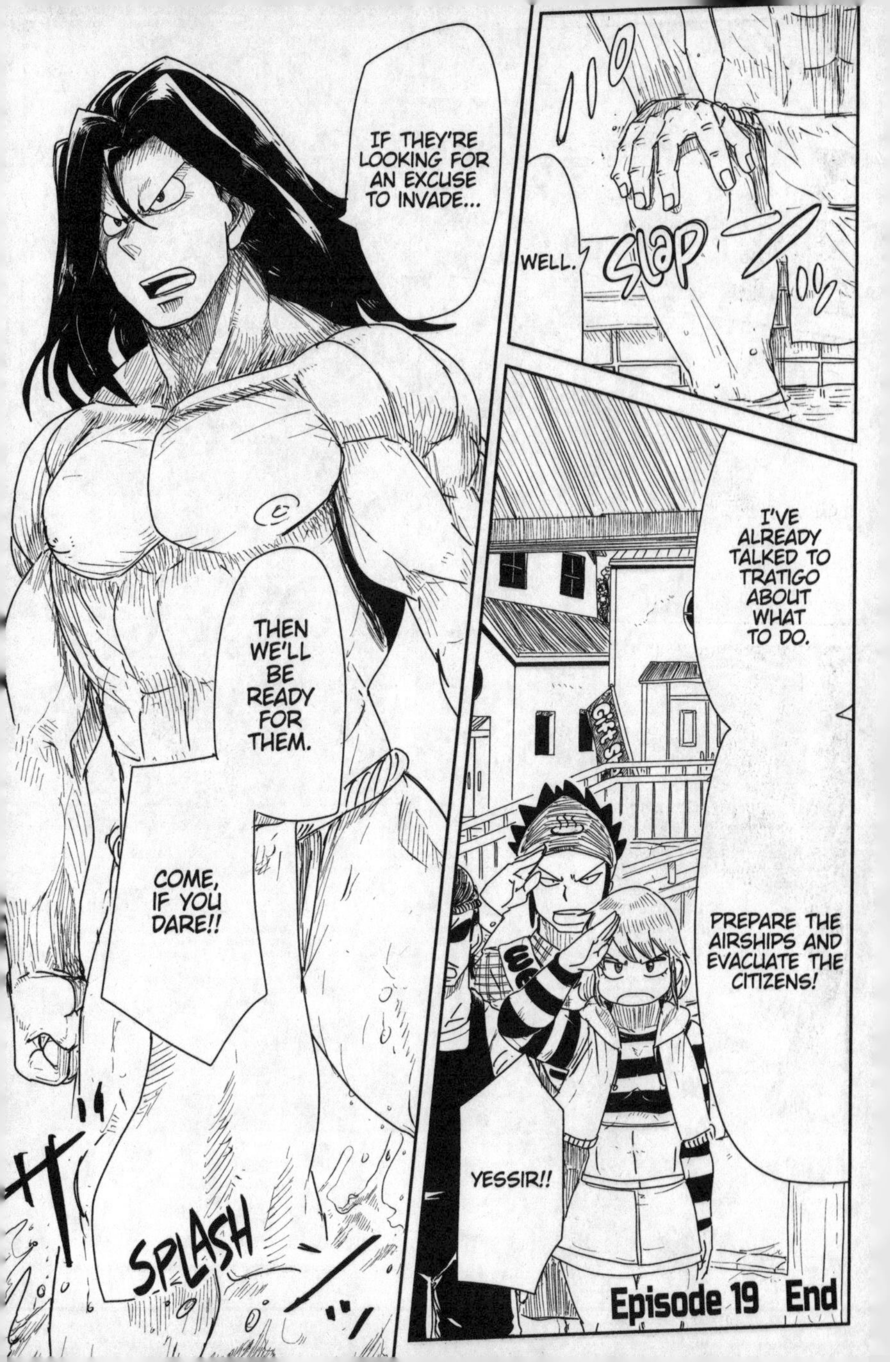

IF THEY'RE LOOKING FOR AN EXCUSE TO INVADE...
THEN WE'LL BE READY FOR THEM.
COME, IF YOU DARE!!
SPLASH
SLAP
WELL.
I'VE ALREADY TALKED TO TRATIGO ABOUT WHAT TO DO.
PREPARE THE AIRSHIPS AND EVACUATE THE CITIZENS!
YESSIR!!
Episode 19 End

LEVEL 1 DEMON LORD & ONE ROOM HERO

Flush~...

Episode 20: The Hero's Dilemma

GIVEN OUR CURRENT SITUATION...

THAT'S ENOUGH.

I'M ANALYZING THE LAXATIVE NOW.

I JUST NEED SOME TIME.

THAT WAS SOME ORDEAL LAST NIGHT.

ARE YOU FEELING BETTER NOW?

OH, MAX.

KLAK

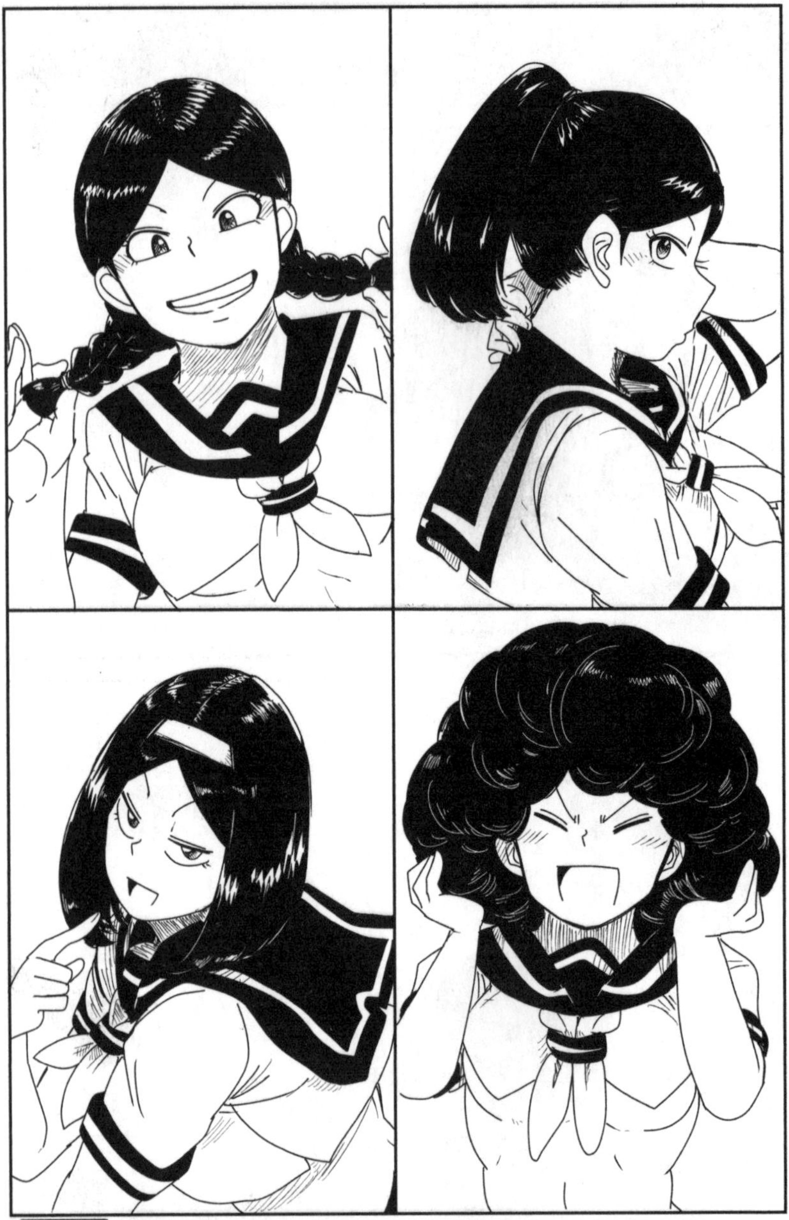

Episode 20 The Hero's Dilemma

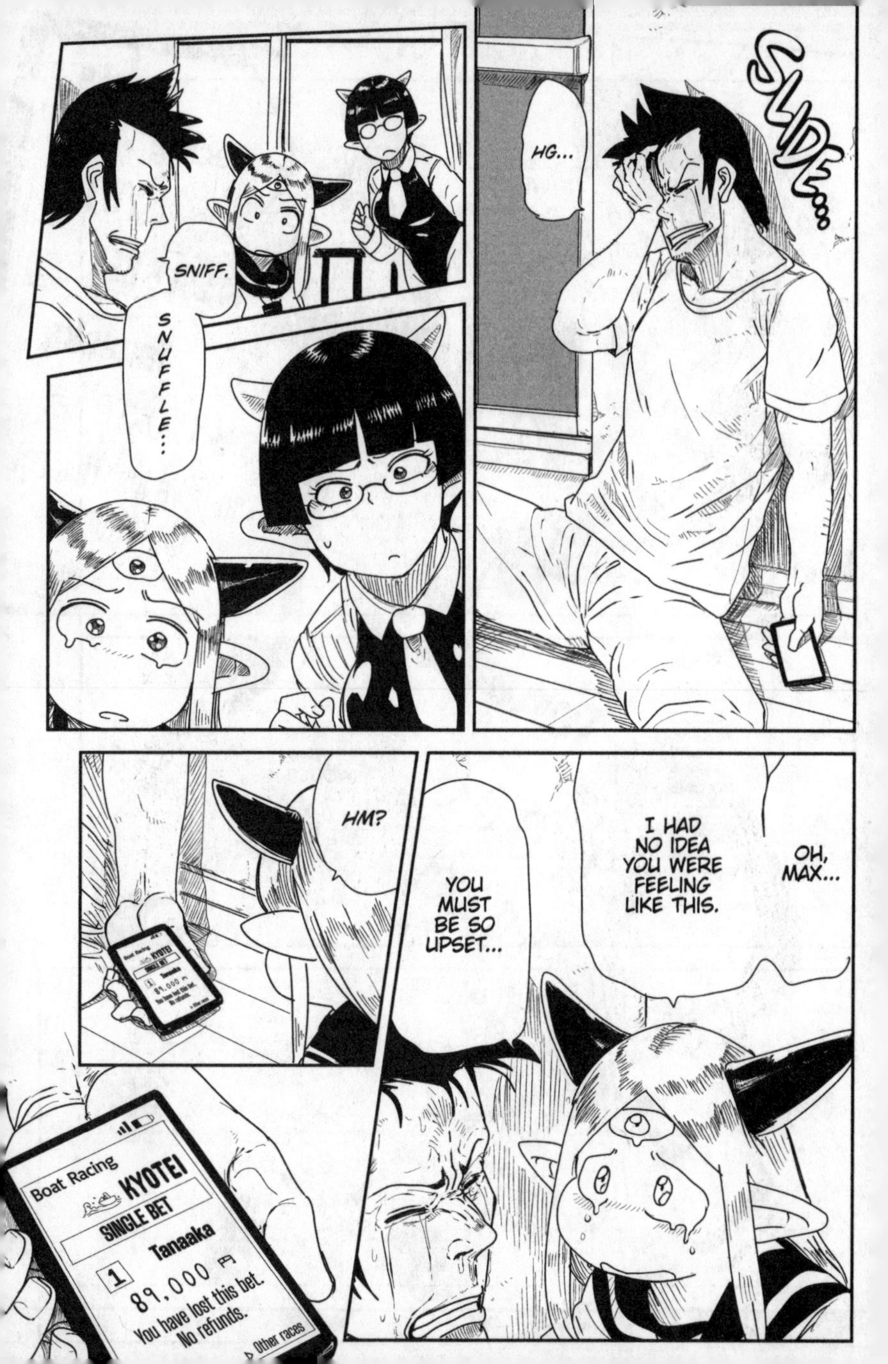
SLIDE...
HG...
SNIFF.
SNUFFLE...
OH, MAX...
I HAD NO IDEA YOU WERE FEELING LIKE THIS.
YOU MUST BE SO UPSET...
HM?
Boat Racing
KYOTEI
SINGLE BET
Tanaaka
1
89,000 円
You have lost this bet. No refunds.
Other races

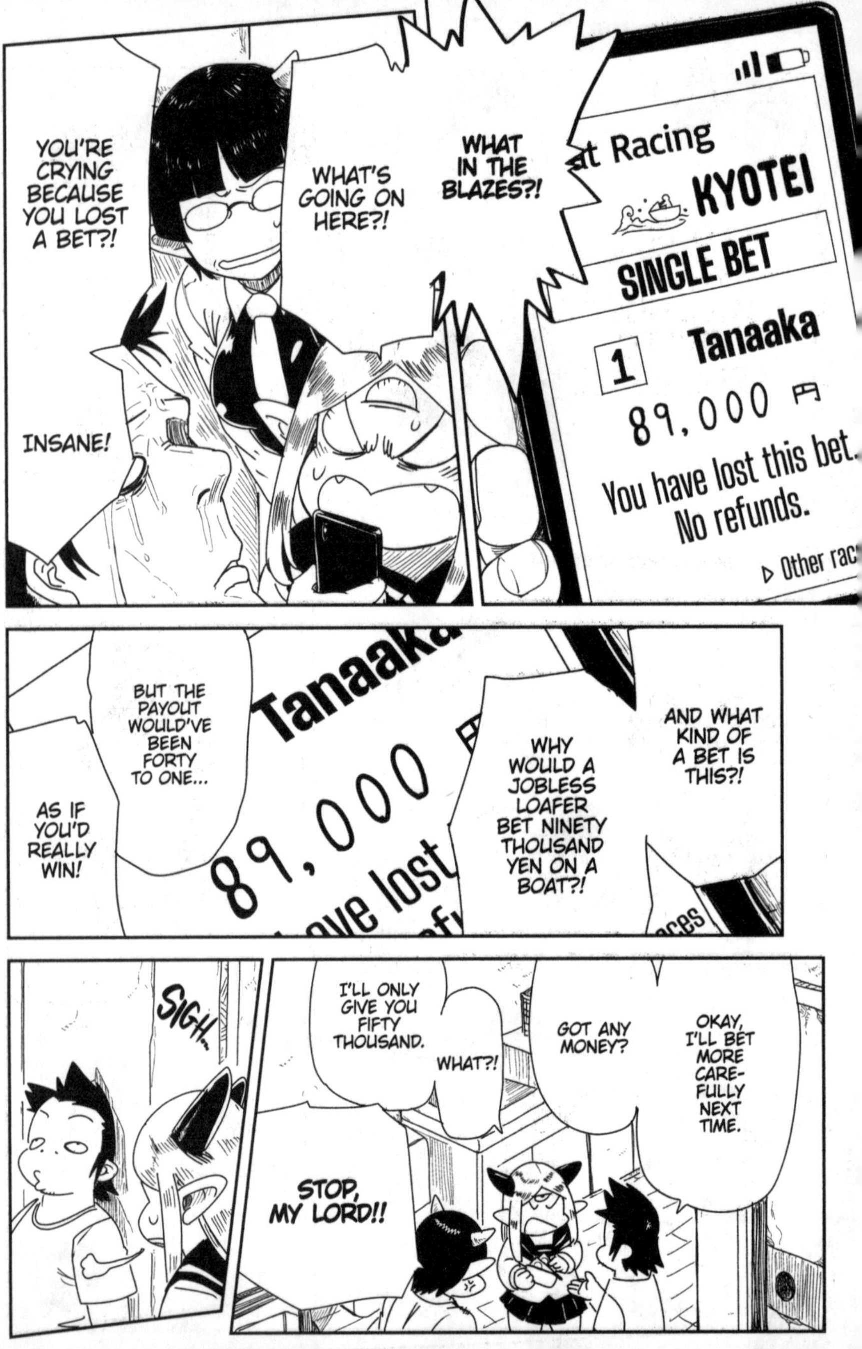

t Racing
KYOTEI
SINGLE BET
1 Tanaaka
89,000 円
You have lost this bet. No refunds.
▷ Other rac
WHAT IN THE BLAZES?!
WHAT'S GOING ON HERE?!
YOU'RE CRYING BECAUSE YOU LOST A BET?!
INSANE!
AND WHAT KIND OF A BET IS THIS?!
WHY WOULD A JOBLESS LOAFER BET NINETY THOUSAND YEN ON A BOAT?!
Tanaaka
89,000
BUT THE PAYOUT WOULD'VE BEEN FORTY TO ONE...
AS IF YOU'D REALLY WIN!
OKAY, I'LL BET MORE CARE-FULLY NEXT TIME.
GOT ANY MONEY?
WHAT?!
I'LL ONLY GIVE YOU FIFTY THOUSAND.
STOP, MY LORD!!
SIGH...

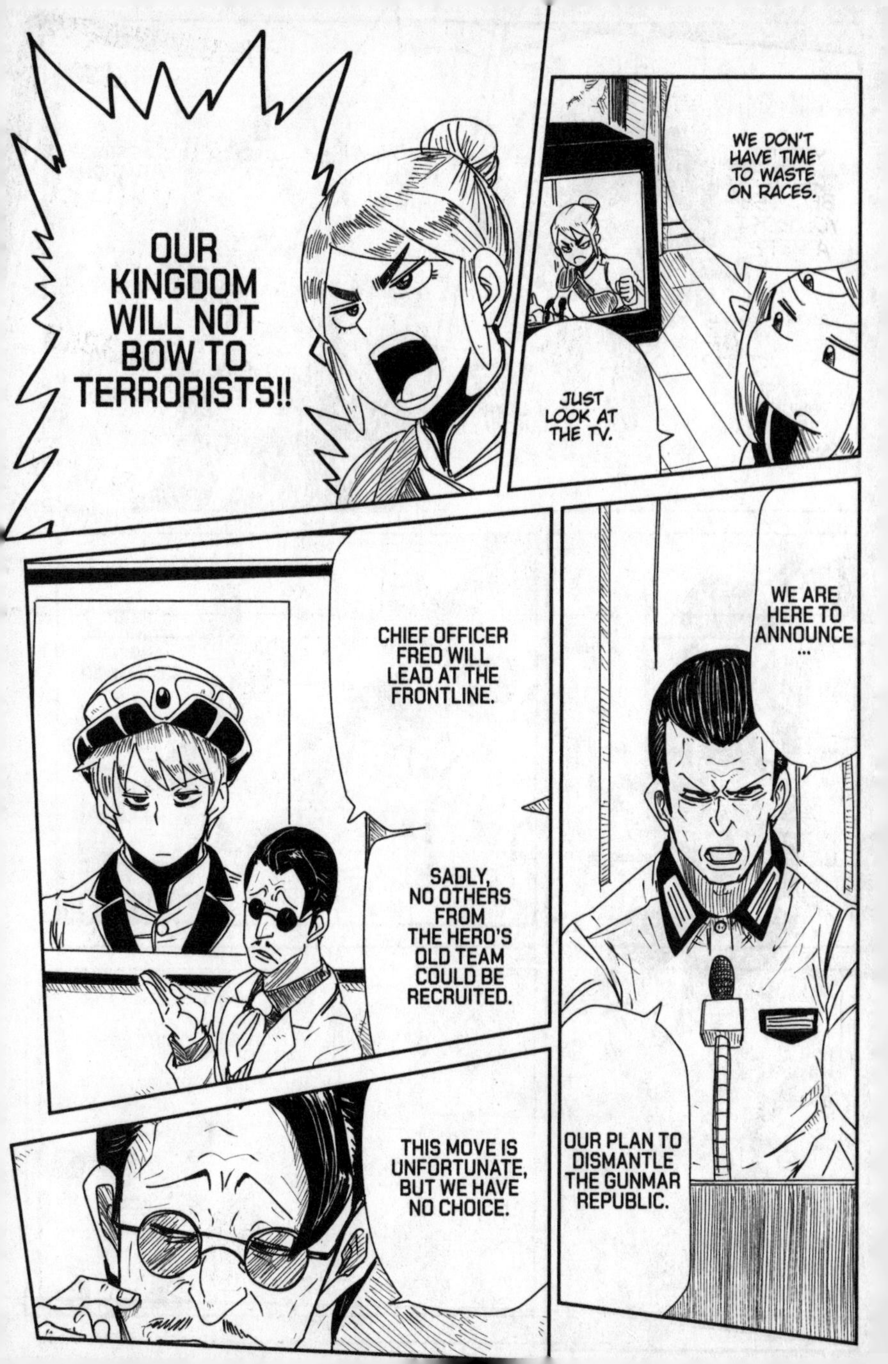
WE DON'T HAVE TIME TO WASTE ON RACES.
JUST LOOK AT THE TV.
OUR KINGDOM WILL NOT BOW TO TERRORISTS!!
WE ARE HERE TO ANNOUNCE ...
OUR PLAN TO DISMANTLE THE GUNMAR REPUBLIC.
CHIEF OFFICER FRED WILL LEAD AT THE FRONTLINE.
SADLY, NO OTHERS FROM THE HERO'S OLD TEAM COULD BE RECRUITED.
THIS MOVE IS UNFORTUNATE, BUT WE HAVE NO CHOICE.

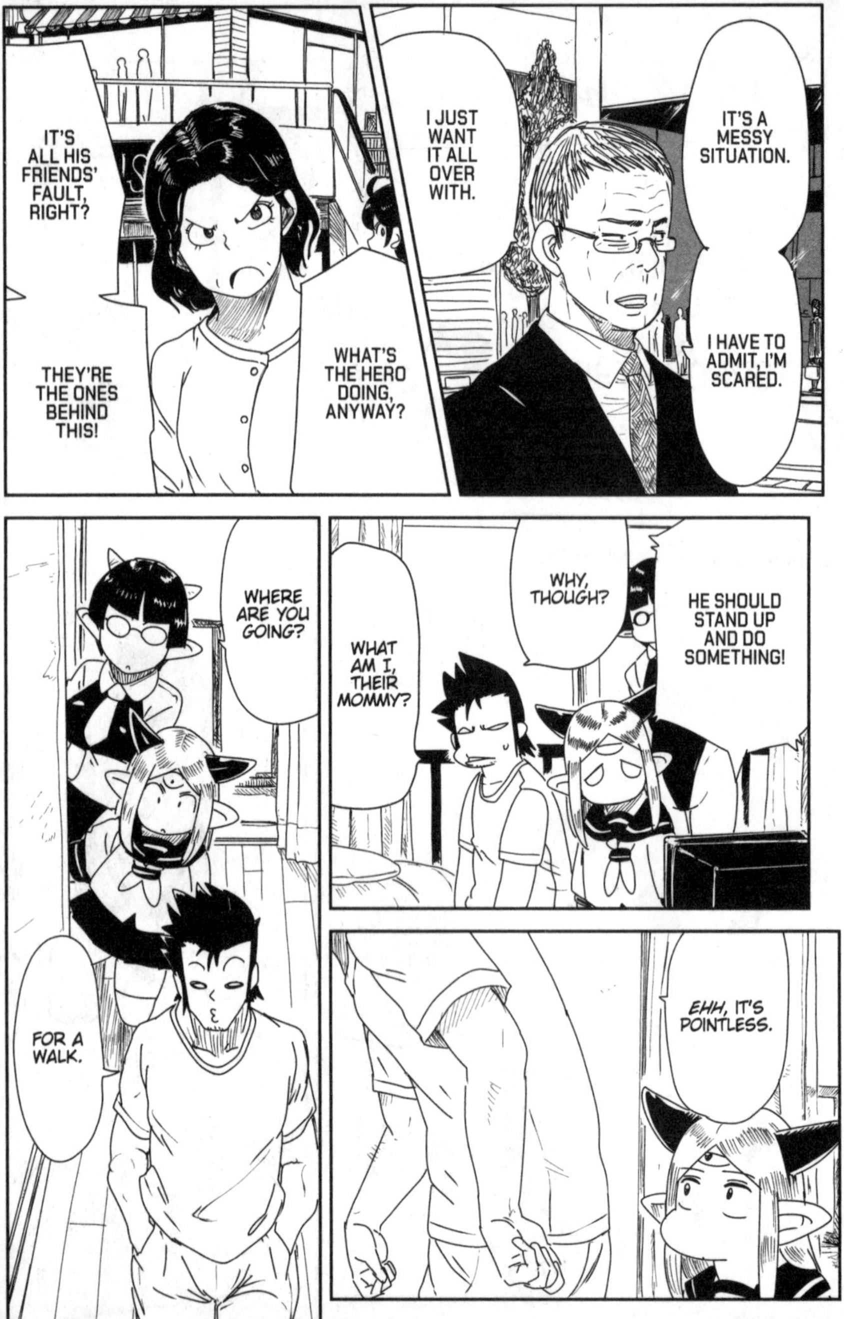
IT'S A MESSY SITUATION.
I HAVE TO ADMIT, I'M SCARED.
I JUST WANT IT ALL OVER WITH.
IT'S ALL HIS FRIENDS' FAULT, RIGHT?
THEY'RE THE ONES BEHIND THIS!
WHAT'S THE HERO DOING, ANYWAY?
HE SHOULD STAND UP AND DO SOMETHING!
WHY, THOUGH?
WHAT AM I, THEIR MOMMY?
EHH, IT'S POINTLESS.
WHERE ARE YOU GOING?
FOR A WALK.

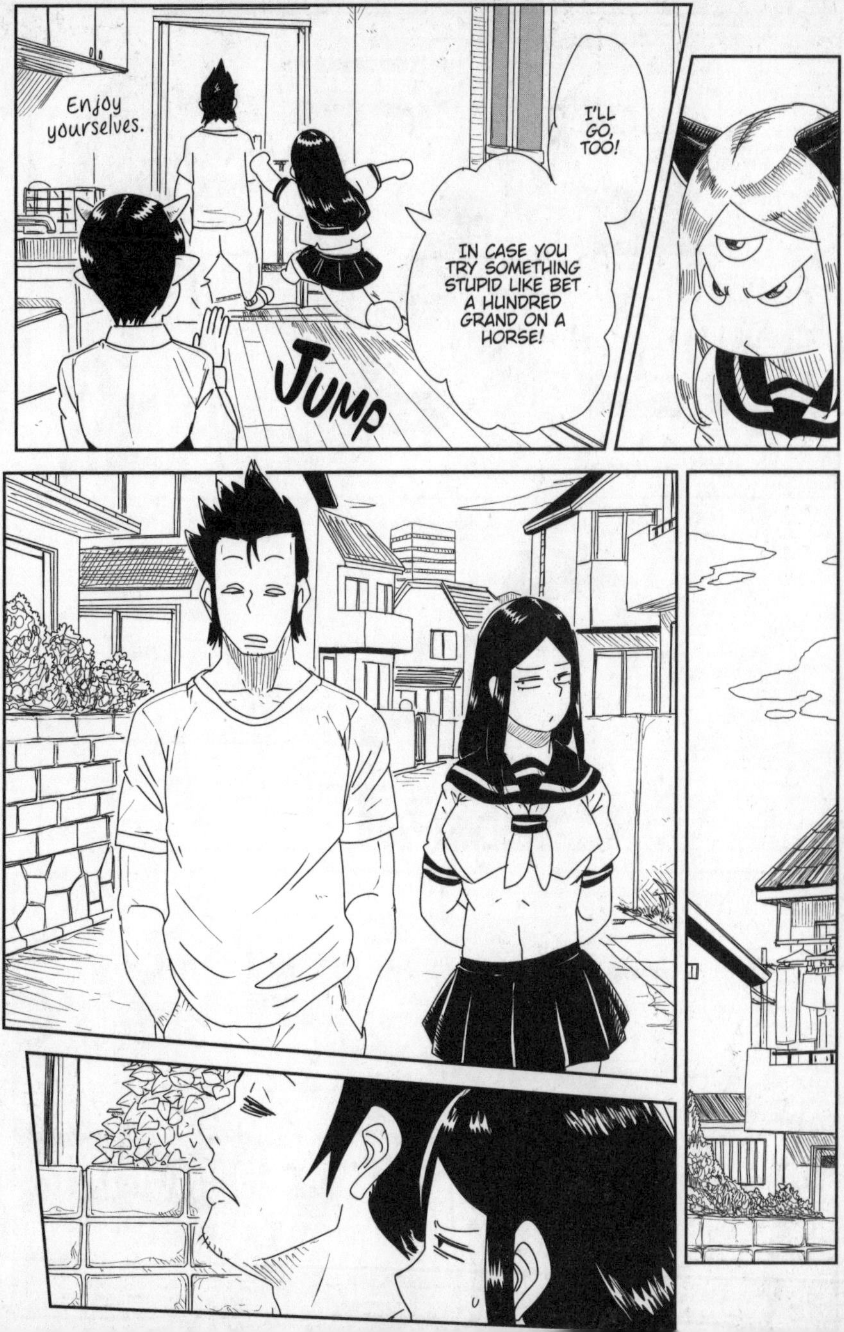
I'LL GO, TOO!
IN CASE YOU TRY SOMETHING STUPID LIKE BET A HUNDRED GRAND ON A HORSE!
Enjoy yourselves.
JUMP

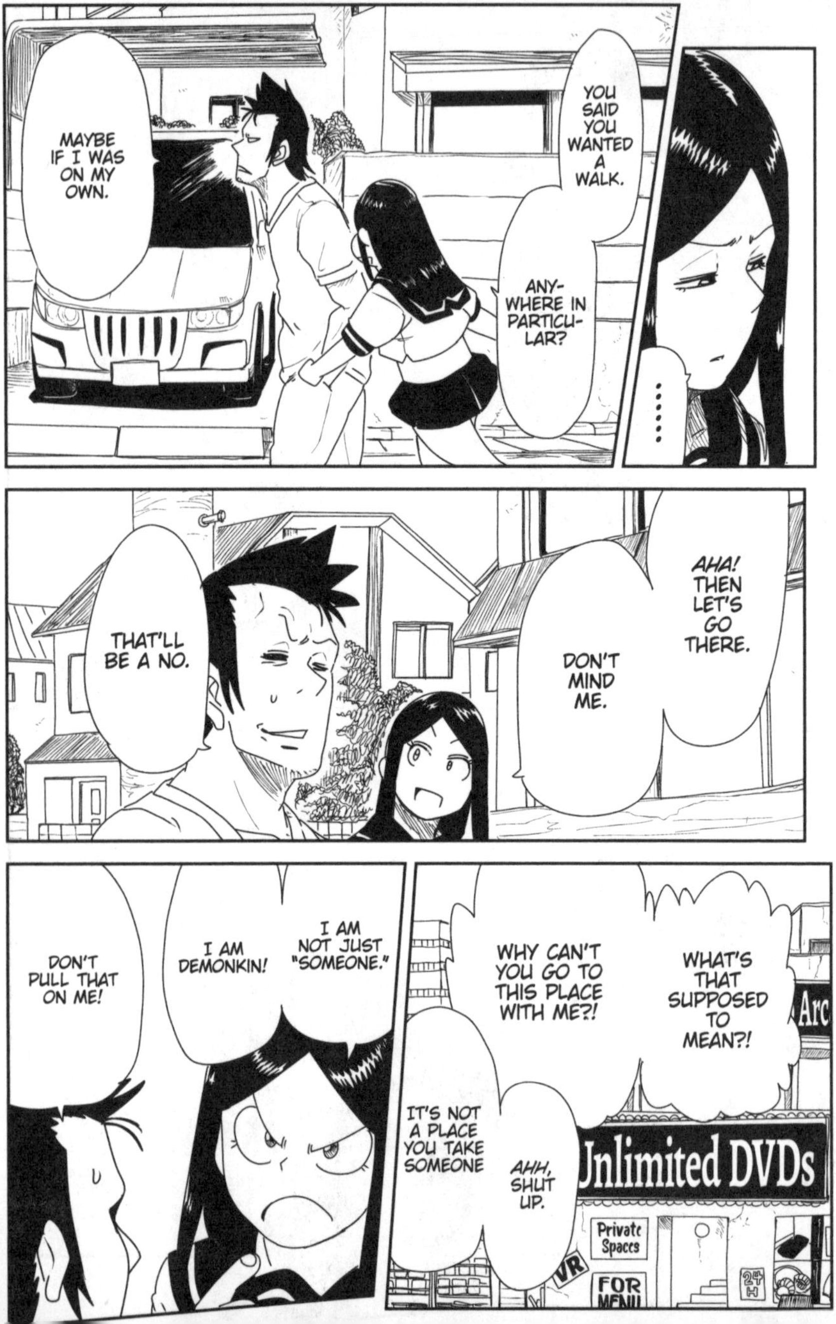
......
YOU SAID YOU WANTED A WALK.
ANY-WHERE IN PARTICU-LAR?
MAYBE IF I WAS ON MY OWN.
AHA! THEN LET'S GO THERE.
DON'T MIND ME.
THAT'LL BE A NO.
WHAT'S THAT SUPPOSED TO MEAN?!
WHY CAN'T YOU GO TO THIS PLACE WITH ME?!
AHH, SHUT UP.
IT'S NOT A PLACE YOU TAKE SOMEONE
Arc
Unlimited DVDs
Private Spaces
VR
FOR MENU
24 H
I AM NOT JUST "SOMEONE."
I AM DEMONKIN!
DON'T PULL THAT ON ME!

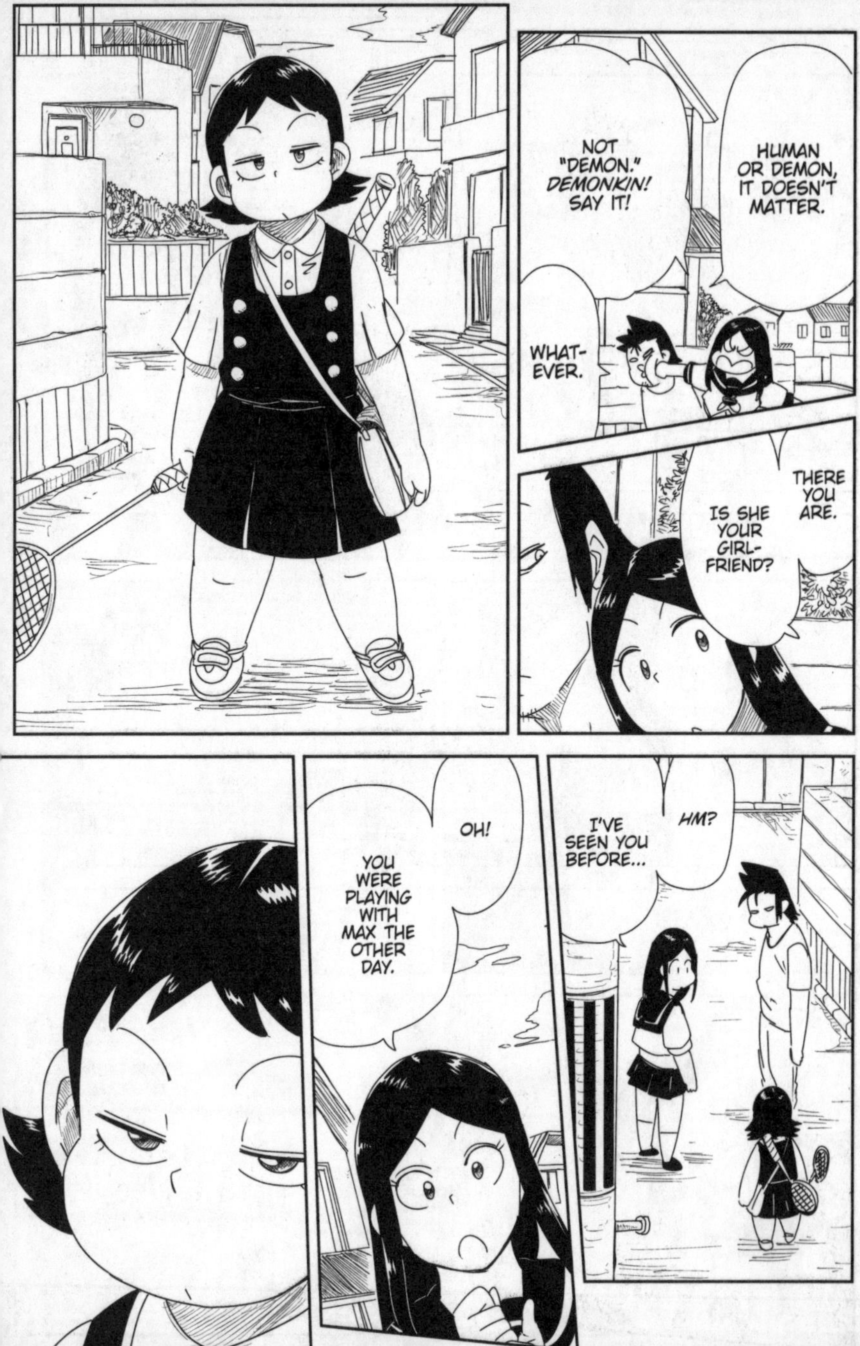
HUMAN OR DEMON, IT DOESN'T MATTER.
NOT "DEMON." *DEMONKIN!* SAY IT!
WHAT-EVER.
THERE YOU ARE.
IS SHE YOUR GIRL-FRIEND?
HM?
I'VE SEEN YOU BEFORE...
OH!
YOU WERE PLAYING WITH MAX THE OTHER DAY.

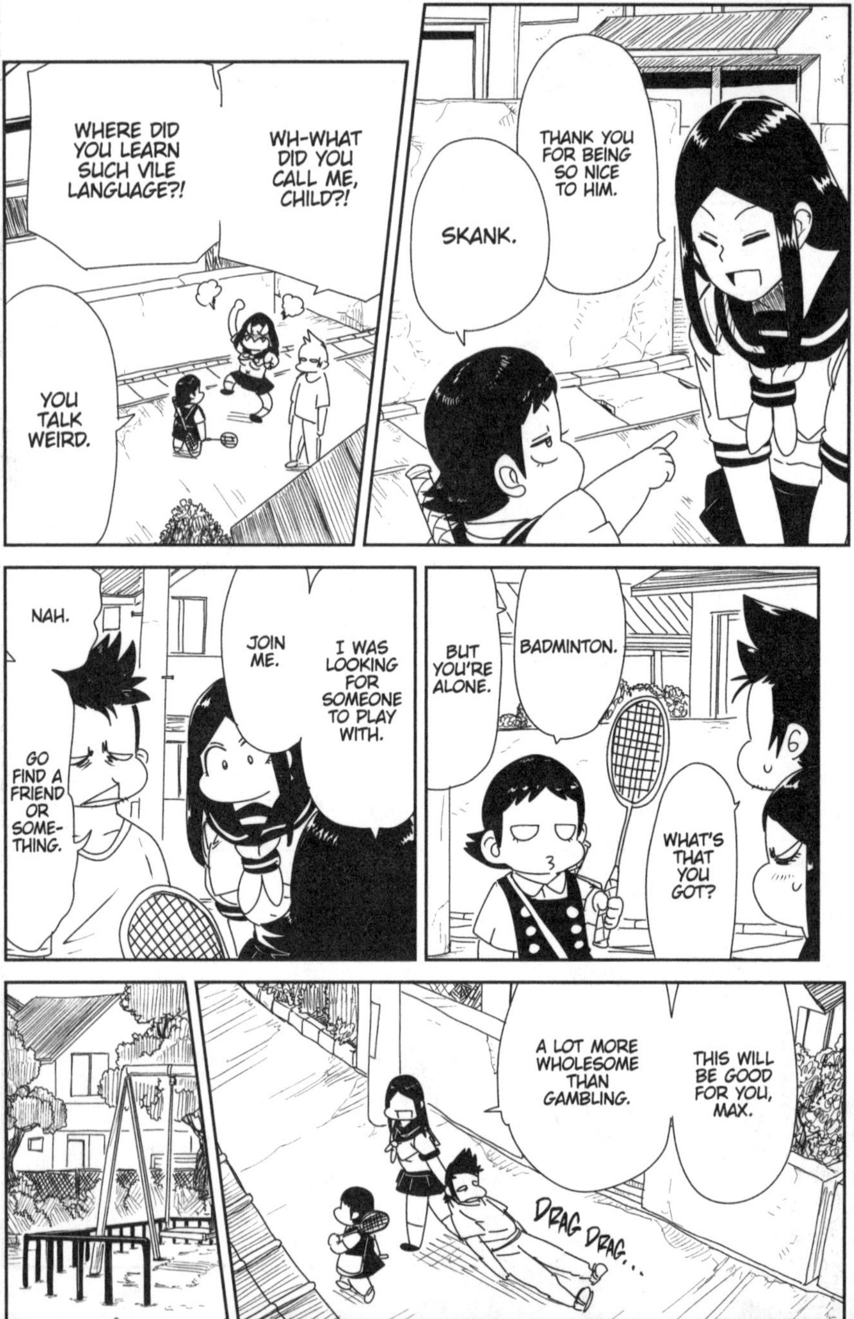
THANK YOU FOR BEING SO NICE TO HIM.
SKANK.
WH-WHAT DID YOU CALL ME, CHILD?!
WHERE DID YOU LEARN SUCH VILE LANGUAGE?!
YOU TALK WEIRD.
WHAT'S THAT YOU GOT?
BADMINTON.
BUT YOU'RE ALONE.
I WAS LOOKING FOR SOMEONE TO PLAY WITH.
JOIN ME.
NAH.
GO FIND A FRIEND OR SOME-THING.
THIS WILL BE GOOD FOR YOU, MAX.
A LOT MORE WHOLESOME THAN GAMBLING.
DRAG DRAG...

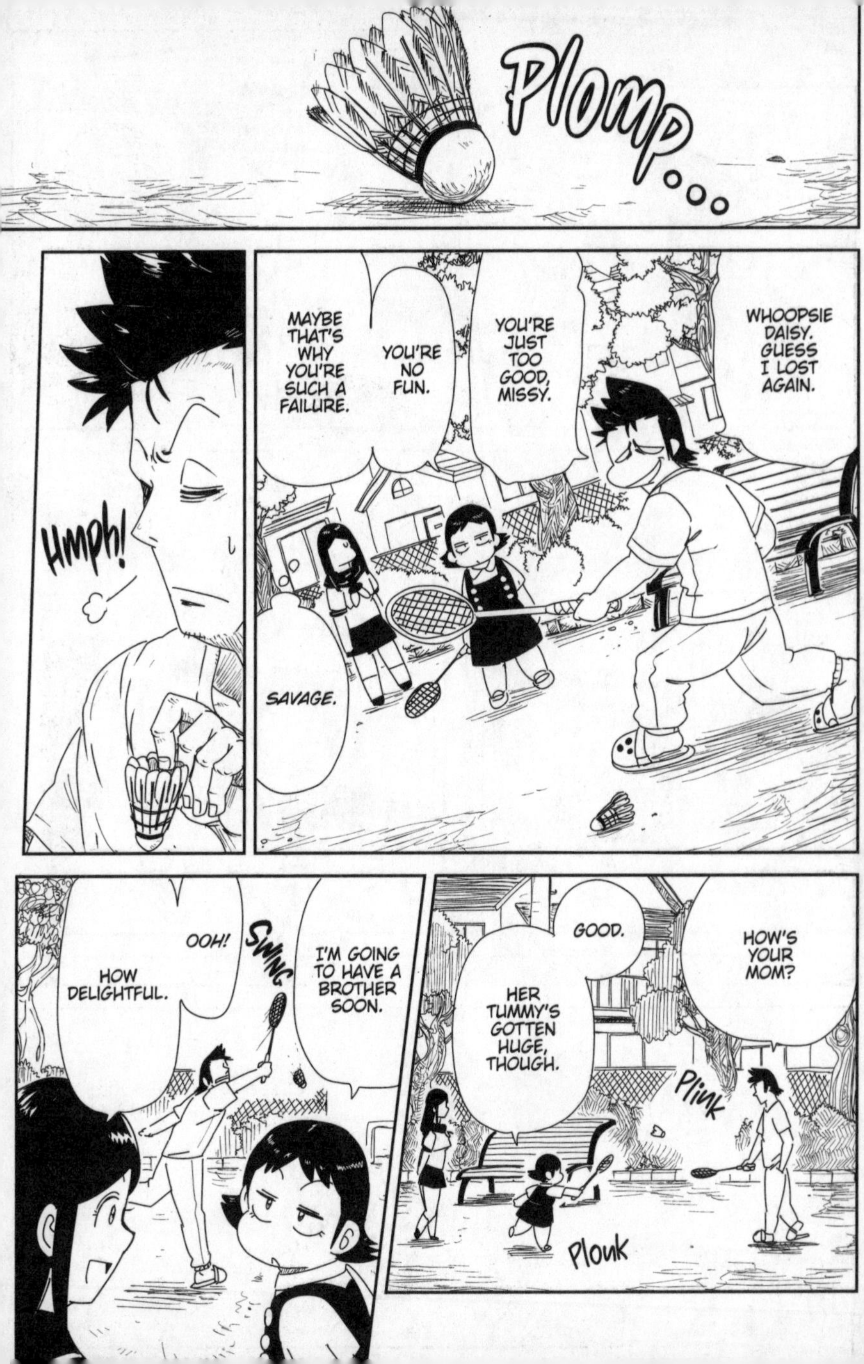
Plomp...
WHOOPSIE DAISY. GUESS I LOST AGAIN.
YOU'RE JUST TOO GOOD, MISSY.
YOU'RE NO FUN.
MAYBE THAT'S WHY YOU'RE SUCH A FAILURE.
SAVAGE.
Hmph!
HOW'S YOUR MOM?
GOOD.
HER TUMMY'S GOTTEN HUGE, THOUGH.
Plink
Plonk
I'M GOING TO HAVE A BROTHER SOON.
SWING
OOH!
HOW DELIGHTFUL.

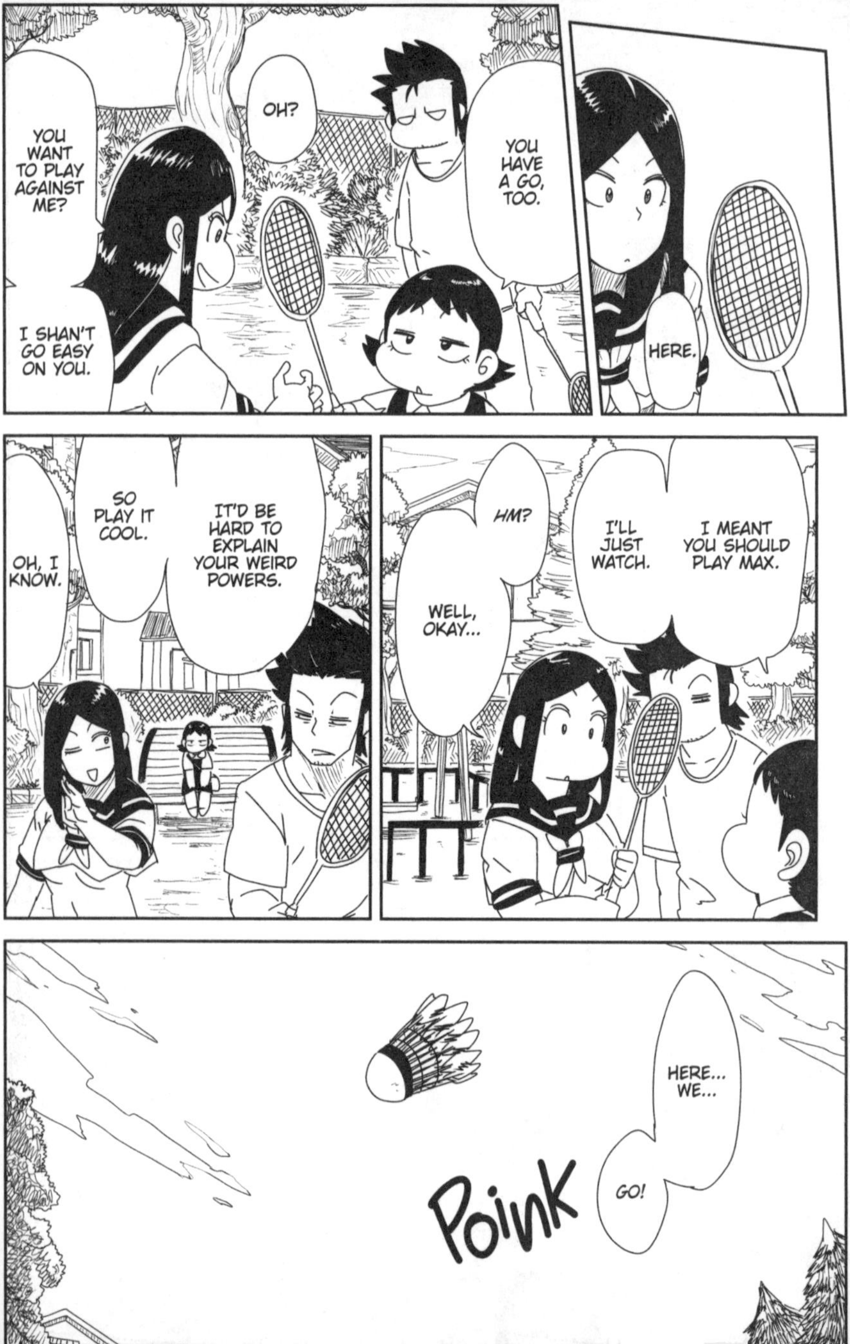
HERE.
YOU HAVE A GO, TOO.
OH?
YOU WANT TO PLAY AGAINST ME?
I SHAN'T GO EASY ON YOU.
I MEANT YOU SHOULD PLAY MAX.
I'LL JUST WATCH.
HM?
WELL, OKAY...
IT'D BE HARD TO EXPLAIN YOUR WEIRD POWERS.
SO PLAY IT COOL.
OH, I KNOW.
HERE... WE...
GO!
Poink

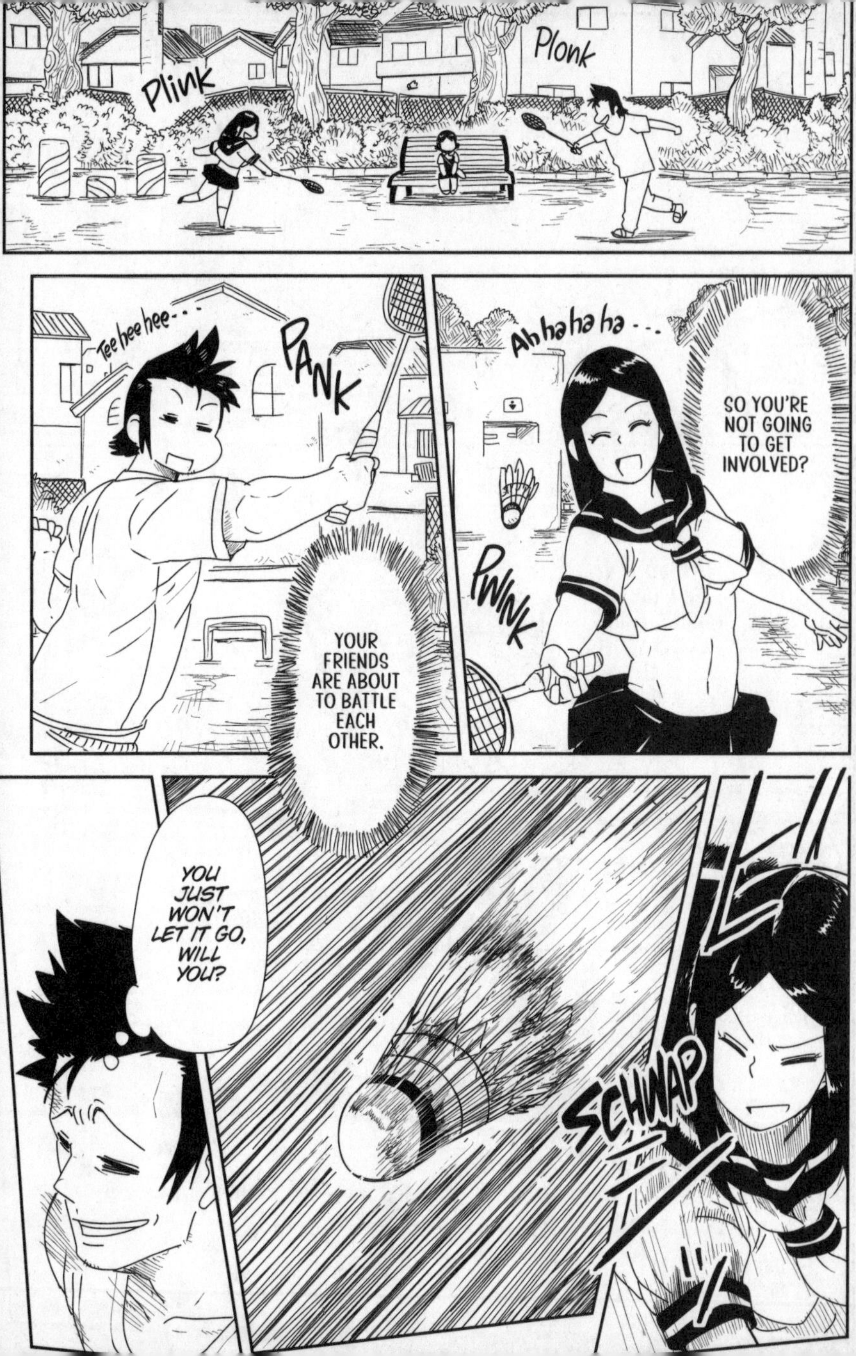
Plonk
Plink
Ah ha ha ha...
SO YOU'RE NOT GOING TO GET INVOLVED?
PWINK
Tee hee hee...
PANK
YOUR FRIENDS ARE ABOUT TO BATTLE EACH OTHER.
SCHWAP
YOU JUST WON'T LET IT GO, WILL YOU?

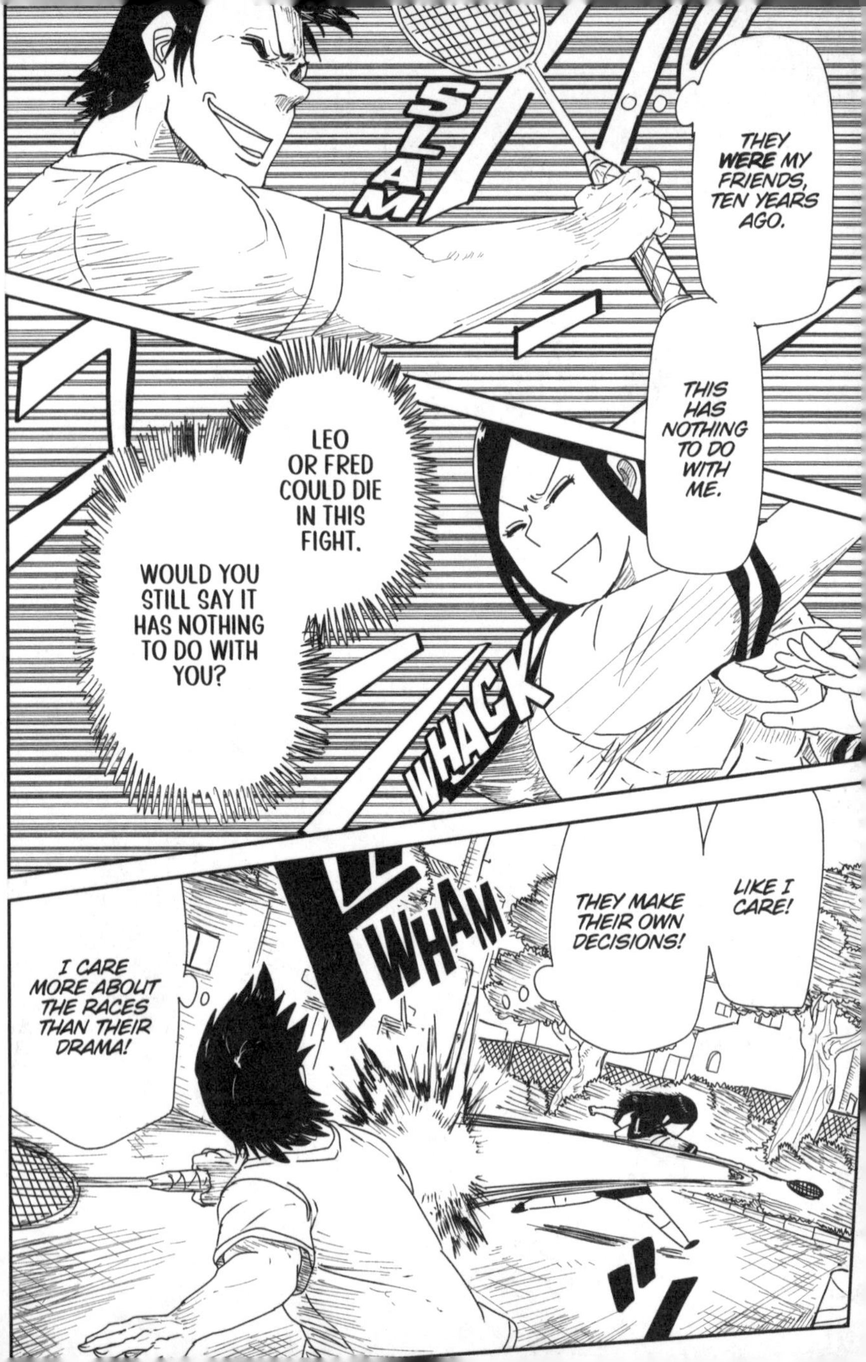
THEY WERE MY FRIENDS, TEN YEARS AGO.
SLAM
THIS HAS NOTHING TO DO WITH ME.
LEO OR FRED COULD DIE IN THIS FIGHT.
WOULD YOU STILL SAY IT HAS NOTHING TO DO WITH YOU?
WHACK
LIKE I CARE!
THEY MAKE THEIR OWN DECISIONS!
WHAM
I CARE MORE ABOUT THE RACES THAN THEIR DRAMA!

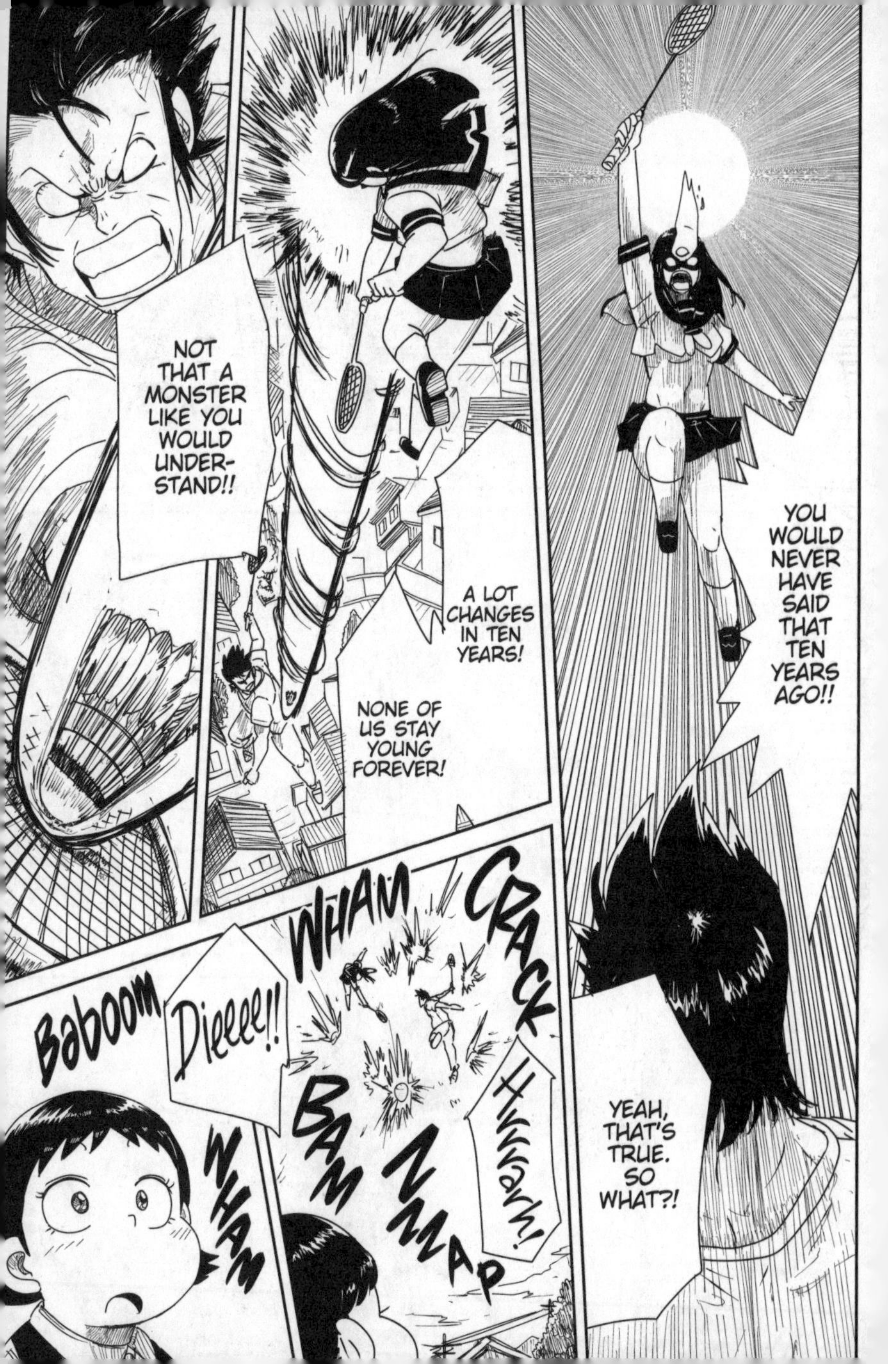
YOU WOULD NEVER HAVE SAID THAT TEN YEARS AGO!!
A LOT CHANGES IN TEN YEARS!
NONE OF US STAY YOUNG FOREVER!
NOT THAT A MONSTER LIKE YOU WOULD UNDER-STAND!!
YEAH, THAT'S TRUE. SO WHAT?!
CRACK
WHAM
Hwaah!
Dieeee!!
Baboom
BAM
WHAM

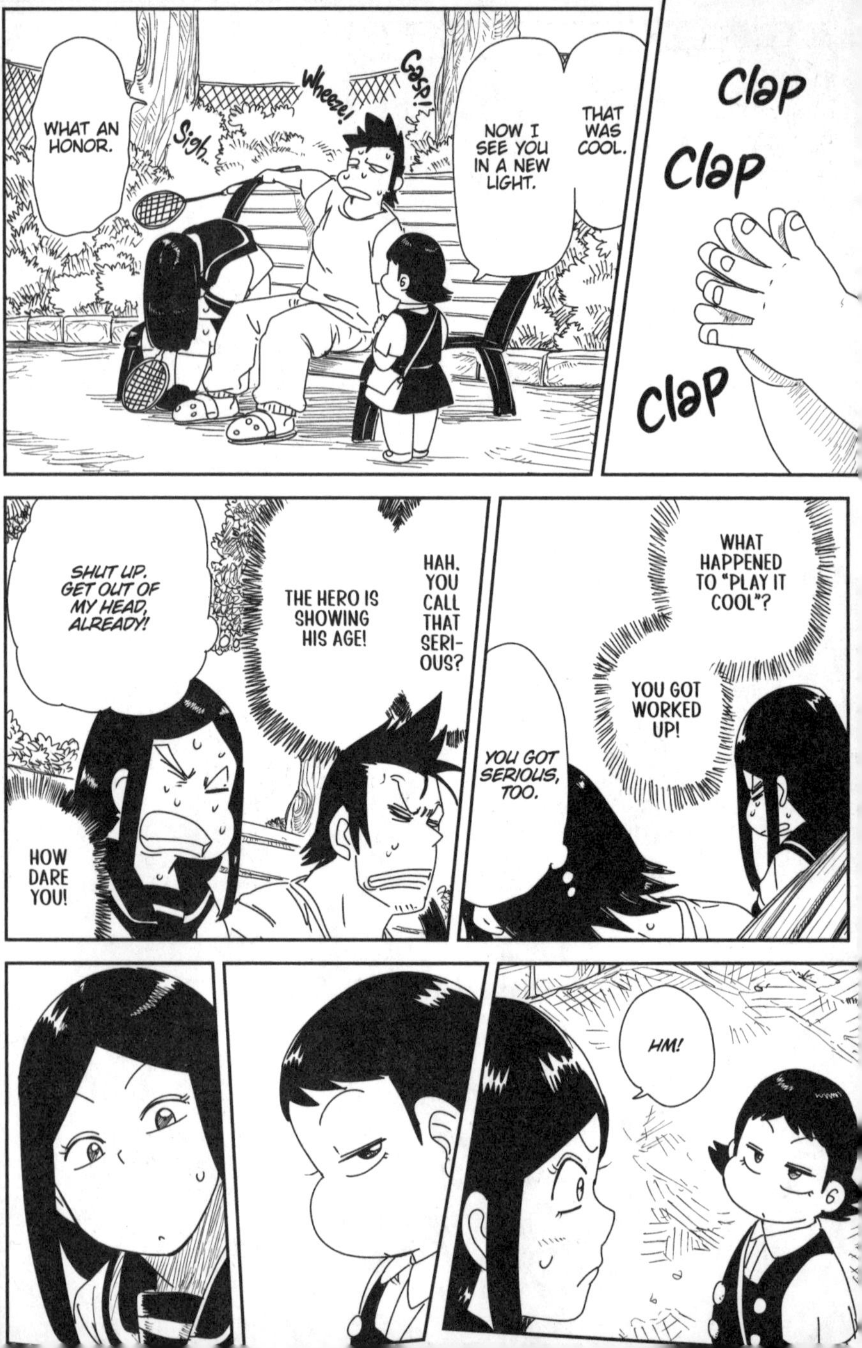
Clap
Clap
Clap
THAT WAS COOL.
NOW I SEE YOU IN A NEW LIGHT.
Gasp!
Wheeze!
Sigh...
WHAT AN HONOR.
WHAT HAPPENED TO "PLAY IT COOL"?
YOU GOT WORKED UP!
YOU GOT SERIOUS, TOO.
HAH. YOU CALL THAT SERI-OUS?
THE HERO IS SHOWING HIS AGE!
SHUT UP. GET OUT OF MY HEAD, ALREADY!
HOW DARE YOU!
HM!

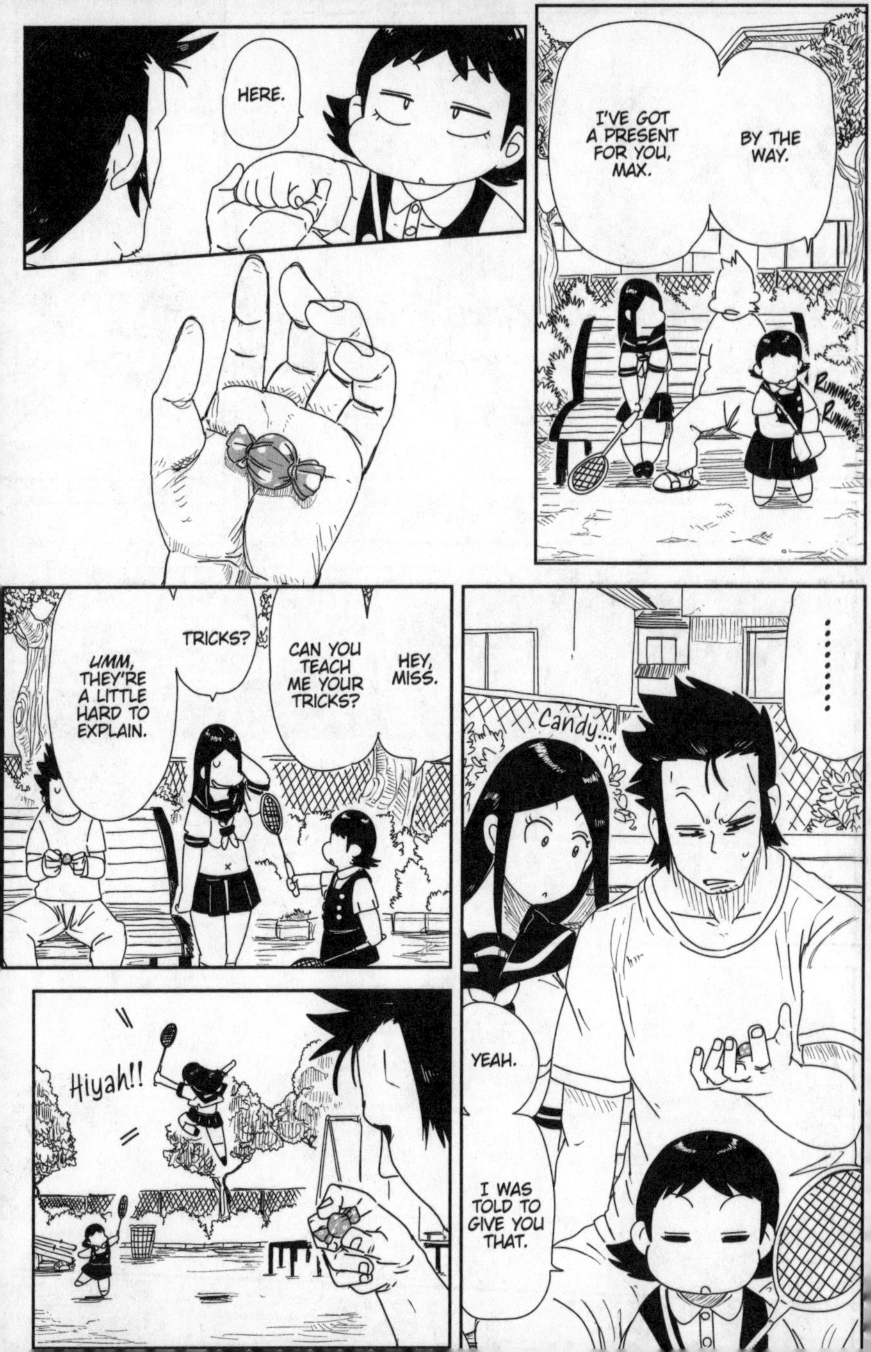
BY THE WAY.
I'VE GOT A PRESENT FOR YOU, MAX.
RUMMAGE RUMMAGE
HERE.
......
Candy...
YEAH.
I WAS TOLD TO GIVE YOU THAT.
HEY, MISS.
CAN YOU TEACH ME YOUR TRICKS?
TRICKS?
UMM, THEY'RE A LITTLE HARD TO EXPLAIN.
Hiyah!!

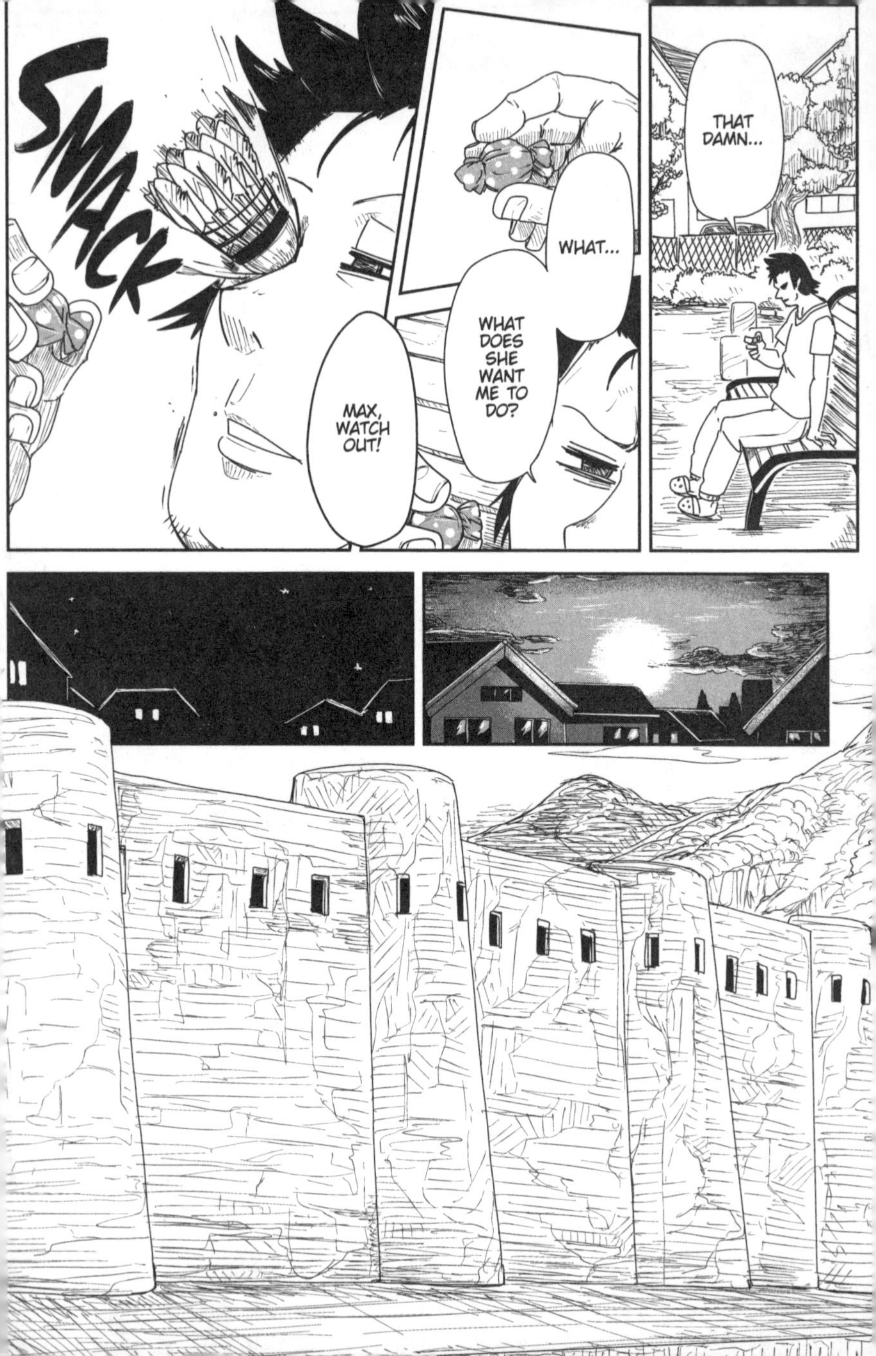
THAT DAMN...
WHAT...
WHAT DOES SHE WANT ME TO DO?
MAX, WATCH OUT!
SMACK

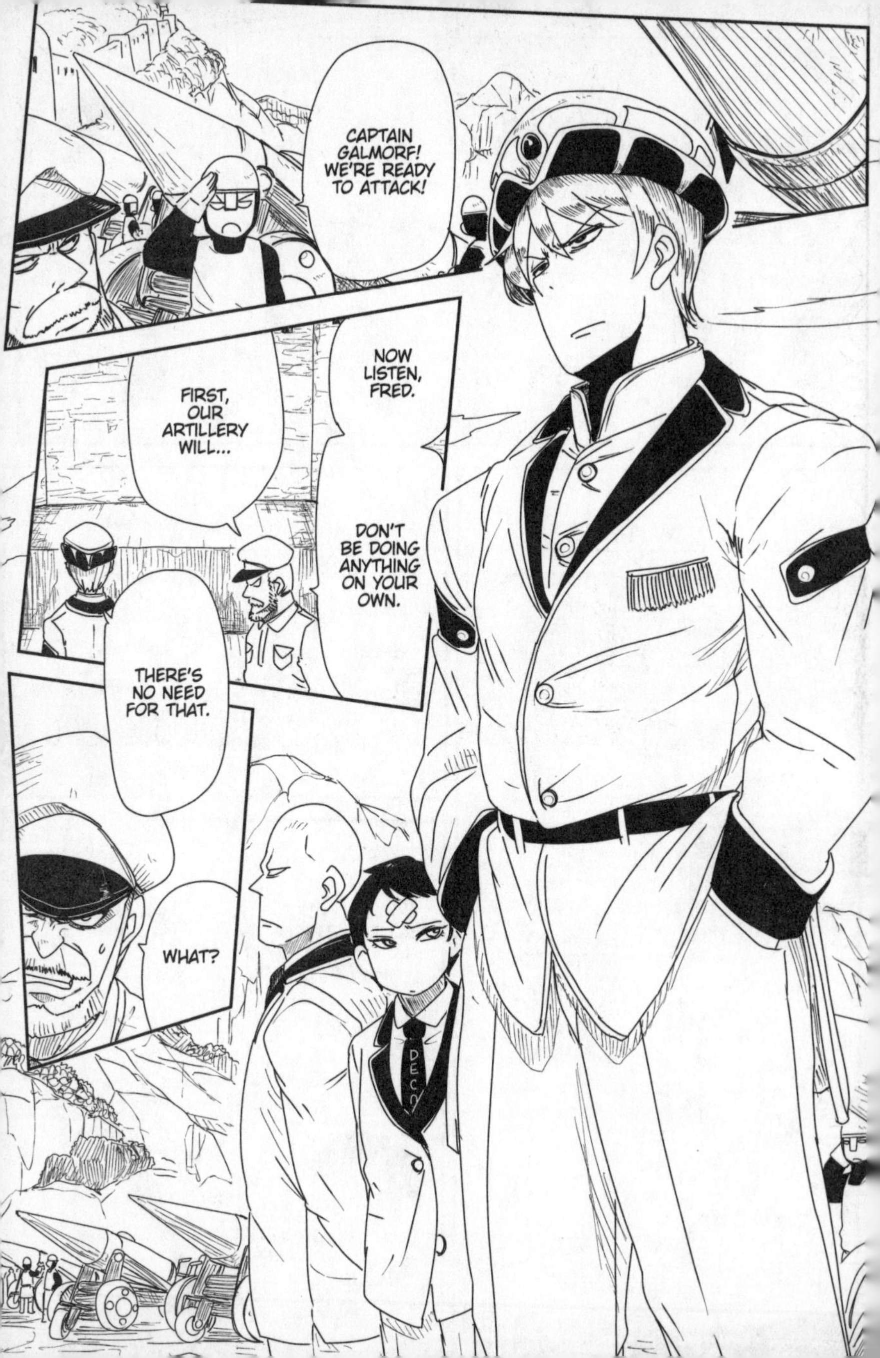

CAPTAIN GALMORF! WE'RE READY TO ATTACK!
NOW LISTEN, FRED.
FIRST, OUR ARTILLERY WILL...
DON'T BE DOING ANYTHING ON YOUR OWN.
THERE'S NO NEED FOR THAT.
WHAT?

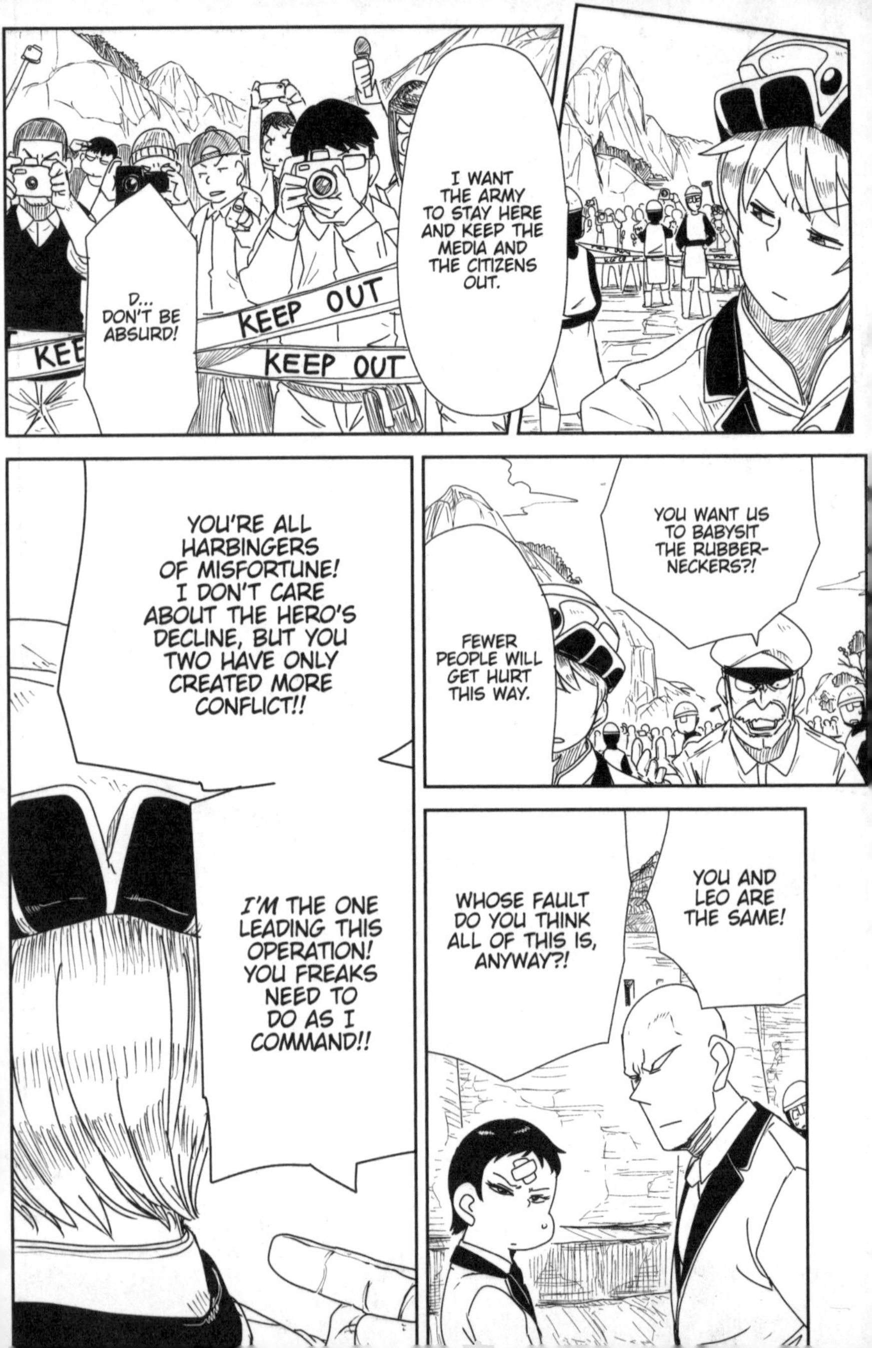
I WANT THE ARMY TO STAY HERE AND KEEP THE MEDIA AND THE CITIZENS OUT.
D... DON'T BE ABSURD!
KEEP OUT
KEEP OUT
KEE
YOU WANT US TO BABYSIT THE RUBBER-NECKERS?!
FEWER PEOPLE WILL GET HURT THIS WAY.
YOU'RE ALL HARBINGERS OF MISFORTUNE! I DON'T CARE ABOUT THE HERO'S DECLINE, BUT YOU TWO HAVE ONLY CREATED MORE CONFLICT!!
YOU AND LEO ARE THE SAME!
WHOSE FAULT DO YOU THINK ALL OF THIS IS, ANYWAY?!
I'M THE ONE LEADING THIS OPERATION! YOU FREAKS NEED TO DO AS I COMMAND!!

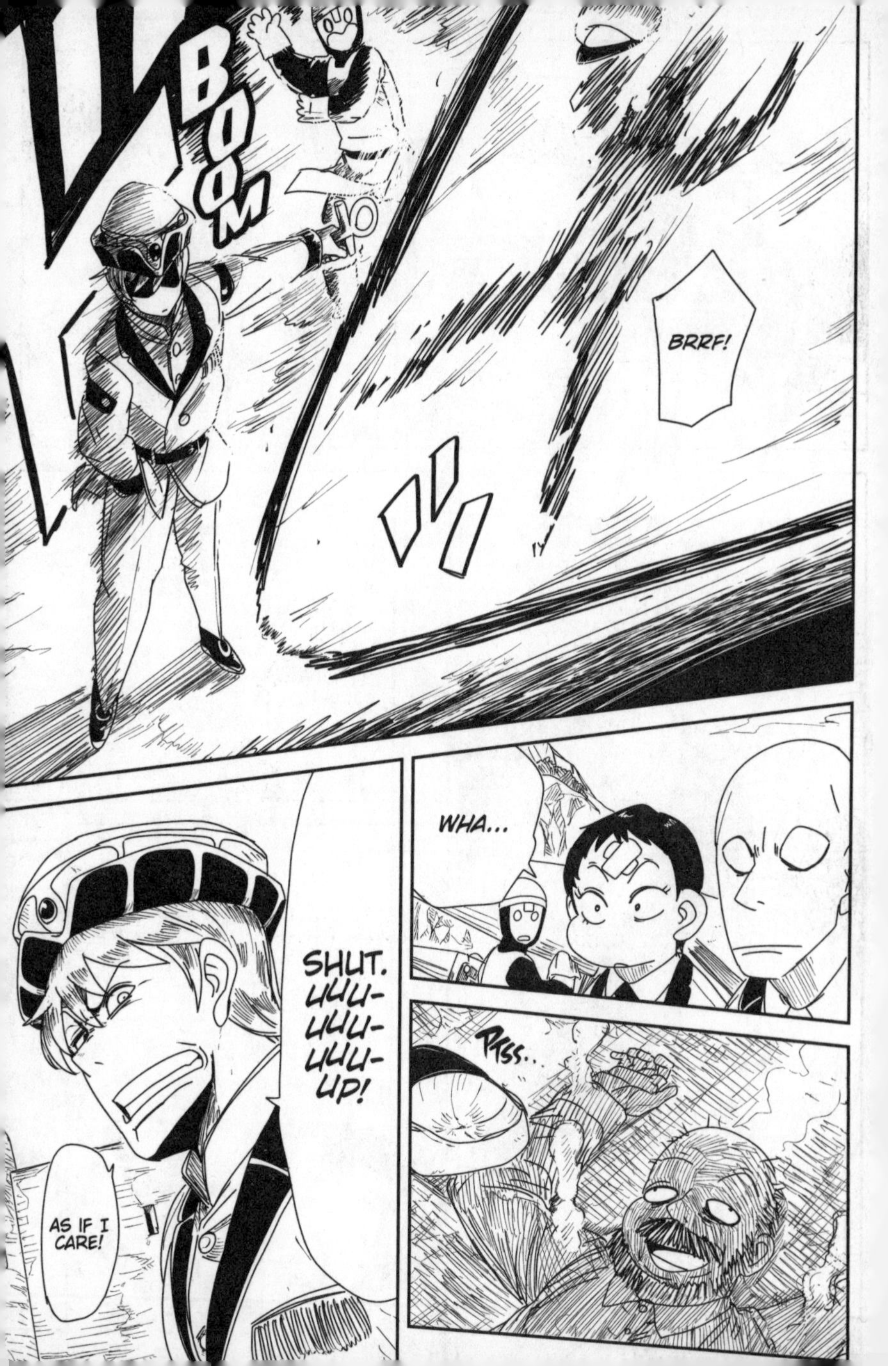
BOOM
BRRF!
WHA...
PSSS...
SHUT. UUUU-UUUU-UUUU-UP!
AS IF I CARE!

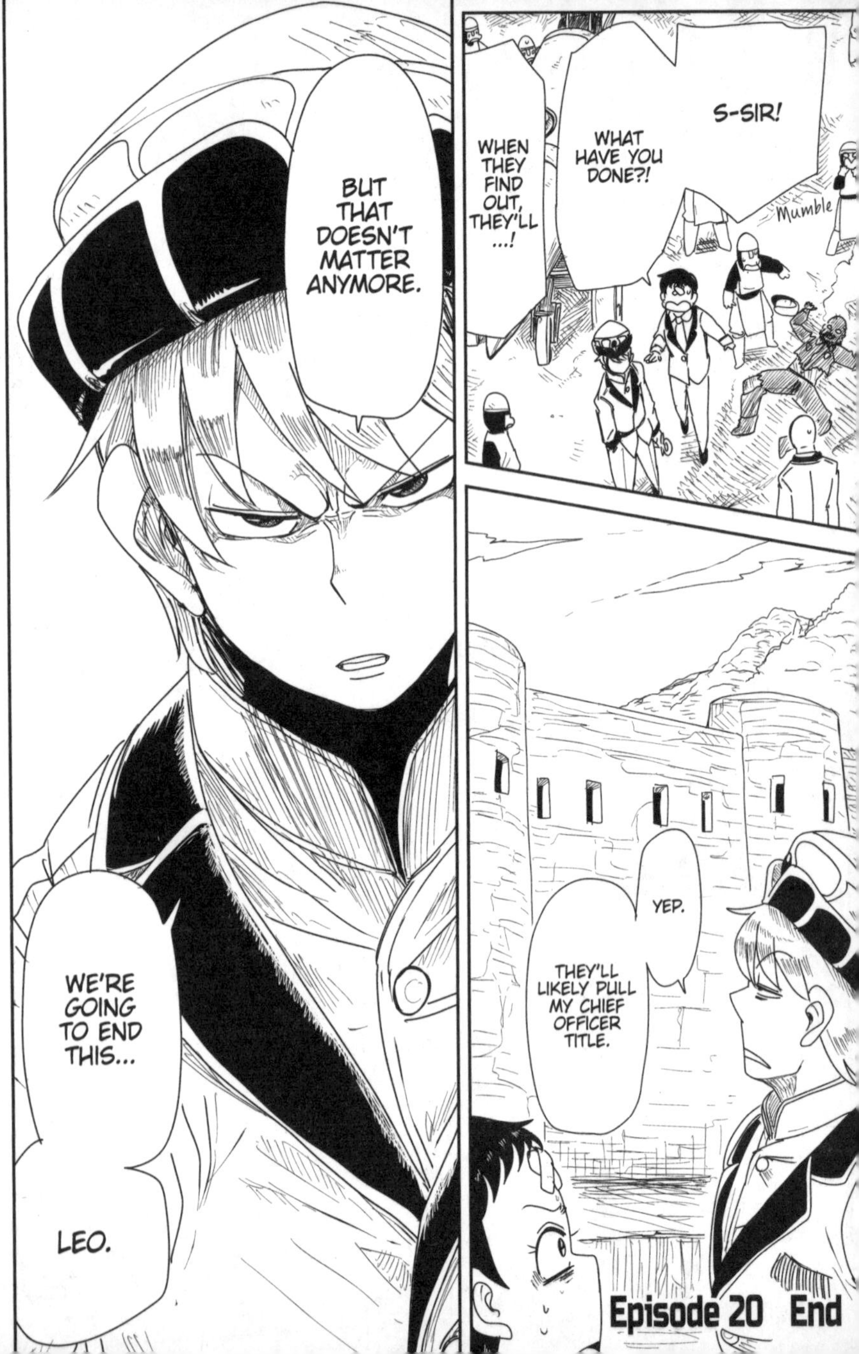
S-SIR!
WHAT HAVE YOU DONE?!
WHEN THEY FIND OUT, THEY'LL ...!
Mumble
YEP.
THEY'LL LIKELY PULL MY CHIEF OFFICER TITLE.
BUT THAT DOESN'T MATTER ANYMORE.
WE'RE GOING TO END THIS...
LEO.
Episode 20 End

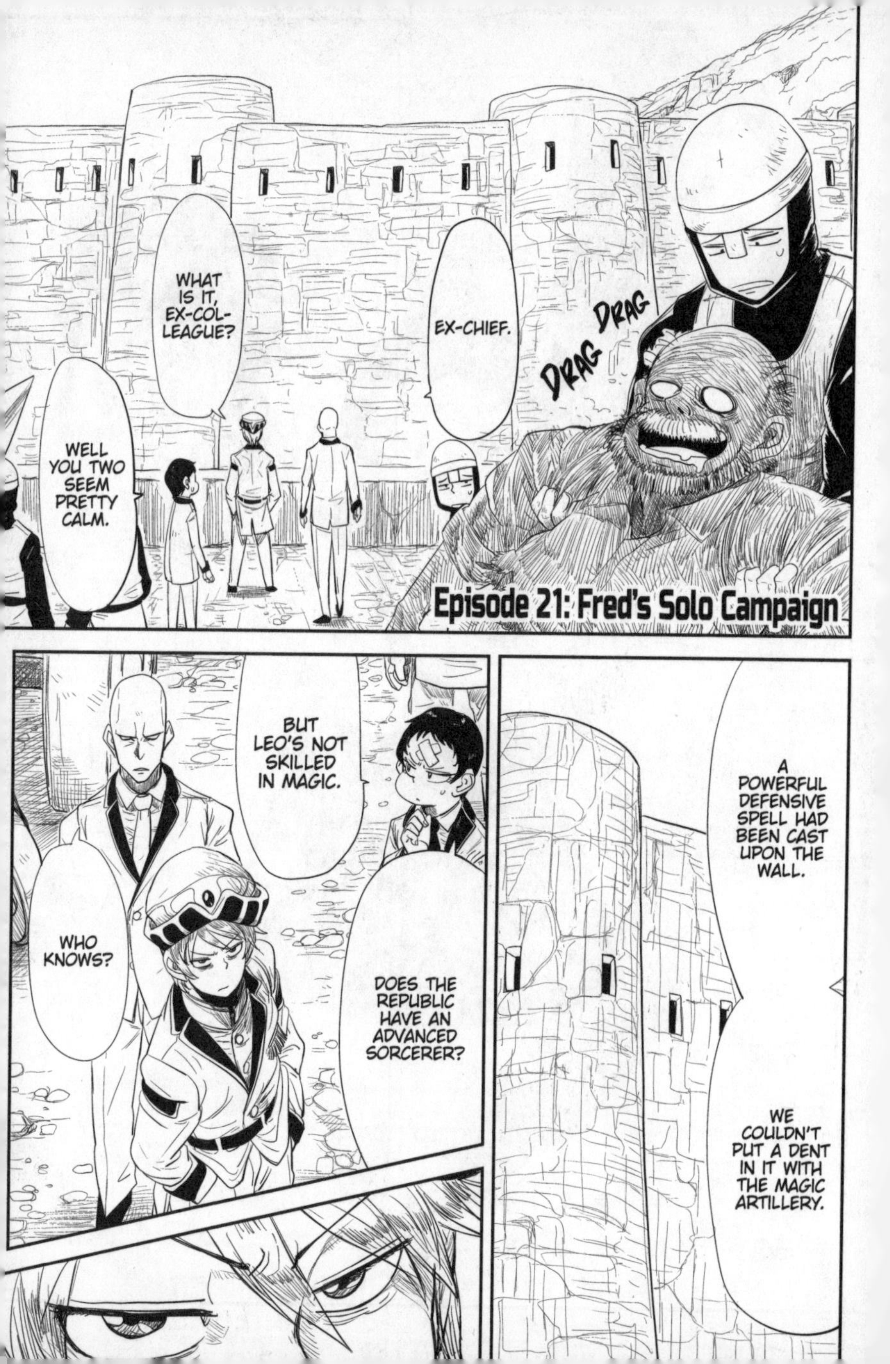
DRAG DRAG
EX-CHIEF.
WHAT IS IT, EX-COL-LEAGUE?
WELL YOU TWO SEEM PRETTY CALM.
Episode 21: Fred's Solo Campaign
A POWERFUL DEFENSIVE SPELL HAD BEEN CAST UPON THE WALL.
WE COULDN'T PUT A DENT IN IT WITH THE MAGIC ARTILLERY.
BUT LEO'S NOT SKILLED IN MAGIC.
DOES THE REPUBLIC HAVE AN ADVANCED SORCERER?
WHO KNOWS?

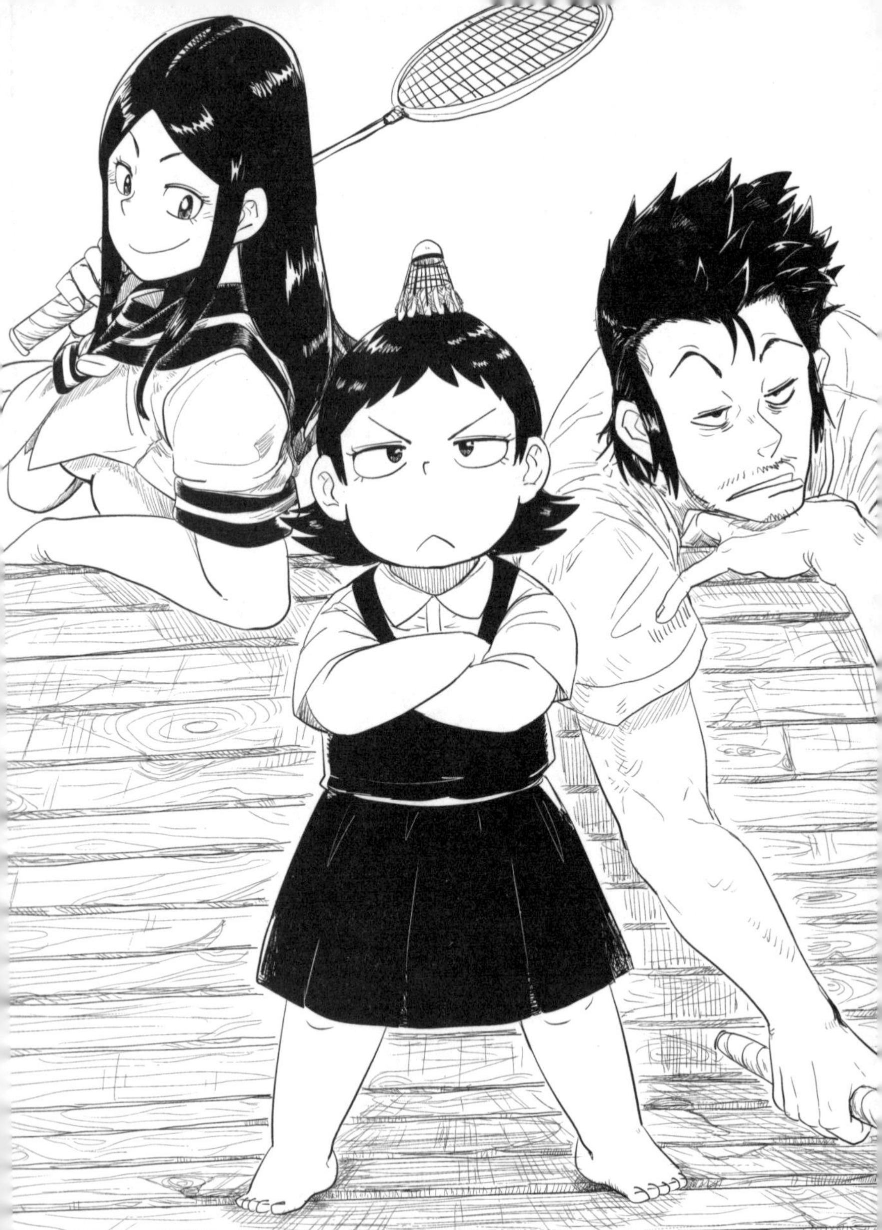

Episode 21 Fred's Solo Campaign

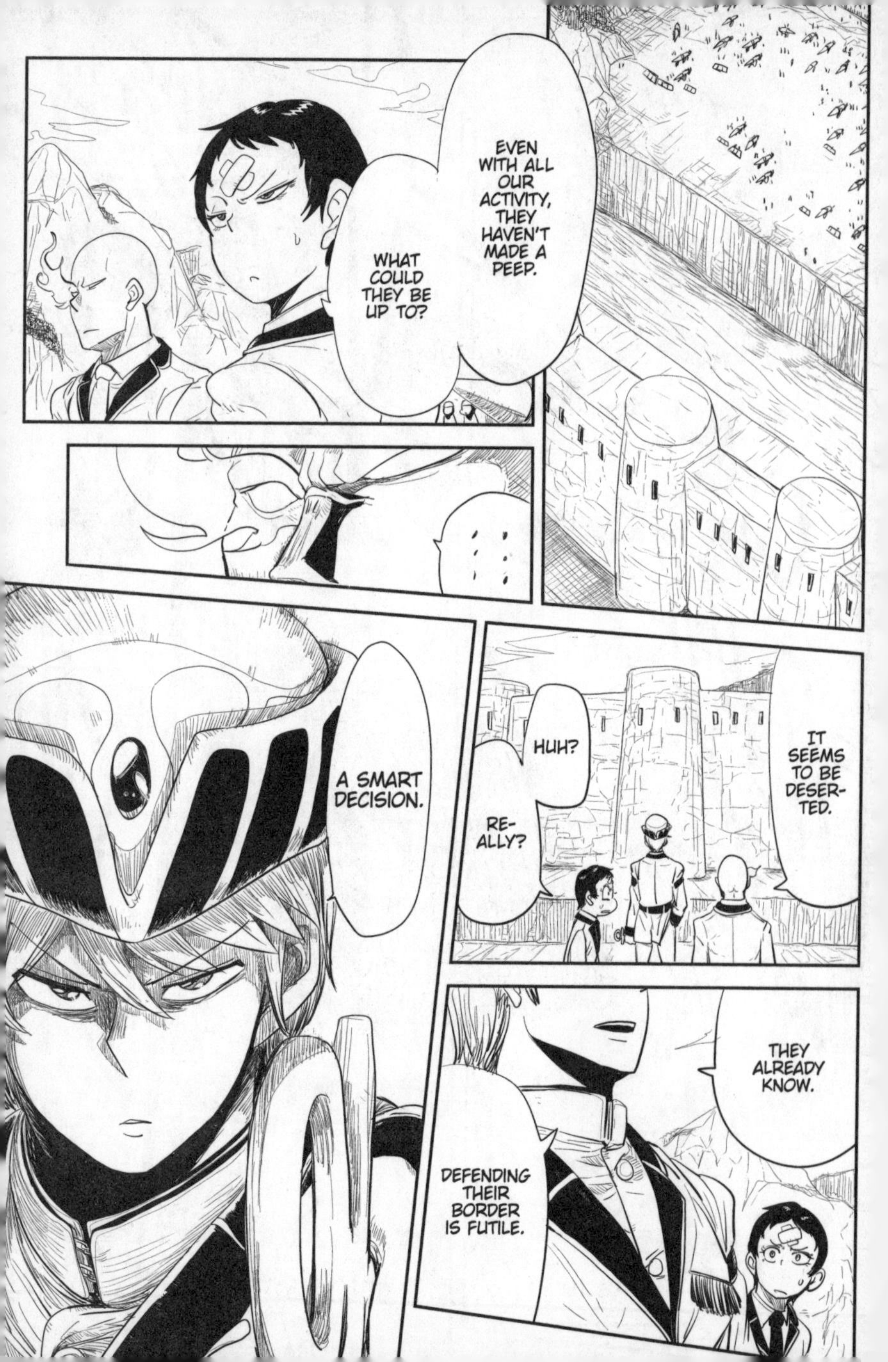
EVEN WITH ALL OUR ACTIVITY, THEY HAVEN'T MADE A PEEP.
WHAT COULD THEY BE UP TO?
...
IT SEEMS TO BE DESER-TED.
HUH?
RE-ALLY?
THEY ALREADY KNOW.
DEFENDING THEIR BORDER IS FUTILE.
A SMART DECISION.

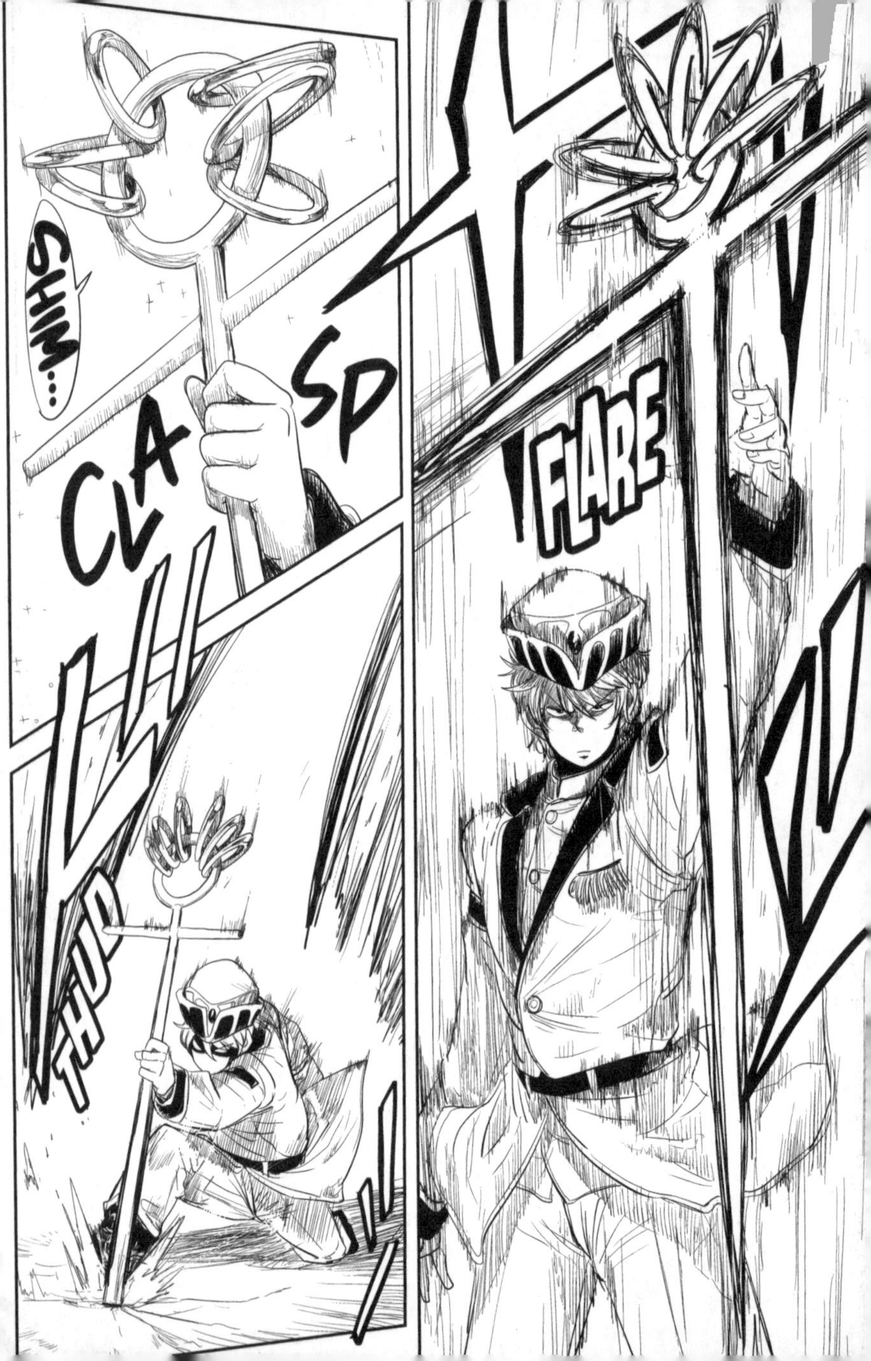
SHIM...
CLASP
THUD
FLARE

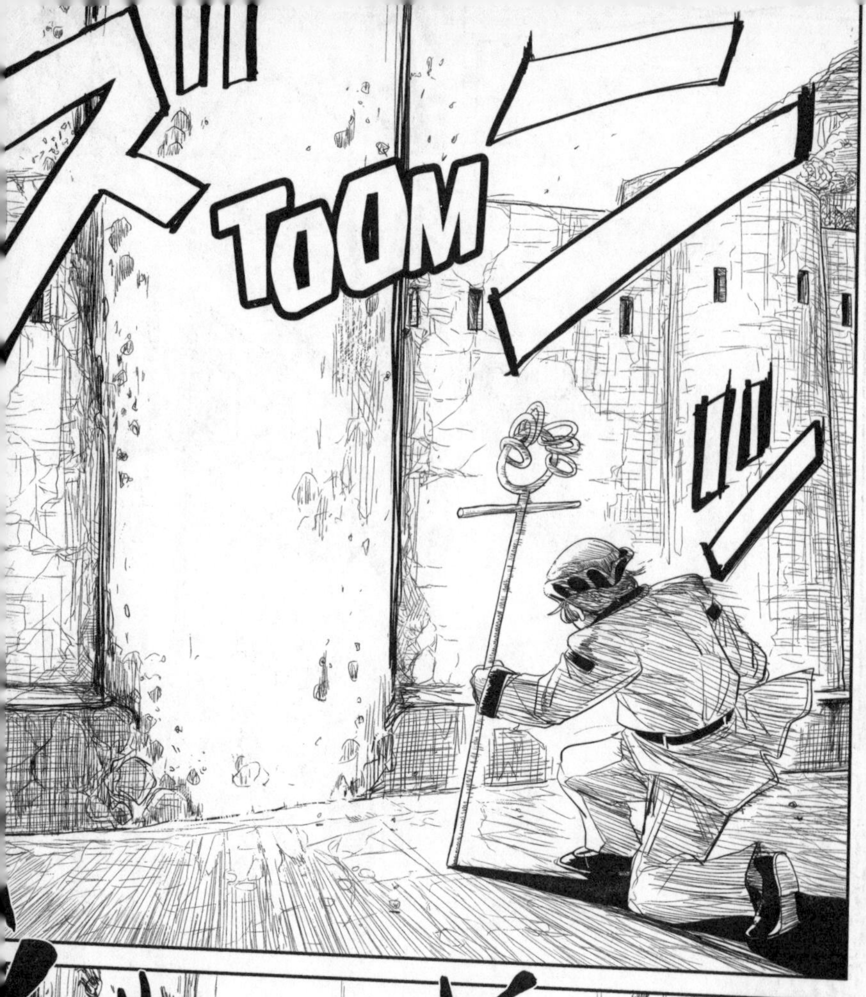
ズ
TOOM
ン

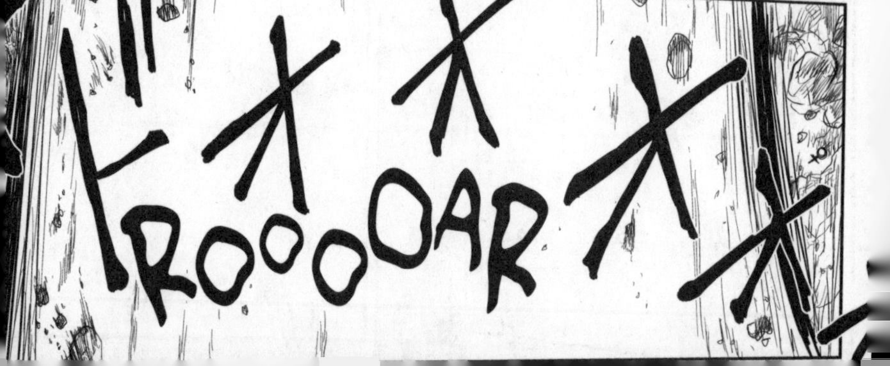
ドオオオオ
ROOOOAR

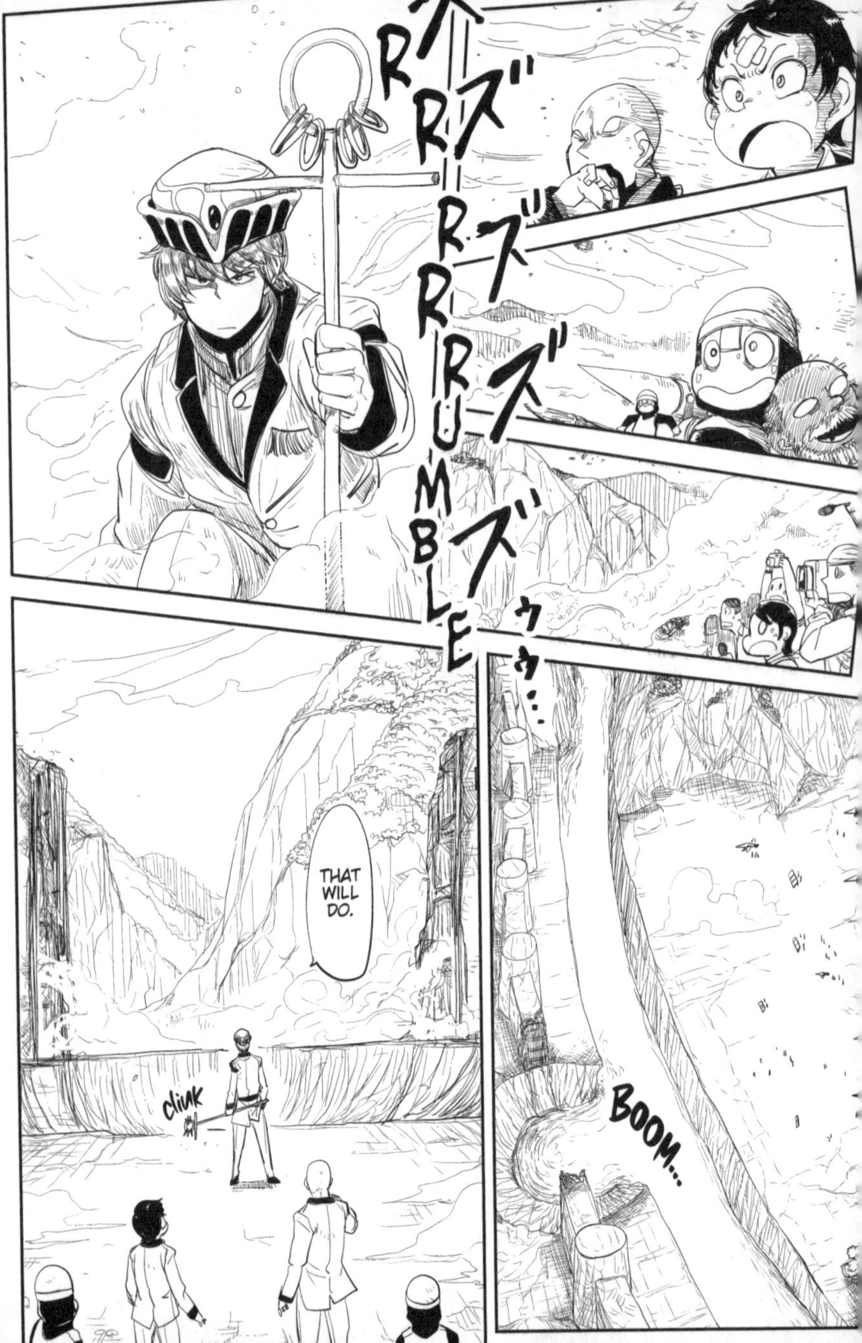
RRRRRRUMBLE
ズズズズ
ウゥ…
BOOM...
THAT WILL DO.
clink

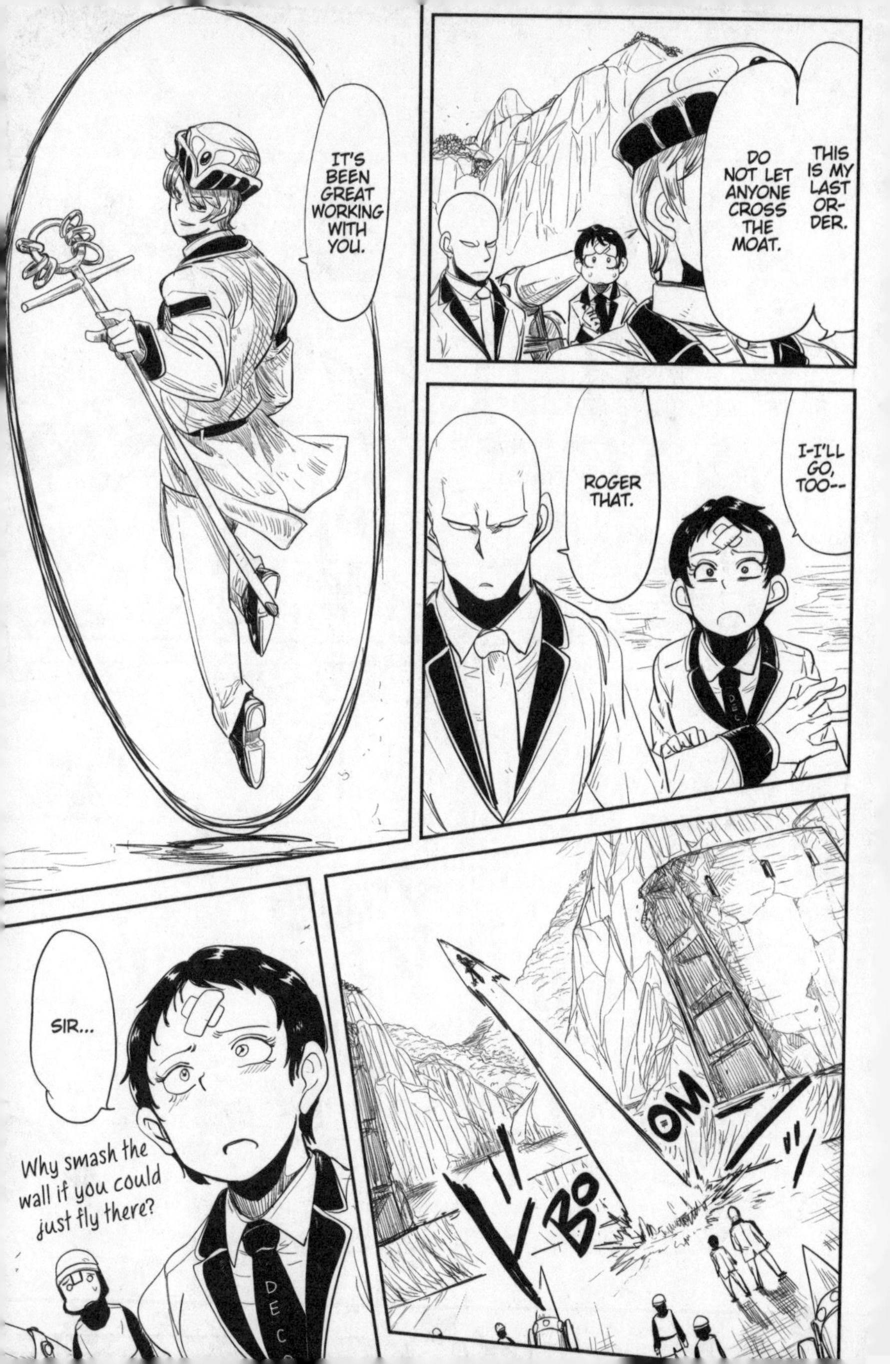
THIS IS MY LAST ORDER.
DO NOT LET ANYONE CROSS THE MOAT.
I-I'LL GO, TOO--
ROGER THAT.
IT'S BEEN GREAT WORKING WITH YOU.
BOOM
SIR...
Why smash the wall if you could just fly there?

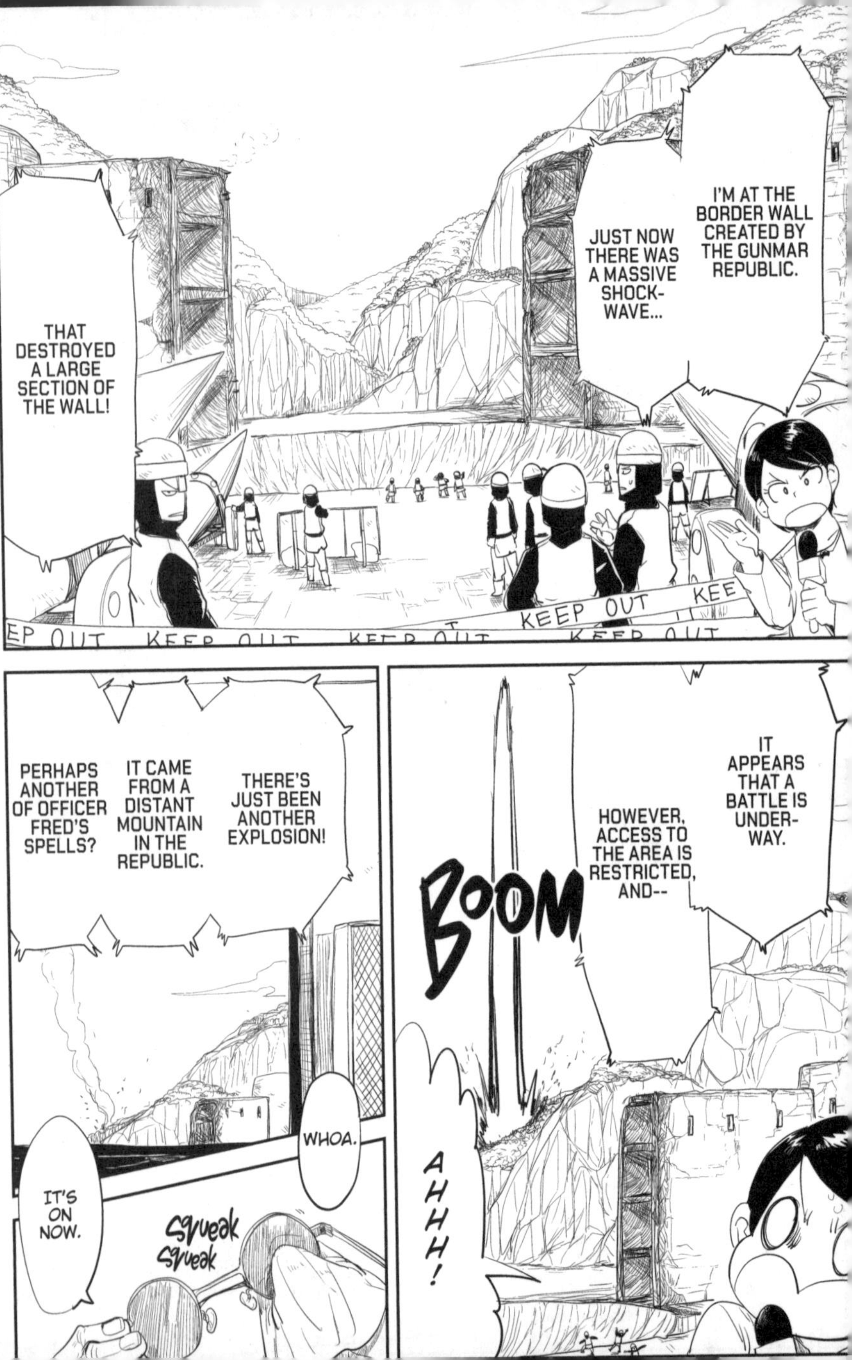
I'M AT THE BORDER WALL CREATED BY THE GUNMAR REPUBLIC.
JUST NOW THERE WAS A MASSIVE SHOCK-WAVE...
THAT DESTROYED A LARGE SECTION OF THE WALL!
KEEP OUT KEE
IT APPEARS THAT A BATTLE IS UNDER-WAY.
HOWEVER, ACCESS TO THE AREA IS RESTRICTED, AND--
BOOM
AHHH!
THERE'S JUST BEEN ANOTHER EXPLOSION!
IT CAME FROM A DISTANT MOUNTAIN IN THE REPUBLIC.
PERHAPS ANOTHER OF OFFICER FRED'S SPELLS?
WHOA.
IT'S ON NOW.
squeak squeak

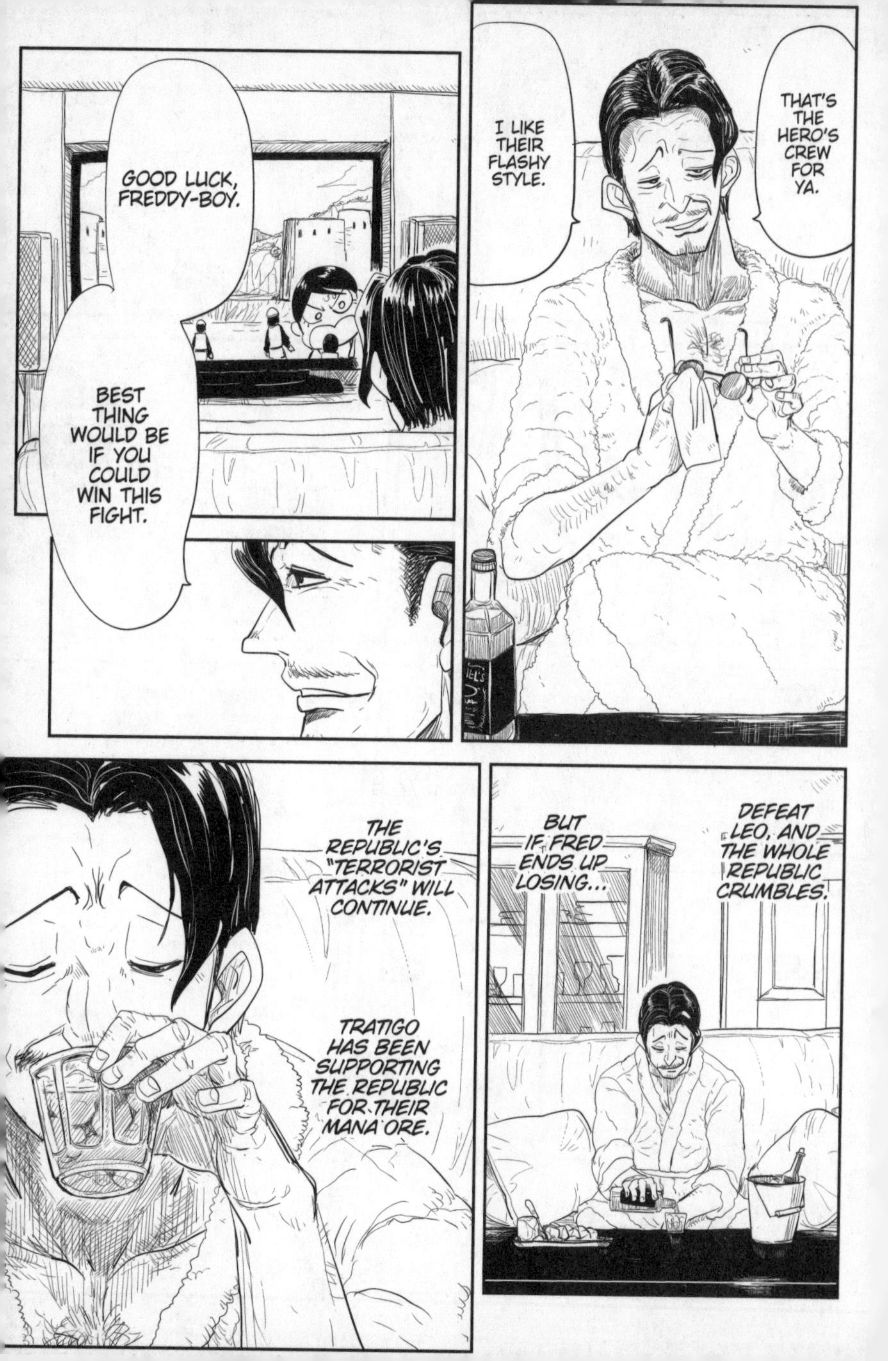
GOOD LUCK, FREDDY-BOY.
BEST THING WOULD BE IF YOU COULD WIN THIS FIGHT.
I LIKE THEIR FLASHY STYLE.
THAT'S THE HERO'S CREW FOR YA.
THE REPUBLIC'S "TERRORIST ATTACKS" WILL CONTINUE.
TRATIGO HAS BEEN SUPPORTING THE REPUBLIC FOR THEIR MANA ORE.
BUT IF FRED ENDS UP LOSING...
DEFEAT LEO, AND THE WHOLE REPUBLIC CRUMBLES.

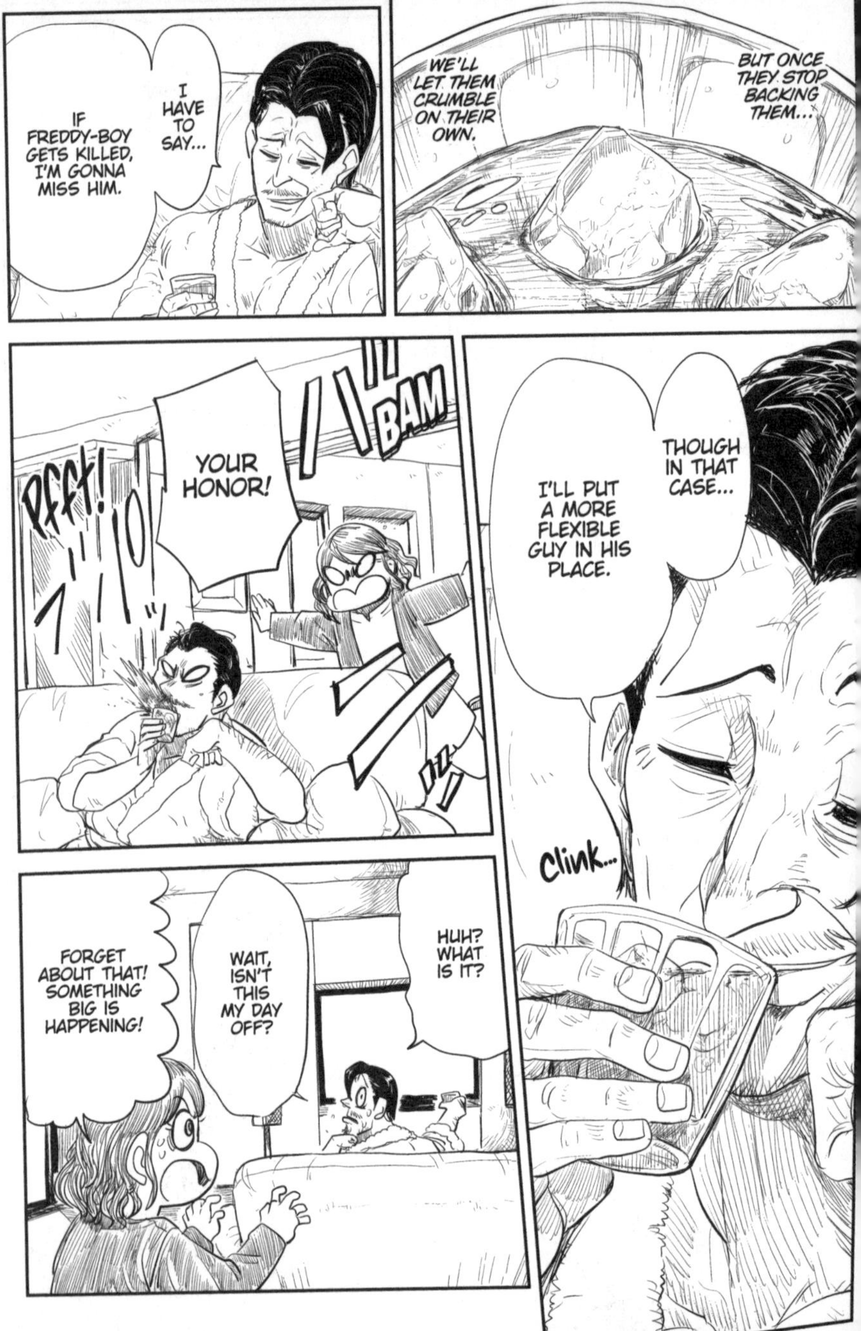
BUT ONCE THEY STOP BACKING THEM...
WE'LL LET THEM CRUMBLE ON THEIR OWN.
I HAVE TO SAY...
IF FREDDY-BOY GETS KILLED, I'M GONNA MISS HIM.
THOUGH IN THAT CASE...
I'LL PUT A MORE FLEXIBLE GUY IN HIS PLACE.
Clink...
BAM
YOUR HONOR!
Pfft!
HUH? WHAT IS IT?
WAIT, ISN'T THIS MY DAY OFF?
FORGET ABOUT THAT! SOMETHING BIG IS HAPPENING!

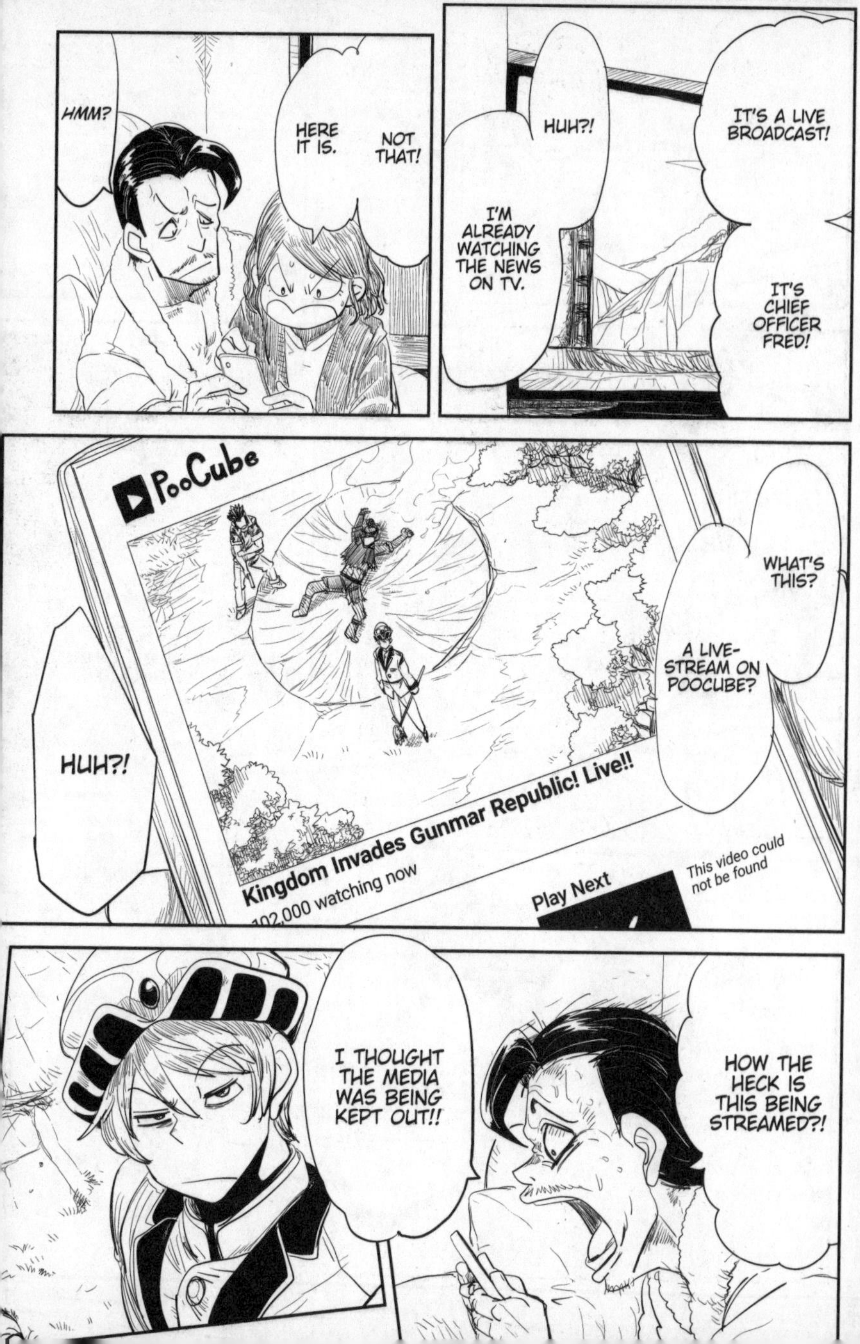
IT'S A LIVE BROADCAST!
IT'S CHIEF OFFICER FRED!
HUH?!
I'M ALREADY WATCHING THE NEWS ON TV.
NOT THAT!
HERE IT IS.
HMM?
WHAT'S THIS?
A LIVE-STREAM ON POOCUBE?
PooCube
Kingdom Invades Gunmar Republic! Live!!
102,000 watching now
Play Next
This video could not be found
HUH?!
HOW THE HECK IS THIS BEING STREAMED?!
I THOUGHT THE MEDIA WAS BEING KEPT OUT!!

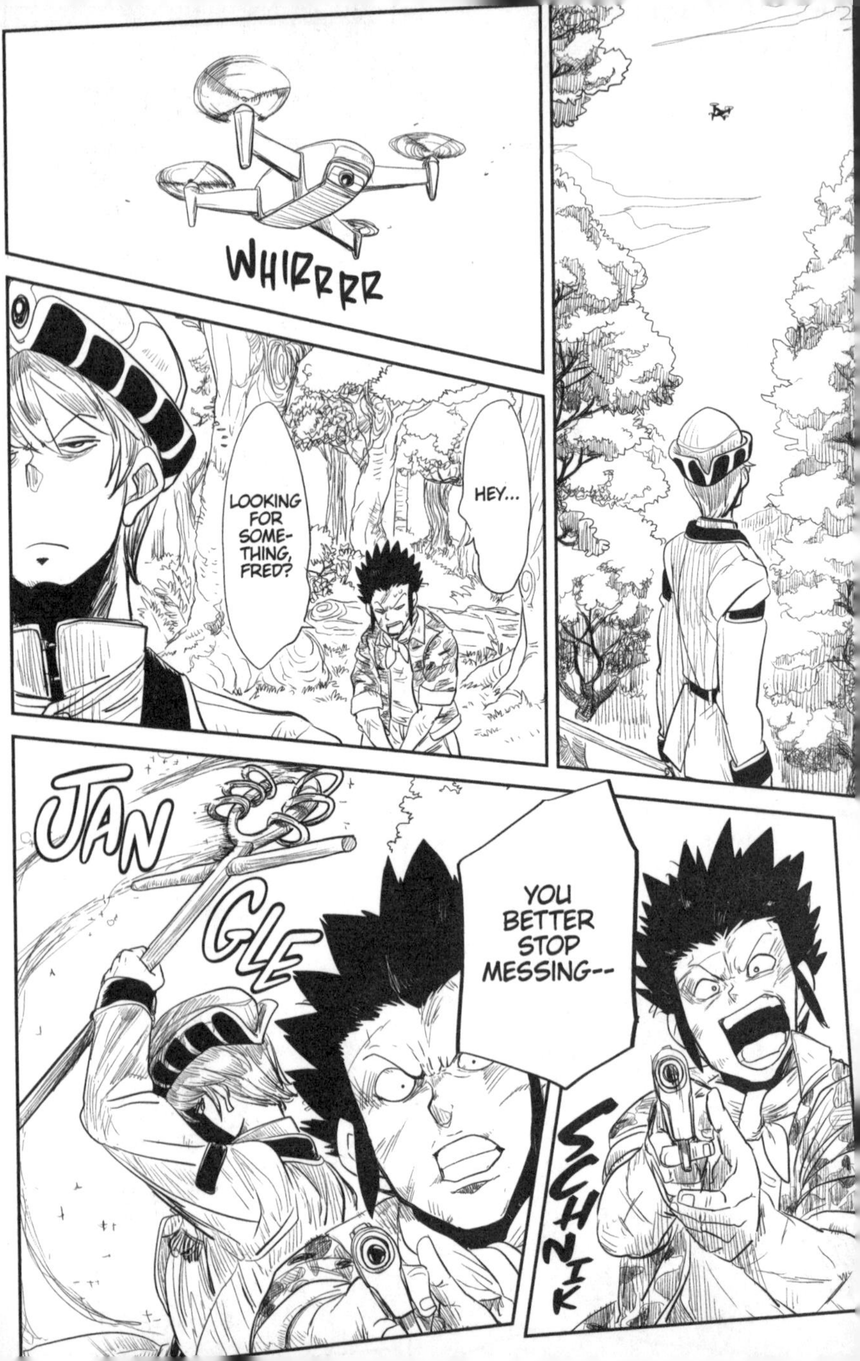
WHIRRRR
HEY...
LOOKING FOR SOME-THING, FRED?
YOU BETTER STOP MESSING--
SCHNIK
JANGLE

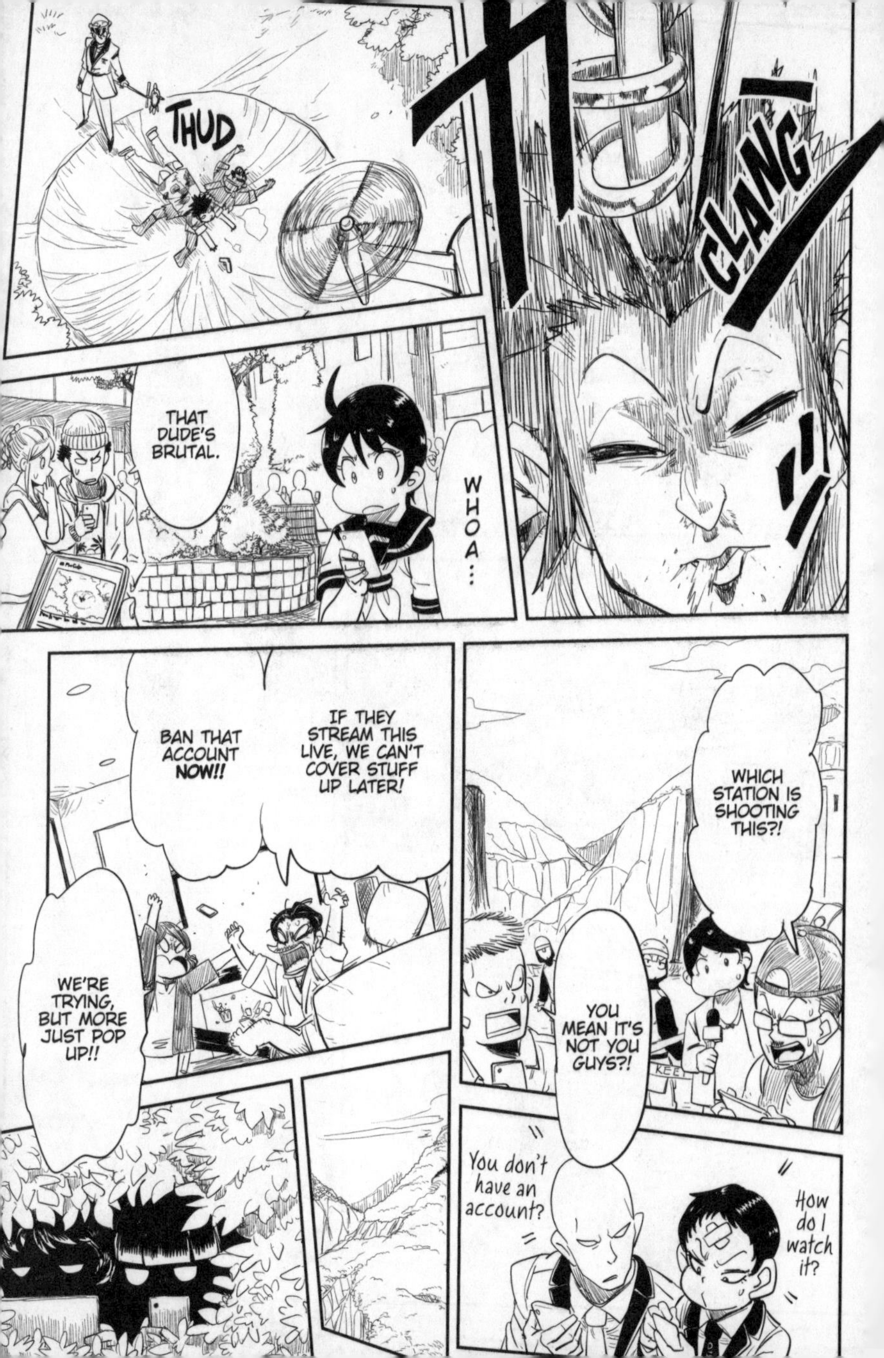
CLANG
THUD
WHOA...
THAT DUDE'S BRUTAL.
WHICH STATION IS SHOOTING THIS?!
YOU MEAN IT'S NOT YOU GUYS?!
IF THEY STREAM THIS LIVE, WE CAN'T COVER STUFF UP LATER!
BAN THAT ACCOUNT NOW!!
WE'RE TRYING, BUT MORE JUST POP UP!!
How do I watch it?
You don't have an account?

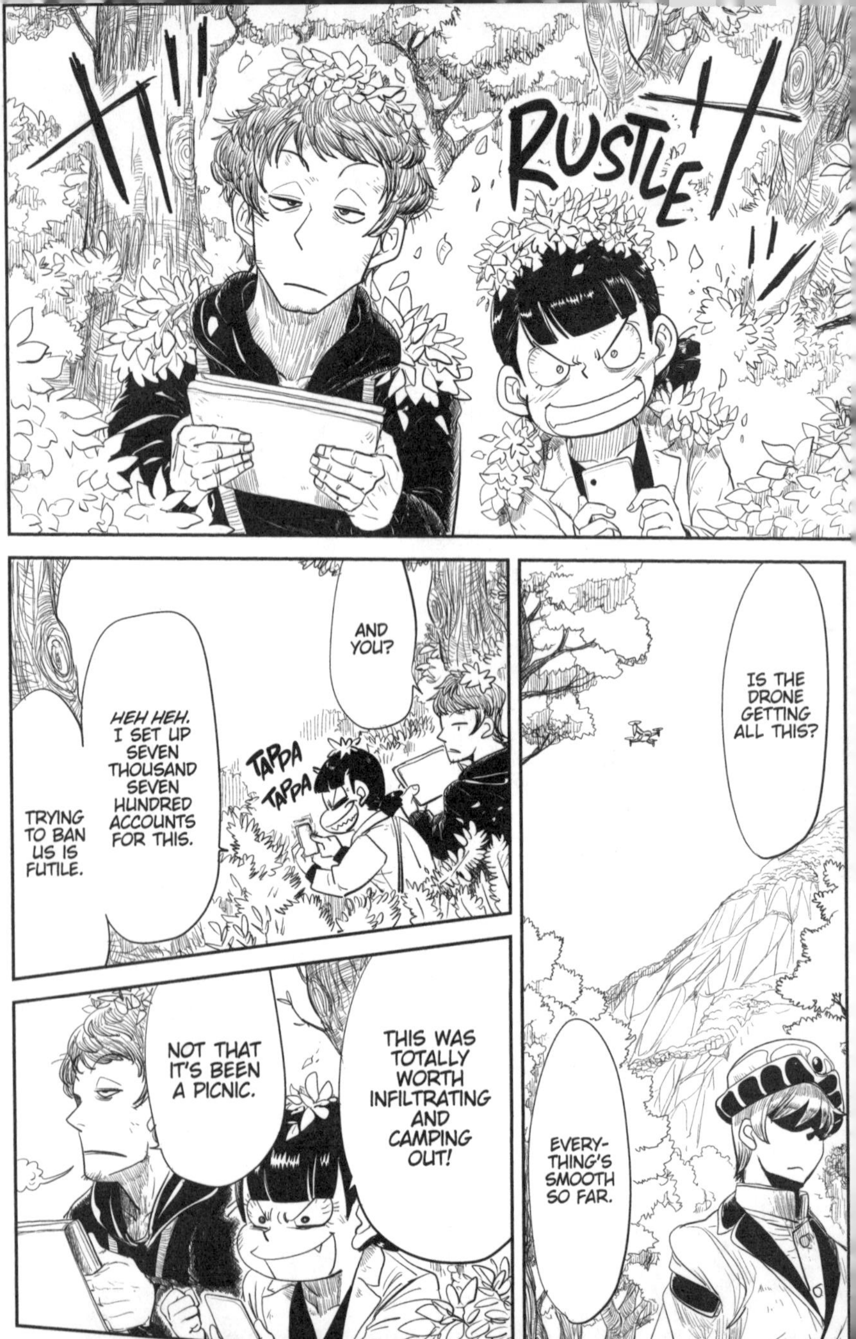
RUSTLE
IS THE DRONE GETTING ALL THIS?
EVERY-THING'S SMOOTH SO FAR.
AND YOU?
TAPPA TAPPA
HEH HEH. I SET UP SEVEN THOUSAND SEVEN HUNDRED ACCOUNTS FOR THIS.
TRYING TO BAN US IS FUTILE.
THIS WAS TOTALLY WORTH INFILTRATING AND CAMPING OUT!
NOT THAT IT'S BEEN A PICNIC.

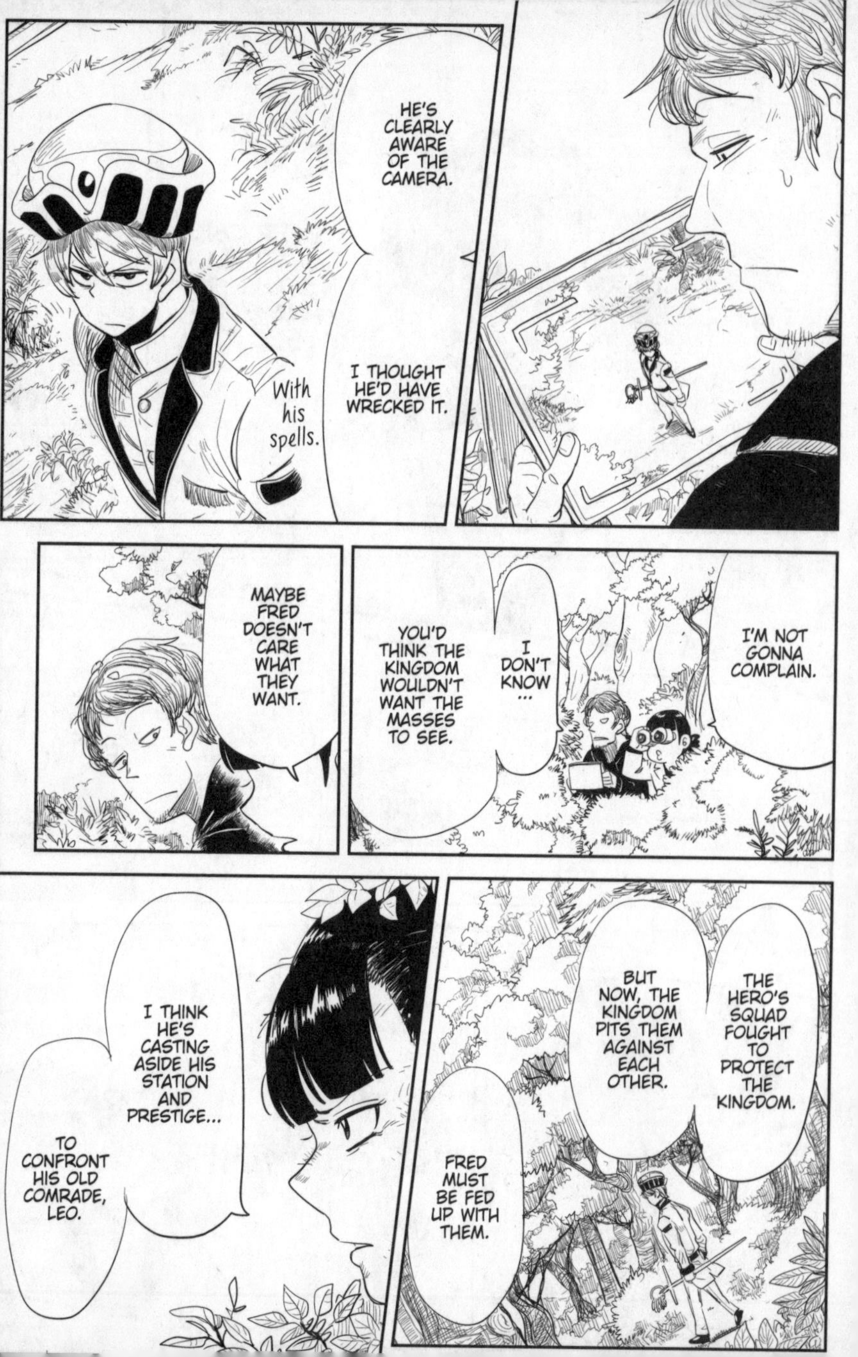
HE'S CLEARLY AWARE OF THE CAMERA.
I THOUGHT HE'D HAVE WRECKED IT.
With his spells.
I'M NOT GONNA COMPLAIN.
I DON'T KNOW...
YOU'D THINK THE KINGDOM WOULDN'T WANT THE MASSES TO SEE.
MAYBE FRED DOESN'T CARE WHAT THEY WANT.
THE HERO'S SQUAD FOUGHT TO PROTECT THE KINGDOM.
BUT NOW, THE KINGDOM PITS THEM AGAINST EACH OTHER.
FRED MUST BE FED UP WITH THEM.
I THINK HE'S CASTING ASIDE HIS STATION AND PRESTIGE...
TO CONFRONT HIS OLD COMRADE, LEO.

| OF COURSE YOU'D SAY THAT. | EVERYONE IS TOTALLY GOING TO WANT TO SEE IT!! | THIS... THIS BAT-TLE... |

| AYE AYE. | WHIRR... THE TRUTH MUST BE BROADCASTED!! | KEEP THAT CAMERA ROLLING! |

HMPH.

TMP TMP

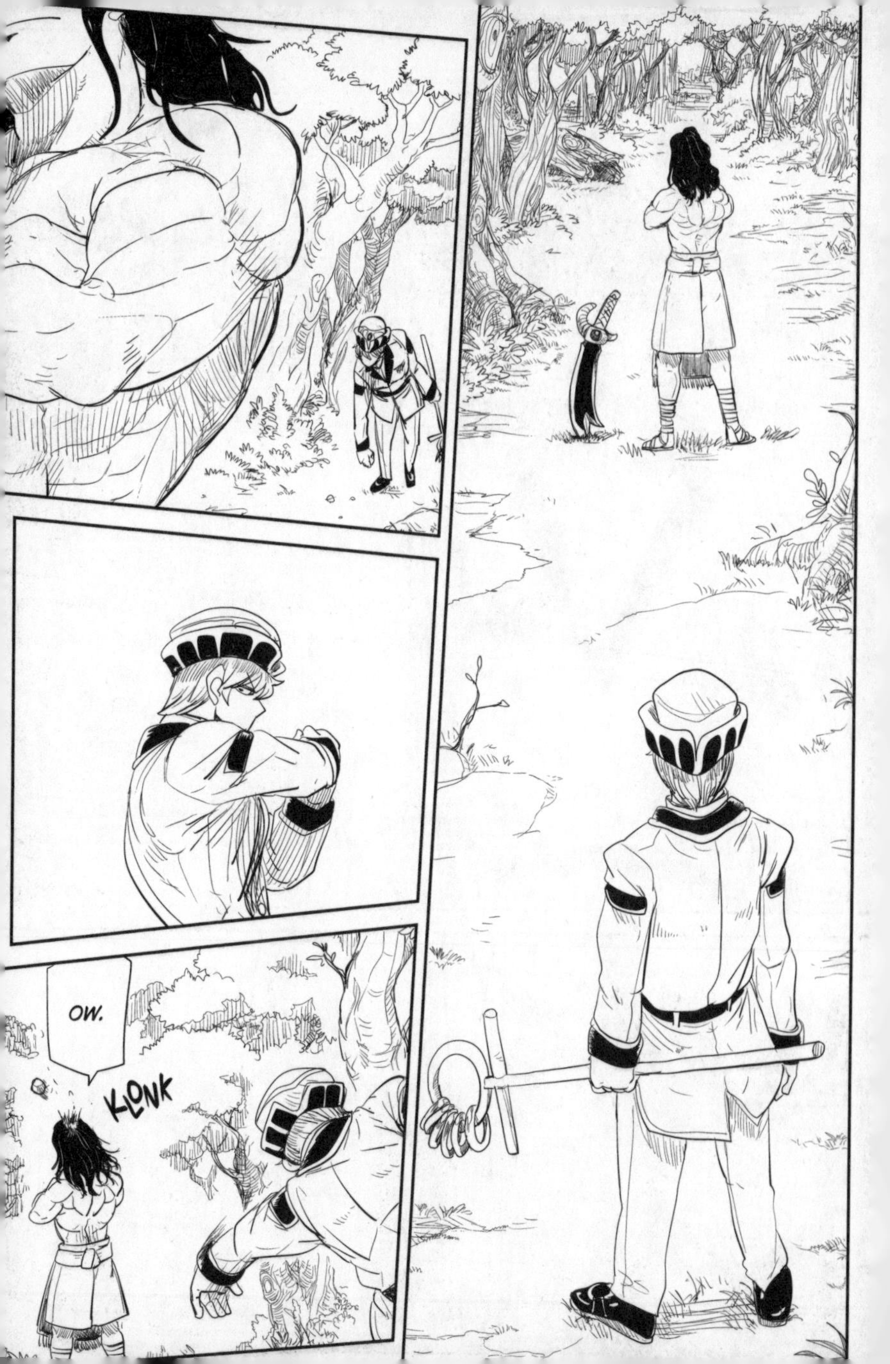

OW.
KLONK

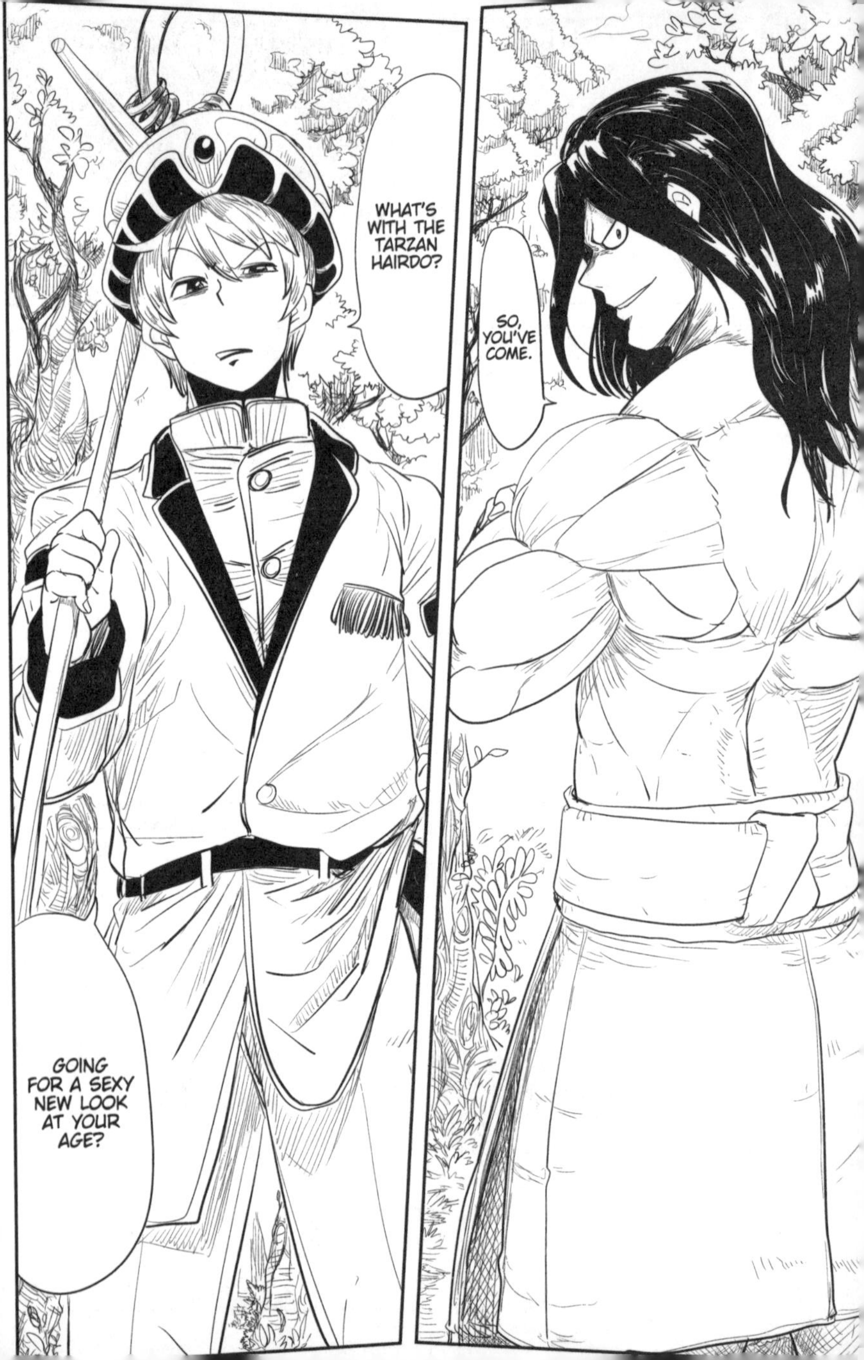
SO, YOU'VE COME.
WHAT'S WITH THE TARZAN HAIRDO?
GOING FOR A SEXY NEW LOOK AT YOUR AGE?

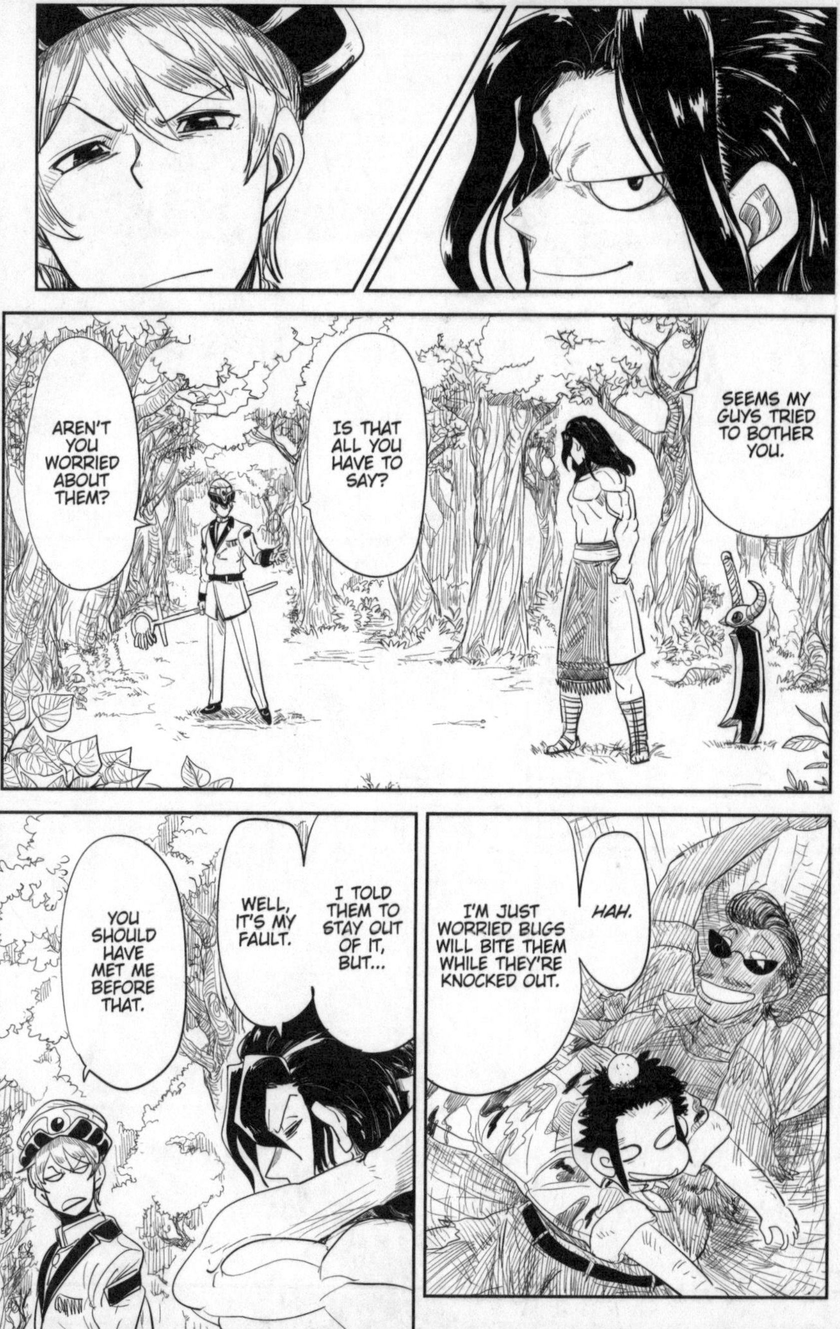
SEEMS MY GUYS TRIED TO BOTHER YOU.
IS THAT ALL YOU HAVE TO SAY?
AREN'T YOU WORRIED ABOUT THEM?
HAH.
I'M JUST WORRIED BUGS WILL BITE THEM WHILE THEY'RE KNOCKED OUT.
I TOLD THEM TO STAY OUT OF IT, BUT...
WELL, IT'S MY FAULT.
YOU SHOULD HAVE MET ME BEFORE THAT.

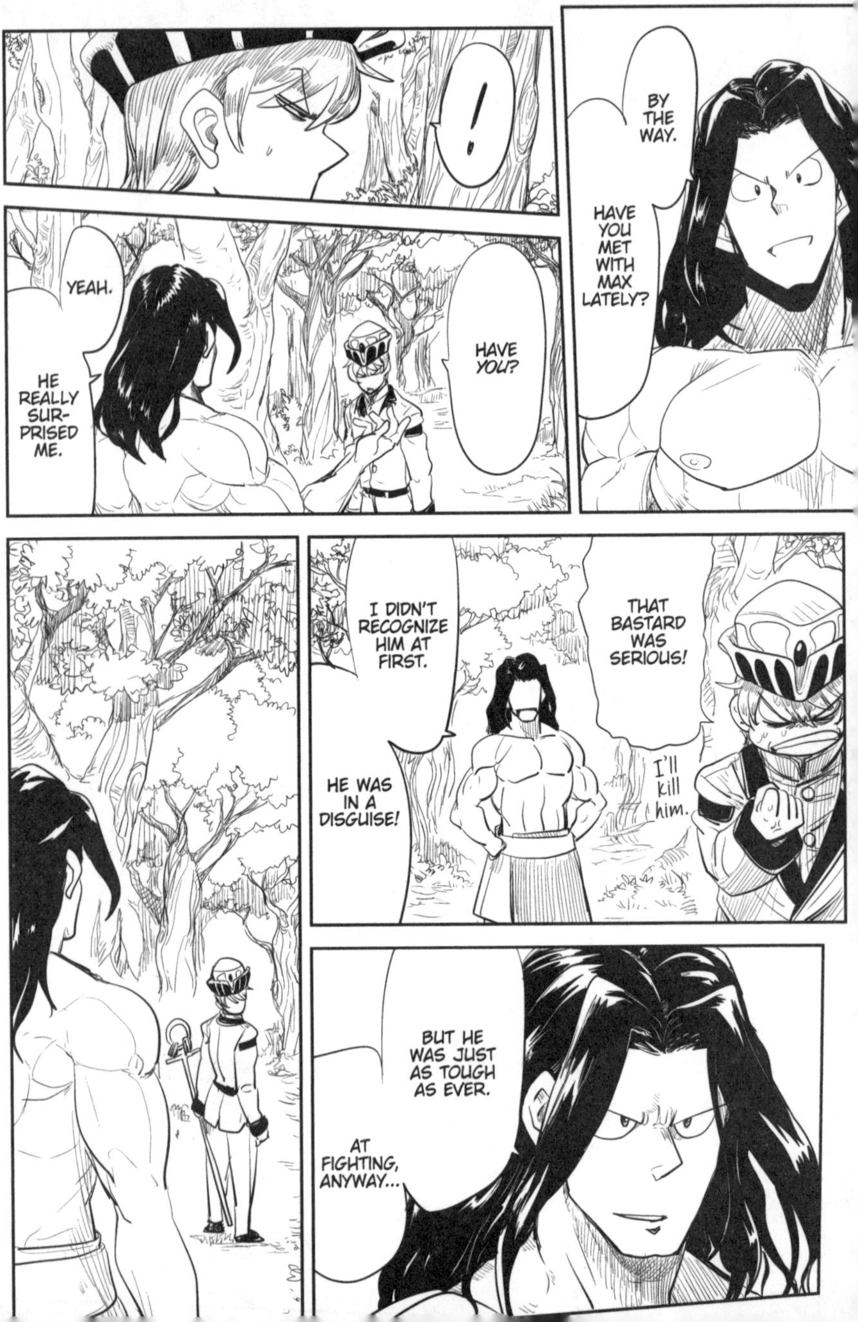
BY THE WAY.
HAVE YOU MET WITH MAX LATELY?
!
HAVE YOU?
YEAH.
HE REALLY SURPRISED ME.
THAT BASTARD WAS SERIOUS!
I'll kill him.
I DIDN'T RECOGNIZE HIM AT FIRST.
HE WAS IN A DISGUISE!
BUT HE WAS JUST AS TOUGH AS EVER.
AT FIGHTING, ANYWAY...

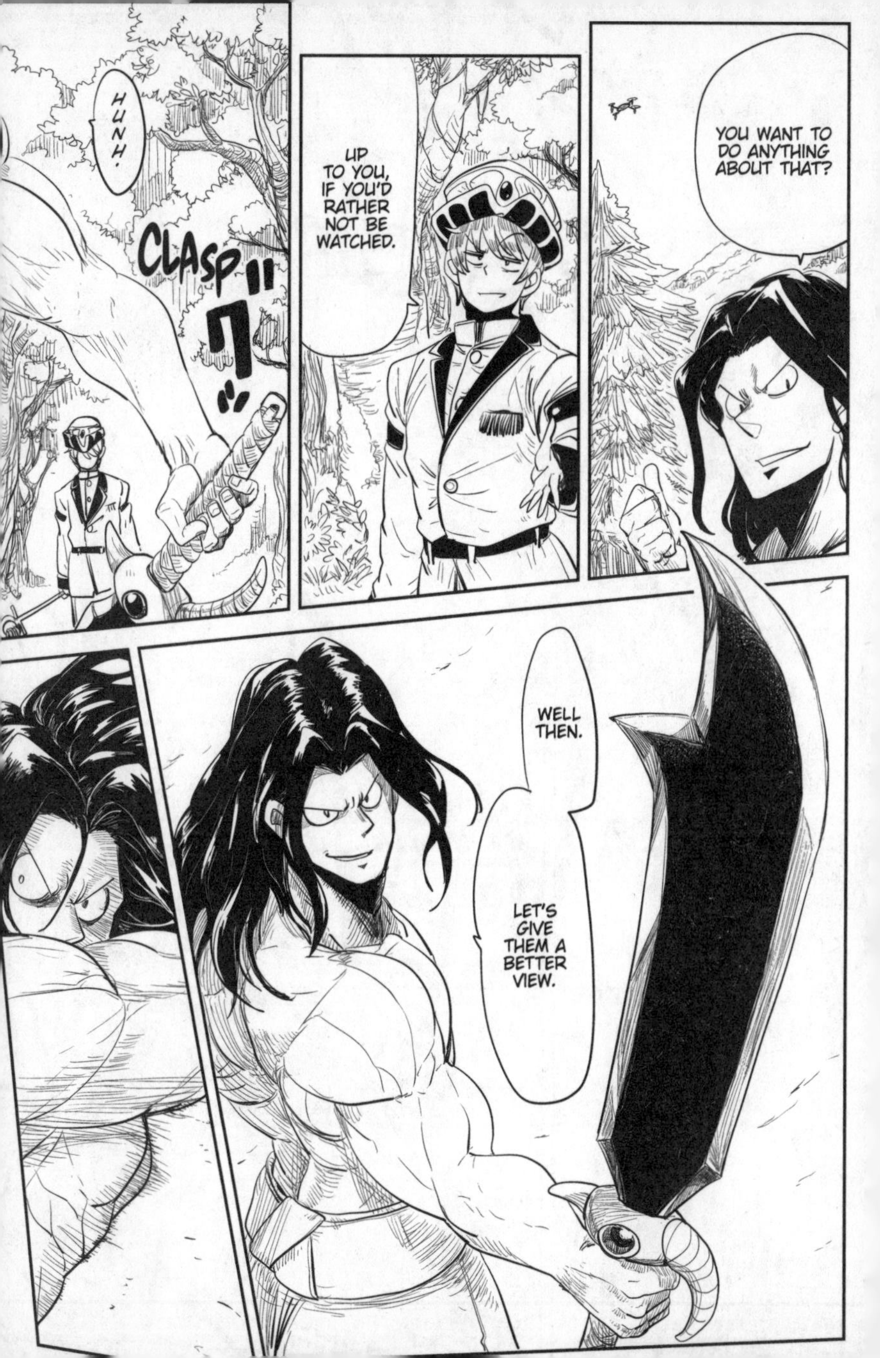
HUNH.
CLASP
UP TO YOU, IF YOU'D RATHER NOT BE WATCHED.
YOU WANT TO DO ANYTHING ABOUT THAT?
WELL THEN.
LET'S GIVE THEM A BETTER VIEW.

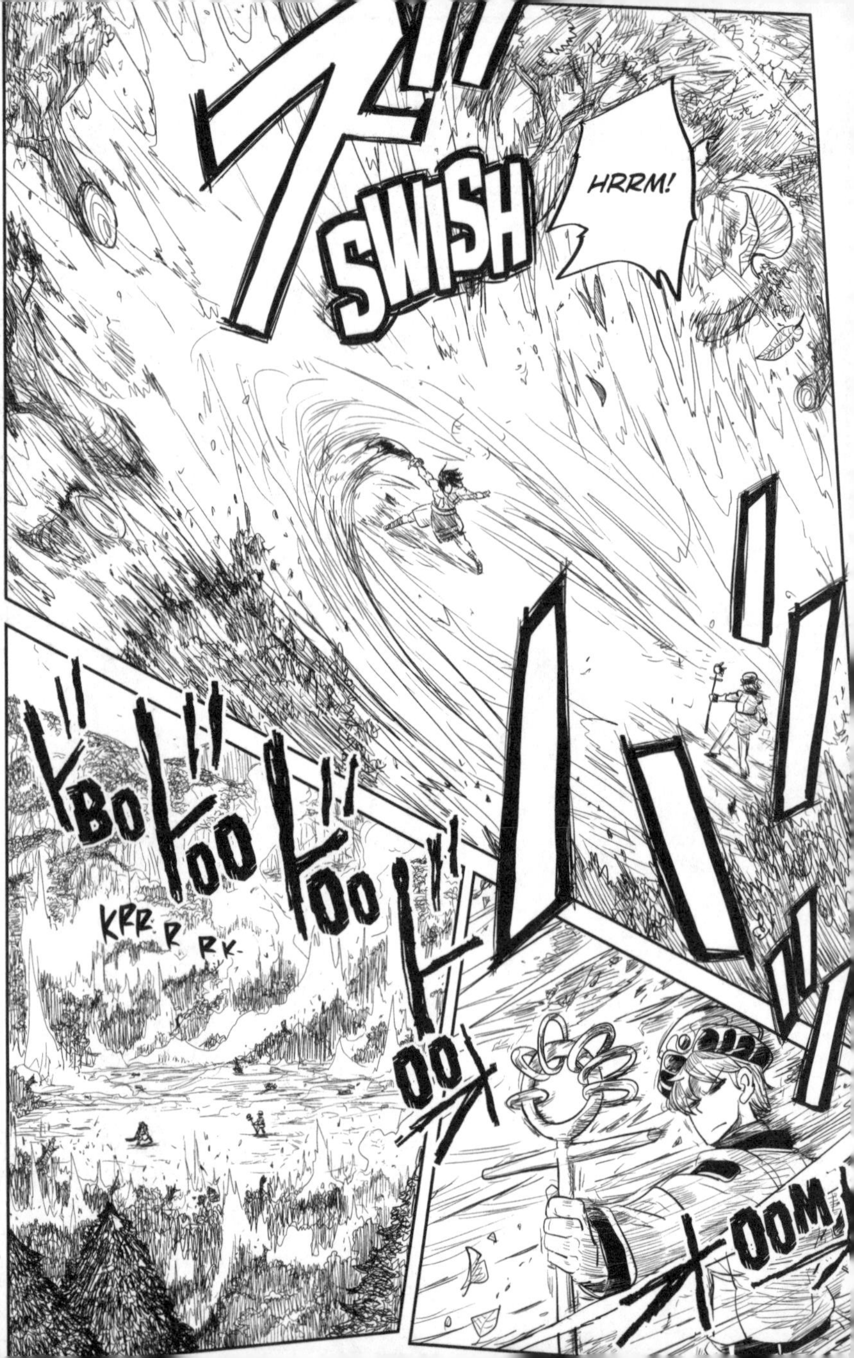
SWISH
HRRM!
BO
OO
OO
OO
KRR R RK-
OOM

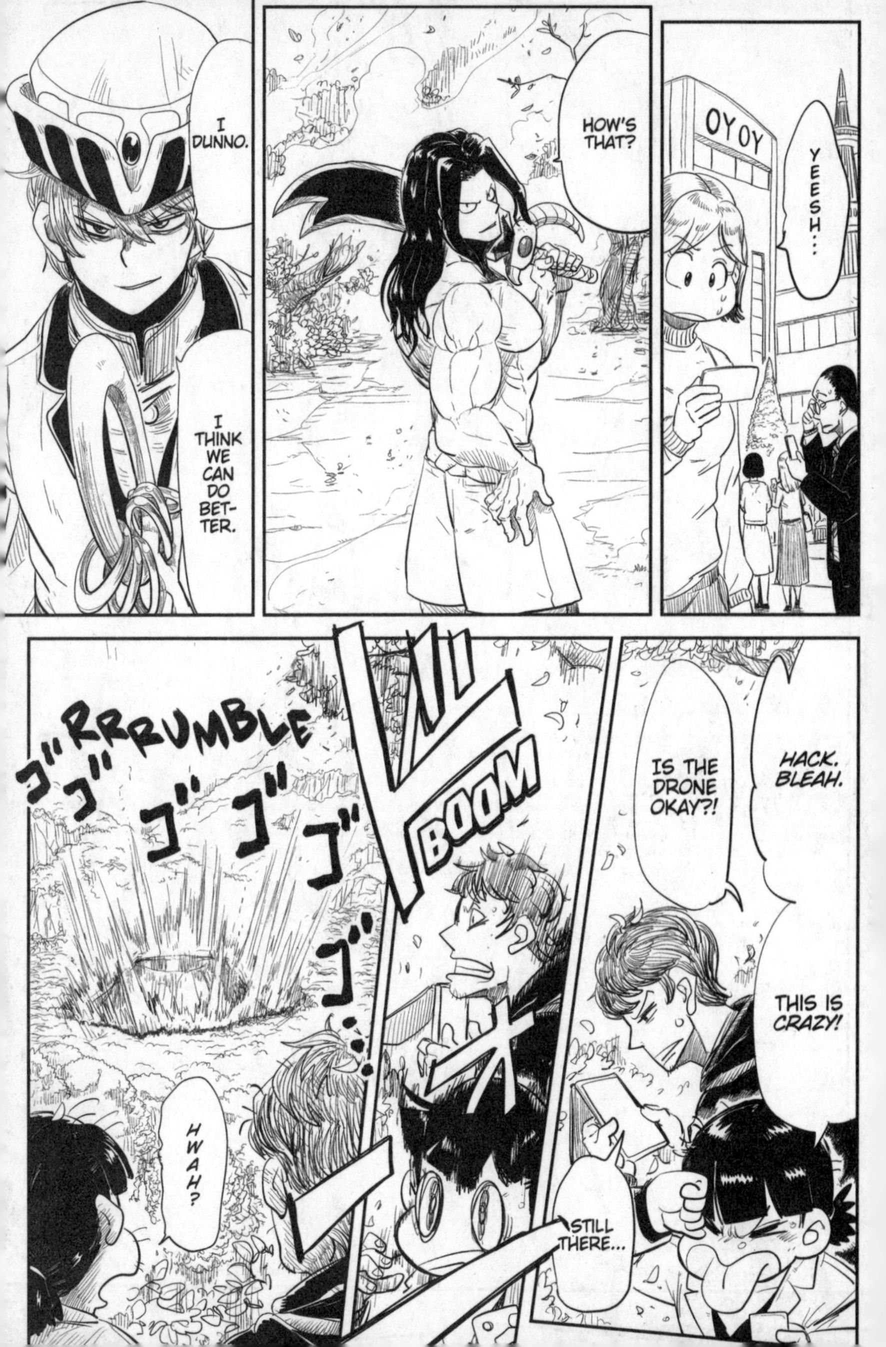
OYOY
YEESH...
HOW'S THAT?
I DUNNO.
I THINK WE CAN DO BET- TER.
HACK. BLEAH.
IS THE DRONE OKAY?!
THIS IS CRAZY!
STILL THERE...
BOOM
RRRUMBLE
HWAH?

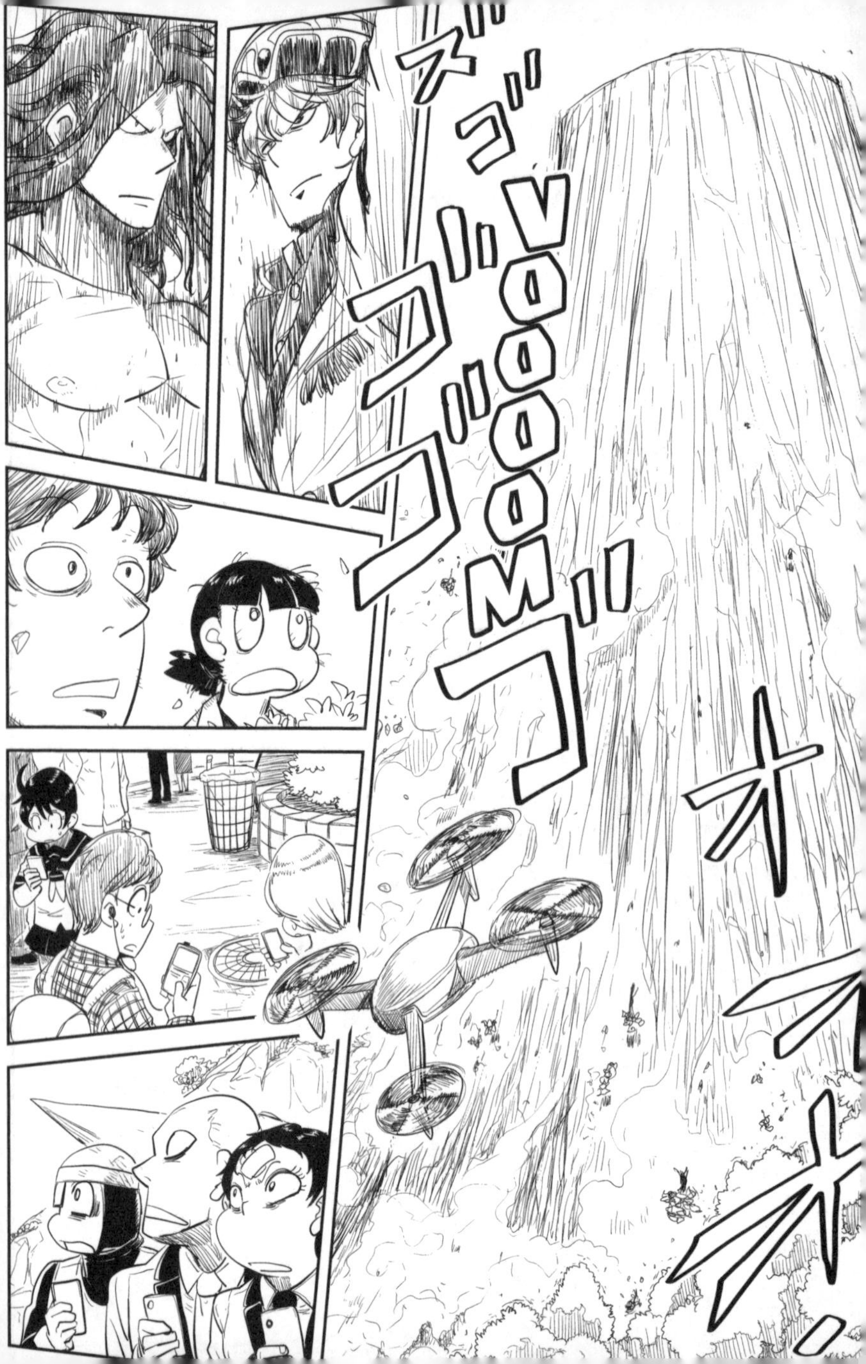
ズゴゴゴゴゴ
VOOOOM
オオオ

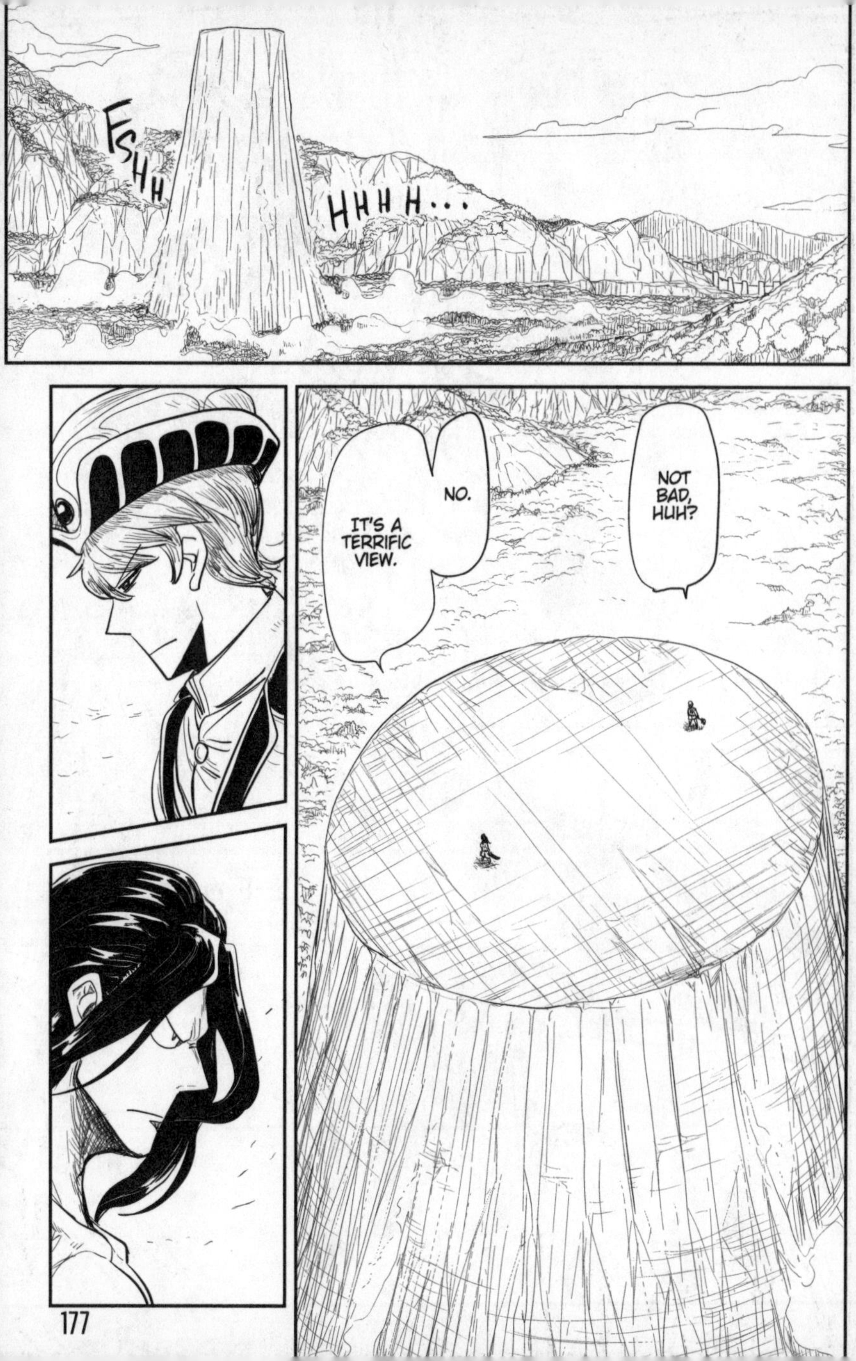
FSHHHHHH...
NOT BAD, HUH?
NO.
IT'S A TERRIFIC VIEW.

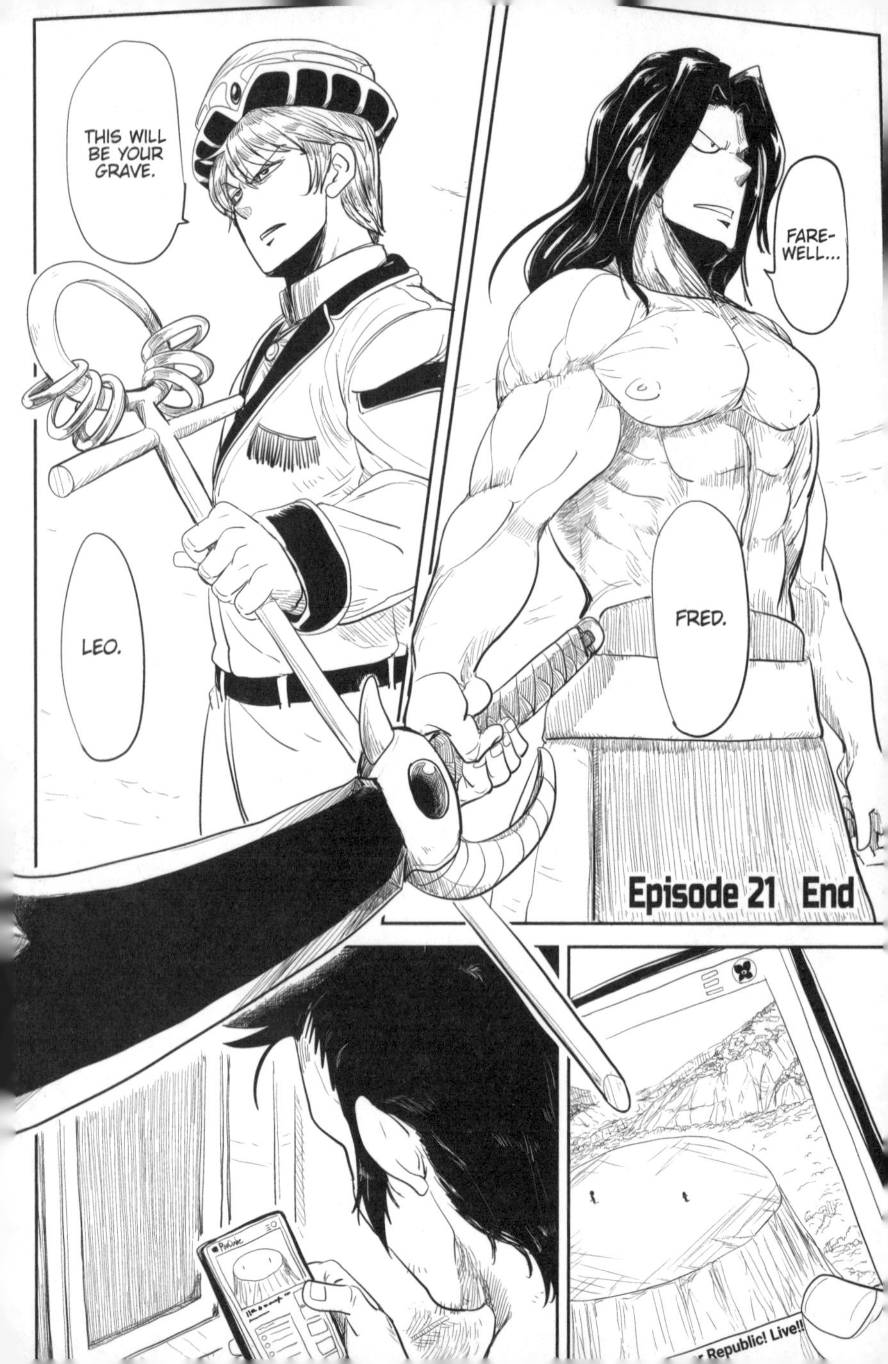
FARE-WELL...
FRED.
THIS WILL BE YOUR GRAVE.
LEO.
Episode 21 End
Republic! Live!!

I never imagined I'd be able to release a third volume.
It was possible thanks to everyone's support.
The story is getting heated now, but will there ever be a chance for poor ol' Max to shine?

Once again, thank you so much.

toufu

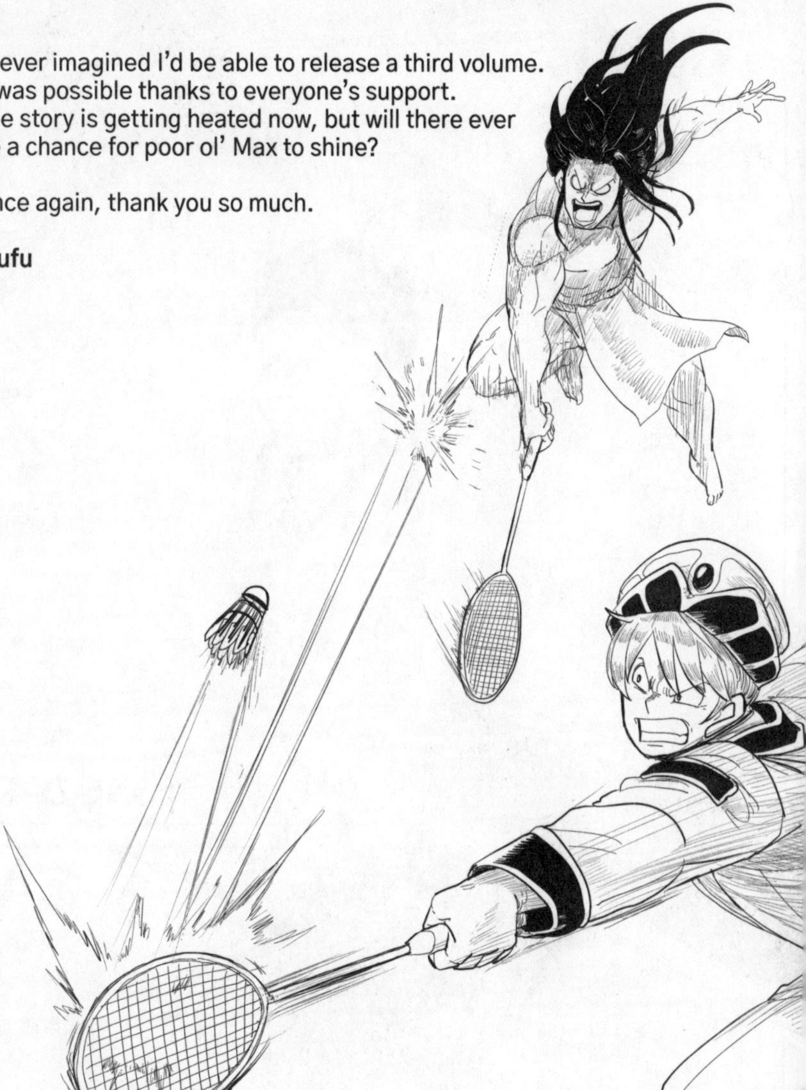

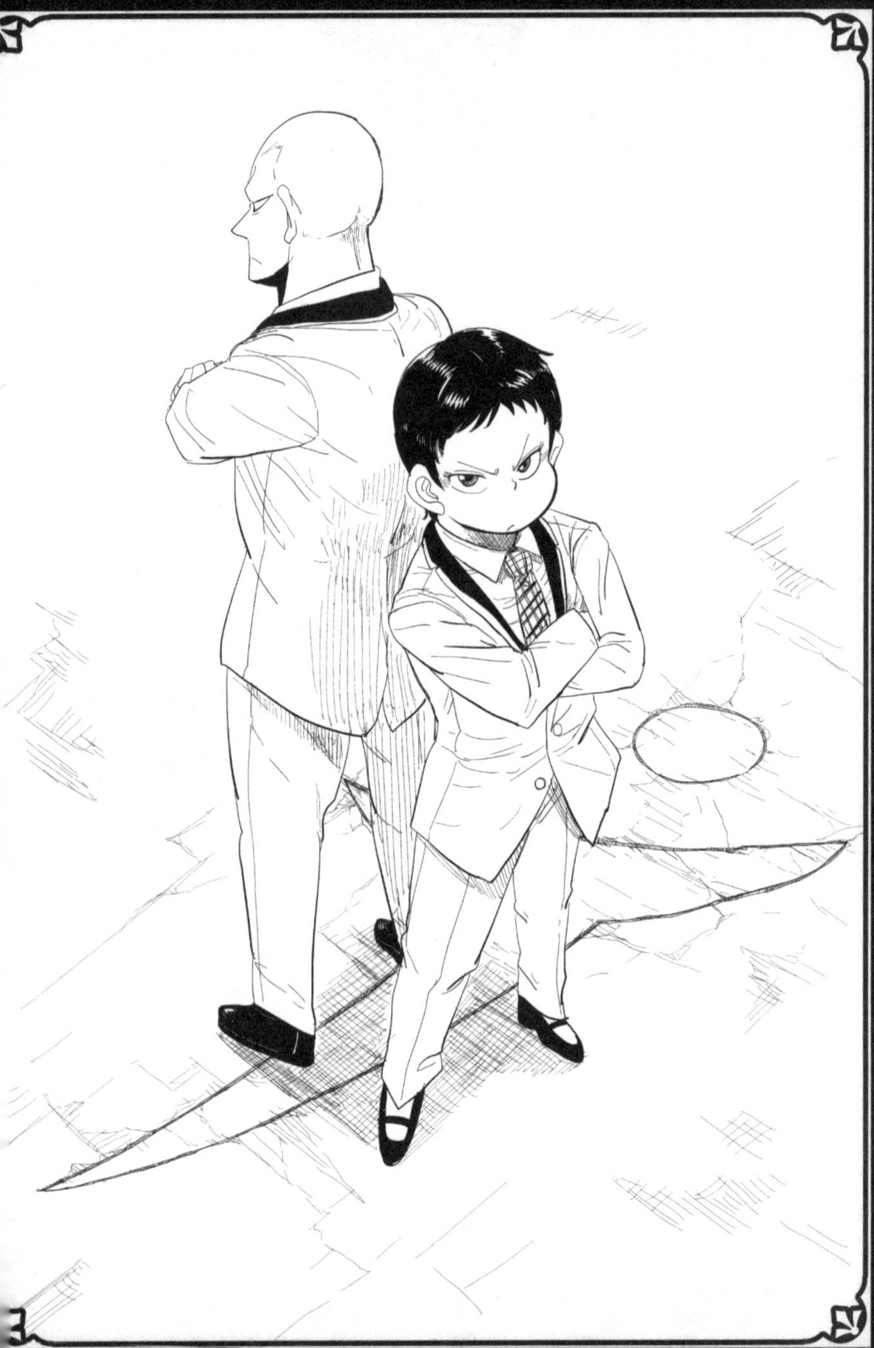

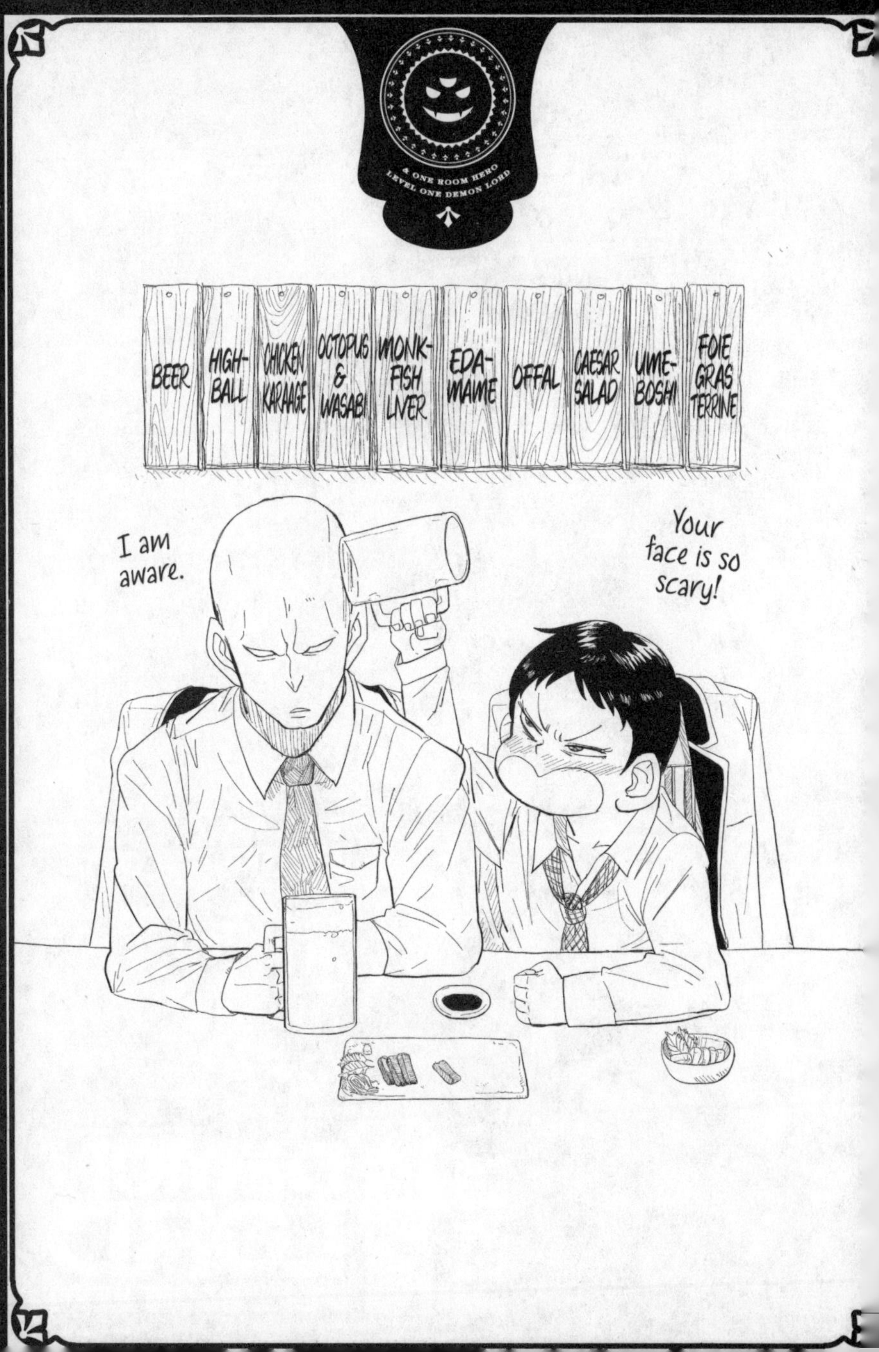

LEVEL ONE DEMON LORD
& ONE ROOM HERO
BEER
HIGH-BALL
CHICKEN KARAAGE
OCTOPUS & WASABI
MONK-FISH LIVER
EDA-MAME
OFFAL
CAESAR SALAD
UME-BOSHI
FOIE GRAS TERRINE
Your face is so scary!
I am aware.

LEVEL 1 DEMON LORD & ONE ROOM HERO

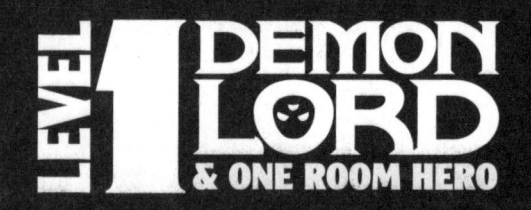

Experience all that SEVEN SEAS has to offer!

SEVENSEASENTERTAINMENT.COM

Visit and follow us on Twitter at twitter.com/gomanga!

SEVEN SEAS ENTERTAINMENT PRESENTS

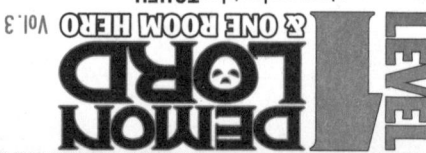

DEMON LORD & ONE ROOM HERO Vol. 3

story and art by TOUFU

TRANSLATION
M. Fulcrum

ADAPTATION
Jeffrey Thomas

LETTERING
Arbash Mughal

COVER DESIGN
Nicky Lim

COPY EDITOR
Dawn Davis

EDITOR
Nick Mamatas

PREPRESS TECHNICIAN
Melanie Ujimori

PRINT MANAGER
Rhiannon Rasmussen-Silverstein

PRODUCTION ASSOCIATE
Christa Miesner

PRODUCTION MANAGER
Lissa Pattillo

MANAGING EDITOR
Julie Davis

ASSOCIATE PUBLISHER
Adam Arnold

PUBLISHER
Jason DeAngelis

LEVEL ONE DEMON LORD & ONE ROOM HERO Volume 3
© toufu 2020
Originally published in Japan in 2020 by HOUBUNSHA CO., LTD., Tokyo.
English translation rights arranged with HOUBUNSHA CO., LTD., Tokyo, through TOHAN CORPORATION, Tokyo.

No portion of this book may be reproduced or transmitted in any form without written permission from the copyright holders. This is a work of fiction. Names, characters, places, and incidents are the products of the author's imagination or are used fictitiously. Any resemblance to actual events, locales, or persons, living or dead, is entirely coincidental. Any information or opinions expressed by the creators of this book belong to those individual creators and do not necessarily reflect the views of Seven Seas Entertainment or its employees.

Seven Seas press and purchase enquiries can be sent to Marketing Manager Lianne Sentar at press@gomanga.com. Information regarding the distribution and purchase of digital editions is available from Digital Manager CK Russell at digital@gomanga.com.

Seven Seas and the Seven Seas logo are trademarks of Seven Seas Entertainment. All rights reserved.

ISBN: 978-1-64827-643-9
Printed in Canada
First Printing: January 2022
10 9 8 7 6 5 4 3 2 1

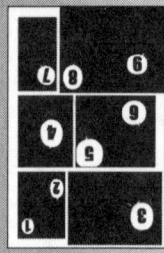

READING DIRECTIONS

This book reads from *right to left*, Japanese style. If this is your first time reading manga, you start reading from the top right panel on each page and take it from there. If you get lost, just follow the numbered diagram here. It may seem backwards at first, but you'll get the hang of it! Have fun!!

Follow us online: www.SevenSeasEntertainment.com